Praise for Cath

"[Thacker] has a knack for ~~...~~
vibrant love."

—RT BOOK ~~...~~

"There's a lot of genuine humor in Thacker's latest, as well as sizzling romance and family drama."
—*RT Book Reviews* on *One Wild Cowboy*
(4.5 stars, Top Pick)

"Thacker's characters and plot are outstanding as usual. The challenges, romance and laughter will keep you hooked to the end!"
—*Affaire de Coeur*

"This wildly romantic tale is a delightful reintroduction to what makes the McCabes Laramie's first family."
—*RT Book Reviews* on *A Cowboy to Marry*

Praise for Linda Warren

"Linda Warren writes a story overflowing with emotional twists and turns that grabs the reader from the first page and doesn't let go until the end."
—*Romance Junkies* on *Once a Cowboy*

"Ms. Warren writes a wonderful romantic read and her characters will burrow their way into the hearts of readers."
—*RT Book Reviews* on *Son of Texas*

"Linda Warren writes about people discovering their strengths and passions. Her gift with dialogue brings the characters to life and compels your sympathy and caring."
—*Fresh Fiction* on *The Texan's Christmas*

A Texas Christmas

Cathy Gillen Thacker & Linda Warren

Previously published as *A Cowboy Under the Mistletoe*
and *The Christmas Cradle*

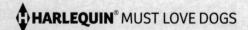 **HARLEQUIN**® MUST LOVE DOGS

If you purchased this book without a cover you should be aware that this book is stolen property. It was reported as "unsold and destroyed" to the publisher, and neither the author nor the publisher has received any payment for this "stripped book."

ISBN-13: 978-1-335-69088-3

A Texas Christmas

Copyright © 2018 by Harlequin Books S.A.

First published as A Cowboy Under the Mistletoe by Harlequin Books in 2010 and The Christmas Cradle by Harlequin Books in 2004.

The publisher acknowledges the copyright holders of the individual works as follows:

A Cowboy Under the Mistletoe
Copyright © 2010 by Cathy Gillen Thacker

The Christmas Cradle
Copyright © 2004 by Linda Warren

All rights reserved. Except for use in any review, the reproduction or utilization of this work in whole or in part in any form by any electronic, mechanical or other means, now known or hereafter invented, including xerography, photocopying and recording, or in any information storage or retrieval system, is forbidden without the written permission of the publisher, Harlequin Enterprises Limited, 22 Adelaide St. West, 40th Floor, Toronto, Ontario M5H 4E3, Canada.

This is a work of fiction. Names, characters, places and incidents are either the product of the author's imagination or are used fictitiously, and any resemblance to actual persons, living or dead, business establishments, events or locales is entirely coincidental.

This edition published by arrangement with Harlequin Books S.A.

For questions and comments about the quality of this book, please contact us at CustomerService@Harlequin.com.

® and TM are trademarks of Harlequin Enterprises Limited or its corporate affiliates. Trademarks indicated with ® are registered in the United States Patent and Trademark Office, the Canadian Intellectual Property Office and in other countries.

Recycling programs for this product may not exist in your area.

Printed in U.S.A.

www.Harlequin.com

CONTENTS

Cathy Gillen Thacker is married and a mother of three. She and her husband spent eighteen years in Texas and now reside in North Carolina. Her mysteries, romantic comedies and heartwarming family stories have made numerous appearances on bestseller lists, but her best reward, she says, is knowing one of her books made someone's day a little brighter. A popular Harlequin author for many years, she loves telling passionate stories with happy endings and thinks nothing beats a good romance and a hot cup of tea! You can visit Cathy's website, cathygillenthacker.com, for more information on her upcoming and previously published books, recipes and a list of her favorite things.

Books by Cathy Gillen Thacker

Harlequin Western Romance

Texas Legends: The McCabes

The Texas Cowboy's Baby Rescue

Texas Legacies: The Lockharts

A Texas Soldier's Family
A Texas Cowboy's Christmas
The Texas Valentine Twins
Wanted: Texas Daddy
A Texas Soldier's Christmas

Visit the Author Profile page
at Harlequin.com for more titles.

A COWBOY
UNDER THE MISTLETOE

Cathy Gillen Thacker

Chapter 1

"You're early."

And not for good reason, Ally Garrett thought, pushing aside the memory of her unsettling morning. She stepped out of her sporty blue Audi, ignoring the reflexive jump of her pulse, and glanced at the ranch house where she'd grown up. The aging yellow Victorian, with its wraparound porch and green shutters, was just as she remembered it.

Unfortunately, she couldn't say the same about the handsome Texas cowboy standing beside her. At thirty-three, the ex-marine was sexier than ever.

Ally got a handle on her mounting tension and turned back to the Mesquite Ridge Ranch's caretaker. Looked beneath the fringe of rumpled, dark brown hair peeking from under his Stetson, and into his midnight-blue eyes. Aware that he was just as off-limits to her as ever, she paused as another thrill coursed through her. "I wanted to get here before dark."

Hank McCabe tipped the brim of his hat back with one finger of his work-glove-covered hand. He regarded her with a welcoming half smile. "You accomplished that, since it's barely noon."

He was right—she should have been at work. Would have been if…

Determined not to let on what a mess her life was suddenly in, Ally bent her head, rummaging through her handbag for her house key. "I gather you got my message?"

Hank pivoted and strode toward his pickup truck, his gait loose-limbed and easy. "That you wanted to talk?" He hefted a bundled evergreen out of the back, and hoisted it over one broad shoulder. "Sure did." As she headed for the ranch house, he fell into step beside her.

The fragrance of fresh cut Scotch pine was nearly as overwhelming as the scent of soap and man. "I'd planned to have the tree up before you got here."

Which was, of course, the last thing she wanted on this last trip back home. Shivering in the bitter December wind, Ally ignored the stormy, pale gray clouds gathering overhead, and held up a leather-gloved hand. "I hate Christmas." The words were out before she could stop herself.

Hank set the tree down on the porch with a decisive thud. "Now how is that even possible?" he teased.

Ally supposed it wouldn't have been—had she been a member of the famously loving, larger-than-life McCabe clan.

Aware that her fingers were suddenly trembling, she paused to unlock the front door, then stepped inside.

The foyer of the 1920s home was just as plain and depressing as she recalled. "My parents weren't big on celebrating any of the holidays. On this ranch, December 25 was just another workday."

Hank hefted the tree over his shoulder again and followed her into the adjacent living room. His blue eyes flickered briefly over the sadly outdated thrift store furniture and peeling horse-and-hound wallpaper, which was at least forty years old. Then he plucked a pair of scissors from the scarred rolltop desk and cut through the webbing on the tree. "That's sad."

Ally shrugged. "That's just the way it was," she said flatly.

Hank shook out the tree and set it in the waiting metal stand. "It doesn't have to stay that way." He moved closer and briefly touched her arm, prompting her to look him square in the eye. "People have the power to change."

Not in her experience, Ally thought.

Although in her own way, she had tried, by leaving Laramie, Texas—and the ranch that had been the root of all her troubles—as soon as she was old enough to do so.

Oblivious to her feelings about the property, Hank strode into the equally depressing kitchen and returned with a beaker of water. He filled the stand, then stood back to admire his handiwork. One corner of his mouth crooked up, as he pivoted back to her and continued his pep talk, with all the enthusiasm of a man who was used to accomplishing whatever he set out to do. "I'm pretty sure you've got what it takes to infuse Mesquite Ridge Ranch with the yuletide spirit it deserves."

That wasn't really the point, Ally thought, as she inhaled the fresh, Christmasy scent. What did it matter if this was one of the most beautiful trees she had ever seen? "To tell you the truth, I'm not really into colored lights and presents, either."

Hank knelt to make sure the tree was settled securely in the stand. He gave one of the metal pins another twist. "Christmas is about more than just giving gifts, and trimming a tree."

"Let me guess." Ally paced over to the white stone fireplace. She turned so her back was to the mantel and took in what otherwise would be a cheerful tableau. "It's about family." Which was something else she no longer had, thanks to the fact that she had been an only child, as had each of her parents. Ally's only remaining link was to the house and the land, and soon that would be severed, too.

"And friends," Hank added, grabbing a cranberry-red throw off the couch and settling it around the base of the tree, like a skirt. "And wrapping up one chapter of your life, celebrating the bounty of it, before moving on to the next."

Unfortunately, Ally thought, she did not have much of anything positive to reflect on...especially this year.

"Although..." He paused, clearly thinking back to the events of last summer that had landed him here, in her absence. He straightened, then closed the distance between them, setting a comforting hand on her shoulder. The warmth of his palm penetrated her clothes, to reach her skin. "...I imagine it's pretty rough for you now, since this is the first holiday since your dad passed."

Ally didn't want to think about that, either. She stiffened her spine and deliberately lifted her chin. "No need for pity."

He studied her with a gentleness that threatened to undo her. "How about a little empathy then?" he insisted softly.

She shook off his compassion, and his light, consoling grip. Taking a deep breath, she gestured carelessly toward the eight-foot-tall symbol of Christmas. "So…back to the tree. If you're doing this for me—" she pressed her lips together, aware all it was going to do was remind her of what she'd never had, and likely never would "—don't."

Something in Hank hardened, too, at the harsh, unwelcoming tone of her voice. "I live here, too, now," he countered. "Or have you forgotten?"

She wished.

Time to get back on track.

To undo all those reckless promises she had made in the throes of an emotion that couldn't possibly have been grief.

Ally sighed, certain that Hank McCabe wasn't going to take the news any better than she was facing the upcoming yuletide. She drew a bolstering breath. "That's what I wanted to talk to you about."

Hank had known from the tone of Ally's terse email at seven-thirty that morning that the meeting was not going to be good. Hoping to delay the inevitable, he followed her down the hall that led to the rear of the sadly neglected ranch house. When they entered the kitchen, he observed, "You must be tired from the drive."

She stepped toward the sink in a drift of orange blossom perfume, her elegant wool business suit and silk blouse in stark contrast to his own comfortably worn jeans and flannel-lined canvas barn jacket. She took a glass from the cupboard and filled it with tap water. "Houston is only four hours from here."

Which meant she'd left moments after she'd sent the email.

Wondering why Ally had dressed so inappropriately for a day at the ranch, he watched as she drained the glass and then continued checking out the rest of the place, her ridiculously high heels making a clattering sound on the wood floor. Ambling after her, his body responding to her nearness, he took in the slender calves, trim hips and alluring thighs. She was five foot nine to his six foot three. Graceful and fit, with a sophisticated cap of sleek, honey-blond hair that framed her piquant features. And a body designed for lovemaking. But it was the sassy cynicism—coupled with the almost unbearable sadness in her wide-set, pine-green eyes—that always drew him in.

Ally rarely said what she was really thinking. She worked even harder to conceal what she was feeling.

Hank respected the need for privacy. He rarely shared his most intimate thoughts, either. But there were times, like now, when he felt she would be a lot better off if she confided in someone. To his knowledge, she never did, but remained determined to prove herself to everyone who crossed her path.

She wanted everyone to know that she was smarter, better, tougher.

That she didn't *need* anyone.

And that she couldn't wait to hightail it out of her hometown of Laramie, Texas.

Which was, Hank noted ironically, where *he'd* finally come back to stay.

Having completed her brief, wordless tour, Ally swung around to face him. Up close, he could see the shadows beneath her eyes. The brief flicker of uncertainty and vulnerability in her expression.

She wasn't as over her grief as she wanted him to think.

He understood that, too.

The need to move on, even when moving on felt impossible.

"I'm putting the ranch up for sale on December 24," she said, leaning against the desk in the study.

Hank had figured this was coming. It was why he'd offered to take care of the place in her absence.

He'd wanted first dibs when it came time for her to let go of the four thousand acres she had inherited from her folks.

Ally folded her arms. "You've got two weeks to vacate the ranch house and move your herd off the property."

Two weeks to place his bid...

"In the meantime, I'm moving in," she added.

The thought of them encountering each other at all hours of the night and day wasn't as intrusive as Hank would have figured. Maybe because she was so damn pretty...not to mention challenging.

"I plan to start emptying the house immediately," she said.

Ally had donated her parents' clothing to a local church. As far as Hank could tell, all their other belongings remained. "You're sure you want to do this?"

"Why wouldn't I?"

Figuring he'd better word this carefully, he shrugged. "Sorting through a loved one's possessions can be difficult." You never knew what you might find.… "The fact that it's Christmastime is only going to make it harder."

Ally curled her hands around the edge of the desk. "I don't plan to celebrate the holiday. I thought I'd made that clear."

Hank wondered how long it had been since someone had engulfed her in a nice, warm hug. Or made love to her slowly and thoroughly. Or shown her any affection at all, never mind made a segue way into her heart. "In other words," he guessed, mocking her droll tone, "your way of dealing with something painful is not to deal with it at all."

Her green eyes flashed with temper. "Thank you, Dr. Phil." She paused to give him a withering once-over. "Not that any of this is your business."

Hank knew that was true. Nonetheless, it was hard to stand by and watch her make a huge mistake that she was bound to regret, maybe sooner than she thought.

Having learned the hard way that some events couldn't be undone, no matter how much you wished they could, later on, he pointed out, "Mesquite Ridge Ranch has been your home since birth."

A flicker of remembrance briefly softened the beautiful lines of her face, before disappearing once again. "I haven't lived on the ranch for eleven years. My life is in Houston now." She swallowed visibly. "Not that what I do with the property is any of your concern, either."

Hank stepped closer. It was time to put his own intention on the line. "Actually," he murmured, "it is very much my business, since I made it clear when I took over the ranch last summer that I wanted to purchase the land from you, if and when you were inclined to sell." He hadn't been sure at the time that would ever be the case.

Ally gestured apathetically, all-business once again. "If you come in with the best offer, it's yours."

That wasn't possible—at least right now, Hank thought pensively. He did his best to stall. "Sixty days is the usual notice given for vacating a property."

Brushing past him, Ally hurried out the front door. He followed her lazily as she crossed the porch and headed toward her shiny red sports car. "If we had a written contract instead of an oral agreement, that would be correct. May I remind you we don't?"

Hank watched her punch the electronic keypad twice and open up the trunk.

"In case you've forgotten, in these parts, a man or a woman's word is good enough for any business deal."

Ally hefted two suitcases over the rim and set them on the ground. With a grimace, she slammed the lid shut. Her honey-blond hair swirled about her pretty face as she pivoted to face him again. "If you remember, I said you and your cattle could stay here *until* I put the property up for sale."

And he'd agreed, not getting into details, because

he had known she hadn't been ready to make a decision of that magnitude last June. And in his estimation, she wasn't ready now. Not during the holidays, when she was still clearly grieving the loss of her family.

"The general rule of thumb is not to do anything major until at least a year has passed. Your dad died just six months ago, your mom eight months before that," he reminded her gently.

In hindsight, if Hank had known Ally intended to act this soon, he would have had his business plan all ready to go.

She sighed dramatically. "And it's Christmas again, or it will be in two weeks, and I don't *want* to be here for the holiday."

Hank wrested the suitcases from her hands and, ignoring her frown of disapproval, carried them to the porch for her. "Then why not wait until spring to put the property on the market?" he pressed.

She shrugged. "I have vacation days that need to be taken before the end of the year."

Something in her expression said that wasn't the whole story. Curious, Hank asked, "The company you work for wouldn't let you hold them over to the new calendar year?"

Ally's eyes became even more evasive. "The one I used to work for, before the merger, would have. The financial services firm I work for now is a lot more hard-nosed."

Clearly, she wasn't happy with her new bosses. "You could always quit," he pointed out. "Work the ranch instead."

He may as well have suggested she take a bath with a skunk.

"Not in a million years," she retorted, stomping around to the passenger side. "Besides, there's no way I'm voluntarily giving up my management position."

She removed a heavy leather briefcase on wheels and a shoulder bag from the front seat, then headed toward the steps.

Hank strode down to help her with them, too. "No doubt you've risen fast in corporate America. And worked hard to get there." He lifted the heavy briefcase onto the porch and set it beside her suitcases. "Your mom used to brag all the time about how well you were doing in the big city."

Hurt turned down the corners of her soft lips. "Just not my dad," she reflected sadly.

Hank opened the front door and set her belongings in the foyer. "We all knew how he wished you'd returned to Laramie to work, after college. But parents don't always get what they want in that regard. Ask my mom. She about had a fit when I told her I was joining the marines."

Ally lingered on the porch, turning her slender body into the brisk wind blowing across the rolling terrain. "Your dad understood, though."

Hank tracked her gaze to the small herd of cattle grazing in the distance, then glanced at the gloomy sky. "Dad rodeoed before he settled down. He understands risk is a part of life, same as breathing. Mom, once she had kids, well, she just wanted to protect her brood."

Turning back to face him, Ally leaned against the porch column. "Yet you came back for good last summer, anyway."

Hank shrugged, not about to go into the reasons for that, any more than he wanted to go over the reasons why he had left Texas as abruptly as he had. "Laramie is my home," he said stubbornly.

Ally's delicate brow furrowed. She jumped in alarm and squinted at the barn, pointing at the open doors. "What was that?" she demanded, clearly shaken.

Hank turned in that direction. "What was what?"

Shivering, Ally folded her arms again. "I thought I saw some animal dart into the barn."

Hank saw no movement of any kind. "You sure?"

"I'm positive!" she snapped, visibly chagrined.

Her skittish reaction clued him into the fact that she was definitely not the outdoorsy type—which did not bode well for ranch activity of any sort.

"What kind of animal?" he persisted. "A fox? Weasel? Snake? Armadillo?"

Ally shivered again and backed closer to the house. "None of the above." She kept a wary eye on the barn.

Hank was about out of patience. "Describe it."

She held her hands out, about three feet apart. "It was big. And brown…"

Which could be practically anything, including a groundhog or deer. Unable to help himself, he quipped, "We don't have grizzly bears in these parts."

Color flooded her cheeks. "I did not say it was a grizzly bear! I just don't know what kind of mammal it was."

Realizing the situation could be more serious than he was willing to let on, particularly if the animal were rabid, Hank grabbed a shovel from the bed of his pickup truck. "Then you better wait here."

* * *

Ally had never liked taking orders.

But she liked dealing with wildlife even less.

So she waited, pacing and shifting her weight from foot to foot as Hank strode purposefully across the gravel drive to the weathered gray barn. Seconds later, he disappeared inside the big building. Ally cocked her head, listening…waiting.

To her frustration, silence reigned. Hank did not reappear.

Which could not be good, since she had definitely seen something dash furtively through those wide doors.

When yet another minute passed and he hadn't re-emerged, she decided to head over to the barn herself. There was no need to worry, Ally told herself. Hank was probably fine. Had there been any kind of trouble, he would have let out a yell.

He probably had whatever it was cornered already—or was trying to figure out how to prompt it to run out the back doors, assuming he could get them open….

Her heart racing, Ally reached the portal. Looked inside. Hank was twenty feet to her right, hunkered down, the shovel lying by his side. With his hat cocked back on his head, he was peering silently into the corner.

"What is it?" Ally strode swiftly toward him, her heels making a purposeful rat-a-tat-tat on the concrete barn floor. And that was when all hell broke loose.

Chapter 2

Hank had seen his fair share of startled animals in the midst of a fight-or-flight response. So the commotion that followed Ally's rapid entry into the shadowy barn was no surprise.

Her reaction to the cornered creature's bounding, snarling brouhaha was.

She stumbled sideways, knocking into Hank, and screaming loudly enough to alert the entire county. An action that caused their unexpected intruder to lunge forward and frantically defend its temporary refuge.

In the resulting cacophony, Hank half expected Ally to scream again. Instead, like a combat soldier in the midst of a panic attack, she went pale as a ghost. Pulse leaping in her throat, she seemed frozen in place, and so overcome with fear she was unable to breathe.

Afraid she might faint on him—if she didn't have a

heart attack, that was—Hank gave up on trying to soothe the startled stray. He vaulted to his feet and grabbed hold of Ally. "It's all right. I've got it under control."

Although she barely moved, her frantic expression indicated she disagreed.

"Just stay here and don't move," he told her, as the frantic leaping, snarling and snapping continued.

He started to move away, but Ally clutched his sleeve in her fist and gave him a beseeching look.

Unfortunately, Hank knew what he had to do or the situation would only get worse.

"Stay here and don't move," he repeated, in the same commanding voice he had used on green recruits.

He pried her fingers from his arm and stepped closer to the other hysterical female in the room. He approached confidently but cautiously, hand outstretched.

"Come on, now. Let's just simmer down." He regarded the mud-soaked coat studded with thorns, looked into dark, liquid eyes. "I can see you tangled with a mesquite thicket and lost," he remarked in a low, soothing voice.

He stopped just short of the cornered animal and hunkered down so they were on an equal level.

As he had hoped, the aggressive growling slowed and finally stopped.

Another second passed and then his fat-bellied opponent collapsed in weary submission on the cold, hard cement.

Ally watched as Hank slowly stood and, talking gently all the while, closed the distance between himself and the intruder. Confidently, he knelt in front of the beast.

The muddy animal lifted its big square head off the concrete and ever so gingerly leaned over to sniff Hank's palm. While Ally stood frozen in place, still paralyzed with fear, Hank calmly murmured words of comfort to the wild animal.

The beast answered his kind welcome with a thump of its straggly tail, then dropped its big nose and licked Hank's palm. A broad smiled creased the cowboy's handsome face. Chuckling, he lifted his other hand to the back of the filthy animal's head and began to scratch it consolingly behind the ears, his touch so obviously gentle and tender Ally wished she could experience it.

Apparently their trespasser felt the same, because it thumped its tail even harder.

Ally stared at the long creature with the drenched and filthy coat and unusually round middle. As she calmed down, she could see that the "savage beast" was actually a big, scraggly dog that had just been looking for shelter from the approaching winter storm. She knew she had just made a pretty big fool of herself in front of the ex-marine. Unfortunately, her fear, irrational as it might have been, was not entirely gone yet, despite the fact that their barn crasher was now putty in Hank's large, capable hands.

Telling herself she would not give Hank McCabe reason to think less of her than he probably already did, Ally willed herself to take several deep breaths. Suddenly he turned his head to look at her. Although he didn't speak, he seemed to be wondering why she hadn't budged from where he had left her.

Good question.

"How did you know that dog wasn't going to bite you?" she asked eventually, hoping to turn McCabe's attention to something other than her embarrassing display of cowardice.

"First, it was scared and upset, not rabid. Second, it's a golden retriever."

Her heart still pounding erratically, Ally discreetly wiped her damp palms on the skirt of her suit. "So?"

Hank regarded her with the ease of a man who was clearly in his element. "Golden retrievers are one of the gentlest breeds." He beckoned her with a slight tilt of his head. "Why don't you come over here and say hello?"

Ally swallowed and eyed the two warily. Hank continued to smile with encouragement. The dog lifted its big head and stared at her, considering.

The memory of another stray dog who had stared silently—then sunk his teeth into Ally's ankle—welled up inside her, followed by yet another wave of uncertainty and fear. "She didn't sound gentle when she came barreling out of the corner," Ally pointed out, taking another reflexive step back.

Hank shrugged his broad shoulders in exasperation. "You startled her. This pretty girl didn't know if you were friend or foe. You'll both feel better if you take the time to make peace with her."

Pretty? He'd called this filthy beast with the large jaws and wary eyes pretty? "And how would you suggest I do that?"

"Pet her. Talk to her. Show her a little kindness," he said as he rubbed the dog's head and neck.

Ally watched as the powerfully built retriever luxuriated in the massage. There was no doubt she was putty in Hank's hands, but animals sensed when humans were scared. And right now Ally was full of fear. Grimacing, she hugged her arms to her chest, not about to let herself be made vulnerable in that way. "I don't think so."

Hank lifted an eyebrow. "I'd ask why not," he replied drolly, "but it's pretty clear you're still as frightened of this big ol' sweetheart as she initially was of you."

His quiet disapproval rankled. "I don't like dogs."

Hank's eyes sparkled with devilry. "Dogs *and* Christmas. Wow. Sure your name isn't Ebenezer Scrooge?"

Ally gave him her most repressing look. "Very funny," she snapped, more annoyed now than embarrassed. "I was bit by a dog that strayed onto our ranch when I was five. I've been leery of them ever since."

Comprehension lent compassion. "That's a shame," Hank said sincerely, shaking his head in regret. "You're really missing out."

Still keeping a cautious eye on the suddenly docile creature, Ally remained where she was. She didn't care how friendly the big mutt looked now—there was no way Hank was getting her to venture over there. "I'll have to take your word for it."

A car motor sounded in the drive behind them. Ally turned to see a Cadillac pulling up in front of the barn. An elegantly dressed, silver-haired man in a gray Western suit, and a Resistol hat emerged from the car.

"Expecting someone?" Hank asked curiously.

She nodded as the stranger strode over to meet them.

I am doing the right thing, she assured herself.

The short, slim man extended his hand and flashed a smile. "Ally Garrett, I presume? I'm Graham Penderson, of Corporate Farms."

So that was why Ally had arrived so early, dressed in a business suit, Hank thought, a mixture of disapproval and disappointment welling up inside him. She'd known she was taking the first step to sell the ranch that had meant everything to her mom and dad.

And now that Corporate Farms was involved, there was no doubt in his mind who would be the highest bidder.

Ally pivoted to face him, her expression as coolly commanding as her voice. "I take it you can handle this situation?" she inquired, gesturing toward the filthy stray.

Hank lifted his free hand to tip up the brim of his hat. If she wanted him to act like the hired help, he'd do just that. "Yes, ma'am," he said, putting as much twang as he could into the words, just to rile her, "I shorely can."

Ally narrowed her eyes and smiled at him deliberately. "All right." She pivoted once again. "Mr. Penderson. This way…"

Hank watched as she led the slick representative toward the ranch house. They were inside the sadly neglected domicile less than two minutes, then walked back out—maps of the property in tow—and climbed into the older man's Cadillac.

Hank looked down at the soaked, shivering dog cuddled against his side. "Well, I didn't expect that, at least not today." He rubbed some of the dirt off a fancy pink rhinestone collar hidden in the fur, which spelled out the first clear hint to the pet's identity. "But I'll deal with it. Meantime, what do you say we get you cleaned up?"

An hour later, Hank was kneeling in the big, old-fashioned bathroom upstairs, toweling off his canine companion, when Ally came down the hall.

She stopped in her tracks when she saw the mess of mud and hair and occasional spots of blood that had been left in the claw-footed tub, the pile of thorns and burrs heaped in the wastebasket.

It had taken some doing, but Hank finally had the animal in decent shape.

He noticed that Ally didn't come any closer than the door frame when she set eyes on the golden retriever. "What's that thing doing in here?"

"Getting a bath," he said shortly.

Ally propped her hands on her slender hips and wrinkled her nose. "And that smell?" she asked.

"Wet dog and my shampoo," he explained.

Ally studied the heap of wet towels next to the tub and made another face. "Ugh."

Hank passed up the opportunity to reassure her he planned to clean everything. Instead, he leveled a matter-of-fact glance her way. "Where's your pal Penderson?" he asked.

She tensed. "He left."

Slowly, Hank got to his feet and braced his own

hands on his waist. "Tell me you're not selling to Corporate Farms."

Ally flushed uncomfortably. "I'm not selling to anyone until I've had a chance to have the property appraised," she told him quietly.

That made sense from a business point of view, he noted. "When is that going to happen?"

Her pretty chin took on a stubborn line. "A broker from Premier Realty in Laramie is coming out later this week, once I've had a chance to get the ranch house in order."

Wishing she'd stop looking so damn kissable, Hank pushed his desire aside and forced himself to concentrate on the very important business at hand. "And once you know what the property is worth?"

Ally swept a hand through her sleek cap of honey-blond hair. "As in all competitions," she replied, tucking the silky strands behind her ear, "the highest bid wins." She let her hand fall to her side and regarded the retriever with a disgruntled frown. "I really wish you hadn't brought him up here."

"First of all—" Hank leaned past Ally "—it's a *she*. And according to the rhinestone-studded collar she was wearing—" he lifted said collar out of the cleansing bubbles in the sink "—her name is Duchess."

Ally leaned closer and inspected the fancy collar without touching it. Then once again her gaze met Hank's. "Who does she belong to?"

"I don't know yet." Ignoring the quickening of his pulse, he knelt and fastened the pink leather strap around Duchess's throat. This was no time to want to bed a woman. Especially when she was his landlord. "It had no ring for metal identification tags." And hence was strictly decorative. But that confirmed Hank's guess that Duchess was a beloved house pet, not your run-of-the-mill stray.

He gave her fur one last rub, then dropped the towel and stood, motioning for the dog to do the same.

Abruptly fearful once again, Ally moved back into the hall. "So what are you going to do next?" she demanded.

"Feed her. Get her a bowl of water." *Come back and clean up this mess. And most of all, stop feeling attracted to you.* Hank moved through the door, and Duchess trotted by his side.

"And then?" Ally pressed.

He paused in his bedroom to remove his damp shirt and pull a dry, long-sleeved henley over his head. He grabbed a pair of jeans and slipped into the bathroom to change. "I already put in a call to my cousin Kurt."

When he emerged, still zipping up his pants, Ally was staring at him as if she'd never seen a man disrobe. Her mouth agape, she watched him fish a pair of wool socks from a dresser drawer.

Hank sat down on the edge of the bed and pulled on the socks. Conversationally, he continued. "Kurt is a veterinarian here now."

Scowling, Ally shook her head as if to clear it. "I know that," she stated irritably.

"Anyway—" ignoring Ally's sudden pique, Hank headed down the stairs, Duchess by his side "—Kurt can't recall a golden retriever named Duchess, but he's having his staff go through the clinic's records to make sure she isn't a patient of one of the other veterinarians in the practice."

Ally followed slowly, her arms clamped defensively in front of her. Giving Duchess and Hank plenty of room, she finally reached the foyer. Lingering next to the newel post, she asked, "And what if that's not the case? Then what?"

Hank shrugged. "Kurt'll put out the word to other veterinarians in the area. I'll notify the Laramie County animal shelter, the newspaper and any other organization I can think of, till we figure out where she belongs." He strode past Ally into the kitchen, with Duchess right on his heels.

Ally followed, again keeping wide a berth from the two of them. She watched Hank pull a stoneware bowl out of the cupboard, fill it with water and set it on the floor in front of the dog.

Duchess lowered her head and drank thirstily.

Ally lounged against the aging laminate counter. "How do you know she wasn't just dumped in the country because her owners decided they no longer wanted her?"

Hank shot her an astonished look. "Seriously?"

He went to the fridge and, for lack of anything better, pulled out a package of smoked ham and several slices of bread. He crumbled them on a plate and set that in front of the dog, too. It was just as quickly and efficiently demolished.

"Seriously," Ally replied in a flat, no-nonsense tone.

Hank debated giving the dog more food, then decided to wait an hour, rather than overdoing it initially and having the food come right back up.

He headed for the living room, and motioned for Duchess to follow. Once there, he glanced out the window at the increasingly gloomy sky, then walked over to build a fire in the grate. The retriever collapsed beside him while Ally lingered in the doorway once again. "Well, for starters, I can't imagine anyone no longer wanting such a beautiful, loving dog," Hank said. "Duchess's temperament and behavior indicate she has been very well cared for up to now, wherever her home was. So it follows that whoever bought her the collar must be missing her desperately, wondering what's happened to her. *Especially* now."

Ally blinked. "What do you mean, especially now?"

Hank glanced at the dog's drooping, barrel-shaped belly. "You really don't know?" he asked in amazement.

Ally waved an impatient hand. "Don't know and don't care. The point is, Hank…" she paused and stared at him defiantly "…the dog can't stay here."

As if on cue, a cold rain began to beat against the windows. After lighting the fire, he looked out at the gloomy sky again and knew the winter storm they had been anticipating had finally arrived. He turned back to Ally, not about to throw out into the elements the dog he had just painstakingly cleaned up. "I don't know why not. It's not as if I'm asking *you* to do anything, Ally. I plan to take care of her." He lit the fire.

Crossing her arms yet again, Ally watched the blaze take off. "I don't want a dog in the house," she stated.

Hank moved his gaze away from the contentious stance of her shapely legs. "Well, I do. And since we have no formal written legal agreement in place banning a pet of any kind—and you already gave me another two weeks before I have to vacate the property—it looks like Duchess *will* stay. You, on the other hand…" he paused to let his words sink in "…are welcome to find a room at the inn."

Ally did a double take. "You're seriously trying to kick me out of my own home?" she asked, aghast.

Hank gave the logs another poke and replaced the screen. Slowly and deliberately, he rose to his feet. Noticing how his large body dwarfed her much smaller, delicate one, he murmured. "I'm just saying you have a choice, Ally. You can stay. Accept that it's Christmas—a time of giving—and that this golden beauty landed on our doorstep, in need of shelter and some tender loving care prior to the big event. Or…"

"*What* big event?" Ally interrupted, her brow furrowing yet again. "What are you talking about!"

Hard to believe this woman had grown up on a ranch. With a sigh of exasperation, Hank took another step closer and spelled it out for the gorgeous heiress. "Duchess is going to have puppies. And judging by the size of her belly, it's going to be soon."

Chapter 3

Ally stared at Hank and the rotund golden retriever curled at his feet, already half-asleep. "Puppies," she repeated in shock.

Crinkles appeared at the corners of Hank's eyes. He gestured magnanimously. "Merry Christmas."

Ally pressed a hand to her temple and sagged against an overstuffed club chair in a hideous floral pattern that clashed with the yellowed horse-and-hound wallpaper.

"This is surreal," she gasped.

Hank strode past her and went back up the stairs, leaving Ally to follow. He went into the bathroom. "More like one of those holiday commercials you see on TV, with all the cute little golden puppies running around. Or it will be, once Duchess delivers her brood."

He grabbed a bottle of spray disinfectant and liberally spritzed the floor and tub. With the ease of a man used to doing for himself, he tugged another clean towel off the shelf and used it to wipe down the dampened areas.

Aware that she was close enough to touch him, Ally stepped back to let him work. "She can't do that here!"

He gathered up the wet, filthy towels and mat, and dumped them into a plastic laundry basket he pulled from the bottom of the linen closet. His sensually shaped lips twisted cynically. "You keep saying that…" he chided softly. He gave her a long considering look, then brushed past her once again, headed purposefully back down the stairs.

Duchess barely lifted her head as he strode by to the mudroom beyond.

Ally worked to retain her outward composure as she watched Hank dump the soiled linens into the washing machine. She clenched her teeth while he added detergent and set the dials. "I mean it," she insisted.

He pulled the knob, then leaned a hip against the washer, and folded his brawny arms in front of him. "Listen to me, Ally." The water rushing through the pipes forced him to raise his voice slightly. "Hear what I'm saying. There is *no way* I'm putting that sweet lost dog in an animal shelter during the holiday season. Or at any other time, for that matter. Not when I've got the capacity to take care of her myself."

Ally had never encountered such fierce protectiveness. Despite the fact that it countered her current request, she couldn't help but admire Hank's gallantry.

Or wish, just a little impractically, that one day someone would feel that way about her.

"Fine." She swallowed, struggling to hold her own with this very determined man. "But the dog doesn't have to stay in the house."

Hank took a moment to scowl at her before he replied. "Where would you have me put Duchess? In the barn?"

That was exactly what her father and mother would have done, had they not run the pregnant dog off the property first. Ally forced herself to hang on to the Garrett family's unsentimental attitude just a little while longer. Coolly, she pointed out, "That was where Duchess was initially headed."

Hank's handsome features tightened in reproof. "Only because it was the best shelter she could find in which to deliver. Fortunately, we spotted her, and came to her rescue. Because if Duchess had given birth out there in the elements sometime in the next few days, with the temperature falling into the twenties at night, there's no way she could have kept her offspring warm enough. All her pups likely would have died—maybe Duchess, too."

Ally's eyes welled with tears at the thought of yet another completely avoidable tragedy. She was responsible for a lot of bad things that had gone down on this ranch. She wouldn't be held to account for this, too. "Fine." She finally relented, throwing up her hands. "But when you're not with her, you're going to have to figure out how to contain the dog so she's not in the way."

Hank shrugged his powerful shoulders. "No problem."

He regarded her in silence.

Another jolt of attraction swept through Ally. Suddenly, the dog wasn't the main danger to her well-being—the sexy cowboy in front of her was. "Well…" She gathered her composure around her like a shield. "I've got to change and go into town…for a preliminary meeting with Marcy Lyon at Premier Realty."

Hank's eyes softened unexpectedly. His assessing gaze took her in head to toe, lighting wildfires everywhere it landed. "No business suit for that meeting, hmm?" he chided.

She fought back a self-conscious flush. "Everyone wears jeans in that office. You know that. Since they deal primarily in ranch property and are always climbing over fences and what not."

Hank nodded and said nothing more.

But then, Ally thought sadly, he didn't have to. He did not approve of her decisions and actions any more than her parents had, when they were alive. Now, as then, she told herself it did not matter. And still knew that some way—somehow—it did.

An hour later, Kurt McCabe stopped by, vet bag in tow. "You were right," he told his cousin, when he had finished his examination of Duchess. "Those puppies are coming soon."

"How soon?" Hank asked.

Kurt shut off the portable ultrasound and folded the keyboard back against the monitor before latching it shut. "The next twenty-four, forty-eight hours."

Hank figured they had time to prepare. "Any idea how many?"

His cousin slid his stethoscope back into his vet

bag. "Looks like ten, from what I could see on the ultrasound, but the way they're packed in there, there could be one more."

Hank knew that was standard for the breed. "You have no idea who she might belong to?"

Kurt shook his head. "My staff and I all asked around. Got nothing. And…" he paused to use the transponder wand that would have detected surgically implanted information beneath the skin "…unfortunately, she's not outfitted with a microchip that would reveal her identity."

"Bummer," Hank said with a frown. Kurt put the portable transponder away, too. "I can tell you that Duchess is definitely purebred. Show quality. On her own, she'd be worth a pretty penny. If those puppies are purebred, too, the whole litter could easily be worth twenty thousand dollars or more. So if that is the case, someone will definitely be looking for her." He stood and shrugged on his yellow rain slicker. "The real question is, how is Ally Garrett taking this? She still as standoffish as I recall her being when we were all in school?"

"Probably more so." Hank slipped on a long black duster.

"A shame," Kurt remarked. Together, they headed out to his covered pickup truck to get the rest of the gear. "She was one good-looking woman." He reached inside the passenger compartment and brought out a whelping kit with printed instructions, and a warming box, handing both to Kurt. Then he picked up a bag of prenatal dog food and two stainless steel bowls. "And since you're in the market for a good-looking woman…" he teased, as they carried their loads back up to the porch and set them inside the front door.

Hank held up a silencing palm. "Just because you are happily married now, cuz—" He turned his back to the cold, driving rain blowing across the wraparound porch.

Kurt grinned even as water collected on the brim of his hat. "Paige and the triplets changed my life."

"Yeah, well," Hank muttered, "save the Hallmark card for later, will you?"

"Can't help it, buddy." Abruptly, Kurt sobered. "I remember how happy you were with Jo-anne, be-fore—"

Again Hank lifted a palm. "That was a long time ago." He had spent ten long years, working to counter the loss. "I'm over it," he stated flatly.

"Glad to hear it." Kurt slapped him on the shoulder. "So maybe you'll start dating again."

The thought of opening his heart to the possibility of pain like that had him clenching his jaw. "I've dated."

His cousin lifted a skeptical brow.

I just haven't found a woman who could take Jo-anne's place. Hank cleared his throat and focused on the situation at hand. "Right now I have to figure out how to hang on to this ranch before Ally Garrett sells it out from under me."

Kurt blinked in amazement. "She's really going to let the Mesquite Ridge go, given how her folks felt about the ranch?"

Hank shook his head in silent censure. "The sooner, the better, in her view." As they headed back to Kurt's truck, Hank told him about the interest thus far from Corporate Farms and the local realty.

"Better get your bid in soon, then," Kurt advised.

He nodded, accepting the advice. *If only it was that simple.*

His cousin headed for the driver's seat. "Meantime, I suggest you read through the handouts in the folder I brought you. You and Ally are going to want to be prepared when Duchess tells you it's time…."

The rain was still falling when Ally drove up to the ranch house early that evening. Telling herself she was relieved to see that Hank's pickup was no longer parked next to the barn, she grabbed her briefcase full of information from the Realtor, her handbag and two small bags of groceries. Lamenting her lack of an umbrella, she headed swiftly for the back door.

The mudroom was as dark and gloomy as the rest of the house as Ally made her way inside. She promptly tripped over something warm and solid, and what felt like a pile of blankets.

A high-pitched yelp matched her own.

Belongings went flying as Ally threw out her arms and attempted to catch herself.

Another high-pitched yelp followed, plus the scrambling of feet on linoleum then a second crash as something hit the opposite wall.

Ally flipped on the light.

Found herself face-to-face with Duchess.

Only this time, instead of looking ferocious, the golden retriever looked hurt and stunned. And to Ally's surprise, very, very sad.

What was it Hank had said? *You'll both feel better if you take the time to make friends with Duchess. Pet her, talk to her, show her a little kindness....*

Ally supposed there was no time like the present to call a truce, especially since the two of them were alone. The last thing she wanted was to get bitten by a dog again.

Swallowing, Ally hunkered down the way she had seen Hank do. Trembling with apprehension, she held out her hand and took a deep, bolstering breath. "I'm sorry, girl. I didn't know you were in here." Which was something else she'd have to talk to Hank about. She had expected him to leave Duchess in his bedroom, not downstairs....

Her back against the wall, the dog stared at Ally and remained very still.

Ally gulped. Determined to establish peace with the lost animal, she forced herself to move closer and continue to offer her palm. After another long hesitation, Duchess dipped her head slightly and delicately sniffed Ally's skin.

Then she lifted her head and looked into Ally's eyes, seeming to want peace between them, too.

Which meant, Ally knew, she had to take the next step and pet the dog, too.

With Duchess watching as cautiously as Ally was watching her, she moved her hand once again.

Ally gently stroked first one paw, then the entire leg, before ever so tenderly moving her hand to the dog's chest, and then the sensitive spot behind her long, floppy ear. Oddly enough, the action was almost as soothing to Ally as it was to the canine. Noting how good Duchess looked with her clean, silky-soft coat, and dark liquid eyes, Ally smiled. And could have sworn the dog smiled back at her.

Maybe this experience would help her—if not actually like dogs, then at least tolerate being around them. And vice versa, Ally thought.

Which, of course, was when the back door opened and Hank strode in.

Pleasure lit his midnight-blue eyes. "Well, now, what have we here?" he boomed in a baritone worthy of ol' Saint Nick. Clearly unable to resist, he teased, "A softening of that stone wall around your heart?"

The heat of embarrassment swept her cheeks. Ally dropped her hand and stood. "Obviously, I had to do this."

Hank took off his wet rain slicker and hung it on the wall, then his hat. "Obviously."

Ally watched Hank run his hands through his disheveled hair. "I startled her," she explained.

He scanned Ally from head to toe, lingering on her rain-splattered trench coat. "And you didn't want to get bitten."

She shrugged out of her own coat and hung it on the hook next to Hank's. "No, I did not."

He kneeled down to pet the reclining retriever. "Hmm."

Ally scrambled to pick up the things scattered across the floor. "Why didn't you tell me you were going to put her in the mudroom?"

He looked at the full food and water dishes in the corner, then gallantly lent a hand. "You weren't here when I left."

Together, they carried Ally's belongings to the kitchen counter. "You could have left me a note."

"I did." He pointed to the message on the blackboard, next to the ancient wall phone. "I assumed you'd come in the front door."

He went back to arrange the pile of blankets in an inviting circle, then motioned for Duchess to come toward him. She moaned as she got up and ambled stiffly forward to collapse on the soft, makeshift bed.

Hank petted her briefly, then came back into the kitchen.

He smelled like winter rain.

"How did your meeting with the Realtor go?"

Not good. Ally unpacked the groceries she'd bought to get her through the next few days. "Marcy Lyon gave me a whole list of things that need to be done to the ranch house before the property goes on the market, if I want to get top dollar."

"Such as...?"

Ally opened the fridge and saw a delicious looking slab of beef from Sonny's Barbecue, a restaurant in Laramie. "Removing all the wallpaper and painting the entire interior, for starters."

While she put items away, Hank got out containers of restaurant coleslaw, potato salad and beans. "You could sell it as is." The mesquite-smoked brisket followed.

Ally ignored the scent of fine Texas barbecue and kept out a container of yogurt, and a crisp green apple, for herself. "And lose thousands of dollars and the potential of a quick and easy sale? No." She rummaged through the drawer for a spoon and filled a glass with tap water. "The look of this place has got to be updated before it officially hits the MLS listings. Marcy gave me a list of contractors to call. Hopefully, one of them will be able to help me out."

Hank added barbecue sauce and a package of freshly baked wheat rolls to the spread on the kitchen table. He shut the fridge door and swung around to face her. Amiably, he offered, "I could help you out if you'd agree to delay the sale for a short while."

Beware unexpected gifts in handsome packages. "And do what?" Ally challenged, ripping off the foil top to her yogurt.

He lounged against the counter, arms folded in front of him. "Give me a chance to pitch my plan to turn this ranch into a money-making operation."

Ally swallowed a spoonful of creamy vanilla yogurt and held up one hand to stop him. There was no way she was ever going to be as impractical and starry-eyed about the land as her parents had been. "I've heard enough plans," she stated simply.

Hank's dark brows lifted. Ignoring his skeptical look, she stirred her yogurt and pushed on. "That was all my father ever did—was come up with one scheme after another. None of which, mind you, was ever implemented…at least not effectively." Hence, the Mesquite Ridge Ranch had become a giant money pit rather than a paying investment.

Hank turned and reached for two plates. "There's a difference. I grew up on a ranch. I come from a family of ranchers. I know I could make this work—to the point I'd be able to pay all the taxes and operating expenses in the meantime—and eventually buy the ranch from you outright. All you need to do is just give me a chance."

Ally couldn't deny it was what her parents would have wanted—for her to sell Mesquite Ridge to someone who loved the land as much as they did. That is, if they could not get her to keep it herself. Which she didn't want to do. She watched as Hank set the table for two.

"Fine," she snapped, irked by his presumption. "If you think you have all the answers and can turn this place around?" She set her yogurt aside and sauntered up to him. "Then show me the numbers on paper. 'Cause I'm not interested in any pipe dreams or half-formed plans. Only the cold, hard facts."

Hank's gaze scanned Ally's face and body, lingering thoughtfully, before returning ever so deliberately to her eyes.

"How long do I have?" he drawled finally, in a way that left her feeling she had somehow come up short yet again.

"Until I officially put the property on the market," Ally answered, mocking his take-charge demeanor. "December 24."

"Fair enough." Hank's broad shoulders relaxed. He stepped back, smiling as if he'd already won her over with his brilliance and the deal was done. "In the meantime, you're more than welcome to join me for supper. As you can see, there's plenty."

There was indeed.

Unfortunately, sitting down with him like this would add yet another layer of intimacy to a situation that was becoming far too familiar, too fast. Ally stiffened her spine. She had come back here, against her will, to end this unhappy saga of her life. No way was she getting sucked back in again, with small town kindness or friendly overtures from handsome men with designs on her family's property.

"No, thanks," she said politely.

"Sure?" His genial expression didn't falter.

Ally chose the one avenue she knew would turn him off—a hit on his legendarily fine character. Ignoring the flutter of her pulse, she stepped away from him and stated in a coolly indifferent tone, "Supplying me with dinner will not give you an edge over any other prospective buyer."

As she expected, he remained where he was. The room was suddenly still enough to hear a pin drop.

His irises darkened to the color of midnight. He stepped closer. "Is that so?" His voice was silky-soft, contemplative. And somehow dangerous in a deeply sensual way.

Ally could see she had insulted him—just as she had intended—and created a real rift between them, simply by making the allegation. Refusing to back down, she folded her arms in front of her. "Yes."

"Then how about this?" Hank demanded.

Before she could do more than draw a quick, startled breath, he had pulled her into his arms. One hand pressed against her spine, aligning the softness of her body to the hardness of his. His other hand threaded through the hair at the back of her neck and tilted her face up. Slowly, he lowered his head toward hers. "And this?" he dared softly, a wicked grin curling the corners of his delectably firm and sensual lips.

As his breath warmed her face, she drew in the scent of wintergreen, and beneath that something masculine…brisk…like the chill winter rain falling outside. His mouth dipped lower still, until it hovered just above hers. "Will this give me an edge?" he taunted.

More like a demerit.

Refusing to let him know how much the near caress was affecting her, Ally smiled at him cynically and narrowed her gaze. "Go ahead and kiss me," she challenged sweetly. "It won't matter, either way."

"Good to know," Hank murmured, lowering his head all the more, until the only way to get any closer was to kiss her. "Because if I wanted to seduce you into selling the ranch to me," he informed her softly and patiently, "I'd do this." His lips brushed hers. Tentatively, then wantonly, as a thrill unlike anything Ally had ever felt swept through her.

"Not just once," he promised, kissing her hotly, "but again and again and again."

Hank kissed her with the steady determination of a marine, and the finesse of a cowboy who knew how to make happen anything he wanted. He was at once masculine and tender, persuasive and tempting. Seducing her in a way that left no room for denial. Ally caught her breath as her hands moved involuntarily to his shoulders and she tilted her head beneath his….

Hank hadn't figured he'd be putting the moves on Ally Garrett, now or ever. It wasn't that he wasn't physically attracted to her—he was. But he knew the two of them were all wrong for each other. And always would be. Yet the coolly provoking way she stared into his eyes, combined with the way she was testing him, made him want to haul her into his arms, and challenge her right back. And damned if instead of getting angry and slapping him across the face—and putting an end to this ludicrousness—she was pressing her body against his and kissing him.

As if she meant it.

As if she hadn't been kissed in a good long while.

As if she needed to feel close to someone again.

And wasn't that the kicker? Hank thought, as his lingering kisses continued to knock her for a loop.

They shouldn't be doing this, and yet he couldn't seem to summon up the urge to put an end to it, either. Not without indulging for a few minutes more....

Who would have thought a totally ill-advised make-out session with a self-serving cowboy could make her feel so good? Ally wondered as Hank wrapped arms around her. He gathered her so close she could feel the hard, hot muscles of his chest pressing against her breasts, and his heart slamming against his ribs.

He opened his mouth, exploring every inch of hers with his tongue, encouraging her to do the same to him.

Whoever would have thought she and the land-loving Hank McCabe would have anything in common? Especially when she intended to go right back to the city, as soon as her task was done....

When he finally came to his senses and released her, he looked as stunned by the passion that had flared up between them as she was.

Hank stepped abruptly. "Fortunately for you—" Hank's jaw tightened with the implacableness she expected from a McCabe "—the only way I'm interested in securing this property is by triumphing over the other bidders, fair and square."

Of course he was thinking about the ranch!

Mesquite Ridge was probably the *only* thing he'd been thinking about during the last five minutes.

Whereas she, Ally noted sadly, had foolishly romanticized Hank McCabe's pass to the nth degree. Damn her foolish heart! "Well, that's good, because 'fair and square' is the only way you'll get it!" she retorted, relying on her inherent cynicism for self-preservation. Legs trembling, she swept up her dinner and her soft leather shoulder bag. She cast him one long, scathing glance before storming past him. "Now if you'll excuse me, I've got some calls to make."

And some incredibly hot, passionate kisses to forget.

Chapter 4

An hour and a half later, Hank was in the mudroom, checking on Duchess, when he heard Ally come back into the kitchen. The sound of cabinets opening and closing followed.

Curious, he stood and ambled in to join her. Ally did not look as if things were going her way. "Need something?"

She rocked back on the heels of her red cowgirl boots. With her honey-blond hair in disarray, she looked prettier than ever. "Coffee. And I can't even find the coffeemaker."

Trying not to notice how nicely the crisp white shirt and gold tapestry vest cloaked the soft swell of her breasts, Hank admitted, "It bit the dust a while back." Briefly, he let his gaze drop to the fancy belt encircling her slender waist, and the jeans molding her hips and

long, luscious legs. Just that quickly, he wanted to haul
her into his arms and kiss her again.

Knowing that would be a very unwise idea, if he
wanted to keep them out of bed, he pointed to the
metal pot on the back of the stove instead. "I've been
using that."

Ally blinked in surprise. "You're kidding."

So she had forgotten how to rough it, Hank concluded. He quirked a brow. "It works fine."

Clearly unconvinced, she sighed.

"I'll make you some," he offered.

Ally lifted her hands in quick protest. "No—I've
got it." She brushed past him in a drift of orange blossom perfume, and checked the freezer. "If I could only
find the coffee."

"It's in the brown canister next to the stove."

"Okay. Thanks." All business now, Ally reached for
the pot and peered inside. Frowning, because it still
contained the remnants of the morning brew, she carried it to the sink, rinsed it thoroughly, then filled it
with two pints of cold water. She swung back to him,
a self-conscious blush pinkening her high, sculpted
cheeks. "Where do I put the coffee?"

"In the bottom of the pot."

Before he could explain further, a quietly grumbling
Ally had opened the canister and dumped six tablespoons of ground coffee into the water. She snapped
on the lid, put the pot back on the stove, then turned
the burner to high.

Aware she still looked frustrated and upset, after a
string of phone calls in the other room, Hank asked, "Any
luck finding someone to paint the interior for you?"

Ally paced back and forth. "None whatsoever! And I called all ten names on the list. No one will take on a job this big so close to Christmas. In fact, almost all the crews are taking time off from now till after New Year's." She whirled. "Can you believe it?"

"Bummer." He pinned her with a taunting gaze. "Or should I say bah, humbug?"

The corners of her lips slanted downward and she narrowed her green eyes. "You're a laugh a minute, you know that, McCabe?"

Hank shrugged, glad to have her full attention once again. "I like to think so."

Ally huffed dramatically. "So it's on to plan B."

Curious, he moved closer. "Which is?"

The fragrance of brewing "cowboy coffee" filled the kitchen.

"Stage the house to the best of my ability, without changing the way the walls look, and put a painting allowance into the contract, for anyone interested in purchasing the property."

Hank eyed the faded chuck wagon wallpaper in the kitchen. It was as bad as the horse-and-hound motif in the rest of the downstairs. Luckily, the rooms upstairs had just been painted many, many moons ago. "You really think that will work?" he asked.

"I'll make it work." Ally flounced back to the stove. Noting that the dark liquid had come to a rolling boil, she grabbed an oven mitt and removed the pot from the flame.

"You may want to—"

Ally cut him off with a withering look and plucked

a mug from the cupboard. Lips set stubbornly, she told him, "I think I know how to pour a cup of coffee."

"I'm sure you do." That wasn't the point. But if she insisted on doing things her own way...

Ally filled the mug, then topped it off liberally with milk from the fridge. She lifted it to her mouth.

He watched her take a sip, pause, then walk back to the sink, where it took everything she had, he supposed, for her to swallow instead of spit.

Hank carried the pot to the sink and set it down on a folded towel. Now that she was listening, he said, "The secret to making it this way is to let it steep for a good four minutes or so after boiling."

"Really," Ally echoed dryly, dumping the contents of her mug down the drain.

He met her gaze. "Really."

She set her cup down with a thud and pivoted toward him. "And how would you know that?"

"Experience." Hank studied her right back. "I made campfire coffee over an open flame all the time when I was in the service. Not too many espresso makers where I was."

"What did you do in the marines?" she asked curiously.

"Flew choppers involved in rescue missions."

"That sounds...dangerous."

And fulfilling in a way that countered the loss he had suffered...

But not wanting to talk about Jo-anne, or the years he'd struggled with residual grief and guilt over his fiancée's death, he filled a cup with icy tap water and finished his tutorial. "Once the coffee has steeped, you add three or four tablespoons of cold water to the pot."

Ally wrinked her nose in confusion and disbelief. "To cool it off?"

He shook his head as he demonstrated the technique. "This settles the grounds to the bottom. And voilà! *Now* it's ready to drink."

She sniffed and tossed her head. "I can't imagine those two things make that much of a difference."

On impulse, Hank reached out to tuck a strand of blond hair behind her ear. "Oh, ye of little faith."

Her eyes flashed. "You're beginning to sound all Christmasy again," she accused.

He lifted his shoulders affably. "Sorry."

"No, you're not."

She was right—he wasn't. He liked teasing her, liked seeing the color pour into her cheeks, and the fire of temper glimmer in her dark green eyes. He poured her a fresh mug, got the milk out again. "Give this a try."

She made a face, but eventually took both from him. With a great deal of attitude, she lightened her coffee, took a sip. Paused to savor the taste on her tongue. Astounded, she met his eyes. "That *is* better," she announced in surprise.

At last, he had done something right. Hank lifted a hand. "What'd I tell you?"

Ally beamed. "I could kiss you for this!" She flushed again, as common sense reigned. "But I won't," she rushed to assure him.

Hank nodded, aware that he was already hard, had

been since she'd walked into the room. "Best you not," he agreed.

Ally's cell phone let out a soft chime. She withdrew it from her pocket, looked at the screen. Immediately sobering, she informed him, "I have to take this." She put it to her ear and walked away.

But not far enough that he couldn't hear some of what she was saying.

"...Calm down, Porter. It's not like we didn't know this was going to happen. We have no choice. Stay busy. You're usually big on Christmas! Go see the boat parade on Clear Lake, or The *Nutcracker* or Handel's *Messiah*... I promise I'll call you if I hear anything at all. Yes! Okay. Bye."

She walked back in to retrieve her coffee.

"Everything okay?"

For a moment, Hank thought Ally wouldn't answer.

Her slender shoulders slumped dispiritedly. "All the middle managers from my firm were ordered to take the next two weeks off, so that the executives in the firm that took us over can decide who goes and who stays." She met his eyes and admitted almost too casually, "The general idea is to keep the same number of clients and financial analysts and advisors while cutting costs...and that means a number of the higher salary employees—like myself—are going to be laid off."

"I'm guessing Porter is a middle manager, too."

Ally grimaced. "He started the same time I did, right out of college. We've worked our way up together. He's going to be absolutely devastated if he is let go."

As would Ally, Hank thought.

He studied her crestfallen expression. "Do you think you're going to make the cut?"

She shrugged. Her expression became emotionally charged. "If life were fair," she stated, "I would. But..." she swallowed, her expression suddenly remote "...you and I both know it's not."

"Hence, the immediate sale of the property," Hank guessed.

Ally shrugged again. "It needs to be done, in any case. Right now I've got the time to get the property listed. After December 26, I may not."

"Because you'll either be very busy with the reorg at work..." He refreshed both their coffees.

"Or pounding the pavement, looking for another job." She added a little more milk to hers. "Obviously, Porter and I both hope it's the former, not the latter."

Hank felt an unexpected twinge of jealousy. Realizing he was more interested in Ally than he'd thought, he stepped closer and asked, "Are you dating Porter?"

She looked surprised, then bemused by the question. "Uh...no. We're just friends."

Hank was relieved to hear that. Yet...he still had to ask. "Are you romantically involved with anyone?"

She rolled her eyes as if the mere notion was ridiculous. "I don't have time for that. But what about you?" she asked curiously. "Has there been anyone since that girl you were engaged to when you graduated from college?"

Hank shook his head.

Ally walked over to test the wallpaper. She found it rigidly adhered to the wall in some places, practically falling off in others. She deposited a strip of paper in the trash, then knelt to examine the linoleum floor. The speckled yellow-green-and-brown surface was clean, but very dated and extremely ugly. "What happened to the two of you, anyway?" She ran her palm thoughtfully over the worn surface.

Hank lounged against the counter. "Jo-anne was killed in a terrorist attack overseas."

Ally stood to face him again. "I'm sorry," she said, genuinely contrite. "I didn't know." She paused and wet her lips. "Is that why…?"

Hank guessed where this was going. "I joined the marines? Yeah."

Another silence fell, more intimate yet. "And since…?" Ally prodded softly, searching his eyes as if wanting to understand him as much as he suddenly wanted to understand her.

"I've dated," he admitted gruffly. He shrugged and took another long draft of strong coffee. "Nothing… no one's…come close to what I had with Jo-anne." He turned and rummaged through the fridge, looking for something to eat. He emerged with a handful of green grapes. "What about you?" He offered her some.

Ally took several. "I was engaged a few years ago, before my mother got sick."

This was news. Hank watched Ally munch on a grape. "What happened?"

"I brought my fiancé home to the ranch. Dexter was a real city boy and I expected him to share my lack of attachment to the place. Instead, he fell in love with Mesquite Ridge and thought we should both quit our jobs in Houston and settle here permanently."

Hank polished off the rest of the grapes in his palm. "Your mom and dad must have liked that."

"Oh, yes." Ally made a face. "The problem was—" she angled a thumb at her sternum "—I didn't. I'd spent my whole life trying to get away from here and—" She stopped abruptly and whirled around, staring toward the mudroom in concern. "Did you hear that? It sounded like…"

A low, pain-filled moan reverberated.

"That's Duchess!" Without a second's hesitation, Ally hurried toward the sound. "She's obviously in some sort of distress!"

You never would have known this was a woman who didn't like dogs, Hank thought as Ally knelt in front of the ailing pet. She looked alarmed as she watched Duchess circle around restlessly, paw the heap of blankets, then drop down, only to get up and repeat the procedure. "What's she doing?" Ally asked.

Hank gave Duchess a wide berth and a reassuring look. "She's trying to make a bed," he said in a soft, soothing voice. "Dams do that for up to twenty-four hours before they deliver."

Ally moved so close to Hank their shoulders almost touched. "How do you know that?"

He resisted the urge to put his arm around her shoulders. "Kurt came by to examine Duchess while you were out. He confirmed she's within twenty-four to thirty-six hours of delivering her pups."

The news had Ally looking as if she might faint.

Hank slid a steadying palm beneath her elbow. "Kurt gave me the handout he distributes to the owners of all his patients, as well as a whelping kit and a warming box. I read through the literature before I went out to take care of my cattle." Figuring Ally would feel better if she was similarly prepared, Hank walked back to the kitchen, with her right behind him. He found the folder and gave it to her to peruse.

She skimmed through the extensive information, troubleshooting instructions and explicit pictures with brisk efficiency. "We can't handle this!"

It if had been a purely financial matter, Hank bet she would have said otherwise. He cast a glance toward the mudroom, where Duchess was still circling, pawing and preparing. "Sure we can." Knowing the importance of a positive attitude, he continued confidently, "It's been about fifteen years, but I've done it before. I helped deliver a litter of Labrador retriever puppies on our ranch, when I was a kid." That had been one of the most exciting and meaningful experiences of his life.

Ally put the pages aside and wrung her hands. "Can't your cousin do this? He is a vet!"

Annoyed by her lack of faith, Hank frowned. "There's no reason for Kurt to do this when I can handle it."

Ally lifted a brow, unconvinced.

Irritated, Hank continued in a flat tone. "Someone needs to be with Duchess during the entire labor and delivery process. Kurt has other patients and responsibilities. He couldn't leave Duchess at home while he's off working with other animals. And if he took her to the clinic, she and her litter would be exposed to the viruses other dogs bring in, and that could be lethal to the newborn pups."

That much, Ally understood. But she was still reluctant to participate. She threw up her hands as if warding off an emotional disaster. "Okay, I get that, but I still can't do this, Hank! It's just too far out of my realm of expertise!"

He had thought it was a bummer that Ally Garrett loathed Christmas. With effort, he checked his disappointment about this, too. "Fine. You don't have to help." Holiday or not, he couldn't magically infuse her with the spirit of sacrifice and giving. No matter how much he wished otherwise...

"Good," she snapped, appearing even more upset. "Because I'm not going to!" After taking one long, last look at Duchess, she handed the folder to Hank, and rushed out of the kitchen.

There was absolutely no reason for her to feel guilty, Ally told herself firmly as she went up to the second floor sewing room and checked out the bolts of upholstery fabric still on the shelves. Not when she heard the canine whimpering coming up through the heating grate.

Or when Hank ran upstairs to raid the linen closet, and hurried back down again.

Or when she heard him rushing back and forth below, his boots echoing on the wood floor.

But twenty minutes later, when a loud whimpering was followed by an unnatural stillness, she couldn't stand it any longer.

On the pretext of getting the tape measure from the

drawer in the kitchen, she went back downstairs to find the table had been pushed to one side.

Duchess was settled in a child's hard plastic swimming pool in the center of the kitchen. Hank knelt next to her. "Come on, girl," he was saying softly, as the animal arched and strained. "You can do it."

Duchess let out a yelp, then looked at her hindquarters with a mixture of alarm and bewilderment. A dark blue water bag had emerged. "Get a couple of the towels. They're warming in the dryer," Hank directed.

Figuring that was the least important of the chores, Ally rushed to comply. By the time she returned, Duchess had heaved again, and the pup was out completely.

Duchess reached around, tore and removed the sack with her teeth, and cut the cord. As soon as that was done, she licked her newborn vigorously. The pup let out a cry.

Ally's eyes welled with tears at the sound of new life.

Duchess turned away from the pup and began to strain again. Hank picked up the whelp, wrapped it in a towel and handed it to Ally. The pup was warm and soft to the touch. The joy she felt as she looked down at the pale gold puppy cradled neatly in the palm of her hand was overwhelming.

Hank set the warming box on the floor, made sure the heating pad was turned to low, positioned it on one side of the plastic incubator, then covered it with a white, terry-cloth crate pad. "We'll give this a moment to warm up," he said, "before we unwrap the pup and put him in."

Too overcome to speak, Ally nodded.

Seconds later, Duchess strained yet again, and the second pup was delivered.

Over the next two hours, eight more were born.

Amid the squeaking and the squirming, Duchess cared for them all.

Until finally, she collapsed with a sigh.

"Do you think that's it?" Ally asked.

"Only one way to tell," Hank said. He counted the pups. "Kurt said there were definitely ten…."

Duchess strained again, ever so slightly.

A dark blue sack, tinier than the others, fell out.

Only this time, Duchess merely nosed the pup and turned away.

Please don't let this last one be stillborn, Ally prayed. "What do we do?" she asked frantically.

"Do our best to save it," Hank muttered. He picked up the sack, quickly figured out which end contained the pup's head, and tore the protective membrane open with his fingers. Amniotic fluid spilled out as he gave the pup's nose a squeeze.

There should have been a cry, as with the others.

But there wasn't.

Knowing there was no time to waste, Hank grabbed the bulb syringe, pressed the air out of it, and then suctioned mucous from the lifeless pup's throat and nostrils. Nothing happened. Again, he suctioned out the fluids. The puppy still didn't respond.

Hand pressed to her chest, Ally watched as Hank lifted the tiny form and made a tight seal by putting his own mouth over the pup's nose and mouth, gave two gentle puffs, then pulled back and assessed her.

Again nothing, Ally noted in mounting despair. No visible sign of life.

Helpless tears streamed from her eyes as Hank repeated the puffing process, then rubbed the puppy's chest while holding her head down.

Still nothing, Ally noted miserably.

Hank used the bulb syringe again, then lifted the puppy and attempted mouth-to-mouth resuscitation once more. And this time, to Ally's overwhelming relief, their prayers were answered.

The sound of that small gasp, followed by a high-pitched, rather indignant squeak, was nothing short of a miracle, Ally thought.

With tears of joy rolling down her cheeks, she watched as Hank gently wiped the moisture from the tiny puppy and wrapped her in a cloth.

Ally drew a quavering breath and edged so close to Hank their bodies touched. "That was…incredible," she breathed, not sure when she had ever been so impressed by a man's gallantry under pressure.

He nodded, looking as amazed and grateful as she felt. "I didn't think she was going to make it," he admitted in a rusty voice.

Ally studied the cute black nose and tightly closed eyes. The pup's ears were as small and compact and beautiful as the rest of her snugly swaddled form. "You saved her."

Yet a trace of worry remained in Hank's blue eyes, Ally noted as he passed her the newborn.

A ribbon of fear slipped through her. She cuddled the tiny pup close to her breast, relieved to feel its soft puffs of breath against the open vee of her shirt. The whelp was breathing nice and rhythmically now, and felt warm to the touch. Yet… Ally searched Hank's face. "What is it?" she asked quietly. "What aren't you telling me?"

His glance met hers, then skittered away, as if he didn't want to be the bearer of bad news. "She's really small," he said finally.

About a third smaller than the others, Ally noted. She nuzzled the top of the puppy's head as she followed Hank back to Duchess's side. "So?" She felt the tiny pup brush its muzzle against her collarbone and snuggle even closer. Unbearable tenderness sifted through her and she stroked the dog gently with her free hand. Was this the connection dog lovers felt? Why many considered canines not just pets but members of their family?

All Ally knew for sure was that she felt fiercely protective of this tiny being. And would do anything to help her thrive. "Isn't there usually a runt of the litter?"

Hank admitted that was so, then frowned. "But it's not just that." He bent down to tend to Duchess.

Ally watched him remove the placenta and gently clean away any remaining afterbirth with the skill of a veteran rancher. "Then what's wrong?" she pressed. She lowered her head and heard a faint purr emanating from the whelp's chest. "I mean, she seems to be breathing okay now." The other ten puppies were okay, too. All snuggled together cozily in the warming box, which had been placed inside the whelping pen, within easy reach of Duchess.

Hank brought a bowl of water to Duchess, and knelt

down next to the golden retriever. Shakily, the dam got to her feet and lapped at the water, before sinking down once again. Surveying her with a knowledge-able eye, Hank said reluctantly, "It could just be that the pup you're holding was the last of the litter to be born. And Duchess was exhausted."

Another shiver of dread swept through Ally.

She watched Hank take a fistful of kibble and hand feed it to Duchess. Wondering what he still wasn't tell-ing her, Ally prodded, "I hear an 'except' in there."

Hank's big body tensed. "Sometimes," he allowed wearily, deliberately avoiding Ally's eyes, "when a mother dog shows absolutely no interest in one of her whelps, it's because the dam knows instinctively there's something wrong with the pup. That it may not survive..."

Shock quickly turned to anger. How could he even say that, after all they'd already been through? Ally wondered. "But the littlest one did survive," she pro-tested heatedly, still cradling the puppy to her chest.

Hank nodded. And remained silent.

"She's going to be fine," Ally insisted, and to prove it, placed the runt in the warming box with the rest of the litter.

Again, Hank nodded. But he didn't seem nearly as certain of that as she wanted him to be.

Chapter 5

Wary of fast wearing out his welcome at Mesquite Ridge in regards to Duchess and her puppies, Hank gathered up the soiled towels and cloths, and carried them to the washing machine. For the second time that night, he added detergent and bleach, and switched it on. He returned to the kitchen, spray bottle of disinfectant cleaner, paper towels and plastic trash bag in hand.

He hunkered down to clean out the plastic whelping bed.

While he worked, Ally knelt on the floor next to the warming bed that contained all eleven puppies. The whelping instructions Kurt had left for them were in her hands. She appeared seriously concerned and incredibly overwhelmed with the responsibility of caring for the dam and her litter. Duchess was right beside

Ally, face on her paws, serenely keeping watch over her brood.

Hank knew there was no need to burden Ally with this, too—she had enough on her plate, with the sale of the ranch, the task of sorting through her parents' things and the possible loss of her job. "I think I can handle it from here," he said gently.

She stopped reading and looked up, as if she hadn't heard right. "What?"

Was that hurt he saw flashing in her eyes? Or just fatigue and confusion? It had been a long day for Ally, too. "I need to walk Duchess for a moment," Hank told her. "But then I can handle it." He paused, wishing Ally would hang out with them a little longer. She was turning out to be surprisingly good company. "Unless you want to stay," he added impulsively.

For a second, Ally looked truly torn about whether to stay or go. "I'll stay until you get them all settled," she said finally.

"Thanks." Deciding to leave her to her thoughts, he headed outside, with Duchess beside him.

The retriever quickly got down to business, then headed back inside. This time she walked straight to Ally.

Hank knew Duchess was waiting to be petted.

Ally didn't.

Recognizing it wasn't going to happen, at least not then, the dog sank down beside her, close enough that her nose was touching Ally's thigh.

Ally looked at Duchess briefly, tenderness flickering across her delicate features. Wordlessly, she smiled and went back to her reading.

Hank folded a clean blanket in the bottom of the whelping pen, then encouraged Duchess to climb back in. "Come on, girl. I need you to get in here so you can take care of your puppies."

Duchess just looked at him, clearly understanding, but in no mood to comply.

At the "standoff" between him and his canine pal, Ally did her best to stifle a grin. Which showed how much she knew.

"You want to try?" Hank asked.

Her eyes twinkling, Ally tilted her head to one side and said drily, "I don't think she's in a mood to listen to me, either. But…" She rose gracefully and moved to the makeshift bed, patting it firmly. "Come on, sweetheart. You'll be more comfortable in here."

Surprisingly, Duchess rose, climbed in and settled down immediately.

Hank was stunned—and grateful. "Thanks."

"No problem." Ally waved the papers still clutched in her free hand. "I think we're supposed to introduce the puppies to Duchess next."

That was indeed the protocol. The only surprise was that Ally—a confessed dog loather—wanted to be present for this, too. But maybe tonight, Duchess and her big brood were changing all that, as well as Ally's feelings about being at the ranch. Which only went to show that miracles did happen at Christmas, Hank thought.

Keeping his feelings to himself, he asked, "You want to do the first one?"

Ally bit her lower lip, abruptly appearing shy and uncertain once again. "Maybe you better."

Figuring the littlest pup needed her mama most, Hank picked her up and laid her ever so gently in front of Duchess.

Once again, the mother dog turned her nose away, prepared to go to sleep.

Hank tried again, with the same result.

For whatever reason, Duchess wanted nothing to do with her tiniest whelp.

Ally shot Hank a look that mirrored his own consternation.

The worry Hank had felt earlier, when they'd been resuscitating the pup, increased. "Let's see if we can get the little one to nurse." He put the tiny pup at a nipple. She suckled weakly and soon fell right back to sleep.

Hank frowned in concern. "Let's see how the rest of them do." He picked up the hardiest pup, a male, from the warming bed and put him in front of Duchess.

The retriever immediately nosed the whelp, kissing and licking him. Encouraged, Hank put him to a nipple. The pup immediately latched on and began to nurse.

And so it went with the remaining whelps, until finally, they were left with eleven pups and ten nipples. Reluctantly, Hank removed the littlest one from Duchess's side, and handed her ever so carefully to Ally. The last puppy took the little one's place and began to nurse vigorously.

Ally cradled the tiniest puppy against her chest. "What are we going to do if she doesn't nurse any better than that?"

Hank studied the sweet-faced golden retriever

curled against the warmth of Ally's breast, and knew they were the castaway pup's last hope. "I'll tell you what we're not going to do," he stated firmly. "We're not going to wait. I'm calling Kurt right now."

To Ally's relief, Kurt McCabe came right out to the ranch, even though it was well past midnight. The personable veterinarian brought a digital scale and his vet bag and checked over the dam and her litter. "Duchess and the whelps all look great," Kurt said when he'd finished recording the weight and sex of all five males and six female pups.

"What about the littlest one?" Ally asked.

"She's definitely a little weaker—as well as tuckered out from her rocky start. That's probably why Duchess initially turned away from her—because she knows instinctively that this pup is going to need more care than the rest, if she's to survive. And on her own, Duchess can't provide that," the vet explained.

Ally glanced at Hank's face, to gauge his reaction. Obviously, this was something the handsome rancher already knew. Which was why he had looked so concerned, and insisted they ask his cousin to make a house call, even if it was the dead of the night.

Her respect for Hank grew.

Ally turned back to Kurt, watching as he gently lifted the littlest one from the warming bed. "Fortunately, the pup's heart and lungs are strong, and there are a lot of things we can do to help her out," he continued.

"Like what?" Ally asked, feeling as protective as if she were the mama herself.

Kurt handed her the puppy. As before, she held the tiny puppy against her chest, and felt it instinctively cuddle close.

"The first thing I'm going to do is give her an injection of replacement plasma to help boost her immune system." Kurt paused to give the puppy the shot.

The little one flinched and let out several high-pitched squeaks.

Ally took comfort in the whelp's strong show of indignation. Judging by the looks on Hank's and Kurt's faces, they also thought it was a good sign.

"It's important you keep her warm. She's going to need to be hand-fed every two hours or so, until she's strong enough to nurse alongside her littermates." Kurt removed several cans of formula and a bottle from his bag, along with another set of instructions. "Come morning, let her try nursing again. Even if it's for only a couple minutes, she'll get colostrum. And of course, keep introducing her to Duchess. Sooner or later they should begin to bond."

And what if they didn't? Ally wondered, exchanging concerned glances with Hank. How would that impact the tiny puppy? Would it alter her chances of survival? Would she grow up feeling like Ally had—as if she never quite fit? Not with her family, not on the ranch, not at school...and now, maybe not even at the job that had been her whole life for the last ten years?

The thought of the defenseless little puppy being rejected made her heart ache.

Mistaking the reason behind Ally's melancholy, Hank stepped closer and patted her arm. "I know this little gal is only twelve ounces—which, according to the weigh-in we just did, makes her roughly twenty-five percent smaller than her siblings. And definitely the runt of the litter." He paused to gaze into Ally's eyes before continuing in a consoling voice, "But often times the smallest one will turn out to be the scrappiest."

"That's true," Kurt agreed.

Realizing worrying about things she couldn't change wouldn't help anything, least of all the tiny puppy cuddled in her arms, Ally began to relax.

Only to see Hank frown again. "The bigger problem is…who do these dogs belong to?"

Kurt nodded toward the wriggling bodies in the warming bed. "These dogs are all definitely show quality purebreds."

Duchess was pretty enough to appear in the Westminster Dog Show, Ally thought, and her puppies were miniature versions of her.

Kurt continued, "Duchess was obviously bred deliberately."

"Which means someone has to be looking for her." Hank knelt down to pet the retriever. He rubbed her large shoulders and stroked behind her ears with so much tenderness Ally felt her own mouth go dry.

"The larger question is how she became separated from the breeder in the first place." The muscles in Hank's own broad shoulders tensed. "Since I'm sure some of these puppies, if not all, have got to be spoken for already."

Surely not the littlest one, Ally thought, then caught herself up short. What was she doing? she wondered in alarm. This puppy wasn't hers to keep! None of them were....

Kurt unhooked the stethoscope from around his neck. "Some dogs want their privacy when they give birth, and slip off to nest in secret. My guess is that's what Duchess did."

"But wouldn't someone have reported her missing by now?" Ally asked.

"You'd think so," the vet replied.

"It's a mystery," Hank concurred grimly. "But one I intend to solve."

Kurt packed up his vet bag. "I'll do everything I can to help." He paused to pet Duchess and several of her puppies. Standing, he glanced wryly at Hank and Ally. "In the meantime, try not to get too attached."

"Easier said than done," Hank muttered beneath his breath.

And for once, Ally knew exactly how Hank McCabe felt.

"So how do you want to do this?" Hank asked her, after Kurt had left.

Ally handed him the littlest pup so she could prepare a bottle of canine milk replacement formula, according to the directions, and set it in a bowl of warm water to heat. Then she checked the items in the emergency kit Kurt had left for them, taking out the unscented baby wipes, cotton balls and petroleum jelly, and lining them up neatly on the table. Lips pursed thoughtfully, she went to the drawer in the kitchen where linens were kept, and pulled out several clean dish towels.

Trying not to notice how cuddly—and fragile—the little puppy felt, Hank followed Ally back to the table. He wasn't sure exactly when the tables had turned. He just knew that she was now the "professional" on the scene. Aware how comfortable she looked in the home she was determined to sell ASAP, he asked, "You want me to handle the feedings tonight?"

Ally shook a few drops of formula on the inside of her wrist, looking up from what she was doing long enough to say, "I can manage the bottle feedings tonight. If we do one now..." She glanced at the clock. It was two in the morning. "...then I'll do another at four, and at six."

Which meant she'd get practically no sleep whatsoever, Hank thought in concern.

He watched her pull out a kitchen chair and sit down. "You sure?"

Ally spread one of the towels across her lap, then held out her arms for the puppy. "I don't mind." Her expression was incredibly tender as the transfer was made. Looking as contented as a new mother, she settled the puppy on her side and gently offered her bottle. "You've got other responsibilities."

No more eager to leave the brand-new litter than she was, Hank pulled up a chair beside them. "So do you."

Ally smiled as the puppy finally got the idea and began to suckle. "Yours are more pressing," she reminded him.

Hank couldn't argue that. It had been raining all night, and the temperature was near freezing. His cattle were going to need extra feed to successfully weather the elements. Plus there were Duchess and the other puppies to consider. They needed help now, too.

"Okay." He rose. "I'll take the ten puppies to Duchess, so they can nurse again, and then get everyone settled for the night."

Fifteen minutes later, all eleven puppies had been fed, licked by Duchess to ensure they would go to the bathroom, and then been cleaned up by their mama. Because Duchess still had no interest in the littlest one, Ally had taken care of the runt. She'd rubbed a moistened cotton ball across her bottom, and after the desired result, had cleaned her up with more cotton balls, adding a protective application of petroleum jelly.

Amazed that a self-professed city girl like Ally could take so early to such a task, Hank moved the puppies away from Duchess and back into the incubator, one by one, where they would be certain to stay warm.

All except the littlest one.

"You want to put her in the warming box, too?" he asked Ally, before he went up to bed himself.

Her gentle smile beautiful to behold, she cuddled the tiny pup to her chest. "I think I'll hold her just a little while longer," she murmured, without looking up.

And Hank knew for certain what he'd only guessed before. Ally was in love. With the puppy whose life he had saved…

"Just a little while longer" turned out to be most of the night. Hank knew that, because Ally was still up, albeit nodding off, when he rose again at five-thirty. "You've really got to get to some sleep," he told her, as he put another pot of coffee on the stove.

Ally yawned and stretched. "You're up."

Hank took the puppies and placed them at Duchess's side, one by one, and made sure they all latched on. "I'm used to staying up all night to nurse sick animals."

Ally shrugged and began preparing another bottle of puppy formula. "Financial analysts pull all-nighters, too."

Hank didn't doubt that she gave her all to whatever she did. Tenacity was something he and Ally seemed to have in common. However, he still thought she needed a break. He closed the distance between them, wishing he could kiss her again. He put his hands over hers, stilling the movements of her fingers. "Seriously, I can handle all the dogs for the next two hours if you want to catch a little shut-eye."

Ally pulled away. "I can't hit the sheets just yet. Gracie is due for another feeding." Her kissable lips assumed a stubborn pout.

Hank pushed away the forbidden image her sweet, soft lips had evoked.

With effort, he concentrated on the problem at hand. "Gracie?"

Reluctant pleasure tugged at the corners of her mouth. "I thought she should have a name, other than 'the littlest one.'"

Their eyes met. Once again, Hank felt a mutual purpose, a bond. The same sort of connection he figured parents of a newborn baby felt. But then she lowered her gaze, and it was gone. He studied the newborn pup's velvety golden coat and scrunched-up face. "Gracie is good. It suits her."

"You're not going to argue with me?" Ally joked, only half-humorously. "Tell me that I shouldn't name a pup I'm only going to have to give away?" She snapped her mouth shut, as if worried she'd reveal even more of her runaway emotions.

Hank shrugged. "I figure you probably already know that. Besides," he said slowly, "Gracie is the runt of the litter."

"What does that have to do with anything?" she demanded, narrowing her eyes.

"Someone willing to pay top dollar for a show quality retriever may not want anything less than perfection. Cute as Gracie is, her size could be a deterrent."

Ally fumed. "Not to me!"

No kidding. Her intense reaction worried him a bit. Ally was becoming personally involved in the situation and was bound to get her heart broken if and when Duchess's owner showed up to claim the litter and their mama. She almost would have been better off if she had continued to loathe the canine species as much as she had when Duchess first showed up.

The sound of a truck motor in the driveway broke the silence. Ally wrinkled her nose and continued cradling the puppy like a newborn baby. "Are you expecting anyone?"

Hank shook his head. "You?"

She furrowed her brow. "At dawn?"

A knock sounded on the back door, and Hank went to open it.

His father was standing there, foil-covered plate in hand.

Hank figured he knew what this was about.

The blessing was, Ally didn't. And if he could help it, she would never have any idea.

Chapter 6

"Might as well get it over with," Hank told his father short minutes later. As the sun rose over the horizon, the two of them emerged from Hank's pickup truck and strode toward the back. Hank opened the tailgate so they could get at the supplemental feed for his herd, and shot his father a knowing glance. "'Cause I know you didn't come here just to say hello to Ally, see the new pups and help me tend my cattle."

"You're right." Shane hefted a big bale of hay and carried it into the mesquite-edged pasture where the hundred cattle had weathered the cold and rain the night before. "I did want to talk to you in private."

Hank cut the twine and separated the feed, scattering it about so the steers could get at it easily. "What about?"

The two of them got back in the truck and drove a

little farther on before stopping and doing the same thing again.

"The word in town is that Corporate Farms is wooing Ally," Shane stated.

Hank shrugged. "She's talking to a Realtor about listing the property, too."

His dad lifted a silver brow. "I thought *you* had a deal with her."

I thought so, too. Which was what he got for letting the arrangement be as convenient as Ally had needed it to be, when he had volunteered to watch over the property for her last summer, in the wake of her dad's death.

Hank went over to check the water supply. Ice had formed around the edges of the trough, so he broke it up with a hoe. "She agreed to let me run cattle here and live in the house, in exchange for my help tending to the ranch." At the time it had seemed the perfect solution for both of them.

Shane studied the property with a horse rancher's keen gaze. "She knew you were interested in buying it?"

"Eventually." *When I had the money.* "Yes." Hank carried another bundle of feed across the rain-soaked ground. "She also figured—rightly so—that I couldn't afford it yet."

Shane followed with another bundle. "I wish you had talked to me before you struck that deal," he said with regret.

Hank's irritation increased. Tired of weathering his father's meddling in his affairs, he squared off with him. "We both know what would have happened if I had!"

"You'd be better off now," his dad countered, his disapproval as evident as his need to help.

"I'd be *better off* if you and the rest of the family stopped trying to coddle me!" Acting as if he were some damned invalid, instead of a decorated ex-marine embarking on the next chapter of his life.

His father grimaced like the take-charge man he was. "We're not doing that," he argued.

Like hell they weren't! "You've done nothing but that since Jo-anne's death," Hank countered.

Shane's jaw set. "You fell apart."

Hank turned his gaze away from the mounting concern in his dad's eyes. "And I've long since put myself back together again."

Shane sighed. Tried again. "The point is, son—"

"The point is," he interrupted curtly, lifting a staying hand, "we shouldn't be having this conversation. Not now. Not ever."

Ally was upstairs in the sewing room when Hank and Shane returned.

It didn't take a rocket scientist to know something had happened while they were gone. The two men appeared to be barely speaking as they parted company. Which was a surprise. Ally had thought the McCabes were a close-knit family through and through. Yet as Hank stood watching his father's pickup disappear from view, he looked as tense and bereft as she had usually felt when dealing with her own parents.

Not that it was any of her business, she reminded herself sternly, returning to the cutting table.

Seconds later, she heard him come in.

Footsteps sounded in the hall. The door to his bedroom closed.

Fifteen minutes later, Hank emerged, looking freshly showered and cleanly shaven. He paused in the doorway of the sewing room. A smile quirked his lips when he glanced at the puppies snuggled together in the warming bed, with Duchess lying on the floor next to it.

An eyebrow lifted in silent inquiry.

Self-consciously, Ally explained, "I needed to do work up here, and I didn't think I should leave them unattended so soon."

Hank nodded, a knowing light in his midnight-blue eyes.

"By the way, the candy cane shaped coffeecake your mother sent over was absolutely delicious." The festive gift had sported a flaky golden bread, cranberry-cherry filling and cream cheese frosting.

Hank folded his arms and propped one shoulder against the frame. "I'll tell her you said so." He nodded at the sophisticated ivory fabric she was measuring. "What are you doing here?"

Ally picked up the shears and began to cut. "Making new drapes for the downstairs windows, to dress up the space."

He came closer, in a drift of sandalwood and leather cologne. "You know how to do that?"

Her gaze flicked over his nice-fitting jeans and navy corduroy shirt, then rose in a guilty rush. "My mother taught me how to sew when I was eight. I helped her make custom slipcovers and draperies." And she needed to stop remembering what it had been like to be held in his arms, kissing him passionately.

Hank hooked his thumbs in the belt loops on either side of his fly. "I didn't realize she had a business."

Ally swallowed around the sudden parched feeling of her throat. "They needed the income she brought in to buy more land."

His gaze roved her face, settling briefly on her mouth. A prickling, skittering awareness sifted through her. "And put you through college?" he added, almost as an afterthought.

Ally tensed and marked off another length. "I did that myself."

Hank did a double take. "Seriously?"

Ally picked up her shears once again. She bent her head, concentrating on her cutting. "They didn't want me to leave Laramie County. They would have preferred I stay on the ranch and build a life here."

He came closer. "But you went anyway."

She sighed. "Like I said, I was determined to do things my own way." She pushed the bad memories aside and turned her attention back to him. "And speaking of parents...what's going on with you and your dad?"

A muscle in his jaw flexed. "What do you mean?"

Ally eyed him pointedly. "I saw the two of you come back. Neither of you looked particularly happy."

Hank shrugged and averted his gaze.

"Does the discord have something to do with the ranch?"

His expression darkened. "Why would you think that?"

"I'm not sure." It was her turn to lift her shoulders. "I just do."

Silence fell. Hank looked as if he was about to say something, but didn't. The quiet continued, fraught with tension.

Aware this wasn't the first time she'd been summarily cut out of a situation—her parents had done it all the time—Ally turned her attention back to her task and cut along the last line she had marked.

Her feelings were hurt, but she wasn't sure why—it shouldn't matter if Hank confided in her or not. She _____ her throat, and added with as much indolence as she could manage, "Anyway, if that's all…"

"Actually—" Hank's frown deepened "—it's not. I've got something I need to do in Laramie."

Could he be more vague?

Could she be more nosy?

Honestly! What was wrong with her today? Just because she and Hank had bonded a little over the birth of the litter, and exchanged one way-too-hot kiss, that was no reason to think they were involved in each other's lives. Because they weren't now, and definitely wouldn't be once the ranch was sold!

"Can you watch over Duchess and the pups a little while longer?"

Trying to hide her disappointment at his sudden remoteness, Ally nodded. "Sure."

And that, it seemed, was that.

"There's no way we can give you a mortgage on Mesquite Ridge without at least ten percent down," the president of Laramie Bank told Hank an hour later. "And given the fact we're talking about a two and a half million dollar loan…" Terence Hall ran a hand over his close-trimmed beard.

Hank had already run the numbers. "I need two hundred and fifty thousand, cash."

Terence rocked back in his chair. "Plus an application fee, closing costs. Money for the survey, inspection and title search. And a real estate sales commission if she lists with a broker, as she currently plans to do."

The situation was getting worse by the minute, Hank thought, as he listened to the Christmas music playing in the lobby of the bank. Only there was no Santa Claus here. Only Ally Garrett, and Gr̶a̶ Penderson from Corporate Farms, who could easily become this year's Grinch, by stealing the property out from under him.

Aware that his holiday spirit was fading as fast as his problems mounted, Hank decided to be straight with the most influential banker in the county. The word in the agricultural community was that if Terence couldn't make it happen, no one could. "I've got only forty thousand saved."

Terence rapped his pen on his desk. "Maybe you could convince Ms. Garrett to do some sort of land contract or lease-purchase agreement."

Hank's hand tightened on the brim of his Stetson. "I doubt it. Besides, even then I'd have only a hundred eighty days max—to come up with the rest of the cash, or forfeit everything I've already put in."

On just the assumption this would work out as I hoped.

"Perhaps if you sell your herd..."

"I'd be all hat and no cattle, with no cash to re-place 'em."

"Sometimes there are sources for cash that aren't readily thought of."

Hank knew where this was heading. He'd already had one argument today with his dad. He wasn't going to have another, with a banker. He lifted a palm and stood, not about to go down that road now. "Thanks for your time," he said curtly. "I'll let you know if anything changes."

Terence followed him to the door. "Maybe you should have another talk with Ms. Garrett," he suggested hopefully.

As it happened, Hank planned to do just that.

The only problem was, when Hank got back to the ranch, a big Cadillac with a Corporate Farms logo was sitting in the driveway.

Frowning, he got out of his truck and walked inside.

Ally was standing next to a ladder in the living room, a spritz bottle in one hand, a putty knife in an-other. In worn jeans, an old Rice University T-shirt and sneakers, with her hair drawn into a clip, she looked younger—and more vulnerable than ever—as Graham Penderson harangued her.

"It's a good offer. Better than you'd get if you went the traditional sale route."

Snorting, Ally sent Graham a narrowed-eyed glance. "That's ten percent less than the asking price suggested by Premier Realty."

You go, girl, Hank thought, pleased to see her standing up to the pushy acquisition agent.

Penderson turned his back on Hank and continued his pitch in a you'd-be-crazy-not-to-accept-this-deal tone. "We subtracted out the real estate commission and other costs. You'd still get the same amount, only without all the hassle and expense of—if you'll forgive my candor—renovating this dog of a house."

It was also, Hank thought, the home in which Ally had grown up.

Not a smart move, criticizing it.

He looked over at her.

Ally's face remained calm, her emotions—whatever they were—camouflaged. She climbed back down the ladder and wordlessly accepted the written offer Graham Penderson was holding out. With a forced smile, she walked over and put the papers on the scarred rolltop desk. "I'll take that into consideration," she stated cooly.

Graham Penderson did not seem to know when to quit. "If you sell to us," he continued, "you won't have to worry about updating anything on the property, since we intend to tear down all existing buildings, including the ranch house and barns, and build something much more utilitarian."

Ally blinked.

She hadn't been expecting that.

"That seems like a waste," Hank interjected, in an effort to buy Ally time to pull her thoughts together.

The agent swung around to him. "It's good business," he countered matter-of-factly. He turned back to Ally. "The offer is good for forty-eight hours," he said impatiently, holding his Resistol at his side.

"So you said." Ally ignored the question in Hank's eyes and gestured toward the door. "Now if you'll excuse me, Mr. Penderson, I have work to do."

The smart move, Hank noted, would have been to take the hint. The agent did no such thing.

"Not if you sell to Corporate Farms. Then, all you have to do is sign on the dotted line, take the money and run."

Clearly unimpressed, Ally stared down the CF representative. "So you *also* said."

Penderson stepped even closer. "I'd hate to see you lose out on what has to be the answer to your prayers."

Ally remained grimly silent. Hank figured this was his cue, and walked toward the agent. "I believe the lady asked you to leave."

Penderson turned. Whatever he was about to say was lost as Hank clapped a firm hand on the small man's shoulder, physically propelling him across the living room, through the dingy foyer and all the way to his car. Hank waited until Penderson drove off, then went back inside. Ally was back on the ladder, spritzing a piece of the loose horse-and-hound wallpaper. If she resented his macho interference, she wasn't showing it.

"You okay?" he asked gently.

Ally set the spray bottle on the platform at the top of the stepladder. Stubbornly pressing her lips together, she eased the putty knife beneath the paper. "Why wouldn't I be?" The wallpaper made a ripping sound as it separated from the ancient drywall.

Hank stepped closer. He grabbed a piece of dampened paper and pulled it off the wall. "Because that jerk was giving you a hard time."

Ally came back down the ladder, picked it up and

moved it another two feet to the left. Resentment glimmered in her green eyes. "I was handling him."

Hank stood with legs braced, as if for battle. "You may *think* you were."

She stiffened. "What is that supposed to mean?"

Here was his chance to bring up what he'd been reluctant to discuss before. "Corporate Farms is more than just an outfit that buys ranches and farms nationwide, or a firm that is angling to create the largest single ranch in the nation. It has a reputation for ruining communities faster than you can imagine."

Ally sobered. "How?"

"Well, first they come in with a lowball offer. Like what just happened. If they fail on the first try—and often they don't—they up the ante. And they *keep* upping it until they get what they want. In fact, they're happiest when they do have to pay more than the assessed value of a property, because that drives up the prices of all the neighboring ranches and farms, and with that, the tax values. A few acquisitions by CF coupled with a bad year agriculturally, and before you know it the neighbors can't pay their taxes."

"Go on," Ally said quietly, suddenly a captive audience.

Hank sighed heavily. "So then Corporate Farms comes in again, and buys the properties in distress, this time for much *less* than what they're worth. The point is, an outfit like CF has vast resources and can move awfully fast. You may not be prepared for how fast. Or the kind of temptation they can exert." His eyes hardened. "Especially since word on the street is they want to eventually buy up every single ranch property in Laramie County and turn it into one big entity."

Ally regarded him calmly. "So in other words, I shouldn't sell to them because they're bad guys. And they're likely to put everyone else around here out of business if I do."

"Exactly," he muttered.

"Which is why your dad was here this morning."

Her insight caught Hank off guard. "That was part of it," he allowed cautiously.

She stepped closer. "And the rest?"

Hank's jaw set. "It's not relevant to this."

Her gaze narrowed. "Why don't you let me decide that? Seriously. You want me to trust you? Then you need to reveal more about what's going on with your situation, too!"

Fair enough. "My parents think I need their help to succeed."

Ally let out a disbelieving laugh. "You? The guy who was Mr. Everything in high school? Student body president, star athelete, class heartthrob—"

Hank focused on the most important of the litany. "Class heartthrob?" he repeated. Was that how she'd seen him back then?

Ally flushed. "Never mind. Forget I said that." She drew a breath and settled on a step of the ladder, turning businesslike once again. "Back to your very implausible story."

Hank's gut twisted with the irony. "It's true," he said, just as quietly. He edged close enough to rest an elbow on the top rung of the ladder. "My parents think I flipped out after Jo-anne's death. That was why I joined the marines and stayed in for ten years."

Ally tilted her head to look up into his face. "Was it the reason?"

His voice was edgy with tension as he answered, "I admit I was depressed and angry after she died. You can't not be if one of your loved ones dies in something as senseless and unexpected as a terrorist attack. But…" He paused reflectively, then shrugged. "I got over it."

The tenderness in Ally's eyes encouraged him to dig a little deeper into his feelings. "I grew up, I guess, came to accept that bad things happen in life to everyone. And what counts is your ability to pick yourself up and make something good happen—even in the worst circumstances—and move on. And that's what my career in the marines was all about. I helped save a lot of lives. Now I'm out…and ready to move on with the next chapter of my life."

Ally stood and moved away from the ladder once again. "But your mom and dad can't accept that."

He watched her amble back to the wall where she had been working, and spritz an area within reach.

Hank picked up a scraper and walked over to help. "My parents blame themselves for my taking off in the first place. They think they failed me somehow, after Jo-anne died. They don't want to be caught short again. And they're afraid if this ranching thing doesn't work out, I'm going to leave again."

For a second, a flash of alarm appeared in her eyes. "Will you?"

Was it possible, Hank wondered, she wanted him to stay around, as much as he was beginning to want her to do the same? "No. Texas is my home and always will be. That's one thing I figured out while I was overseas."

She scowled at the piece of wall covering she was working on, then tilted her head up to his. "When you say Texas," she murmured, looking at him from beneath her fringe of thick lashes, "do you mean Laramie, or anywhere in the state?"

"I got a hundred head of cattle, and I have to find somewhere of my own to graze them." At the moment, Mesquite Ridge was the only ranch available for lease or sale in Laramie County.

"So if it's not here...?"

Hank studied the way she was biting into her lower lip. "It'll be somewhere."

"That's all very interesting." She ripped off the stubborn piece of wallpaper with more force than necessary and dropped it into the trash can. Then she whirled around and chided, "But it doesn't explain why you just acted so protectively toward me."

He'd been wondering when she would bring that up.

Hank refused to apologize for giving Graham Penderson the old heave-ho. "I wouldn't think I'd have to explain that," he answered drily.

She lifted a blond brow. "Apparently," she said, perfectly mimicking his deadpan tone, "you do."

Was it possible? Was he really that hard to read that Ally had no clue how he was beginning to feel about her?

"Then how about this for an explanation?" Hank said, leaning in for a kiss.

Chapter 7

His move wasn't all that unexpected. The woman in Ally had known Hank was going to kiss her again. She just hadn't known when—or where.

The question was, Ally mused, as his arms wrapped around her and drew her close, what was *she* going to do? Was she going to acknowledge the rapid thudding of her heart and the weakening of her knees, and give in to the ever so slow and deliberate descent of his lips to hers? When the professional businesswoman in her knew she should not—at least until the matter of the sale of Mesquite Ridge was settled? Or would she go with her feminine side, and the instinct that told her to grab this opportunity to see if their chemistry was as good as she'd suspected?

Unable to keep herself from slowing things down a little and speaking her piece, Ally planted a palm in

the center of Hank's chest. She drew in a quick, bolstering breath and looked him square in the eye. "This
won't change anything, you know."

Grinning, Hank threaded a hand through the hair
at her nape. "I know *you* think so," he murmured, just
as confidently.

And then all heaven broke loose as his lips finally
took command of hers....

My goodness, did this man ever know how to kiss!
With finesse and depth and stark male assurance. He
kissed her as if kissing was an end in itself, and there
was no one but the two of them in the entire universe.
He kissed her as if he meant it—and always would.
He kissed her as if she was the most incredible woman
he'd ever been privileged to know.

And darn it all, Ally thought, as she threw caution to the wind and rose up on tiptoe to meet him
with every ounce of womanly passion she had. She
felt the same!

She never wanted this moment to end.

She wanted to stay just like this, with his arms
wrapped around her, his strong body pressed ardently
against hers.

She wanted to savor the peppermint taste of his
mouth, and the incredible heat that exuded from every
sexy inch of him.

And she wanted more. Much more than she had
ever wanted in her life...

Right now. Right here.

And since it was Christmastime, and she had no
other gifts headed her way, why not present herself
with the most thrilling experience of all?

Ally broke off the caress to murmur, "I want you."

Hank looked down at her with a mixture of affection and longing. He threaded both his hands through her hair and tenderly cupped her face between his palms. "I want you, too, but only," he said soberly, "if you're sure."

Ally had never been impulsive. Until now. And darned if she wasn't enjoying the experience. "I'm sure," she said, just as earnestly.

He nodded and swung her up in his arms. "Then we're going up to my bedroom and doing this the way it should be done."

"And how is that?" Ally asked, her recklessness soaring with every step he took, until at last Hank set her down next to his neatly made bed.

"Slowly." He paused to kiss her again, even more deeply this time again. "And with great attention to detail."

She liked his approach. It kept her from thinking too much about her feelings. Emotions could be her undoing. Better to think about the task at hand....

"Detail's good." Ally let her head fall back as he nibbled his way down her neck, lingering over her collarbone. She shivered when he eased her old college T-shirt over her head, letting it fall to the floor. His eyes darkened as he took in the curves of her breasts, spilling out of the lace of her bra.

"Very good," Hank murmured thickly, as he eased the fabric from her arms and reached behind her to undo the clasp.

The lace slid away. He bent her backward over his arm. Cool air assaulted her nipples and her breasts tingled in anticipation. Unable to bear the excitement, Ally let her eyes flutter shut. She felt the warmth of his mouth, the caress of his tongue, the nip of his teeth, while his hands conducted a very thorough exploration of their own. Despite her efforts to keep this a purely physical experience, feelings welled up inside her, mixing with the sensations. The combination of the two was overwhelming and incredibly enticing....

Ally's heart slammed against her ribs and her breathing grew short. It was suddenly imperative, she decided, that they both get out of their clothes.

Hank seemed to have the same thought, because he was guiding her upright again so he could use both hands to unbutton and unzip, and help ease off her boots and jeans.

"You, too," she said, jerking the shirt hem free of his jeans, working at the fastenings, spreading the fabric wide. His chest was every bit as sleek and hard and masculine as she had imagined it would be. Swirls of dark hair covered his flat male nipples and arrowed down past his navel.

Anxious to discover more, she let her hands move to his belt buckle.

Hank kissed his way from the shell of her ear down her neck. "I thought we were taking this slow."

Ally eased both her hands inside the waistband of his jeans. He was throbbing, ready, full. Heat poured through her, curling her toes and she rose up to meet him. With her heart slamming against her ribs, she kissed him full and hard on the mouth. Given the way she felt... "We are."

He grabbed her close and kissed her back, just as

ardently. The hot skin of his muscular chest pressed against her bare breasts. She felt his urgency. And still he kissed her thoroughly. As if she was the most beautiful, wonderful woman on earth, and he was the only man for her. It felt as if they were meant to be together, meant to celebrate the upcoming holiday in just this way. And though Ally had never liked Christmas, never let herself want presents, she did want this.

What did it matter if it wasn't destined to be anything but a fling? she told herself practically. Something that felt so good had to be right.

Hank must have felt so, too. Otherwise he wouldn't be letting go of her long enough to step out of his boots, jeans and briefs, wouldn't be ripping back the covers on his bed and lowering her to the warm flannel sheets.

Slipping both hands beneath her, he urged her knees apart and eased his weight between her thighs. More kisses came, slower and more sultry than before, and only when she was trembling and arching and gasping for breath did he release her lips and kiss his way down her body. Lingering over her breasts, moving past her ribs, to patiently explore her navel…

Seeming more content than she had ever imagined he could be, he explored the hottest, wettest part of her, through the lace of her panties. Holding her hips, he made her wiggle and moan. And then his hands were inside the elastic, steadily easing that last bit of cloth from her. The intensity of his exploration left them both shaking.

At some point the tables were turned and her hands

were on him, causing him to inhale sharply and bury his head against her throat.

"Enough playing," Hank murmured. Turning her onto her back, he stretched out overtop, his hot breath scorching her neck.

"Agreed." She put her palms on his hips and wantonly pulled him toward her.

A second later they were one, fitting together as if they had been destined to join forces just like this, his fullness generating another roller coaster of want and need. Forcing her to open herself up and wrap her arms and legs around him and be closer yet. And still they kissed, the two of them moving together, burning hotter, until they were soaring out of control. The force of the pleasure consumed her, prompting her to arch and shudder and cry out. And Hank, sweet unbelievable gift that he was, found his pleasure, too, surging into her just as rapaciously, taking her along for the ride.

Ally lay on her side, her eyes closed. She wasn't sure when she had ever felt so completely, utterly fulfilled…or so drained. Physically, she was exhausted. Emotionally was another matter. Her heart was in as much of an uproar as her senses. Every inch of her felt alive, appreciated and more vulnerable than she knew what to do with.

With a long, luxurious sigh that sounded like pure contentment, Hank rolled so his body was cuddled up next to hers.

Spooning was something Ally had never done, either. Yet with Hank's arm clamped snugly around her, his strong body pressed against hers, she didn't have the will to move away.

So she lay there, eyes shut, trying not to think about what had just happened or what it might mean. Now or in the future.

And she was still "not thinking" about it some time later when she awakened and found herself naked and alone in Hank McCabe's bed. Ally sat up with a start, clutching the sheet to her breasts. Her naked state, and the just-loved tingling of her body, made it official. She hadn't dreamed this tryst with Hank. Or her newfound, never to be repeated, recklessness. Fortunately for both of them, *he* had apparently come to his senses, too, and left the room before she roused. Which meant she could get dressed in solitude.

With shaking hands, Ally pulled on her clothes and went into the bathroom to splash cold water on her face.

The woman staring back at her in the mirror, with the bright eyes, flushed cheeks and kiss-swollen lips, looked different.

One roll in the hay with Hank and she felt different, too.

But Ally wasn't going to think about that, either.

She was going to go down and see to Duchess and the puppies, because she should have done that a good half an hour ago. Ally ran a brush through her tousled hair, twisted it up into a clip and hurried down the stairs to the kitchen.

Only to find the puppies already curled up to Duchess's side, suckling sweetly. All except Gracie, who was cuddled on Hank's lap, taking her formula from a bottle in his hand.

His dark hair was mussed, his jaw lined with late-afternoon shadow, and he, too, had the glow of someone who had just been well and thoroughly loved.

Ally pushed aside the notion of what it might be like to have him home with her like this every evening. No matter how much she might fantasize that, or wish for it in her dreams, it wasn't going to happen, she told herself firmly.

She didn't care how sexy he was.

She was not going to return to the place that had held so much loneliness and uncertainty in her youth.

To a place that held nothing but bad memories for her now.

"Why didn't you wake me?" Ally asked.

Hank looked at Ally tenderly. "I know how hard you've been working. I wanted you to get some sleep."

She had to admit she did feel better for the rest. "You didn't have to do that."

Something shifted in his expression, though the affection in his eyes remained. Appearing as if he had half expected just this kind of reaction from her, he favored her with a reassuring smile.

"I know that," Hank returned, just as quietly. "But I wanted to."

Just as, Ally thought wistfully, he clearly wanted to make love to her again. She swallowed, her fear of being hurt stronger than ever. "The thing is," she reminded them both, "I'm only here temporarily."

The look in Hank's eyes said he clearly felt otherwise. "So you're telling me I'm nothing more than a fling to you?"

Ally wished it were that uncomplicated. She could already feel herself being drawn to him again, heart and soul. The problem was, they were all wrong for each other. "We want different things from life," she told him in a low, measured tone.

His gaze narrowed. "Ranchers marry city girls all the time," he returned casually.

Marry! Telling herself they were speaking hypothetically, Ally concurred. "But in those cases, the city girls move to the ranch." Which was clearly not going to happen here. She edged closer to make her point as gently and kindly as possible. She put up a staying hand. "I'm not saying it wasn't great…"

"That's good to hear," Hank interrupted, looking her straight in the eye. "Because it was—" he paused, letting the words sink in "—great."

Ally flushed at the new heat in his midnight-blue eyes. "But it's not going to happen again," she continued, standing her ground determinedly.

He lifted a skeptical brow. "Sure about that?" he teased.

Ally nodded. She did not want to be hurt and instinct told her that, whether he wanted to admit it or not, Hank McCabe had the potential to break her heart. She gulped, moved closer still and inclined her head toward the adorable puppy he held in his arms. "So what's going on here?"

To her relief, Hank let the discussion about their lovemaking end.

"Well," he drawled, his attention returning to Duchess and the puppies, too. "You're not going to believe what just happened," he said. He finished giving Gracie the bottle, then held her up tenderly, to look into her cute little face and still-closed eyes. "Is she, Gracie?"

Ally could have swore the pup gave a tiny squeak in response.

But maybe that was wishful thinking, too.

"What happened?" she asked in concern.

Hank smiled and gently set the littlest puppy down in front of Duchess, who promptly began nuzzling the runt of the litter affectionately and cleaning her, with her tongue. That much attention from her mother was new, Ally noted with a start.

Hank beamed like a proud papa, and languidly rolled to his feet. "Gracie nursed at her mama's side for a good three minutes at the start of the feeding before she got too tired and fell off."

Nursing from the mother was much harder, physically, than taking formula from a bottle. Which meant that Gracie was not failing, after all, but getting stronger. "That's nearly three times as long as she did this morning!" Ally noted, impressed.

"Not only did she get much needed colostrum and immunity from her mama," Hank reported happily, "but she drank most of this bottle, too."

Finished, Duchess nosed Gracie away from her and turned to the next puppy who needed her attention.

Hank reached over and picked up Gracie, handing her to Ally to cuddle. As she held her, Gracie made the same sounds the other puppies were making—like the quiet purr of a well-tuned motor. The males were a little larger than the females. All the puppies, including Gracie, seemed a bit more adept at wiggling and scooting around today. Duchess seemed attached to every one of them, even the littlest one.

"Gracie is getting stronger, too." Ally could feel it in the way the little puppy nestled against her.

Hank regarded her seriously. "It won't be long at all—maybe the end of the week or so—before Gracie can take her nourishment with her siblings, and give up the hand-feeding entirely."

Which meant, Ally realized with a pang, that Gracie wouldn't need her.

"That's great," she choked out, telling herself that the pup's coming independence, as well as Hank's wordless departure from the bedroom, was to be celebrated, not mourned. Ever so gently, she pressed a kiss on the top of Gracie's head and handed her back to him.

Their fingers brushed during the transfer. The tenderness of his touch told her he knew just how vulnerable and exposed she felt. A humiliating sting of tears pressed against the back of Ally's eyes. She knew she had to get out of there. Now. Before she gave her heart away to more than just Duchess and the puppies.

Determined not to reveal herself even more, she whirled around. Reminding herself she could not stay in Laramie, no matter what happened with her job in Houston, Ally found her coat, purse and keys. *I'm a city girl now. And that being the case...* "I have to go into town."

Hank's eyebrows went up. "Right now?"

Not trusting herself to speak, Ally nodded.

He looked...disappointed.

The odd thing was, she was disappointed, too. But she knew it was for the best. Despite Hank's protests to the contrary, their fling was just that—a one-time event never to be repeated. Ally forced herself to hold Hank's steady, assessing gaze, and said in the most even voice she could manage, "Since I can't find a crew to do it for me, I've decided to go ahead and strip and paint at least the living room and foyer myself. Hopefully, the kitchen and mudroom, too. I'm going to pick up some paint samples before the hardware store closes, and decide on a color this evening."

Hank settled Gracie in the warmer and began adding the other puppies, too. "Want company?"

Yes, as a matter of fact, she did. Which was another part of the problem. She was used to weathering life's difficulties alone. Hank was going to be in her life for only twelve more days. It would be a mistake to count on him more than she already had. And an even bigger mistake to put herself in situations with him that could only lead to further intimacy.

"Thanks for the offer," she said briskly, "but no." For both their sakes, she flashed a too-bright smile. "I think we've imposed on one another enough."

Much more, and she'd begin to think they were in some sort of relationship. And that was not the case.

"And I thought the situation couldn't get any worse," Ally's coworker told her over the phone in an anxious tone two hours later. "Unfortunately," Porter continued unhappily, "I was wrong."

I'm not sure I want to hear this.

Ally stopped her car at the end of the road leading

to the ranch and rolled down her window. She checked the post and took out several pieces of mail, all for Hank. She set them on the seat beside her and rolled up her window again, speaking into the microphone attached to her earpiece. "What do you mean?" she asked, doing her best to remain calm.

"The powers that be have decided to notify everyone of their job status—or lack thereof—by email!" Porter railed. "If we're laid off, we're not even going to be permitted back in the building. They're going to ship our personal belongings to us."

Ally turned her car into the lane, the golden arc of her headlights sweeping through the darkness of early evening. On either side of the gravel path were heavy thickets of mesquite that further obscured her view. In no hurry to get back to Hank, she drove carefully. "I'm sure the new CEO thinks it will be easier that way," she told Porter.

"Maybe for them," he argued. "For us, it's all the more humiliating! And *depressing,* since the messages are all going out simultaneously on the morning of December 23!"

Good thing I've never been much for Christmas, or my holiday would be completely ruined.

"Couldn't they at least have kept us around until after the holiday?" Porter complained.

Ally winced as her Audi bumped through a water-filled rut that spanned the width of the gravel lane.

Was there no place on this ranch not needing repair? she wondered. Then said practically, "For accounting reasons, the company has to wrap this up before December 31. You know that. Anyway, the last I heard, the plan was to keep at least a few of the old middle managers around, to help with the transition. So you could still have a job when the dust settles, as could I."

"I'm not counting on it, which is why I'm already sending out my résumé as we speak." Porter paused. "At least you have a substantial financial cushion with the ranch."

Not as much as people probably thought, given the size and value of Mesquite Ridge. Unless they had looked at her financials...

"All you have to do is sell to Corporate Farms or whoever and—"

Holy cow! Ally blinked in astonishment as she reached the clearing that surrounded the ranch house and barn. If she hadn't known, she would have sworn it wasn't her home! She'd been gone only a little over two hours, yet half a dozen pick-up trucks and cars were parked there.

Inside the 1920s domicile, lights blazed.

Clearly, a party was going on.

Why hadn't she been invited?

Or at least advised that it was happening?

"...Whereas I will probably end up having to sell my condo," her coworker continued. "Unless I end up getting another job right away. If we're lucky enough to get a little severance, along with our pink slips—"

"Porter," Ally interrupted, "I've really got to go."

"Okay. Call me."

"I will." She turned off her phone and dropped the earpiece into her shoulder bag.

Gathering up Hank's mail, she drew a bolstering breath. And emerged from her car just in time to see Hank stride out of the front door and head straight for her.

Chapter 8

Grinning, Hank strolled toward her, one hand behind his back. "Ready for a surprise?"

Was she?

Before Ally could protest, he produced a red Santa hat and slid it over her head, so the white fur trim obscured her vision. Trying—and failing—to hold on to her pique regarding both his cheerful antics and the party obviously going on in her absence, Ally drawled sarcastically, "Is this necessary?" The furry brim tickled the bridge of her nose.

"Yes, ma'am," Hank bantered back. "If you want to get in the holiday spirit…"

Ignoring the tremor of excitement soaring through her, Ally let him guide her. "I thought I told you I wasn't big on holidays."

Hank's warm hands closed over her shoulders. Purposefully, he steered her in the direction he wanted her to go. "Yet," he interjected, as if he expected that attitude to fall by the wayside as quickly and easily as her resistance to him had.

Talk about a one-track mind! Determined not to let him know how much she hated having to rely on him to get anywhere, Ally scowled as he helped her up the steps, onto the front porch. Her skin tingled from the contact. "You're not going to be able to change me, you know."

His laughter had a masculine, confident ring to it. "Famous last words," Hank whispered in her ear. He propelled her through the front door, turned her toward the living room and whipped off her Santa hat.

"Merry Christmas!" everyone said in unison.

Ally blinked. Thanks to Hank and the twenty or so working guests, the ugly horse-and-hound wallpaper that had dominated most of the first floor was almost completely gone. The unadorned wallboard provided a clean slate. For the first time in her life, Ally had an inkling of what the space could be like. "Thank you!" she whispered, overcome by the unexpected generosity shown her.

"Don't thank us. Thank Hank. He's the one who pulled it all together on short notice!" Hank's baby sister, Emily, came forward. The feisty twenty-eight-year-old beauty was chef and owner of the Daybreak Café. She had one of Duchess's puppies in her arms. "Hank told me you're in love with the littlest one, Gracie, and I have to tell you, Ally, I completely understand! I'm in love, too. In fact, I think I'd rather have a dog than a man. They're *much* more loyal and dependable."

Ally couldn't help but laugh, as did everyone else gathered around.

Jeb McCabe, Hank's older brother, came down off a ladder and sauntered forward. "Hey, Ally," he said. "Good to see you!" The former rodeo star gave her shoulders a casual squeeze, then turned back to his sister. "As for you—you wouldn't have trouble in the love arena if you picked good guys to begin with."

Emily scowled.

Apparently, Ally thought, this was an old and familiar argument.

Holden McCabe, Hank's younger brother, joined the conversation. Serious and responsible to a fault, even before his best friend's untimely death a year before, the horse rancher regarded his baby sister kindly. "If you'd just let the men in the family vet your choices first…"

"He has a point," Hank said protectively. "There's no way you'd end up with losers if the three of us put them through the gauntlet first."

Emily glared at all her big brothers. "What you mean is there's no way I'd ever have another date in my life, if the three of you were involved! Although," she declared cantankerously, as the front door opened and closed, "I'm not sure that would be such a bad thing!"

Behind her, Lulu Sanderson swept in. Gorgeous as ever, the sophisticated former prom queen made a bee-line for where Hank and Ally were standing. Unlike everyone else in the room, dressed for manual labor, Lulu was wearing a Stella McCartney suede jacket, skinny jeans and Jimmy Choo heels.

The petite brunette smiled at Ally. "Hank told me

you were back! And here I am, too, doing what I said I'd never do—working for my dad's barbecue restaurant."

This was a surprise, given that Lulu had gone to an Ivy League college and business school and—last Ally had heard—was successfully climbing the career ladder on the East Coast.

"Anyway…" Lulu turned back to Hank. She reached into her carryall and pulled out a piece of paper. "You can kiss me now, because I found a crew, and they'll have half a dozen workers here tomorrow to paint the entire interior. They think they can do it in two days, as long as you email them before six tomorrow morning to let them know the color choice."

Ally blinked in surprise and scanned the information handed her. "How did you manage that?"

Lulu lifted her hand in an airy wave. "Oh, I have connections all over the place. The crew is coming from San Angelo." Correctly guessing the reason behind Ally's concern, she continued, "And don't worry about the cost. Hank has it covered."

Ally turned back to him in stunned amazement.

He reassured her with a sober glance. "I know you want it done, as soon as possible, and I figure it's the least I can do since you let me stay here rent-free the last six months."

"Don't let him fool you," Emily McCabe interjected. "Hank is just trying to soften you up so you'll let him buy Mesquite Ridge."

Was that the case? Ally wondered. Was that the only reason he was being so incredibly generous and nice? His expression gave no clue.

* * *

While Hank walked Lulu out, Ally retreated to the kitchen to see what she could do about rustling up some refreshments for all the people who had turned out to help her. Emily tagged along, the puppy still in her arms. She knelt to replace the little dog in the warmer and pet Duchess and the other pups for a moment. Then she went to the window overlooking the side yard, where Hank stood, hands in his pockets, conversing privately with Lulu Sanderson.

Moving to the sink to wash her hands, Emily inclined her head toward the window and muttered, "I wish I could figure out what's going on with the two of them."

Me, too. Ally pushed aside the whisper of jealousy and worry floating through her. Why should she care who Hank chatted up?

Emily stood on tiptoe to get a better view. "They're not dating, and yet...they seem almost intimate on some level. It's like they've got something secret going on between them."

Like Hank and me? Ally wondered, reflecting on the way they'd recklessly kissed...and later made love. No one knew about that, either, Ally thought uneasily. Not that it would have been appropriate to talk about, given the matter-of-fact way they'd hooked up.

Ally turned her attention back to Hank's sister. Clearly, Emily was worried about Hank in a way Ally had never seen her be with her other two brothers. Was Hank right? Did every member of his family still treat him with kid gloves and think he needed extra protection from whatever life threw his way? It certainly seemed so.

Curious, Ally dug a little deeper. "I gather that bothers you," she remarked casually.

Emily shrugged and turned away from the window. She knelt down to survey the puppies, many of which were twitching in their sleep, or squirming to get more comfortable. "I never thought Lulu was Hank's type." She smiled at the velvety soft little animals sleeping in a tangle, heads pillowed on each other's backsides.

Then she sighed. "Or that Hank was Lulu's type, either, since the guy she married was a very savvy investment banker. Of course, he cheated on her and they're divorced now. And the rumor is Lulu got quite the financial settlement. So maybe she's just looking for someone steady and dependable, who also wants to live in Laramie." Emily chewed her lip anxiously. "And heaven knows, Hank is that. Once he commits to a woman, he's hers, heart and soul. The only problem is, he hasn't actually *committed* to anyone since Jo-anne died...."

But he had hooked up. With Ally. And maybe other women, as well. Ally realized too late that she and Hank hadn't even discussed exclusivity, or the lack thereof. She had just assumed he was single and unattached when he made his move on her. And even though they didn't plan to continue their relationship past the next few weeks, and maybe not even then, the thought of him with another woman rankled.

Maybe she *was* getting in too deep. With Duchess and the puppies. The ranch. Hank.

Ally arranged fresh fruit slices on a tray. "He thinks the family worries about him."

Emily followed Ally's wordless directions and arranged cheese and crackers on another tray. "I think we all just want to see him settled again with someone, even if it's not the kind of wildly-and-passionately-in-love kind of relationship he had with Jo-anne." She frowned. "Because honestly, until he has another woman in his life, long term, who wants the same things that he wants, I don't think he is going to ever be really happy again."

If that was true—and Ally had no reason to think it wasn't—then she was definitely out of the running to be the next woman in Hank's life. So maybe it was best the two of them kept to friendship and, despite the temptation, didn't hook up again. Because Hank needed a woman who loved this ranch and the lifestyle that went with it, every bit as much as he did.

"So what do you think?" Hank asked Ally, nearly two days later. Late that afternoon the painters had packed up and left, their check from Hank in hand.

Ally couldn't stop looking at her surroundings. In many ways, it was like having a new house, 1920s style. All the old blinds and worn area rugs had been removed. As per her instructions, the entire interior had been coated in sophisticated shades of gray that soaked up the light pouring in from the freshly washed windows. The original wide plank floors contrasted nicely with the newly painted high white ceilings and trim.

"I have to tell you I wasn't sure about the colors you

selected." Hank surveyed their surroundings with a keen eye. "But now…wow."

"I knew it would work," Ally replied absent-mindedly, as she hung the long damask drapes she had made at the front windows. "The varying shades of gray are neutral enough to appeal to a buyer of either sex, and support a rainbow of color schemes for the various rooms." Ally climbed back down the ladder. "I'd say we just upped the value of the property by a good twenty thousand dollars."

Abruptly, concern flickered in Hank's eyes.

Her usual hard-edged business sense gave way to an unexpected flood of guilt. Regretfully, Ally guessed, "Which puts the asking price even further out of your reach?"

Hank shrugged, confident once again. "Not necessarily."

What did he mean by that? Had he found a way to obtain the money, the same way Lulu Sanderson had managed to do the seemingly impossible and scrounge up a painting crew? Maybe through one of his many family or friends in the area? His expression gave no clue. Yet there was something on his mind. Something mysterious and suddenly…almost merry in intent.

"Want to go for a ride?"

Now they were back to the chase. With Hank pursuing her, and Ally wanting nothing more than to relent. What possible good could come of this? she wondered. But found herself asking curiously, "What kind of ride?" Why did he seem so happy, when she was another step closer to selling the ranch house out from under him? Without having to resort to a sale to the greedy, undercutting Corporate Farms?

Hank shrugged, all indifferent male again. "You haven't really seen the ranch in a while, and I need to put out some feed for my herd." He gestured widely with his large, capable hands. With pure innocence he looked her in the eye. "You could help, if you like."

Ally hesitated. There didn't seem to be a sexual motive in the invitation. She tilted her head and continued studying the inscrutable expression on his handsome face. "Are you asking me to be a cowgirl?" Was this his new approach? Get her to love the ranch so much she'd be unable to sell it?

Hank shrugged and hooked his thumbs in his belt loops. Holding her gaze, he rocked forward on his toes. "A windshield cowgirl, maybe."

What was she—a one-hundred-forty-pound weakling unable to hold her own with one of the indomitable McCabes? Or a strong independent career woman capable of handling herself in any situation? Figuring it was time to remind Hank who he was really dealing with, Ally allowed, "Actually, some fresh air would be nice. Just let me change and check on Duchess and the pups first...."

He nodded. "I'll do the same and meet you out by the barns."

Fifteen minutes later, Ally was still in the kitchen, kneeling next to the puppies.

Hank strode back in, impatient to get going. "I knew I'd find you here," he said.

She refused to be rushed. "Gracie needed some

more cuddling before I put her back in the warming bed with her littermates."

"Um-hmm." Hank bent down to pet Duchess's silky head. He angled a thumb at Ally, then told the dog in mock seriousness, "That gal over there. She's showing favoritism. Which normally would not be cool. But your littlest one needs some extra attention, so we're going to forgive Ally for her blatant unfairness."

Ally rolled her eyes. "I can't help it. Gracie needs me."

Still keeping a hand on Duchess, Hank reached down into the warmer and lovingly petted each of the other pups in turn. "Keep it up," he warned, "and Gracie's going to think you're her mother, not Duchess."

His criticism would have been easier to take if she hadn't caught him sneaking into the kitchen to do the same thing. Ally got down on the floor with Hank and, still holding Gracie close, used her free hand to pet the other pups, as well.

Deciding maybe now was the time, she broached what was on her mind. "I could be Gracie's mother if I were to adopt her."

"I thought you didn't like dogs," he teased.

Okay. It was time to come out and admit… "Obviously," Ally murmured, "I was wrong. I do like dogs. In fact…" she paused and cleared her throat "…I think I actually might…love them."

Hank grinned. "Me, too."

Which was another thing they had in common. Not that Ally was keeping score….

"The only problem is," Hank continued seriously, "that none of these dogs are ours to keep."

Ally wasn't convinced about that. "Kurt has used all his connections as a vet to put out the word, state-wide now. And no one has turned up to claim them." She knew, because she checked with the vet daily.

"Yet. They still could."

Ally watched Hank rise and give Duchess a final pat on the head. "Now who's got the bah, humbugs?" she prodded.

He frowned. "I'm just being realistic."

"Christmas is not about reality. Christmas is about hope and joy. And before you argue with me," Ally added, her voice ringing with emotions, "I'd like to point out that you are every bit as attached to Duchess as I am to Gracie!"

For once, Hank didn't deny it. "You going to help me feed the cattle or not?"

Ally kissed Gracie on top of her tiny head and reluctantly put her back in the warming box, next to her littermates. "I'm coming with you," she muttered as she shrugged on her old shearling-lined denim jacket. "How long is this going to take, anyway?"

Hank slipped a hand under her elbow as he escorted her out the back door toward the barns. "As long as we want it to take."

Ally looked up at him and smiled. It was a beautiful winter afternoon, with a slight breeze, crisp cold air and blue skies overhead.

And that suited her just fine.

The Mesquite Ridge Ranch property ranged along the Laramie and Mesquite Rivers, an occasional barbed wire fence setting it off from the surrounding six ranches. Hoping Ally would appreciate what she was about to give up, once she absorbed the rugged beauty around them, Hank drove slowly along the gravel road, past thickets of juniper and holly, through acre after acre of mesquite and cedar choked hills.

He half expected Ally to complain about their unhurried progress. Instead, she settled back in her seat, and studied their surroundings in silence.

Hank wondered if she had any idea how much work he'd done the last six months, or how much more was going to be required to turn this ranch into the showplace it should be. Her pensive expression held no clue; the only thing he was certain of was that the tour was as unexpectedly thought-provoking and important for her as it was for him.

Realizing they had only an hour or so before dark, Hank finally turned the truck and circled back around to the grassy pasture that housed his herd. Ranging in size from six hundred to nearly eighteen hundred pounds, the cattle grazed sedately.

"I've always liked black Angus more than longhorns," Ally murmured, with an appreciative glance at the healthy steers.

As he cut the engine and they got out of the cab, Hank realized how little he really knew about her, how much more he wanted to learn.

"How come?" He came to her side.

Ally thrust her hands in the pockets of her old farm jacket, one he recalled her wearing in high school. Now, it was something to work in. Back then it had been her one and only coat.

She grinned up at him. "Black Angus don't have horns, and that makes 'em look cuddlier."

"Not exactly a word I'd use for cows and steers," Hank countered drily, thinking that if anyone here was in need of a cuddle, it was Ally. And not because a cold winter wind was blowing against them, inducing shivers.

It was more in the vulnerable way she held herself.

Knowing how completely she could give, when it came to physical intimacy.

Emotionally…well, emotionally was another matter. For every step she took nearer to him, she seemed to take another one away.

Her cheeks pinkening in the cold, Ally lazily closed the distance between them. Unable to help herself, she taunted, "And here I thought you were the more romantic of the two of us."

As soon as the words were out, she blushed. "I meant…sentimental…when it came to ranching per se…" she choked out.

Hank chuckled. "You might be a tad sentimental and romantic, too," he teased right back.

"I wouldn't count on it."

"I'm sure you wouldn't."

Looking more like a cowgirl than ever with one booted foot crossed over the other, Ally leaned against the side of the truck, while Hank opened the tailgate. "How many cattle do you have?"

"One hundred." He flashed a wistful grin, aware that for the first time in a very long time he actually cared what a woman thought about him. "Or two hundred less than required to have what is considered a working cattle ranch."

Ally shot him a respectful glance from beneath her lashes. "I have every confidence you'll get there," she said quietly.

Hank knew he would. The only question was where would his cattle be housed. Here on Mesquite Ridge, or somewhere else by default.

Ally tugged on the leather work gloves Hank had loaned her. "They look healthy," she observed.

Beaming with pride, Hank carried a bundle of hay out into the pasture and cut the twine. "I've had good luck so far."

Ally took handfuls of alfalfa and spread it around, so the cattle didn't have to fight for feed.

"It's more than luck," she remarked. A bitter edge underscored her low serious tone. "It takes skill. Dedication. The willingness to study up on animal husbandry and do all the things necessary to keep the cattle in top form."

Hank carried another bundle over and set it down. There was an undertone to her voice that bore exploration. "Why do I have the feeling we're not talking about me any longer?" he asked casually.

She sighed and shook out more hay. "It's no secret my dad was a lousy cattleman. All he and my mom ever cared about was expanding the ranch."

"He eventually owned four thousand acres. Given the fact he started from nothing, that's quite an accomplishment."

"But no surprise," Ally muttered resentfully. "Every cent we had went to buying more and more land. To the point that we wore sweaters instead of running the furnace in winter, and did without practically everything because every penny spent was a penny we wouldn't have to buy more land."

"And you hated it."

"Of course I hated it!" She stomped back to the truck and tried to reach another bale. "I couldn't participate in any of the extracurricular activities at school because I was expected to go home and help out with my mother's sewing business."

Hank reached past her to pull the hay to the edge of the truck bed. "Surely your parents were proud of you when you got that big scholarship to Rice University."

"Honestly?" Ally shrugged and walked with him back out into the pasture. "They would have preferred I stay and work the ranch with them. But I had to get out of here." When they reached another open space, perfect for feeding, she paused to cut the twine that held the hay together, and exhaled wearily. "So I left...."

Together, they threw out the shredded grain, as additional cattle ambled toward them. "And you never came back, except to visit," Hank surmised when they'd finished their task.

Ally nodded grimly as they walked away. "And I didn't do that much, either, until my mother was diagnosed with Parkinson's disease." Ally strode to the fence, where she paused to examine the thick strand of mesquite on the other side. Trees up to thirty feet high and nearly as wide sported dense, tangled greenery studded with long thorns. The heavy rain a few days before had brought forth another wave of fragrant white flowers. In the spring, the mesquite would bear fruit in the form of beanlike pods that wildlife and cattle would eat.

Right now, Hank could tell, the overgrowth was just one more mess Ally would prefer not to have to deal with.

"But you did come back, when she was sick." Hank remembered his mother talking about that, and the fight between Ally and her parents that had evidently ensued.

Sorrow turned down the corners of Ally's mouth. "I told them about this new protocol being developed at a hospital in Houston. I wanted them to come and live with me, so Mom could get the best treatment." She inched off her gloves and stuck them in the belt at her waist. "I knew the isolation of the ranch was no place for anyone with the kind of neurological disease my mother suffered from, that as time went on she would need more and more care, and that—like it or not—it was time they gave Mesquite Ridge up, in favor of my mother's health."

"But your parents didn't agree with that."

"No." Ally's low tone was filled with bitterness. "They didn't. They insisted they didn't need my help, unless I wanted to move back home and take over the sewing business. That, they would accept." Her eyes gleamed with moisture. "Anything else…" she recalled in a choked voice, "forget it."

Hank took off his gloves, too, and went to stand behind her, resting his hands on her shoulders. "That wasn't fair to you."

Ally tilted her head back and relaxed against him. "I had worked very hard to get where I was in the company. I was a first line manager, about to be promoted to the next tier…on the fast track to an early vice presidency…." She swallowed. "So I said no, and I sent them money to get a caregiver to help out with my mother, instead."

Hank didn't recall anyone saying anything about nursing care. He paused, then tensed. "Tell me they didn't…"

She looked as if she had just taken an arrow to the heart. "They bought another ten acres."

"You must have been devastated," he observed quietly.

"I was furious." Ally blinked back tears. "And scared." She pushed away from Hank. Hands balled into fists, she began to pace. "With as much difficulty as my mother was having, getting around at that point, I was afraid she was going to have a fall."

"Which," Hank recalled sorrowfully, "she eventually did."

Ally swept her hands through her hair. "Unfortunately, my dad was out on the ranch, tending to his cattle, when it happened, and it was hours before he found her. By then, Mom had lapsed into a coma and she never came out of it." Ally gestured in despair as more tears fell. "My dad never recovered. I think that's why he had the heart attack last summer. Because… he couldn't forgive himself."

Hank drew Ally into his arms. "The question is, can you forgive yourself?" he asked softly.

Chapter 9

No one had ever asked her that. Could she forgive herself? Was it ever going to be possible?

Ally looked deep into Hank's eyes. "I'm not sure," she said finally, knowing it was past time she confided in someone. The understanding glint in his dark blue eyes gave her the courage to go on. "There are times I have so much guilt I feel like I'm suffocating. Guilt because I couldn't convince my parents to handle my mother's illness any differently. I would give anything to have gotten them the help they needed, when they needed it. Instead of failing them at the toughest, most crucial moment of their lives...."

"Do you think they would have been happy in Houston?"

Her face crumpled. "No." More tears flooded her eyes.

Hank settled his palms on her shoulders. "Do you

think if they'd known they were coming to the end of their lives, they would have wanted to be right here, on the ranch?"

A sob rose in Ally's throat. She was so choked up she could barely breathe, never mind get words out. "I don't think there is anywhere else they'd rather have been."

He threaded a hand through her hair. "I know you miss them."

Tears blurred Ally's vision as pain wrapped around her heart. "I do."

Hank's hands shifted to her back and he pulled her close. Unable to hold back a second longer, Ally buried her face in the solid warmth of his shoulder. And cried the way she hadn't cried when her parents had died. She cried for all the times she had had with them…and all the things that were left unsaid, for the way she had disappointed them, and the way they had disappointed her. But most of all, she cried because she loved them anyway, with all her heart, and missed them so much she felt her whole being would shatter into a million pieces. And through it all, Hank held her close and stroked her back, letting her sob her heart out.

Ally had no idea how long they stood like that. She only knew that when the storm finally passed and she lifted her head, he wiped her tears away with the pads of his fingers and gently lowered his head to hers.

The touch of his lips was everything she had ever wanted, everything she needed. Ally kissed him back, pouring her feelings into the sweetly tender embrace.

For the first time in her life, she was really and truly happy to be right where she was. And it was all due to Hank.

He made Mesquite Ridge a different place for her.

It was still a wilderness, with so much of the four thousand acres uncared for and untamed. But when she was with Hank and saw the ranch through his eyes, she also noted the richness of possibility of the house and the land.

She saw the wonder to be had in a life here, with him.

And that made her want to be held, to be loved, to love in return.

It no longer mattered how much was holding them apart. She wanted to be with Hank again, even if only for a brief period of time.

And he wanted her, too.

His kiss, the warmth and tightness of his embrace, told her that.

And that was, of course, when the purr of a car motor came up behind them.

Ally and Hank let each other go, turned in unison and saw Graham Penderson, of Corporate Farms, get out of his Cadillac and stride toward them.

"I haven't heard from you," the small man said, as slick and falsely charming as ever. "So I thought I'd stop by to get your answer in person."

Ally felt Hank tense beside her. Knowing it would be a mistake to show any weakness to the CF agent, she resisted the urge to take Hank's hand and hold on tight. Deliberately, she held Penderson's eyes. "Thank you for the offer—" which, technically, was about to expire "—but my answer is no."

Ally wasn't surprised to see Penderson's expression grow more conciliatory than ever. "You understand ours is a one-time offer. Six months from now, if you still haven't sold on the open market, we won't be back with anything near what we are offering now."

But Hank would still be there, Ally thought, wanting the land.

If his "plan" to acquire it had been put together by then…

She stopped herself. She could not allow herself to think that way; otherwise she'd be no better a business person than her father had been. And it was up to her to see the ranch sold—for a good price—so her own future would be assured, no matter whether she got laid off from her job or not.

This was her chance to obtain the financial security that had always eluded her in her youth.

But she was going to do it her way. Not Corporate Farms'.

"I understand," Ally said calmly. "The answer is still no. I'm not selling until I get an offer that matches what the land is worth."

Penderson's glance narrowed. "We already gave you that."

"No. You didn't," Ally countered equably. "Fortunately, I have every confidence someone else will."

Especially now that renovations on the ranch house are under way.

"Fine, then." Penderson gave one last disparaging look at the acres of untamed land, resettled his hat on his head and stalked back to his Cadillac. "You'll be waiting a long time to realize more than what we've already offered, for property that is in such poor shape. And I'm not just talking about the house, which we planned to tear down anyway. No one can run cattle on pastureland this overgrown! The mesquite thickets alone are a hazard."

Ally and Hank stood in silence, watching him drive off.

"He has a point about that," she said with a sigh, as her mind returned to business. "There is mesquite everywhere and the trees are covered with two-inch thorns that can do a lot of damage to people and cattle."

Hank wrapped a companionable arm around her shoulders. "First of all," he soothed, "cattle are smarter than you think."

"Is that so?"

"It is." Hank squeezed her warmly and continued his tutorial. "They know enough to stay away from anything that is going to injure them. Second, the trees don't just sport fragrant white flowers in the spring and summer, they also produce long bean pods that the cattle can graze on, and provide shelter when it's cold, and light shade in the hottest parts of the day. Mesquite adapts to almost any soil that isn't soggy. It's heat and drought tolerant, helps prevent erosion and fixes nitrogen in the soil."

Ally thought about what the untamed growth would do to the bottom line. "Mesquite is still not popular with ranchers, since it readily invades grazing sites, and is virtually impossible to get rid of once it takes root."

Hank tipped back the brim of his hat and gave her the sexy once-over. "And here I thought you didn't know anything about ranching."

"I know enough to realize that a controlled burn is needed on vast parts of the ranch, to ensure the long-term health of the land. But as much as I'd like to rid the ranch of all the old dead grass, cedar, mesquite and so on, to germinate different seeds and promote steady, even growth, I'm not sure blackened land would be the best thing for any property on the market."

Hank inclined his head. "Nonranchers might not understand."

"And since everyone who is anyone wants a ranch these days, just so they can say they have one—even if they never really visit it…"

"It makes sense to leave the land wild and untamed, for now."

"Right."

They studied each other.

Ally knew Hank still didn't want her to sell to anyone else, but to her surprise, he didn't look the least bit relieved about what had happened earlier.

"Aren't you going to tell me I made the right decision regarding Corporate Farms?" She didn't know why, exactly; she just wanted to have Hank's approval about that.

He shrugged and walked toward the back of his truck. "It's not over yet."

Perplexed, Ally trailed after him. The intimacy they'd felt earlier was gone, just like that. "What do you mean?"

Hank slammed the tailgate shut. "I know what it looked like just now, but Corporate Farms has not given up. They will wait a few days and go into phase two."

Oh, really? "And what the heck is that?"

"First, they tried to take advantage of you. That didn't work, nor did playing hardball with you. So, figuring the third time is the charm, the next time they'll come back to woo you. And give you an offer you'd be nuts to refuse, with absolutely no time limit on deciding."

Ally shook her head. "I don't think so. Graham Penderson was pretty clear just now, that this was it—they wouldn't be back."

Hank folded his arms in front of him. "We'll see who's right. The question is, what are you going to do if they come back with a much higher offer?" He scanned her face. "Will you sell to them, knowing what you do about their overall intent, and how they do business? Or wait for another buyer?"

Hank had hoped—unreasonably, he knew—that Ally would have had time by now to really think about what she was going to do, and commit to selling to him. If only because he had the ability and the drive to turn the ranch into the financial success it always should have been.

Instead, the hard-edged business person in her kicked back in. "If Corporate Farms were to come back with another offer, I would of course listen to what Graham had to say. Just like I will consider any and all offers that Marcy Lyon at Premier Realty brings to me, after the property is listed. And should you come to me with a serious offer that meets my asking price, of course I'll listen to that, too."

Hank's gut tightened with disappointment. "But in the end the highest dollar wins," he guessed.

Ally nodded reluctantly. "I may not have a job in another ten days. This property still has a mortgage on it. Up to now, I've been making the payments and paying the utilities out of my savings, but I can't keep doing that when I have no revenue of my own coming in. Even if I somehow manage to keep my job, it's still too much of a stretch to continue for very much longer."

Hank understood.

"I suspect the people at Corporate Farms suspect that, which is why they thought they could come in with a low offer and I'd jump on it."

Hank's cell phone rang. Frowning, he pulled it out of the leather holder attached to his belt. Looking at the screen, he saw his cousin was returning his call. "I've got to get this. Hi, Will…"

Hank listened as Will confirmed the details. "Yeah. Eight tomorrow morning. The usual deal. Okay, thanks, see you then." He ended the call.

Trying to figure out how much he could tell Ally, without betraying the confidentiality of the business deal under way, Hank explained, "My cousin, Will McCabe, owns a charter service out at the Laramie airstrip. It used to be just private jets, flying in and out of there, but since I came back to the area he's added a helicopter to his fleet. So whenever he gets a request— usually from a big oilman or one of the other prominent business people in the area—I fly the chopper."

"Sounds lucrative."

It was. "The revenue from those gigs is responsible for all the cattle I've bought thus far, and the additional money I have saved."

Ally eyed him with respect. "How long will you be gone?"

Long enough to get the deal done, Hank thought resolutely. But wary of telling Ally anything before the plan was set, he replied cautiously, "I'm not sure. The person I'm taking wants to go to Dallas, with a couple of stops along the way, stay overnight, and then do the same thing the following day, en route back. Which brings me to the next question. Are you going to be able to handle Duchess and the puppies, or do you want me to bring someone else in to care for them?"

Ally glowered. "Seriously?"

"I did promise it wouldn't be your responsibility," Hank reminded her.

"Yeah, well, it's not the first promise around here that hasn't been kept."

Hank let that one pass.

She lifted her hands in a placating gesture. "Sorry. It just seems that whenever something goes wrong in my life, it happens here at Mesquite Ridge."

Hank tugged Ally close for another long, thorough kiss. Only when she was putty in his arms did he lift his head. "Things have gone right here, too, Ally," he whispered.

Very right. And one day he hoped she would see that.

Greta McCabe appeared on the ranch house door-step at six o'clock the following evening. Hank's mother smiled warmly as Ally ushered her in out of the cold. "I tried calling before I came over, but there was no answer."

Ally didn't mind her stopping by without an invi-tation. It had been a little lonely since Hank had left for his trip early that morning. "I must have been out walking Duchess," she explained.

Greta cast an admiring look at the newly painted woodwork and walls, then turned back to her and handed over a large paper bag bearing the insignia of Greta's restaurant in Laramie.

"You didn't have to do this." Ally beamed with pleasure.

"I figured you'd be too busy to cook, given all you have to do around here," Greta said.

She was right about that. Ally had been working hard all day, making washable canvas slipcovers for the living room furniture.

"I wasn't sure what you liked so I put in a couple of different entrées. Just follow the reheating directions on the foil containers when you're ready to eat," Greta said. "And of course, the salads and desserts are ready to go."

"Thank you. This is so nice." Ally basked in the thoughtfulness.

"So how are Duchess and the puppies?" Greta asked.

Ally gestured toward the kitchen. "Come and see for yourself."

While Ally put the food in the fridge for later, Hank's mother knelt to say hello to the golden retriever and all eleven of the newborns. Nearly a week had passed since Duchess had given birth. All the pups except Gracie, who still lagged a little behind, were now close to two pounds in weight. And although their eyes were still sealed shut, they were getting about with increasing mobility, rolling and squirming across the warming bed when they were awake. Right now, they were all sound asleep in a pile of puppy arms and legs.

Greta smiled at the sound of the soft, gentle snoring. "I can't believe no one has stepped forward to claim them yet," she said.

Me, either, Ally thought.

The woman stood and regarded her with a soft, maternal expression. "So. How are you doing, dear?"

Ally swallowed. "Good," she lied. Then added, more honestly, "Considering."

Greta gently patted her arm. "This must be really hard for you, coming home for the first time after the funeral."

Ally nodded—it had been. Happy to have some female company, she picked up the coffeepot off the stove. "Would you care for some coffee?"

"Love some," Greta said.

Relieved that Hank's mom appeared in no hurry to go, Ally poured two mugs of the fresh brew and brought out a tin of sugar cookies from the grocery store. As they enjoyed their snack, they talked about the progress Ally had made thus far, updating the ranch house.

Greta cast her an appreciative glance. "It's not just the house that has benefited from your presence. Hank seems to be really flourishing since he's been around you, too. Bringing in a Christmas tree..."

Which was still undecorated, Ally thought, a little guiltily.

Greta ran a hand through her silver-blond curls. "Organizing that wallpaper removal party..."

Ally rubbed the edge of her plate with her thumb. "I was really surprised." And maybe a little thrilled.

Greta studied her over the rim of her mug. "He feels for you," she observed tenderly. "Probably because he knows what it is to lose a loved one."

Was that all that was drawing him to her? A mix-

ture of empathy and lust, with a healthy dose of property hunger, thrown in? Ally wondered.

Oblivious to the nature of her thoughts, Greta ran
a nicely manicured hand over the tabletop, lamenting, "We never thought Hank would get over losing
Jo-anne. But the years in the marines, and now this
ranch, have brought him back to life."

And Hank's mom was happy to see that, Ally noted.

"I know you're getting ready to put the ranch on
the market...."

If I don't sell it to Hank first, Ally thought, wishing
all the harder he would find a way to make a decent
bid, so she could accept it and move on. She would
have peace of mind knowing the property was in the
right hands to make it thrive, the way it should have
all along.

Greta patted Ally's hand. "I know the process can
be difficult, particularly when it comes to sorting
through your parents' belongings. It can be a lot to
take on alone, as well as very emotional, so if you need
help...let me know. And before I forget, Shane and I
would very much like for you to come to the annual
open house at our ranch, on December 23...."

The day she was supposed to hear about whether
or not she still had a job. Ally hesitated. "I'm not sure
that will be a great time for me," she said.

"Nonsense. You have to eat. In the meantime, if
you need help with anything at all, you let Hank's father and me know. We're only eight miles down the
road. And it's not just a family thing that has us making the offer—or the fact that Hank is temporarily
absent. It's part of the code of survival around here.

Ranchers help each other out." She smiled warmly at Ally. "But having grown up on Mesquite Ridge, surely you know that."

Actually, Ally didn't. Her parents had always kept pretty much to themselves, and never asked for help for themselves—or gone out of their way to assist anyone else, even their closest neighbors. But maybe it was time that changed, too, she thought. For as long as she stayed in the area, anyway...

She thanked Greta again and walked her to the door, then went back to get Duchess and take her out into the yard.

As she went back inside, she noticed the message light blinking on the answering machine. There were two calls from Premier Realty and the title company, another from Porter, wanting to know if she'd heard anything more about the layoffs, and finally, one that was definitely not for her.

"Hank, honey, it's Lulu. Are you ready for dinner?" the chic divorcée asked enthusiastically. "'Cause I'm starving after the day we've had together! Oh, wait, I think I just dialed your home number instead of your cell. Never mind. I'll just come and find you." *Click.*

Ally sat staring at the phone. The call had come in at six-fifteen, when she was out walking Duchess in the yard. The screen ID said the call had come from a luxury hotel in Dallas.

So that was where Hank had gone! Ally realized, stunned. Lulu Sanderson was the client he was flying around? And now they were in Dallas together, sharing a hotel, if not a room? What in heaven's name was going on?

Chapter 10

Hank knew something was going on with Ally when he returned home the following evening. He just wasn't sure what had her suddenly ignoring his calls.

He shrugged out of his leather aviator jacket and walked through the downstairs. It was clear she had been as busy and productive in their two days apart as he had. Custom slate-gray canvas slipcovers now gave the sturdy but ugly furniture a classy new look. A new area rug, colorful throw pillows and lap blankets had been strategically added.

There was still no real feeling of Christmas in the ranch house, since the tree and mantel remained undecorated. Hank was determined that, too, would change.

Thinking Ally might be with Duchess, he walked into the kitchen. All the puppies were cuddled up together in the warmer, sleeping contentedly. Duchess was lying next to it. She lifted her head and wagged her tail when Hank approached. He petted her silky head and scratched her behind the ears. "Looks like all is okay here with you and the kids," he murmured. Was Ally okay, though?

Hank gave the sleepy Duchess a final pat and headed on up the stairs.

Ally was standing in her bedroom in front of the mirror, blow-drying her honey-blond hair. Her slender form was covered by a satin robe with a tie sash. Her feet were encased in fuzzy slippers. Beneath the knee-length hem, her legs were bare.

Hank's pulse picked up a notch.

Was this all for him?

He hoped so.

He strode into the bedroom. Ignoring her indifferent reception, he asked, "Did you get my message?"

Ally curved the ends of her hair around a brush, held it against her chin and moved the dryer back and forth. "All six of them," she answered, sounding distracted.

Okay, so maybe he'd been a little eager to talk with her. But it had been thirty-six hours since they had seen one another. He had missed her. Had she missed him?

Aware that Ally hadn't exactly invited him in, Hank folded his arms and lounged against the chest of drawers. He was beginning to feel a little defensive, which seemed unwarranted, given all he had been doing behind the scenes on their behalf. "Why didn't you call me back?" he asked quietly.

Ally brushed her hair into place and spritzed it with hair spray. She steadfastly averted her gaze. "The message that you were coming home by six this evening didn't exactly warrant a reply."

Annoyed that he'd fallen so hard and fast for a woman who seemed easily able to do without him, Hank lifted a brow and said nothing in response.

Still doing her best to ignore him—although he was pretty sure she could see him out of her peripheral vision—Ally grabbed a dress out of her closet. Chin high, she headed for the bathroom across the hall. Over her shoulder, she added, "And I was busy."

Irked by her swift, inexplicable change of attitude toward him, Hank waited for her to come back out.

She looked as incredibly sexy as he expected in a cranberry-red dress. The V-neck exposed the lovely slope of her throat and the hint of décolletage; the fabric clung closely to her breasts, waist and hips before flaring out slightly. Ally rummaged in a drawer and pulled out a package of panty hose. "As were you, I take it."

He had been, with extraordinarily good results.

Not that she wanted to hear about it. At least not yet…

Ally disappeared into the bathroom again. When she emerged, she wore a pair of black stilettos that made her legs look spectacular.

Which made him wonder what else she had on under that sexy dress. And how hard would it be to get her to take it off for him.

Ally applied lipstick in front of the mirror. Then mascara, eyeshadow and perfume.

She was so beautiful. And clearly, so determined to make him jealous.

Despite his pique, he couldn't stop watching her, couldn't draw his gaze from the loveliness of her features.

When she opened a velvet case and removed a gold pendant necklace, he finally gave in to curiosity. "I presume you're going out this evening?" he drawled.

"Yes." Ally fastened the clasp around her neck and let the teardrop pendant fall between her breasts. She returned to the box for matching earrings and put those on, too. "My dinner companion should be here shortly."

"Dinner companion," Hank repeated.

Finished, she gave her hair a final pat and turned to him. Her green eyes held a glacial frost. "Was there something you wanted?"

Yes, Hank thought. *You.* But aware how that would likely go over, he decided to cut to the chase, and asked instead, "Just for the record. Are you angry with me?"

"Why would I be angry with you?" Ally replied sweetly.

I have no idea. Wanting peace between them, Hank guessed, "For leaving you alone with Duchess and the puppies?" *And not getting you extra help with them despite the fact you insisted you did not need it?*

Ally shot down that theory with a decisive shake of her head. "I adored being with them."

So... "It's me you'd rather not spend time with," Hank concluded.

"Bingo."

Another silence fell between them, and then the doorbell rang.

"That's for me!" Ally grabbed an evening bag and a black velvet jacket and headed for the stairs.

Hank ambled after her.

He was not happy when he saw her "date" for the evening.

Judging by the determined look on her face as she sailed out the door, Ally knew that.

"Everything okay?" Graham Penderson asked Ally as they took their seats in the Lone Star Dance Hall.

I wish you had chosen another place to dine, she thought. But it was no surprise—Greta McCabe's restaurant, with its lively atmosphere and superb food— was *the* place to spend a social evening in Laramie. And it was clear that Graham Penderson—and by extension, Corporate Farms—were now going all out to woo her, just as Hank had predicted they would.

"Everything's fine," she answered. *I just wish I'd had time to quiz Hank about his trip with Lulu. It would have been interesting to hear what he had to say.*

Not that she wanted or needed to know, since she and Hank were history.

Still…

"We've had a chance to review the initial property assessment on Mesquite Ridge and think we might have come up a little short in our first offer," Graham said.

No surprise there, either.

Ally turned her full attention on her dinner partner, adopting her most hard-edged business demeanor. "I'm not going to be pushed into responding to *any* offer from Corporate Farms."

"We realize that was a mistake."

"Any future offer that comes with a timeline will be immediately rejected."

"Understood," Graham assured her.

Ally folded her hands in front of her. "That said, I'd like to talk with you about what figure *might* be acceptable...."

The CFS agent pulled an envelope from his pocket, and handed it to her. Inside, typed on their letterhead, was an astounding figure. One that would leave her set for a good while, job or no job....

Throughout the rest of the meal, Graham spoke with her about the benefits of a sale to Corporate Farms, and the various ways they could accommodate her to make the transition easier. Despite herself, Ally was impressed.

She knew what the impact on the community would be, should the company get a toehold in the area with the acquisition of Mesquite Ridge. And while the sentimental, compassionate side of her would not even consider such an offer, the businesswoman in her knew she would be a fool not to.

What happened to the other ranches in the area was not her responsibility. Her own future and financial security was.

And yet...

"Naturally," Graham concluded with finesse, "although we want you to have as much time as you need, we are going to want to follow up on this...."

"And I," an oh-so-familiar male voice said, " would like to speak with you about your dessert options for this evening."

Ally's heart skipped a beat. She turned and saw the familiar red shirt, blue jeans and black Lone Star Dance Hall apron on a very fine male form. Already knowing which handsome face she was going to see, she lifted her gaze and looked up into Hank McCabe's midnight-blue eyes.

Hank ran through the options with the finesse of a guy who had grown up waiting tables in his mama's restaurant. "We've got a fine cranberry-cherry pie, as well as a chocolate peppermint torte that is out of this world. And of course, the traditional banana pudding, pecan pie and peach cobbler. You can have ice cream with all of those. Coffee, too."

"What are you doing here?" Ally snapped. And why did he have to look so superb? She couldn't help but note he had gone to the trouble of showering and shaving before coming in. He'd even applied the brisk, wintry aftershave she liked so much.

Hank ignored the glare he was getting from the agent, and pointed to the black change apron tied over his jeans, and the Lone Star Dance Hall badge that bore his name. His smile widened. "I'm helping out. My mom's shorthanded tonight."

Helping out, my foot! Ally lifted a brow in wordless dissension. It looked as if they had plenty of waitstaff, as usual. "Um-hmm," she said.

"Good to see you have a job to fall back on, *Mc-Cabe*," Graham Penderson said. "You're going to need it, since the ranch where you house your cattle is about to be sold out from under you."

Hank locked eyes with Penderson, all tough ex-marine and veteran cowboy.

Talk about a Renaissance man, Ally thought.

Hank smiled. "I wouldn't count on it if I were you."

Penderson ran a smug hand across his jaw. "I would."

Wincing, Ally squirmed in her seat.

Given the high-stakes volatility of the situation, she wouldn't have been surprised to see Hank forget his manners and pull Penderson out of his chair by the knot of his necktie.

But as it happened, his expression did not change— if you discounted the slight darkening of his irises. He merely stepped an inch closer. Flashed a dangerous crocodile smile. "Still waiting on that dessert order. *Penderson.*"

Ally swallowed. She could see this situation fast getting out of hand.

She stuffed the papers the agent had given her into her handbag and shut the clasp, then held up her hands. "Actually, I don't think I want any dessert," she told them both.

"I do," Graham said. "And I want McCabe here to bring it to us, since he's so eager to help."

Out of the corner of her eye, Ally saw Hank's mother step out of the kitchen. Greta sized up the situation, hands on her hips. Sighed.

"Why, it'd be my pleasure," Hank drawled. "But..." He turned with a flourish and signaled the DJ running the sound system.

The man nodded and promptly started a song by Lady Antebellum entitled "One Day You Will."

"Well, what do you know, Ally." Hank slid his order pad and pen back in his apron pocket. He reached down and took her hand in his, and in one smooth motion, drew back her chair and pulled her to her feet. He winked at her. "They're playing *your* song. Sorry, Penderson."

The next thing Ally knew they were on the dance floor. Hank's left hand splayed warmly across her spine, and his right hand clasped her fingers as he two-stepped them around the floor to the strains of the romantic ballad.

Ally tried but could not stop the thrill rushing through her. "Cute, McCabe."

He grinned, all confident male. "Like the lyrics?"

Despite her decision to remain unaffected by his chicanery, his sense of humor was contagious. "Especially the part about if I left town and never came back," Ally retorted drolly.

He leaned close enough to whisper in her ear. "Like the song says, you'd be missed." His warm, minty breath caressed her cheek. "But if you just hang in there…and wait awhile…"

"The sun will shine again and," Ally paraphrased, "I'll find love and peace and the real me."

The laugh lines around his eyes crinkled. "Exactly."

If only he knew how much she wanted to believe that. As it was, the powerful lyrics combined with the soul-stirring music were drawing her in, every bit as much as the wonderfully comforting and enticing sensation of being in his arms again. Deciding she needed to reestablish some emotional boundaries, Ally lifted her chin.

Now that he had picked her tune… "What's your song?"

"Coming right up." Hank again signaled the DJ. One tune segued into another.

Ally listened a moment to the lively beat, then looked down the bridge of her nose at him. "'You Take My Troubles Away'?" *Seriously!*

He two-stepped her around the dance floor. "Appropriate, don't you think?" His lips brushed her temple.

Another thrill swept through Ally. "If this is supposed to be a message for me…" she warned.

"It is." Hank's voice was low and hoarse. All the pent-up affection she ever could have wished for in his gaze.

Ally had spent her high school years wishing something this out-of-control exciting and romantic would happen to her. But that didn't mean it was a good idea for Hank McCabe to go all possessive on her in the middle of a business dinner at his mother's restaurant! Particularly after what he'd done in Dallas the day before. She blushed and attempted without much success to resurrect the protective barrier around her heart. "Everyone is looking at us."

Hank's arm tightened around her waist. Their thighs brushed as they moved to the beat. "That's no surprise. You look incredibly beautiful tonight. But then…" his voice dropped another inviting notch "…you know that."

She felt beautiful—in Hank's arms. Ally struggled not to give in to the overwhelming emotions rising up within her. "And for the record, what on earth possessed you to pick out his-and-her songs for us?"

He shrugged and brought their clasped hands even closer to his heart. "I wanted the excuse to dance with you tonight."

That sure had done the trick. She was here in his arms, feeling like there was no place she'd rather be.

Ally cast a look over Hank's broad shoulder. "Penderson is livid."

"He'll get over it. It won't stop Corporate Farms from making good on their latest offer, if that's what you're worried about."

"How do you know there's been another offer?"

"Because Corporate Farms sees what I see in terms of the rich potential of the ranch. They don't want Mesquite Ridge to get away."

"So that's why you're doing all this." Ally did her best to keep the sadness from her voice.

"No. I'm doing this because I want you to know I'm sorry for leaving you alone for two days. And I don't want you to do anything stupid to get back at me, just because you're mad at me."

So he sensed she was onto him! Figuring she'd use the opportunity to get the answers to all the questions she had, but hadn't asked, Ally inquired sweetly, "Why would I be mad?"

Hank paused, revealing nothing, then said finally, "You tell me."

For a second, Hank thought Ally wouldn't answer. Then something shifted in her expression. A little of the fight left her slender body. "I don't want to have this discussion here," she said quietly.

Neither did he, if it was half as intimate as it appeared it was going to be. "Then let's go home." Or at least where he wished their home could be. In another week, he was well aware, that might not be the case for either of them.

Another silence fell, as the song they were dancing to came to an end.

They stood there, not moving, still holding on to each other.

"And let me drive you," Hank murmured.

Ally glanced over at Penderson.

The agent looked even more incensed. And Hank knew, whether Ally realized it or not, the stakes for the ranch had just been raised. Corporate Farms would be more determined than ever to steal the property out from under him. Which was too bad, because they weren't going to get it; his new plan guaranteed that.

"All right," Ally said eventually. "Just let me say good-night to Mr. Penderson."

Hank returned his apron and badge while Ally walked across the dance hall.

Hank's mother pulled him aside before he could duck out. "Are you sure you know what you're doing?" she asked.

"Don't I always?" he quipped. He refused to entertain the notion of failure.

Greta blocked his way. "I don't blame you for going after Ally Garrett. She is a lovely young woman. But she deserves better than the shenanigans you pulled just now."

Hank thought that was a little like the pot calling the kettle black. His own father had called for a duel, in the street in front of the dance hall, while working to win his mother's heart. The outlandish maneuver infuriated—and captivated—his mom to this day.

Where women were concerned, there was one thing Hank knew. You had to go public with your feelings if you wanted a real chance with them. He figured he had done that tonight.

He gave his mother a perfunctory smile. "I know Ally deserves only the best, Mom."

Greta lifted an elegant silver-blond brow. "Do you?"

Hank was tired of family interference, no matter how well meant. "My situation with Ally is complicated." Too complicated, he added silently, for a regular courtship at a regular pace.

Greta patted his arm with maternal affection. "Life is always complicated, Hank. That's what makes it so interesting." She paused to make sure she had his full attention. "It doesn't mean that Ally deserves any less than your best. Especially given all she's been through the last couple of years."

And was still going through, Hank thought, watching her converse quietly with Penderson.

Was his mother right? Was he making a mistake by going all Texan on Ally? All Hank knew for sure was that Ally looked tense and unhappy now—and that she had appeared to be doing okay before she knew he was on the scene....

"Everything all right?" Hank's mother asked Ally kindly, as she joined them in the employees-only alcove between the dining room and kitchen.

Ally stepped aside to let a server prepare a tray of drinks, and flashed a too-bright smile. "I told Mr. Penderson to feel free to stay and have dessert and coffee without me, since our meeting this evening is concluded and I've got another ride back to the ranch. Thus far, he's refusing...."

Greta lifted a hand. "I understand, dear. I'll talk to him and see what I can do. In the meantime, I want you to know I've asked Hank to escort you to our open house out at the ranch, on the evening of the twenty-third."

Ally's mouth dropped open in surprise. "I—"

Way to go, Mom, Hank thought, even more resentfully. It wasn't enough she was advising him—without his consent—on his love life. Now she was arranging it for him, too.

Across the dining hall, Penderson lifted a hand as if to signal a waiter.

Greta patted Ally reassuringly on the arm. "I'll take care of that." She glided off.

Hank looked at Ally. She appeared as shocked and peeved as he felt. Which in turn prompted him to say matter-of-factly, "It looks like we have a date." One arranged by his mother, no less!

Ally knew the matchmaking could not stand. So the moment they started the drive back to Mesquite Ridge, she looked at Hank and blurted, "I know your mother feels sorry for me because it's Christmas and I have no family of my own."

"That's not it," Hank interrupted, with the arrogance of a man who always thought he knew better—at least where his own family was concerned.

Ally argued back, just as insistently, "It's exactly why she asked me to go to the open house yesterday. And why, when I hedged instead of just accepting her invitation on the spot, she put additional pressure on me tonight, by asking you to escort me. Because she knew it would be impossible for me to say no to the both of you. I'd be outnumbered and out…whatever."

Hank exhaled in exasperation. He pulled the truck off the road, into an empty parking lot at the edge of town. He put it in Park, leaving the lights on and the motor running, and turned toward her, draping his arm along the bench seat. "First of all…left to my own devices, I would have asked you to the party myself and provided transportation to and from the event."

Ally looked out the window. "You don't have to do that, either. I'm fine on my own."

Hank slid a hand beneath her chin and guided her face to his. "No doubt. I still want to escort you. It's a fun party. A lot of people come, and we always have a good time."

Exactly why I wouldn't fit in, Ally thought. *I've never been a party person. And certainly not on a scale with the famously loving and outgoing McCabe clan.*

"Furthermore," Hank continued in a low tone that sent shivers up and down Ally's spine, "my mom arranging for me to escort you has nothing to do with the sympathy she feels regarding your loss."

"Then what is it?" Ally asked, her voice tight with apprehension.

"She doesn't trust me to be able to handle another romance, after the way I screwed up with Jo-anne."

"What are you talking about?" Ally demanded. "The two of you were engaged! Plus, everyone knows you were madly in love each other." Just hearing about it had made her envious.

Hank exhaled. "No one knows this, but we were on the verge of breaking up when Jo-anne left to go overseas. You see, I asked her to marry me the week we graduated from college. She said yes. The only problem was, she had already accepted a job at an American hotel abroad. She still wanted to go and work there for a year, *then* come back and marry me later."

"And that put a wrench in your plans…." Ally guessed.

He nodded. "Pretty much. But I didn't want to stand in her way. She'd never really been out of Texas, and this would have allowed her to spread her wings and travel through Europe, on her time off work, for very little money. She wanted me to try and get a job there, too, so I could get the same perks and discounts at other hotels in the chain, as she did. But I wasn't interested in being a bellboy…which was all they had available."

"So what did you do?" Ally asked curiously.

"After Jo-anne went overseas, I took a job on a ranch in Colorado and started thinking about what I really wanted to do with my life, which was join the military and become a chopper pilot. And then eventually acquire my own ranch. When I told Jo-anne, she thought it would be great. After all, she was all for adventure and living life out of the ordinary. And we figured we could both request assignments overseas and see the world together that way…"

He swallowed hard. "Things were finally back on track between the two of us. I had almost saved enough money to go and visit her for a couple weeks and then…she got killed in that terrorist bombing."

Ally understood a lot about grief and guilt. "And you had a hard time forgiving yourself," she presumed softly.

He nodded. "We wasted a lot of time arguing about things that could have been worked out a whole heck of a lot easier, if the two of us had just figured out what we had to have to be happy and been willing to compromise sooner."

Ally bit her lip. "There's one thing I don't understand. If your parents knew you were already thinking about enlisting, then…"

"I hadn't told anyone but Jo-anne of my plans, or her reaction. After she was killed, I didn't want to talk about what might have been, just what I was going to do next."

That made sense. Ally studied Hank's tortured expression. "So your mother thinks…"

"The same thing my dad thinks—that I need the family's help if I'm going to achieve anything— whether it be in ranching or romance. And that's why Dad is always stopping by the ranch to see if I need his help with anything, and why Mom is trying to help our relationship along."

"Because your dad wants to know you're okay, business-wise, and she's concerned about your personal life, and…for whatever reason…wants to see the two of us together."

Or, as his sister had said, the family just wanted to see Hank with someone again, settled down with a family of his own to love.

He grimaced. "It would appear so."

Ally thought about that on the rest of the drive home. It was nice that she had the approval of the McCabe family, or guessed she did—otherwise they wouldn't be pushing Hank and her toward each other. However, it was not so nice that once again she wanted what she could never seem to get—the sense that she was more important to those closest to her than Mesquite Ridge ever would be.

As they walked into the ranch house, she and Hank stopped in the kitchen to check on Duchess and the pups. All were sound asleep.

They continued on into the living room, where Ally saw the message light blinking red, and a big shopping bag from Neiman Marcus underneath the un-adorned tree.

His expression abruptly serious, Hank shrugged out of his coat. "We still haven't talked about what upset you while I was gone," he reminded her kindly.

No, Ally thought, they hadn't. And at this point she wasn't sure she wanted to. After all, she had no official claim on Hank, or he on her. It didn't matter that the two of them had kissed a few times and reck-lessly made love once. They were both single, and she'd made it clear she was selling the ranch to the highest bidder and leaving Laramie on December 24.

If Hank wanted to see someone else, especially with Christmas on the horizon, that was his business.

Hanging on to her pride by a thread, she fibbed, "I think I just had a touch of cabin fever. I'm not used to being out here all alone."

Hank looked at her dress, the way she'd gone all out with her hair and makeup and hooked his thumbs through his belt loops. "Now why don't I believe that?"

Anxious to keep from spilling the truth, Ally looked at the answering machine. "Maybe we better see what that message is about.

"Let's not."

Ignoring his frown, Ally stepped forward and pushed the button, anyway.

As she had feared, Lulu's voice rang out loud and clear. "Hank, where are you? *I'm so excited!* I want to know when we're going to get together next! Hopefully, tomorrow. Call me, will you, honey? And do it soon!" *Click.*

Jealousy reared its ugly head.

Hank lifted a hand in damage control. "I know how that sounds, but it's not what you think."

Ally sure as heck hoped not!

Nevertheless, before she could stop them, words came pouring out of her mouth. "Well, now that we're on the subject, *honey,* messages like that one might have something to do with my pique."

Astonishment mingled with irritation on his handsome face. "Lulu and I are just friends."

"Uh-huh." Ally folded her arms and pinned him with a withering look. "Such good friends you spent the night in a hotel with her in Dallas last night?" The minute the accusation was out, Ally regretted it. For the sake of her pride, she had never meant to let on that she knew. But now the reckless words were out, there was no taking them back.

Recognition turned Hank's eyes a deeper blue, and he deliberately closed the distance between them. "First of all, Lulu and I weren't together, not in the way you're obviously thinking. And second of all, how did you know that?"

"The machine. She called here, looking for you, last night at dinnertime." *Probably accidentally on purpose, so I'd know,* Ally thought resentfully.

"Is that why you went out with Penderson this evening?" Hank looked at her as if he wanted nothing more than to make love to her, then and there. "Because you wanted to make me as jealous, as you are obviously feeling?"

"I went out with Penderson because he asked me to go." Ally spoke as if to a dimwit. "So he could apologize for putting the pressure on me regarding the sale of the ranch."

"And make another offer," Hank added tersely.

"And make another offer," Ally confirmed. "Just as you said he would."

Hank paused and searched her face. Once again he seemed able to read her mind. "Did you accept it?"

"I'm still hoping something better will come in," she replied honestly.

"Me, too." He smiled as if he knew a secret.

Ally recalled what Emily had said about Lulu getting a substantial financial settlement from her divorce. She shifted uneasily. "Back to Lulu…"

Hank gave her a stern look. "I repeat, she is just a friend."

"Who had a crush on you all through high school."

The tension in his broad shoulders eased slightly. "We never dated."

"To Lulu's lament."

Hank scrutinized Ally with unremitting interest. "There's nothing for you to be envious about," he insisted.

She scoffed. "I'm not envious. Just curious." As to why he still hadn't explained what exactly what was going on between him and Lulu…and why they had been together in Dallas the night before. Was Lulu the client Hank had been ferrying about for the last two days? Or had the two of them just happened to be in the Metroplex on business at the same time, and decided to have dinner together? And what were he and Lulu going to see each other about next that had her so excited?

Hank studied Ally, looking impossibly handsome and determined in the soft light. He gestured amicably. "Okay. *If* that's the case," he challenged audaciously, "then prove it."

Ally pushed away another wave of desire and held her ground with effort. Why did she suddenly feel she had a tiger by the tail? "How?" she asked, just as casually.

Hank held his arms wide. "Come here and kiss me like you mean it."

Chapter 11

"Kiss you?" Ally echoed.

Hank came closer, until they were near enough to feel each other's body heat. "You asked me not to bother you with half-formed plans," he stated in a soft, decisive voice that coaxed her closer still. "I haven't and I won't. I'm asking you to trust that, given another week or two, I will meet my objective and make a formal offer on Mesquite Ridge that tops the one you've already received from Corporate Farms." He regarded Ally. "If you are willing to believe in me, in here—" he put his hand over his heart "—then demonstrate your faith in me and kiss me."

It was clear from the expression in Hank's eyes that the cynic in him expected her to do the opposite—assume the worst about his time with Lulu, and move away. And had she not spent the last week with him, and seen close up what a decent, loving and honorable man Hank had become, she would have done just that.

But she knew he was good and kind.

And although maddeningly self-contained at times—as his parents very well knew—not the kind of person to make promises he felt he could not deliver on.

Hank was not the only one who could take risks, Ally thought, as she went up on tiptoe and wreathed her arms around his neck. He promptly wrapped his arms around her and used the flat of his palm to bring her all the way against him.

Their lips met. She moaned softly, tangling her hands in his hair, never wanting him to stop. And he didn't. Their tongues intertwined and his hard body pressed resolutely against her. Ally surged forward, surrendering all, until she was kissing him back more passionately than ever before. She reveled in his warmth and strength and the myriad sensations soaring through her. She knew it was Christmas, and that before this she had considered their lovemaking an unexpected gift, a salve for her loneliness. But it was so much more than that. She wanted him so much—wanted the companionship and understanding, and yes, the feeling of belonging that he offered. She knew he hadn't said anything about loving her.

It didn't matter.

She loved *him*.

Loved him enough to trust him, to take his hand and lead him up the stairs to her bedroom. Loved him enough to undress him and kiss him again, long and hard and deep.

She wanted him…so much.

Wanted him to tumble her onto her bed and disrobe her just as playfully as she had just done to him.

Her body was as ready for him, as his was for hers, and she reclined on her side, taking this gift for what it was, a coming together that was also an act of hope and faith, a moment in time to be cherished.

Hank trailed a hand over her side, the indentation of her waist, the curve of her hip, the line of her thigh. Her breath grew ragged as he caressed her abdomen, going lower still.

"I missed you," he whispered as he explored the tip of her nipple with the pad of his thumb, and followed it with a kiss.

"I missed you, too," Ally said, her pulse pounding, her senses in an uproar.

Shifting her onto her back, he draped a thigh over hers and continued caressing her, studiously avoiding the part she most wanted him to touch. Until she moaned, arched her back and opened her thighs, aware that nothing had ever felt so right....

Hank had never imagined he'd be in a position to use the chemistry he had with Ally to break down that stone wall around her heart. But Ally was so guarded and her time on the ranch with him so short that he had no choice but to use whatever advantage he had to get close to her. He wanted her in his life. Not as some long distance or occasional lover, but as a real, viable part of his everyday existence. He wanted to go to sleep with her every night and wake up with her every morning. He wanted to roam the ranch with her, and then hunker down inside, before the fire. Spend lazy afternoons in bed, when the mood struck, and work side-by-side all night when that was necessary, too.

It was more important for him to get her to stay than for him to own the ranch. If she ended up selling Mesquite Ridge to someone else, so be it. There was always more land in Laramie County. There was only one Ally.

Only one woman who could make the impossible happen, make him ready and willing to love again. Not the selfish way he had in his youth, but in the completely giving way of a man.

And she sacrificed for him, too, drifting lower, giving him what he needed, letting him know with each soft, sensual kiss just how much she cared.

Loving the no-holds-barred way she surrendered herself to him, he knelt on the floor in front of her and guided her to the edge of the bed. She caught her breath as he nudged her legs farther apart.

"Oh, Hank," she whispered, shivering as he breathed in the sweet musky scent of her and explored the petal pink softness. Satisfaction unlike anything he had ever experienced roared through him. Tightening her hands on his head, she allowed him full access, letting him stroke the pearly bud again and again. Until she was calling his name and coming apart in his hands, and he was moving upward once again, not waiting, taking her the way she yearned to be taken, until there was no stopping. Until she was clamped around him, shaking with sensation, bringing him to a shuddering climax and then slowly, sweetly down again.

Hours later, dawn streamed in through the bedroom windows. Ally was curled up next to Hank, her head on his chest, his strong arms wrapped around her. Her thigh nestled between his legs, and the warmth of his body pressed against hers. She inhaled the masculine scent of his skin and hair, and reflected on the passionate lovemaking that had kept them awake—and aroused—most of the night.

Hank stroked a hand through her hair. "What are you thinking?" he murmured, kissing her temple.

Easy. Aware she had never felt so safe, or so cherished, Ally let her eyelids flutter shut.

"I never knew it could be like this." *Never knew I could fall in love so hard and fast...or want to be with someone so very much.*

Was it just that it was Christmastime—and she was leaving Mesquite Ridge for good—that had her in desperate need of a connection? Ally wondered. Or was it because she had never had anyone so invested in making sure she was okay? All she knew for certain was that Hank was as tender and considerate as he was sensual, and that he had brought out a side of her she hadn't realized existed. He'd made her feel it was okay to be vulnerable. He'd helped her realize it was all right to need to be touched and held and cherished, in the way only he could.

"I...hoped...it could." His touch grew more loving and his husky voice dropped a notch. "But for the record..." his expression radiated a soul-deep happiness that mirrored her own "...I never imagined anything could feel this right, either."

Ally had only to look into Hank's eyes to know how true that was.

Disconcerted by the intensity of her feelings and

the fluttering of her heart, she reverted to her usual cynicism. "Maybe it's a yuletide miracle," she teased.

The corners of his lips lifted. "Or just a plain miracle," he drawled.

The raw affection in his tone made her catch her breath. "Must you always have your way?" she murmured back.

He pressed his palm to hers. "Once a marine, always a marine at heart. And now I'm a Texas rancher, too."

With no ranch to call his own. Yet.

Where had that thought come from?

He wasn't using her as a means to an end! He was not like that.

Hank had a lot more in his life, and on his mind, than the need to acquire land. He was a McCabe, and McCabes valued family and the people they loved above all else.

And even though Hank hadn't said he loved her, any more than she had confessed she loved him, she felt the connection between them. Knew they were on the cusp of something very moving and profound....

Whether or not it would last, she couldn't say. But she was going to be here for another week. She intended to spend that time enjoying Hank's company, seeing where this would lead....

He disengaged his hand from hers and chucked her beneath the chin. "I wish you wouldn't worry so much."

She wished so much wasn't at stake. How much easier it would be if Mesquite Ridge wasn't standing between them. She squinted at him. "I'm not worrying."

"The wrinkle between your brows says otherwise." Hank leaned over to kiss her temple. "All you have to do is trust me and give me a little more time, and I promise you, everything will be all right."

Hank stayed to take care of Duchess and the puppies, then headed off to feed his herd and "do what he needed to do" to be able to make her a solid offer on the ranch.

Which meant, Ally thought, as she headed to her father's den to begin the task of going through his many papers, Hank would likely be spending time with Lulu Sanderson.

Ally knew she shouldn't be jealous.

Hank was an honorable man, and he had shown her how he felt about her, the night before.

She had to do what he had asked of her, and trust in his power to achieve his goals.

She reassured herself that, unlike her parents, Hank knew what he was doing when it came to the business side of ranching. Certainly he had the connections through his family to get any expertise, advice and probably even financing that he needed.

Yet as Ally plowed through her father's notes about one crazy, ill-formed plan after another to make Mesquite Ridge profitable, her mood went downhill fast.

She was close to putting her head down in despair when Hank strode into the den, a fistful of mistletoe in his hand, a grin as big as Texas on his handsome face. "You look…happy," Ally murmured. Really happy.

He set the mistletoe down and sat on the edge of the

desk facing her, his long legs stretched out in front of him. "And you look like you just lost your prize cow."

Ally flushed. "I don't have a prize cow."

"Exactly." He swiveled slightly, so the side of his denim-clad leg pressed against hers. "But you could, if you hang with me long enough." He paused to survey her from head to toe, before returning his gaze ever so deliberately to her face. "Seriously…" his voice dropped to a compassionate murmur "…what's going on?"

Ally rocked back in the ancient wooden swivel chair and sighed. "I was going through my dad's papers, trying to figure out if there was anything I should save."

Hank's brows knit together. "And…?"

"See for yourself." Feeling like she could use an impartial opinion, Ally handed over a folder. "These are his plans to put Mesquite Ridge on the map. First there was the dude ranch idea. He spent several years on that, when I was in elementary school, but learning how much it would cost to get an operation like that up and running eventually put an end to that notion."

She handed over another folder. "Then there was his grand idea to open up a rock quarry on one end of the property and harvest limestone for builders."

Hank frowned. "I imagine hauling the rock to the cities made the cost of that prohibitive."

Ally sighed. "Exactly." She picked up another box of meticulously kept folders. "For the next few years after that he tried to find a way to buy or build a giant telescope, and put a pay-per-view planetarium on the property for tourists or star lovers passing through."

"Hmm." Hank glanced through the pages and pages of papers. "That's actually kind of interesting."

"If completely impractical," Ally added impatiently. "Next up was the idea to build a wind farm and somehow connect it up to an electrical power plant."

Hank raised his hand in the age-old gesture of peace. "He was just ahead of his time there. That's the wave of the future."

That, Ally knew. She wet her lips. "The point is… in all of this, you know what you don't see?"

Hank shrugged. "What?"

Ally drummed her hand on the scarred wooden desktop. "Books on cattle or grass management. Data on the latest breeding practices. Or anything related to what he was supposed to be doing all along, which was building a cattle operation."

Hank cocked his head. "He had a herd."

"A small one that never amounted to much. You can see when you drive around the property how he let the land go to seed. There's mesquite and cedar everywhere. And everyone knows you can never get rid of mesquite. Cut it down, and it comes right back up."

"Hey. That's not such a bad thing." Hank set her father's folders in one neat pile, on the far side of the desk. "All of that untamed brush has not only kept the topsoil intact, it's added to the nutrient value."

Ally scowled. "You're just like him. You look at the land and you see value."

Hank grinned. Clasping her hands in his, he stood and drew her to her feet. "I sure do. And you know what else I see?" He winked playfully, refusing to allow her glum mood to spread to him. "A promise I need to keep."

The devilry in his blue eyes was almost as exciting as his lovemaking had been. "And what 'promise' would that be?" Ally found herself asking.

Hank picked up the half-dozen sprigs of mistletoe he had brought into the house, and clutched them in his fist. "Finding the perfect places to hang these."

"You're sure we need *six* sprigs of mistletoe?" Ally asked as she and Hank set off to find the perfect spots to hang the holiday greenery.

Hank followed, admiring the view. There was no question Ally looked good in her chic city clothing, but she really filled out a pair of jeans and a sweater, too. "What number would you have us use?" He paused to secure one just inside his bedroom door.

Ally's heavenward glance told him what she thought about the subtlety of that. "One."

"But then—" Hank continued on down the hall, stopping at her bedroom door. He stepped inside the sanctuary that had been hers for the first eighteen years of her life, and tacked one there, too. "—You wouldn't have one here."

Merriment sparkled in her green eyes. "What makes you think I want mistletoe in my bedroom?"

Her teasing brought a smile to his face, too. She'd been so serious and bereft when she'd arrived at Mesquite Ridge the week before. It was good to see her loosening up and letting go of the grief and rigidity that had ruled her life prior to this holiday season. He winked again. "You never know when you might get the impulse to kiss someone. And need an excuse."

Ally sauntered past him, leaving a trail of orange blossom perfume. "If I want to kiss someone, I don't need an excuse."

"Ah," he said, thinking of the time when he would make love to her again, and get her to commit to more than just a momentary diversion or holiday fling. "Good to know."

Electricity shimmered between them. Ignoring his instincts, which were to make love to her then and there, Hank continued on down the hall. Determined to give her the emotional space she seemed to need, and show her they could have a good time simply hanging out together, he stopped midway down the staircase and put one there, too.

"Now that's an interesting place," Ally murmured.

"Isn't it?" Hank fantasized about having her beneath him, her arms and legs locked around his waist, and him so deep inside her he didn't know where he ended and she began. He continued to the front door and placed one just above it, in the foyer. One of these days, they'd make love without the sale of the ranch, and what that might or might not mean, between them.... One day soon, he'd be able to tell her how he really felt....

Oblivious to the passionate, possessive nature of his thoughts, Ally tilted her head. She studied the decoration over the portal, decreeing whimsically, "Not as original, cowboy."

Loving the way the unexpected endearment sounded rolling off her lips, Hank pressed the remaining greenery in her hand, relishing the soft, silky feel of her palm. "There's two left. Knock yourself out."

"Hmm." Accepting his humorous challenge, Ally sauntered off.

She paused next to the unadorned but fragrant Scotch pine and looked around. Then, grinning, she hurried across the room and stopped in the doorway between the living room and the hall that led to the kitchen and mudroom. "How about right here?"

"Expecting an earthquake?" Hank quipped.

"Door frames can be nice to lean against—" she batted her eyelashes flirtatiously "—should you want to lean, of course."

Hank liked this side of Ally. She was incredibly uninhibited and playful, deep down. The problem was that side of her didn't surface all that much. So far. If he had his way, that would change as readily as their relationship. "One left."

"Obviously, we know where that will go." Ally sashayed on down the hall and into the big country kitchen.

The plastic baby pool that served as a whelping pen had been pushed to one side of the room. Duchess lay contentedly on the blanket lining it, her back against the side. The warming box, which contained all eleven puppies, was nestled beside the mother dog.

As Ally approached, Duchess lifted her head and thumped her tail happily.

Smiling in return, Ally handed the remaining sprig to Hank. "This should go in this room because you never know when one of us is going to want to kiss Duchess or a puppy."

Hank chuckled. He got out the step stool and fastened the mistletoe in the center of the eight-foot ceiling. "How's that?"

Ally stopped petting Duchess long enough to study the result. "Perfect."

"Maybe we should try it out."

"You're right." Ally gave the dog a final pat and turned her attention to the pile of slumbering puppies. She picked up the tiniest one and lifted her gently to her chest. "This one definitely needs a kiss."

Hank chuckled. "I'll make sure I give her one," he drawled. "But first this…" He wrapped his arms around Ally and, being careful not to squish Gracie, captured Ally's lips with a tender kiss that conveyed everything he was feeling and could not say.

She kissed him back just as ardently.

When he finally lifted his head and looked into her eyes, she nudged him with her knee. "You are so bad."

"You haven't experienced the half of it." They exchanged sexy grins.

Hank felt a surge of heat, content to wait. But it turned out his competition for Ally's attention was not.

The puppy lapped at her hand with her little pink tongue, let out a familiar squeak of hunger and began to squirm.

Smiling tenderly, Ally tore her gaze from Hank's. She glanced down, then gasped. "Oh my gosh, Hank! Look at this!"

Chapter 12

"Her eyes are open!" Ally cried in amazement. She had grown used to seeing the puppies in constant play, with their eyes shut tight. Being able to look into Gracie's dark eyes forged yet another unexpected yet highly emotional connection. To the point that Ally knew leaving her was going to be excruciatingly hard.

For Hank, too, judging by the depth of affection on his handsome face. He came closer and leaned in for a better look. "Right on schedule, too." He grinned triumphantly, then turned to Ally, his warm breath brushing her face. "I told you that Gracie might be little, but she's mighty."

Ally glowed with pride, knowing that just ten days ago the pup nearly hadn't made it, and now she was leading the pack in development. Except... Ally frowned. "She doesn't seem to be focusing."

Hank brushed a gentle hand over Gracie's soft head and scratched her lovingly behind the ears. "She won't be able to track an object for another two weeks, but between now and then, she'll see a little more every day."

Ally's spirits took a nosedive as the realization hit. "Unfortunately, I won't be with her when she can see more than a blur when she looks at me. I'll be back in Houston. With or without a job…trying to put together my life there." Ally's face crumpled as another wave of sadness moved through her. "Gracie will never really get to know me." She blinked back tears. "Not the way I've come to know—and love—her."

Hank wrapped a comforting arm about Ally's shoulders. He kissed the top of her head and flashed her a consoling smile. "She knows and loves you."

Ally luxuriated in his tenderness, even as she questioned his assertion. "How? Puppies' ears are closed when they're born, too. It takes several weeks before they can hear a loud noise. According to the handouts your cousin gave us, their lack of vision and hearing is Mother Nature's way of insuring they get enough sleep in the newborn phase."

Hank's eyes glimmered. "But their other senses—touch, smell, and taste—are there from the outset. Trust me on this, Ally." He tightened his grip on her protectively. "Gracie knows you, same as she knows her mama."

Ally supposed that was true.

Which made leaving the tiny puppy all the harder.

Ally blinked back a tear as Hank knelt beside the box. The other puppies were beginning to waken, squeaking and swimming and rolling around in the search for their mother. A few more were trying to open their eyes, too.

His expression unbearably sweet, Hank lifted them one by one and put them next to Duchess to nurse. Reluctantly, Ally settled Gracie against Duchess, too, then went to prepare a supplemental bottle of puppy formula.

Not that Gracie seemed to need the extra calories as much anymore, as she was able to nurse alongside her littermates, with nearly as much vigor...

Hank held the last puppy to wake up, cradling and petting him while he awaited his turn to nurse. Duchess lay contentedly, keeping one eye on the puppy Hank held, and watching over the others snuggled at her side.

"It's amazing how fast they're all growing," Ally murmured. Or how content she felt, watching them. She had never thought of herself as much of a ranch person. This experience was changing her mind. She liked being around animals more than she had thought.

Hank nodded agreeably. "In another week they'll be standing. A week after that running and scampering about."

Ally sighed. "Sounds lively." And she would miss that, too....

The doorbell rang.

Ally looked at Hank. "Expecting anyone?"

He shook his head. "You?"

"No." She went to get the door. Seconds later, she returned with Kurt McCabe. He had his vet bag in one hand, a file folder in another. Encompassing them both with a friendly grin, Kurt told them, "I thought I'd stop by and check on Duchess and the puppies while I was out this way. And give you the news while I'm here...."

That, Hank thought, could not be good. Trusting his cousin to be objective, in a situation where he might not be, Hank asked, "Did you hear something about Duchess and her puppies, and who they might belong to?"

"Maybe." Kurt set his bag on the table. "I had a call at the clinic a while ago that sounded a little sketchy. It was from a lady in Wichita Falls named Frannie Turner."

"That's two hundred miles from here!" Ally said.

Kurt obviously shared their consternation. "Anyway, Ms. Turner said she had agreed to watch Duchess for her sister-in-law, Talia Brannamore, who had been called off on an emergency with her great-niece's family in Nashville, Tennessee. Something about a house fire and Christmas and all the presents going up in smoke, and the family having small children and nowhere to go but a hotel, and it all being very short notice. Apparently, there was a lot of confusion, both before Duchess was dropped off with Ms. Turner, and during the first day Duchess was there."

Ally's eyes took on a cynical glint. "Kurt, this sounds like a hoax!"

Hank agreed.

"That's what I thought." Kurt knelt next to the whelping pen, stethoscope around his neck. "Except for one thing. This woman who claimed she was keeping the female golden retriever named Duchess, knew the retriever was pregnant and about to deliver eleven whelps. We didn't put that information in any of the flyers we sent out."

Ally blinked. "Why not?"

Hank explained, "The dogs are valuable. It's Christmas, and the demand for puppies—even those not quite ready to go home yet—is higher than at any other time of year. And these are purebred, show quality dogs. They're worth a lot."

Kurt started examining the puppies one by one. "So the fact that Frannie Turner in Wichita Falls knows that we have a golden retriever named Duchess is great. The fact she has no proof of ownership—no papers, or pictures of this dog—gives rise to a lot of question. She says it's because Duchess isn't hers, and she was just doing a favor. And that the dog got out of her house accidentally and ran away."

Ally pressed her lips together, clearly skeptical. "We're two hundred miles from Wichita Falls, guys. That's an awfully long way."

Hank draped a consoling arm across Ally's shoulders. "Duchess was pregnant, about to deliver. She could have been trying to make her way home to San Angelo to deliver her puppies, and ended up here."

Her expression thoughtful, Ally turned into Hank's embrace. He squeezed her, then let her go.

"You hear about that sometimes," Ally murmured. "Dogs surmounting impossible odds—and doing whatever they have to do to get home."

More than one movie had been made about this kind of true life event, Hank knew.

"And it could have happened in this case," Kurt said

as he checked Duchess. Finding everything in order, he put his stethoscope back in his bag. "Pregnant dogs have a desire to nest, and a lot of them instinctively go off in private to deliver. But it's also possible Frannie Turner could have gotten the information elsewhere. Everyone in the community is talking about it. And they're all telling their friends and family. So it's possible this woman is trying to pull a scam on us."

Ally's brow furrowed with emotion. "So now what?"

Kurt sighed. "Apparently, Frannie didn't tell her sister-in-law the dog was missing, because she had enough to deal with and Frannie didn't want her to get upset with her. The sister-in-law is a very serious professional dog breeder, she claims. Now that Frannie knows we found the dog and that the puppies are all okay, she's not afraid to tell Talia Brannamore." He locked eyes with Hank and then Ally. "So Frannie told me she would call Talia in Nashville, and see if she can't get us some sort of proof."

"How long is that going to take?" Hank asked, impatient to get this resolved before he or Ally became any more emotionally involved with Duchess and the pups.

Kurt stood. "She's already done it. I spoke to the breeder right before I got here. Talia Brannamore reiterated everything Frannie already told me, but said she doesn't have any proof with her. It's all at her house in San Angelo. And she won't be back there until December 23. Talia offered to drive through Laramie on her way home, since she'll pass right by here, and see Duchess. If her story is true, and Duchess is hers, then the retriever should immediately recognize her. If not, and we think a fraud is being perpetrated… well, I've already talked to my brother Kyle, and we'll have someone from the sheriff's department ready and waiting."

"But you think it might be true, don't you?" Ally asked, clearly upset.

Kurt shrugged. "All I can tell you is that the woman from San Angelo was really concerned about her pregnant dog being lost and not knowing anything about it. She is exceedingly grateful to you and Ally and the vet clinic, and prepared to compensate us all for our troubles."

Which went to confirm the value of golden retrievers, Hank thought.

He cast a sideways look at Ally. Her face had a crushed expression that mirrored his own feelings and tore at his heart.

He watched her kneel down and pick up Gracie, cradle her tenderly. He knew he'd do anything to make Ally happy. "What about the pups?" he asked.

Kurt knew where this was going. He shook his head. "They're all spoken for, every last one."

Hank swore silently to himself. "Including the runt of the litter?" He had to make sure.

Kurt nodded and confirmed grimly, "Gracie, too."

Ally sat in the kitchen, devastated, while Hank walked his cousin out. She had known this could happen. She had just been hoping that it wouldn't….

Hank strode back in, an old-fashioned hatbox, emblazoned with his name, clasped in his hands. Wordlessly, he set it on the table and came around to where she was sitting. He knelt in front of her, like a knight before a queen, and covered her hands with his warm ones.

Ally lifted her head. How easy it would be to depend on him this way. And how foolish. Since she wasn't staying, and he wasn't about to leave, and the sale of the ranch still stood between them...

Hank searched her face. "Are you okay?"

Embarrassment heated her cheeks. "Why wouldn't I be?" she countered grumpily.

"You've gotten attached to Gracie."

Against all common sense, she reminded herself unhappily. "And you're attached to Duchess. And we always knew this would happen." She drew a deep breath, then added honestly, "I wished it wouldn't. I just hoped I'd be able to find a way to keep the littlest one. But that's not going to happen," she said, the bitterness of old coming back to haunt her. Like every other situation at Mesquite Ridge, this event had a bad ending. For her, anyway...

Hank looked into her eyes as if he shared her heartache. "You can get another puppy," he murmured softly, as if there was no place on earth he would rather be.

She gripped his hands, drawing on his strength despite herself, and blinked back tears. "I know," she said thickly.

But it wouldn't be the same, Ally knew. *Just like making love with another man won't be the same. Not after you.*

With effort, Ally pushed her melancholy thoughts

away. Hank was right—she could get another puppy. Someday. In the meantime, she had four days left in Laramie. She wasn't going to let the bleakness of her future life ruin what she had today. She was going to do what she'd never been wise enough to do before. Enjoy the here and now, and forget about whatever tomorrow might bring.

Swallowing, Ally nodded at the box in Hank's hands, determined to try to get back in the holiday spirit and be cheerful if it killed her. "What's that?"

"My mom sent it over. Kurt almost forgot to give it to me."

Okay, that told her absolutely nothing, except that his mother apparently liked fancy hatboxes, and this one looked as if it had been around for a while. In fact, there was even a little dust on it. "Aren't you going to open it?" Ally prodded.

Hank shrugged, as maddeningly determined as she was impatient to learn more. "Sure. If you want." He flashed her a grin that upped her anticipation even further. "That is—" he leaned forward intimately, more than ready to lend a little sensual distraction "—if you're ready to do *your* usual thing and get your bah, humbug on."

Hilarious. "Can't wait, cowboy." Ally dared him with a glance. "Do your best to get me in the spirit."

Hank chuckled as if it were already a fait accompli. He took the lid off the hatbox. It was filled with a breathtaking array of amazing and unique ornaments. Some wrapped in tissue, some not. He picked up a ceramic Western-boot-wearing Santa Claus driving a sleigh filled with presents. "I got this one when I was five."

Ally could imagine him hanging it on the tree, as an adorable little boy. "Cute," she murmured, intrigued by this glimpse into his holidays past.

Hank fingered a Nutcracker soldier and reflected fondly, "This came from Dallas the year I turned eight. Mom and Dad took the whole family to see the ballet at Christmastime."

The wooden figure was exquisite, even without the beautiful memories. "So everything in here has special meaning."

He nodded, then gathered the box in one arm, took her by the hand with the other and led her into the living room.

Belatedly, Ally realized there were electric lights on the tree. Hank had to have put them up. When, she wasn't sure.

Chuckling at her surprise, he leaned over and plugged in the cord. The tree lit up with a rain of tiny sparkling lights.

He reached for the box and fished out an ornament with a picture of him as a gap-toothed first grader on it. He walked over and hung it on the tree they had yet to decorate. "When I was a teenager, I found this photo hideously embarrassing."

Ally sauntered closer. "And now?"

He brushed his thumb across her cheek. "It brings back memories. Good ones." He paused. "I guess this isn't so great for you, though." He started to remove the ornament. "Maybe we should just stick to the decorations I bought at Neiman Marcus."

Ally looked over at the shopping bag he had brought home days before. "We can use those," she told him happily, returning to the hatbox full of memories. "But let's use these, too." It was fun, hearing his stories. Learning about his childhood made her feel closer to him in a way she hadn't expected.

Hank studied her with concern. "It's not really fair to have a tree for us that says everything about my childhood and nothing about yours, though."

For us. She liked the sound of that.

Ally raised a hand, promising cheerfully, "We can rectify that. Wait here." She darted upstairs, anxious to surprise him, too. She came back several minutes later with a cloth-covered shoebox, and opened the lid. Inside was a collection just as unique.

His dark brow furrowed. "I thought you said your family didn't celebrate Christmas."

Ally sent him a wry look. "They didn't." She unwrapped a paper chain and another of artificial popcorn and cranberries, aware she was sentimentally attached—to every ornament of her youth, as he was to his. She smiled, belatedly realizing that "Christmas" was found in the unlikeliest of places. Like here, with Hank.

"But the teachers at school did," she continued, surprised to find herself eager to share her past with Hank. "And when I was younger, we made stuff in art class, too." She had tucked it all away, in the very back of her closet, where it would be safe.

Hank's eyes locked with hers.

"I used to get it all out and look at it over the holidays," she confessed.

He gathered her in his arms, intuitively giving her all the comfort and reassurance she needed. "That's... sad."

She had thought so, too...until now. "Not really." Ally had a brand-new way of looking at things. She lifted her chin. "Not when you consider how much joy these little trinkets brought me."

Tenderly, he drew a knuckle across the bow of her lips. "So there is a heart inside that Grinch exterior, after all."

Ally grinned and wound her arms about his neck. Playfully, she went up on tiptoe. "Just don't tell anyone about it."

He regarded her in a way that left no doubt they would be making love again very soon. "Not to worry," he whispered. "Your secret is safe with me." As if to prove it, he captured her lips in a kiss that was so unbearably tender it had her melting against him. "Although," Hank drawled finally, smoothing a palm down her spine, "you may not be able to keep it secret much longer...."

Ally chuckled and splayed her hands across the warmth of his chest. "Just decorate the tree!"

An hour later, they had all the remnants from their youth hanging next to the beautiful glass ornaments from Dallas's top department store. It was an eclectic tree, rife with meaning. Ally knew she had never seen anything more beautiful.

Hank stepped back to admire the pine. He braced his hands on his hips. "All we need now is something for the top."

Suddenly, Ally wanted to do more than just be

dragged into participating. "Why don't you let me handle that?"

"Sure?" Hank teased her with a kiss to the brow. "Wouldn't want to ruin your rep as a holiday curmudgeon."

She rolled her eyes. "Trust me, there's very little chance of that!"

"I don't know...you're looking awfully happy right now."

Her heart pounded against her ribs. "I'm feeling awfully happy." Which was odd, given the fact that she was about to lose the puppy and the mama dog she had fallen in love with. Closer still to unwillingly forfeiting her job and selling the home she'd had since birth. By all rights, she ought to be flat-out miserable tonight, and crying her eyes out. She wasn't. There was only one reason for that.

He knew it. And was coming closer once again, to claim her. Fully, this time. Hank took her into his arms, lowered his mouth to hers. Their lips were just about to touch when his cell phone rang.

Hank grimaced, looking very much like he didn't want to answer the call. Then again, it was late, and generally people didn't phone at eleven at night unless it was important....

He let her go reluctantly. "This will just take a second. Hank McCabe..." He listened intently, frowned some more. "You want to meet *now?*" he asked, his tone incredulous. "Of course... I understand. Time is of the essence. Fifteen—twenty minutes okay? See you then." He ended the call. "I've got to go into town."

"Let me guess." The words were out before Ally could stop them. "Lulu again?"

To his credit, Hank didn't back away from the facts. "She's an integral part of my plan to buy Mesquite Ridge."

Ally's heart sank. "I heard she got a lot of money in her divorce settlement."

Hank acknowledged that with a brief nod, but did not comment, before once again glancing at his watch. "I've got to go." He paused, the inscrutable look coming back into his deep blue eyes. "I'm not sure how long this will take."

Jealousy and anger twisted inside her. "Don't worry." Ally flashed the most nonchalant smile she could manage. "I won't wait up."

Hank was out the door a few minutes later.

Ally paced the room. The tree that had seemed so festive moments earlier appeared flat and unexciting now.

She guessed the old saying was right—beauty was in the eye of the beholder. The question was, how did Hank see Lulu? As his savior?

Ally didn't have a big bank account. If she did...

But she didn't. She might not even have a job.

She glanced at the clock again. It was late, but chances were, Porter was still up. She went to get her phone. Seconds later, her call went through, and her colleague answered on the first ring. "Hey, stranger," he said. "About time you returned any one of the half-dozen calls or email messages I left for you."

"Sorry. I've been a little busy. How are things with you?"

"Glum. The current job market in Houston is bleak. I might have to go back to Phoenix, where I grew up."

"Do you have a lead?"

"On several things, as a matter of fact. With all the retirees still moving to the Sun Belt for their golden years, the demand for financial analysts and advisers is growing every day. I can give you the name of the recruiting firm I'm using. It might not be so bad if we both got jobs and moved there at the same time."

To Arizona? "I don't know, Porter. I'm a Texas girl, born and bred...." To date, she had never thought much about it. But now...? "I'm not sure I want to live anywhere but the Lone Star State."

"Look. You don't have to decide anything tonight. Just send in your résumé and a cover letter to the contact I emailed you this morning. Think of it as insurance. Chances are, if a firm in Arizona gives you an offer, you won't lose your job in Houston."

Chances for success were definitely better if they had multiple options, instead of just the one. Ally forced herself to be practical. "I like the way you think."

Porter chuckled. "Thank you."

She paced back and forth. "Any further word on the layoffs?" Unlike her, Porter always had his ear to the ground for workplace gossip. If there was something to know, her friend would be aware of it.

"Nope. Just that the new management intends to keep a skeleton crew on to manage the transition, and the rest of the cuts are going to be massive, and brutal."

Which meant, Ally told herself sternly, she *had* to be practical. She couldn't just follow her heart....

She thanked Porter for the info. They chatted some

more and then hung up. Restless, she took care of Duchess and the puppies. By the time she had finished, it was well after midnight, and there was still no sign of Hank.

He was not off making love with Lulu. Or looking for a liaison. Lulu was probably just using her connections to help Hank find the additional financing he needed to be able to make an offer on Mesquite Ridge.

But on the off-off chance that Hank was out doing something that would signal the end of Ally and him… She figured she better do as Porter advised and develop a much better plan B.

Hank tiptoed in at 3:00 a.m. Ally had said she wouldn't wait up, and she hadn't. She was fast asleep on the living room sofa, an angelically peaceful look on her face—and what appeared to be a half-finished quilted Christmas stocking in her hands.

Hank considered picking her up and carrying her to bed, but knew he'd wake her, and then he'd want to make to love to her. Trouble was, given the time and where he'd been, it was unlikely that Ally would welcome his advances.

So, he figured, as he went upstairs and got one of the blankets off her bed and covered her up, this would have to do.

Kissing her would have to come later.

In the meantime, he needed a little shut-eye himself. He had a lot to accomplish and a short amount of time to get it all done, if he were to make Ally's dreams come true and give her a truly merry Christmas, to boot.

Chapter 13

The sound of footsteps jerked Ally from her reverie. Her heartbeat accelerating, she turned to see Hank striding toward her, two steaming mugs in hand. He greeted her with a cheerful smile. "You're up bright and early."

And you, Ally thought, as she put the fabric samples she had been studying aside, *got home awfully late.*

Determined to keep her hurt feelings to herself, she waved off his offer of a fresh cup. "Thanks." She forced herself to be polite as she rose from the living room sofa. "I'm already at my limit." For caffeine and a lot of other things....

A knowing look on his face, Hank set the beverage he'd brought for her on an end table, safely out of harm's way. "In case you change your mind," he said casually.

Not likely, now that another potential investor was in the picture, Ally thought, with unprecedented resentment simmering deep inside her.

Ally had *promised* herself she would never again get in a situation where the acquisition of land took precedent over everything else. The fact that Hank could ditch her on a moment's notice at eleven o'clock at night, when they'd been close to making love again, proved that he felt otherwise. Clearly, the ranch was more important to him than the two of them.

So Ally had no choice. She had to take a step back from the fierce attraction she felt for Hank, and think about what was in her best interests.

It didn't matter how capable and kind he seemed, standing there in the morning light. Or how good he looked and smelled, fresh from his shower. She could not allow herself to forget her own need for long-term financial security, throw caution to the wind and make love with him again.

Not when his obsession with acquiring the ranch had him putting Mesquite Ridge first, her second. Or maybe, considering Lulu Sanderson's involvement, even third…

Hank inclined his head at the bolts of fabric scattered across the living room. "What's all this?"

"I'm still planning to put the ranch on the market on December 24."

Ally ignored the shadow that passed over Hank's face. This was business—not personal, no matter how much he might want her to think otherwise.

Deliberately, she pushed on. "The broker from Premier Realty, Marcy Lyon, is coming out to do a walk-through inspection and take some photographs for the MLS listing on the 22. She and I will nail down the final asking price at that time, which as you know could be quite a bit higher or lower than the tax appraisal Corporate Farms is using. I want it to be higher, of course, so I'm trying to do everything I can, within the constraints of my budget, to get the place looking the best."

Hank glanced around in admiration. "You've already had the place painted, and made draperies as well as slipcovers for all the furniture in here."

"We still need splashes of color to brighten up the space. And I don't want to buy any more fabric—I'd prefer to use the remnants from my mother's sewing room. So I'm trying to figure out which to use for pillows and a throw. I'm even thinking about making a wall hanging or two, since we don't really have any art, and the walls are looking a little bare. It would be easy enough to do."

Hank pointed to several bolts of colorful cloth with a splashy modern art motif. "I don't know if you want my opinion, but I like those."

Ally nodded. Call it coincidence, but they were the ones she had chosen, too.

Hank stepped closer, his expression intent. "Look, I know we said we wouldn't talk about the offer I'm planning to make on the ranch until I get everything pulled together—"

She cut him off with a quick lift of her palm. "It's still a good idea."

Hank gave her a steady, assessing look. He *wanted* to confide in her. What did she want? The answer to that was easy enough. She wanted to protect her heart and get her life back on a secure track once again.

"Are you sure?" he asked finally.

Ally nodded. It hardly mattered whether Lulu was drawing on her handsome divorce settlement and personally loaning Hank the money he needed to make a down payment on a mortgage, using her business school connections to line up another investor to help him out, or going in on the ranch with him. All options left Ally feeling like a third wheel. It didn't matter whether she wanted to be with Hank or not. She couldn't live like that again.

"Well, I must say," Marcy Lyon concluded when she had finished the tour of the property, "you have done an incredible job in a short amount of time, fixing up the interior of the ranch house."

Ally had to admit it looked better. The soft gray walls and gleaming white trim showed off the wide plank floors. Ivory slipcovers covered a multitude of sins on the aging furniture. Antique Texan accessories, throw pillows and fabric wall hangings provided color throughout. And of course, there was the Christmas tree she and Hank had decorated. It still lacked something on top, and Ally reminded herself she still needed to take care of that.

"Unfortunately, it's not enough," Marcy said reluctantly. "The plumbing, electrical and roof are all forty years old. There's no dishwasher or disposal. The kitchen is nice and big, but the linoleum floors and counters are terribly dated, and the appliances are ancient. The bulk of the acreage is in similarly bad shape."

She sighed with regret. "This puts Mesquite Ridge squarely in the category of a fixer-upper, and lowers the price a good ten percent. That, combined with the commission you'd have to pay on what should be a two point five million dollar property—but currently isn't— minus the existing mortgage debt… At the end of the day you'd have very little."

Ally felt her heart sink. "So in other words, the last offer I received from Corporate Farms…"

Marcy looked her square in the eye and put her pen back in her briefcase. "Is really unbeatable, if money is your only criteria."

Ally watched her continue to pack up her belongings. "And if it's not?"

She closed the clasp on her briefcase with a snap, then pressed her lips together. "May I be blunt?"

Nodding, Ally said, "I need you to be as direct with me as possible."

Marcy began to pace. "You can't expect to sell to Corporate Farms—knowing full well they intend to drive everyone else out of business so they can create an outfit bigger than the King Ranch right here in Laramie County—and think it will be okay."

"If I were to do that…" Ally swallowed and looked the real estate broker in the eye "…I'd never be able to come back, would I?"

Marcy shook her head. "I don't see how you could."

Hours later, Hank walked into the living room where Ally sat beside the Christmas tree. Duchess was curled up next to her. The puppies were sleeping in a comical heap across her lap. It was a blissful scene, except for the faintly troubled look in Ally's eyes.

Hank tossed his leather jacket over the back of the chair and loosened the knot of his tie. He wished he could tell Ally about the meeting he'd just been to. But like everything else about the negotiations he was involved in, the details were top secret until the deal was set. And that wouldn't be for another thirty-six hours.

In the meantime, though…moments like this didn't come along all that often. He took out his cell phone, determined to capture the moment. "Hang on a minute. I've got to get a picture of this."

For a second he thought Ally might burst into sentimental tears, which was not surprising, given how attached she had gotten to all the dogs. Then she got that fiercely independent look in her eyes he knew so well. She mugged dramatically, then picked up Gracie and held her to her chest. She used her other hand to soothe the equally hyperalert Duchess. "Since when are you into taking pictures?" she chided.

The walls were coming up around Ally's heart again, higher than ever. Hank wanted to tear them down.

"Since I found the perfect Christmas card photo." *And the perfect woman.* "And because," he added honestly, "this is something I want us all to remember for a long time to come."

Some of the fight drained out of Ally. "You really think the dogs are going to remember?" she asked softly, pressing a kiss on top of Gracie's head.

The pup opened her eyes and looked up at Ally.

If Gracie wasn't focusing on Ally's face, Hank decided, she was darned close…. Certainly, there was love and affection reflected on her cute little mug as she snuggled there.

Realizing Ally was still awaiting an answer to her question, he said, "I'm sure the dogs will recall all the love and attention they've received from us. In fact," he predicted, working to disguise the small catch in his throat, "I think they are going to be as sad to leave Mesquite Ridge tomorrow as we will be to see them go."

To his chagrin, Ally noticed the unusual huskiness in his voice. She made another face and teased, "I didn't think ranchers got emotional about stuff like this."

For some, the acquisition and loss of pets was a normal part of the ebb and flow of ranch life. Something accepted without much thought. For Hank, dogs were part of the family. Which was why he'd been thinking about getting one as soon as he had his own ranch.

"What can I say?" He shifted angles to make sure he captured the tree and the fireplace in the next frame. Smiling, he joined their makeshift family. Holding the cell phone out in front of him, he took a photo of all of them together. "You bring out my sentimental side."

This time Ally's smile was from the heart. "And your familial one," she added softly.

That was true, too, Hank noted. Never had he wanted to have a family of his own more than he did right now, with Ally, Duchess and Gracie…

Whenever she let her guard down, Ally seemed to want that, too.

Silence fell as they looked into each other's eyes.

Ally sobered, as if suddenly recalling all that still remained unsettled, all that could drive them apart. She
was right to be concerned, Hank admitted reluctantly
to himself. It was time to have a serious discussion,
at least about the things they could talk about at this
juncture.

Such as her meeting with Marcy Lyon.

Hank pocketed his phone once again. Figuring this
was one conversation best had with no distraction, he
helped Ally return the puppies to the warming box,
next to Duchess in the whelping pen. The warming
box was situated next to the mother dog. When they'd
all settled down to sleep once again, Ally motioned
for Hank to follow her.

"So how did your meeting go?" he asked, while
they walked back into the living room.

She sank down on the sofa, propped her feet on the
coffee table and released a long, slow breath. "Premier
Realty's appraisal did not come out as I had hoped."

Hank tensed, not sure whose side he was on—hers
or his. Maybe both... He sat next to her, being careful
to give her plenty of room. "How bad was it?"

Ally passed a weary hand over her eyes. "So bad
Marcy is refusing to list the ranch for me, because she
doesn't want every bit of profit I might make from the
sale of the property to go toward her commission."
Briefly, she explained, then looked over at him and
shook her head in exasperation. "What kind of person
shoots themselves in the foot professionally that way?"

Hank replied frankly, "The kind who lives in Laramie, Texas. Neighbors here help each other out. They
don't take unfair advantage for personal gain."

"Like Corporate Farms would."

Hank nodded, knowing he would give anything to find a way to keep Ally in his life. Even his dream of one day owning this ranch, if that's what it would take. Because she was worth any sacrifice to him. The question was, what was he worth to her?

She released a beleaguered sigh and turned toward him, tucking one foot beneath her, her other knee nudging his. Her green eyes were full of strength and wisdom. "I'm a financial analyst." She shifted closer, the fragrance of her hair and skin inundating his senses. "I know the smart thing to do, fiscally, would be to accept CF's deal and not look back."

Hank gazed at her thoughtfully, really wanting to understand her. "And yet…?" he prompted softly.

She tensed, seeming on guard once again. "They'd destroy the house, the barn and everything that is familiar about this place."

And that, Hank noted, was something Ally couldn't bear. He reached over and covered her hand with his. "I thought you hated Mesquite Ridge."

Her fingers grasped his and she bit her lip. "I did, too. At least I thought I did." She paused to look deep into his eyes. "But now that I've been here again and started fixing up the house, I'm remembering some not so bad times." She shrugged. "Like sewing with my mother. Learning the ins and outs of finance and bookkeeping with my dad. As much as I hated their frugality, I have to admit no one could stretch a dollar better than the two of them." Ally pushed her free hand through her hair, mussing the silky strands. She shook her head, her eyes glimmering moistly. "I feel like I have no good options."

Unable to bear seeing her in so much distress, Hank shifted her onto his lap and wrapped his arms around her. "That's not true. You have me. I am this close—" he held his index finger and thumb half an inch apart "—to being able to help you." *This close to being able to tell you everything I feel...everything I want us both to have.*

She scowled briefly. "Please don't say that," she begged, splaying her hands across his chest. "Really. I can't bear any more half-baked promises. Not tonight."

Tenderness swept through him. Not sure when he had ever felt such devotion, he shifted her closer still. Heaven help him, he wanted to make love to her here and now. And one day soon, their time would come.

"Then what can I do?" he asked quietly.

The caution that she'd been feeling the last few days, about the two of them, fled. She leaned into him and allowed herself to be vulnerable to the undeniable sparks between them once again. "Help me to forget I may soon have to sell the only real link to family that I have left. Or that tomorrow I'm going to find out whether or not I'm going to be laid off from my job." Her voice cracked emotionally. She looked at him with raw need. "And that Duchess and Gracie and the rest of the puppies are going to be taken away...."

She was facing tremendous loss, Hank knew. But she wasn't going to lose him. Not if he could help it. And lowering his mouth to hers, he set about to show her that.

One kiss turned into two, then three. She shifted

around on his lap so she was straddling him. The softness of her breasts pressed against his chest as she
nuzzled his neck.

Hank unbuttoned her blouse, eased it off and di-
vested her of her lacy bra. She shuddered as he palmed
her nipples, teasing them into tender buds. His hands
drifted lower, to release the zipper on her skirt.

Deciding the sooner there was nothing but pure heat
between them the better, he shifted her again, so she
was on her feet. And then she took the lead, stripping
sensually, helping him do the same. She touched and
kissed him with a wild rapture, pushing him toward
the edge. In a haze, he suddenly found himself sitting
on the sofa again, with Ally straddling his lap.

"Now," she said determinedly, tangling her fingers
in his hair.

"Not until you're ready." He held her wrists in one
hand, using his other to touch, stroke, love. She quivered, as he kissed her again, vowing to make this last,
to make it so incredible she would never want to pull
away. Her skin grew flushed, her thighs parted to better accommodate his. And then she was wet and trembling, ready, wanting, needing, and Hank was lost in a
completeness unlike anything he had ever known. His
heart pounding, he caught her hips. Brought her flush
against him. Ally closed around him, her response
honest and unashamed. Surrendering entirely, she took
him deep inside her, resolutely commanding everything he had to give. And when she would have hurried
the pace even more, he held back, making her understand what it was to feel such urgent, burning need.

Until there was no doubt that this holiday season,

the two of them had every dream fulfilled, in their lovemaking, in each other. Until she was giving him every ounce of tenderness and passion she possessed, just as he was to her.

For the first time Hank knew what it was to come home to where the heart was, to have every detail of his future happiness laid out in front of him, his for the taking.

He wanted to tell her how he felt. But with the business of the ranch still between them, he knew he had to wait. So Hank tried to show her instead, with kisses full of longing, touches full of need. Until she was shivering with pleasure, until she drew him toward the brink and was crying out hoarsely as he thrust inside her, the friction of their bodies doubling the pleasure. Her hands were on his skin, and his were on hers, and nothing mattered but the two of them. Their mouths and bodies meshed until every bit of her was sweet and wild and womanly. And all his... Beautifully, magically, wonderfully his.

All they had to do was make it another thirty-four hours.

Until late Christmas Eve.

When he would finally be able to tell her the truth.

And give her the security and sense of belonging she had always craved.

Chapter 14

Ally clapped a hand over her heart and stared at the litter. Her pretty face glowed with a happiness that would have been hard to imagine just two weeks before. "I can't believe it, Hank! They're actually *standing*."

"Before they fall over, that is." Hank chuckled as the puppies—all roughly three pounds each now—struggled upright, tottered and then fell, only to get right back up again. It seemed once Gracie had the idea, all her bigger littermates wanted to follow her example.

"It's going to be so quiet here without them," Ally mused tenderly.

Even quieter without you, Hank thought. *If you choose to leave. I'm still hoping a Christmas miracle will happen and you'll decide not to return to Houston, after all.*

Pushing his own concerns aside, he asked, "Have you heard about your job yet?"

Ally paled. "Word was supposed to be sent out via email at seven this morning."

Hank glanced at his watch. "It's seven-thirty."

She acknowledged this with a slight dip of her head. "I know. I should check. But..." she lifted her slender shoulders in a shrug "...I'm afraid to look."

Hank knew it was his job to lessen the tension. He flashed her a consoling grin, and drawled, "You know what they say..."

"I'm sure you're going to tell me," Ally replied, mirroring his deadpan expression.

"Burying your head in the sand doesn't give you anything but grit up your nose."

She burst out laughing. "And here I thought you were going to go all Churchill on me and say something like—" she lowered her voice to a booming alto "—Now, Ally, there's nothing to fear but fear itself!"

"That, too." He moved a strand of hair from her cheek, and tucked it behind her ear. "Why don't you have a look?" he encouraged gently. For her sake, he hoped she got what she wanted—continued employment and a steady salary coming in. "I'll have the champagne ready."

She looked as if she was going to need a hanky instead. "I'm going to be fired," she worried out loud.

Hank shook his head. "Not if they're smart."

Ally gave him one last glance, then swallowed and went to the desk. She switched on her laptop computer and brought up her email. Waited impatiently, her hands trembling slightly all the while. Finally, she drew a long bolstering breath, typed in a command, then another. And promptly burst into tears.

Hank swore silently to himself and reached for the tissue box.

"Porter lost his job," Ally sobbed. She accepted the tissues he handed her and wiped her face. "I kept mine."

Hank was ambivalent, to the say the least, since this meant she would be leaving Laramie—and him. His need to be a decent and chivalrous human being demanded that he once again put his own concerns aside, and congratulate and wholeheartedly support Ally on her career success. "Well, that's good, isn't it?" he countered enthusiastically.

Ally's face crumpled. She slumped back in her chair and wearily ran a hand over her damp eyes. "It means I have to be back in Houston for an 8:00 a.m. managers meeting on December 26."

Which meant she would be leaving Christmas Day, if not sooner, just as she had initially planned. Not so good. Still, Hank didn't want to be a jerk. "Congratulations," he said, meaning it with every fiber of his being.

"Thank you." Ally closed her eyes and exhaled slowly, looking even more distressed. Finally, she straightened. "I have to call Porter."

"I'll manage things here," Hank promised as another round of puppies stood, wobbled and fell into a wiggling pile.

Ally stepped outside on the wraparound porch to speak in private.

Just as she finished, Talia Brannamore arrived. Ally greeted her, then brought her inside.

Hank had been prepared to loathe the breeder who'd managed to put Duchess in the care of someone so obviously incompetent. Who could lose such a precious dog who was about to give birth? But it was clear Talia Brannamore had been through a little bit of hell herself. Her face was haggard with fatigue, her middle-aged body drooping.

Duchess thumped her tail in recognition and panted happily when she saw her owner, but didn't rise to greet her, as Hank would have expected her to do after such a prolonged absence.

Talia shook her head at the puppies tumbling over each other in an effort to get to their feet and stay there. She knelt and picked them up one by one, examining each in turn. "The nose is a little short on this one," she noted with a discerning frown. "I don't like the look of these ears. Now this one…this one is darn near perfect. And what happened here?" Talia stopped when she saw Gracie, who weighed in at only two and a half pounds, instead of the three sported by all her littermates. "What a little runt she is!"

Ally's jaw dropped. She squared off with the woman unhappily. "I don't know how you can say that! I mean…she's on the small side, but she's absolutely beautiful!"

Talia sighed. "Only because you know nothing about show dogs. This one would not win Westminster. Now this one…" she picked up a particularly robust male puppy "…would." The breeder set the puppy down with barely a pat of affection. She rocked back on her heels. "Fortunately, most of my customers aren't interested in showing their dogs. They just want their pet to look like he or she could be competitive enough to win first place." That said, Talia Brannamore looked back at Gracie and shook her head in obvious disappointment.

"If you don't want her, I'll take Gracie!" Ally blurted.

Again, Talia shook her head. "I can't do that. These dogs have all been presold for months now. And even though they won't be able to go 'home' for another seven weeks, I've promised their new owners they'll be able to come and visit their puppy on Christmas Day. So I've got to talk compensation with you, and then load them up and get going."

Saying goodbye to all of them was tough, even for Hank, but saying goodbye to Gracie was heart-wrenching. Ally's lower lip trembled and tears rolled down her face as she kissed the smallest puppy on the head and then gently put her in the flannel lined warming box with her littermates. The box was plugged into the power outlet in Talia Brannamore's station wagon.

The breeder patted the blanketed cargo area. "Come on, Duchess, let's go."

The retriever looked at Talia and then Hank, and went to stand next to him. Taking his hand in her mouth, she tugged him toward the back of the station wagon.

She seemed to be urging him to get in with the puppies.

Then Duchess went to Ally and gently mouthed her hand, doing the same.

Ally cried all the harder.

The lump in Hank's throat got even bigger. "Well, I'll be darned. She wants us to go with them," he muttered in awe.

"Honestly," Talia said, exasperated. She patted the cargo bed vigorously and commanded, "Duchess! Inside! Now!"

Duchess gave another last long look at Hank and Ally, then did as ordered. She settled next to her puppies, as if knowing this was where she had to be. The breeder shut the back, then turned to them. "Thanks again. Y'll have a merry Christmas now!" She got in and drove off.

As the station wagon went down the lane, they could see Duchess press her head against the window, looking back at them.

Hank had grown up around animals. He knew that there was a cycle to things, and this cycle had ended— at least for him and Ally. It still hurt almost more than he could bear. He turned to her and could tell at a glance that it was all she could do not to run after the station wagon and beg Talia Brannamore to let all the dogs stay.

He felt the same way.

On top of that, he was about to lose Ally, too! Talk about yuletide misery. She apparently felt it, too, for she pivoted, saw his eyes gleaming with moisture, and promptly lost it.

There were times, Ally knew, when a person needed to be held. And right now she needed not just to be held, but for *Hank* to hold her. And he knew it, too.

She thrust herself into his arms. He caught her to him and buried his face in her hair, offering low, consoling words and the sweetest solace she had ever felt. Then the tears came, in an outpouring of grief she could not seem to stop.

Ally cried because they'd lost the dogs they both loved so much. She cried because she had kept her job, and that meant she had to leave. She cried because she wasn't quite sure where she stood with Hank. And most of all, she cried because for the first time in her life she felt like she just might belong somewhere, with someone. And she wasn't sure that was going to last, either. All she knew for sure was that she was drenching his shirt, and that he made her feel so safe and cared for. And that he probably thought she was an utter fool, for reacting so emotionally around him... again.

Sniffing, Ally forced herself to pull herself together and draw back. She dabbed at her eyes. "They're going to be fine," Hank told Ally firmly as they walked back into the ranch house together.

"Of course they are," Ally agreed.

Hank laced a protective arm about her waist. "Duchess wasn't our dog to begin with."

Ally shrugged out of her jacket. "We knew that from the outset."

Hank went to tend the fire in the grate. "Looking out the window that way was just Duchess's way of saying goodbye to us."

Ally battled a new flood of tears.

Hank paused, abruptly looking as utterly bereft as Ally was feeling. Ally drew a bolstering breath, aware her hands were shaking. She wrung them together. "I'm not sure what you're supposed to do in a situation like this."

Hank replaced the screen on the fireplace. "I know what we do in the military when we lose a comrade—and in this case," the corner of his lips crooked ruefully "—we just lost 'twelve' of 'em. We raise a glass in our lost friends' honor." He rubbed his chin with the flat of his hand. "The only problem is I think I drank the last beer several days ago, and since it's only eight in the morning, I doubt any of the bars in town are going to be open. Although I guess we could hit the grocery store…"

Ally didn't even want to think what the talk would be if she and Hank showed up together, looking for even "medicinal alcohol" at that time of morning.

And while she was soon leaving, to go back to her job in Houston, Hank would have to stay and face—not just the gossip—but the million and one questions from his parents.

"I think I might know where there's a bottle." She dragged a chair over to the cabinets and stepped from that onto the countertop. Sidling carefully, she opened the very uppermost storage cabinet, above the sink. Inside, wedged in the very back, was the bottle—just where her mother had put it, the day the gift from a grateful client had arrived.

Ally removed it and blew off the thin layer of dust. "Voila! Peppermint Schnapps!"

Hank wrinkled his nose.

Happy to have something that would ease the sorrow in her aching heart, if only temporarily, Ally waved off his disdain. "Buck up, cowboy! Beggars can't be choosers."

She turned to hand off the bottle and found Hank's hands anchored securely around her waist. He lifted her down, as easily as if she weighed a feather. "You're right," he acknowledged, looking like a marine, ready for action. "In this case, a drink's a drink."

Her heart racing, for a completely different reason this time, Ally handed the pint to Hank. He ripped off the seal, took off the cap. Sniffed. His expression perplexed, he offered the bottle to her. "Is it supposed to smell like this?"

Ally dutifully inhaled the mixture of peppermint-scented vodka. "I don't know," she said with a shrug. "I've never had it."

He grinned. "Me, either."

It didn't matter how tough life was, Ally noted. Being near Hank always made her feel better. "Well, let's give it a try." She got down two water glasses, the nearness of him and the intimacy of the moment filling her senses. "You want it over ice or straight up?"

His eyes darkened seductively. "Straight up, probably while holding my nose."

Ally wrinkled her nose at his joke, glad for the distraction of their 'toast'. She poured an inch in each glass.

Hank lifted a brow. "That's a little stiff."

Moving closer, Ally breathed in the masculine fragrance of his skin and hair. "I can handle it."

He met her gaze and their fingers brushed as he accepted his drink.

He lifted his glass, his deep blue eyes glittering

with ardor. "To Duchess and Gracie and the rest of the cute little darlin's. May they have all the happiness they brought us."

"Amen to that." Ally touched her glass to his and took a hefty drink. The liqueur burned on its way down. She coughed a bit while Hank grinned, then poured another inch for both of them. They lifted their glasses again. "And to Mesquite Ridge," Ally toasted softly, wanting this said. "I'm glad I came back, after all."

Two hours, a good portion of the pint—and a plate of Christmas cookies later—Hank and Ally were lounging side by side on the living room sofa. They'd pulled off their boots and had their feet propped up on the coffee table. Hank had put a CD of Christmas music on, turned the lights on the tree and built a fire in the grate.

The whole scene was like something out of a holiday movie. Ally felt her heart swelling with joy.

As she tilted her head slightly to the left, to look around, the top of her cheek brushed the hardness of Hank's shoulder. She reveled in the contentment. She still missed the dogs—and knew he did, too—but it still felt so right, being with him this way.

Like they could handle any challenge that came their way, as long as they stuck together...

"I know I didn't make that many changes, but the ranch house seems so different now," she murmured.

Hank nodded and shifted position slightly, so the natural thing for Ally to do was let her head rest on his broad shoulder. "It's much nicer."

Relaxing all the more, she cuddled against him and admitted, "It makes me want to keep going. You know, redo the kitchen—at least the countertops, floor, and appliances—and bring in some better furniture, like the kind I have in Houston."

"So it'll feel even more like home to you," Hank guessed, regarding her in a reverent, possessive manner.

Ally studied his expression—aware she hadn't dared share the solution forming in her mind with anyone just yet. "You know, don't you?"

Blue eyes crinkling, he looked over at her as if he wanted nothing more than to make love to her, as thoroughly and ardently as he had the evening before. He took her hand in his and kissed the inside of her wrist. "Know what?"

Ally tingled with a longing for him that went soul deep. She savored the warm seduction of his touch. "That I'm having second thoughts about selling the house," she explained.

His expression sobered.

She pushed on. "Not the ranch land—that still has to go. But I'm beginning to think I might want to keep the house and the barn and ten acres or so around them. Just sell the other three thousand nine hundred and ninety acres."

The joy she had expected to see on his ruggedly handsome face did not materialize.

Hank took a moment to absorb what she'd revealed, then replied in a low, implacable tone, "Corporate Farms is going to want the whole thing."

Determined to do the right thing, for everyone involved, Ally retorted, "Corporate Farms is going to want a lot of things they aren't going to get."

Hank went very still. "You've decided not to sell to them?"

Ally's stomach fluttered with a thousand butterflies. "I'm not doing anything until I see what all my options are." And that included whatever it was Hank—and/or possibly Lulu Sanderson—were getting ready to propose to her.

Hank nodded with a mixture of approval and relief. "The important thing is, you don't have to rush to make a decision now."

"That's true." Ally traced the knee of her jeans. "Now that I know I still have my job, I do have some time." And the opportunity to develop the plan of her own, that had been brewing ever since Marcy Lyons had set her straight on the financial inadvisability of a traditional sale by broker....

"And we do need to sit down together and have a serious talk about it," Hank stipulated, smiling broadly, as if he had a secret. "Say, tomorrow at noon?"

Ally wanted to do that, too. She only hoped that he would be as open to a nontraditional arrangement as she was, at this point. Because she knew now, more than ever, that he was the one who should run cattle on Mesquite Ridge. A twinge of uncertainty tightened her middle. Would the ranch finally help change her luck—and bring her happiness at long last?

She searched Hank's expressive blue eyes. "You're okay with the two of us having a business meeting on Christmas Eve?" If anything could tempt fate...

He captured her hands with his. "When it's this important to both of our futures, absolutely."

His words hinted at a permanence Ally found very exciting.

"But right now," Hank continued tenderly, using the

leverage of his grip to bring her even closer, "I have something even more important to ask." He shifted her onto his lap. "I know you're due at work on the 26...and I respect that. But I'm hoping you'll stay and spend Christmas with me."

For the first time in her life, Ally found herself looking forward to celebrating the holiday, with nary a bah humbug in sight. "I'd love to." She smiled and reached for the buttons on his shirt. "In the meantime, though, we have much more important things to do..."

Hank groaned in pleasure as she undid them, revealing his powerful chest and spectacular abs. While her hands explored the chiseled contours and warm satiny skin, he bent his head and slowly kissed her neck. "Looks like the celebrating is starting early...."

And celebrate they did, with tender kisses and hot caresses. And a roll in the sheets that was completely devoid of words—and utterly glorious.

Ally had never realized lovemaking could be so incredibly fulfilling. Never knew touch alone could communicate so much! Or guessed that anyone could make her feel so warm and safe, and so wanted and revered. Was it any wonder she was driven to take their pleasure to a new plateau, and make love over and over again?

Before long she was giving herself over completely, tempting him to do the same. Until at last she knew what made their connection so special. It wasn't just that she had finally given her whole heart and soul to Hank. It was that he made her feel he had fallen impossibly, irrevocably in love with her, too.

Chapter 15

Ally awakened slowly. Late afternoon sunshine poured across the rumpled covers of the bed. She could hear the shower running across the hall. Knowing she had never been so thoroughly loved, she stretched languidly. Then burrowed even deeper in the sheets, the crisp percale shifting smoothly across her bare skin.

A minute later, the water shut off and the shower curtain was swept back.

Ally opened her eyes and propped her head on her upraised hand. Smiling, she watched Hank saunter into the room.

Towel knotted low on his waist, he padded barefoot to the bed. As he sank down by her side, his towel-clad hip nestled warmly against her thigh. "How's your head?" he asked, running a hand down her arm.

Beginning to regret the morning lazing around, imbibing peppermint schnapps, but not what happened afterward, Ally groaned. "Throbbing. Yours?"

Hank grinned. "Better since I took some aspirin."

He lifted a staying hand, then went back to the bathroom. He returned, bottle of aspirin and water glass in hand. "This will help."

Ally took two pills before lying back among the pillows, as eager to make love again as she had been the first time. She waggled her eyebrows at him. "So would not getting up at all."

Briefly, Hank looked tempted. Very tempted. "We'll have to work on that part later." He bent and kissed the curve of her shoulder. "We've got an open house to go to tonight." He straightened while she was still tingling. "Remember?"

At his parents' ranch.

His eyes spoke volumes as they locked on hers. "I really want you to be part of my family's annual Christmas gathering."

Two weeks ago, Ally would have been totally intimidated by the notion of going to Greta and Shane Mc-Cabe's open house. Now she was looking forward to it. Hoping that someday she would be part of the loving clan…and not just an invited guest. The telling expression on Hank's face indicated he felt that way, too.

Bursting with joy, Ally flung back the covers. "I'm headed for the shower right now."

An hour later, they were heading out the door.

"One question," Ally said, when they arrived at their destination. She knew what their relationship felt like in private, but in public she needed to be clear—in case questions arose. "As far as everyone else is concerned…are you just my ride for the evening?" Or was he as ready as she was to go public with their romance?

Hank's gaze drifted over her before returning ever so slowly to her face. He made no effort to hide the emotion brimming in his eyes. "Are you kidding?" He pulled her close and kissed her tenderly. "You're a lot more than that, Ally Garrett. You're my future."

And you, Ally thought, *are mine.*

Smiling, he took her hand and led her toward the front door.

Moments later, they were mingling inside.

Ally couldn't help but note that Lulu Sanderson kept catching Hank's eye. Every time the divorcée did she flashed a secret smile. The confident way Hank looked at her in return told Ally there was *something* going on between him and Lulu.

Pushing aside the niggling feeling of uneasiness, Ally continued making her way among the guests, at first with Hank, then by herself after his father asked for his help bringing in more firewood.

Hank's mother appeared at Ally's side. Looking as beautiful and put-together as always, Greta engulfed her in a hug. "How are you doing, darlin'?"

Ally basked in the easy maternal affection and smiled back. Greta would be a dream mother-in-law. Not that anyone was anywhere close to talking marriage yet.

"Good," Ally replied. *At least I was before we walked in the door and I saw whatever-it-is going on between Hank and Lulu again…. Whatever he's chosen not to share with me. Again….*

Greta arched a silver-blond brow. "That son of mine treating you right?"

Ally noted the matchmaker's gleam in her eyes. Obviously, Hank's mom had either been told or figured out on her own that Ally and Hank were romantically involved. That had to be a good sign, didn't it?

Greta clasped her arm and leaned in close to confide, "Just so you know, honey… I haven't seen Hank this happy in years. And it's all due to you. So keep up the good work. It's about time someone put a spring in that boy's step and a light in his eyes."

I hope it's all due to me, Ally thought, looking at Lulu, who was standing next to a group of her old high school friends at the buffet table. But what if it wasn't? What if the real reason behind Hank's happiness was the ranch? And the fact that she couldn't sell it via the traditional route, and had decided not to sell to Corporate Farms?

Oblivious to the troubling nature of Ally's thoughts, Greta checked out the fast-diminishing spread on the buffet with a frown. She propped her hands on her hips. "Speaking of loved ones, have you seen my husband lately?"

Ally nodded, glad to talk about something else. "He stepped outside a few minutes ago with Hank, to get more firewood."

"Would you mind getting Shane? Tell him to meet me in the kitchen when he does. I need his help carving the brisket."

Ally nodded. "No problem."

Given the crowds of people, she figured the easiest way to reach him was to go out the front door and walk around. Ally grabbed her coat and headed outside. She was halfway around the porch surrounding the entire first floor when she heard the rise in men's voices.

"I don't understand why you won't take our money, if the Garrett ranch is what you want," Shane said, sounding as if he had very little patience left.

Hank harrumphed. "I don't need it, Dad. I've worked out everything on my own."

"Then the rumors going around town are true?" Shane demanded, sounding even more upset. "You *are* going to marry Lulu Sanderson for her money."

A brief silence followed. "If I was going to marry anyone for her money, I'd marry Ally Garrett," Hank snapped. He was obviously exasperated. "But that's not necessary with the plan I have."

Of course it wasn't, Ally thought, reeling backward in shock. She was ready to give Hank everything he could ever want, without so much as a promise of a ring on her finger. But Hank didn't know that yet.

Deciding the conversation was over, she started forward once again, only to hear Shane McCabe say, "But Lulu is involved in this plan of yours...."

The grim note in Shane's voice stopped Ally in her tracks once again.

"Not that it's any of your business," Hank retorted, just as tautly, "but yes, Lulu is an integral part of my future plans, too."

Ally's heart sank. She ran a trembling hand over her eyes.

"You have to see you can't have Ally and a deal with Lulu, too," his dad argued.

"I don't see why not," Hank scoffed, confident as ever.

"It'll never work," Shane insisted with the paternal wisdom for which he was known.

"Yes," he argued, as tears misted Ally's eyes, "it will, Dad. The real question is when are you going to start believing in me again—with the trust and faith you gave me when I was a kid?"

And when, Ally mused, was she going to learn she would always—*always*—take second place to the family ranch?

"I do believe in you, son," Shane insisted.

"Then why are you standing here tonight, trying to loan me the down payment and whatever collateral I need to purchase Mesquite Ridge?" Hank countered bitterly.

And why wouldn't he take the offer? Ally wondered. Surely receiving money from family was better and more honorable than whatever it was Hank had cooked up with Lulu Sanderson.

"Your mother and I want you to be happy," Shane soothed. "We want you to have kids. You and Ally seem like a good match."

Ally leaned against the side of the house. *I thought so, too.* Obviously, she'd been wrong. Otherwise Hank would have confided some of this to her.

The voices came a little closer. "Lulu and I are a good match, too, Dad. Just not in the way you'd expect."

Or want to hear, Ally thought.

Realizing she had witnessed enough, she marched briskly on around the corner of the house. Both men took one look at her face and realized she'd overheard enough to be deeply disturbed. Knowing she had to talk to Hank privately first, Ally said quietly, "Shane? Greta is looking for you. She needs your help in the kitchen."

He nodded briefly at Ally, his glance conveying a thousand apologies as well as compassion. For Shane, too, knew what it was like to be emotionally shut out of Hank's life at precisely the moment when Hank should have been opening up the most. To family, friends and especially the woman in his life. The woman he had pretended meant everything to him! Not, Ally thought miserably, that Hank had ever come right out and said he loved her, either. What if he didn't? What if it was just passion keeping them together? A passion that might not last?

Ever the gentleman and congenial host, Shane said, "I'm sorry if I misstepped or have in anyway said or done anything to make you uncomfortable here this evening." Shane cast another meaningful look at his son. "I was only trying to help."

There was no question of the elder McCabe's gallantry. Ally dipped her head in acknowledgment. "I know. I appreciate what you were trying to do, sir." Even if Hank didn't.

With a last rueful look at his son, Shane went inside. Ally stood facing Hank. She put her wounded feelings aside and faced him like the savvy business-woman she still was. "Is it true that Lulu Sanderson is going to be an integral part of the deal you're proposing to me tomorrow?"

Hank shrugged and ambled up the steps toward

her. To her amazement, he now appeared to be annoyed with her! "I told you I've been talking business with Lulu."

Ally warned herself to resist jumping to further conclusions. "I thought—hoped—you were just getting advice from her, or making use of her considerable connections in the venture capital and banking community, since she went to an Ivy League business school and worked in the financial sector before she came back to take over her dad's restaurant."

Hank stepped closer. It was clear from the look on his face that he wanted to tell her everything but for some reason still couldn't. Or still wouldn't. Frustration welled up inside Ally, as potent as hurt. "I've given you no reason to mistrust me."

Hadn't he? "Those glances Lulu has been giving you all evening say otherwise."

Hank's jaw set with the resolve of an ex-marine. "I've told you before. You have no reason to be jealous."

Ally threw up her hands. Her feelings had been constantly dismissed and disregarded by her parents. No way was she letting it happen to her again.

She regarded Hank coldly. "I have every reason, given how happy Lulu is and how *unhappy* I am right now."

"It's just business."

How many times had her parents told her that, while excluding and ignoring her? How many times had she been expected to just go away quietly and wait for the crumbs of their attention? "Then why can't you tell me about it right now?" Ally countered with a burning resentment she could no longer contain. "Why are you treating me the way you're treating your parents and heaven only knows who else?" Ally ignored Hank's dissenting frown and rushed on miserably. "By only telling us what you feel we have a right to know at any given time, and yet still expecting us to magically understand what is going on in your mind and your heart?"

Hank's spine stiffened. "When you really care about someone, you take things on faith," he returned gruffly.

Like Lulu apparently was?

"Your dad is right," Ally warned flatly. "You can't have intimate relationships with both Lulu and me simultaneously."

Hank folded his arms in front of him deliberately. "I know what you're thinking and you're wrong, Ally. Lulu and I are just friends."

Maybe not physically…at least not yet…

Ally set her jaw and took a stance. "I saw the way Lulu's been smiling at you all evening, Hank."

He lifted a hand. "She's excited!"

Jealousy flared inside Ally. "I bet!"

Hank's eyes narrowed. "I need you to believe in me, Ally."

No doubt he did, Ally thought. But he wasn't the only one with requirements for personal happiness. "And I need a life where I don't feel excluded by ranch business, the way I did when I was growing up!"

More to the point, *she* had wanted to be an integral part of Hank's efforts to purchase and build up Mesquite Ridge. Not Lulu. Ally had even, through clever financial analysis, found a way to do so that would meet both their monetary needs. For all the good it had done them.

Ally gestured dismissively. "Whatever the deal with Lulu is, I won't accept it."

Hank scowled. "I've spent days working on this," he warned.

How well Ally knew that! "I don't care. It's pulling us apart, and you have other options."

A muscle ticked in his cheek. He stared at her as if she were a stranger. "You're not even going to give me a chance to lay out the proposal for you tomorrow at noon?" he asked incredulously.

"Not if the plan involves the participation of Lulu Sanderson or any of her money or ideas." Because there was no way Ally was playing second fiddle to another woman, or being shut out by Hank and Lulu in the way she had been emotionally shut out by her folks. Especially over ranch business.

Hank studied her a long moment. His expression was grave. "You're serious."

"Dead serious," Ally stated bluntly.

Anger flashed in his blue eyes. "I wish you'd made this clear a lot earlier."

"Me, too," Ally said bitterly, as the tears she'd been holding back spilled over and ran down her cheeks. "Because if I had," she choked out, unable to hide the depth of her distress any longer, "you and I never would have made love. We never would have come here together tonight."

"You can say that again." Hurt and resentment scored his low tone.

With effort, Ally gathered her dignity. "But not to worry, Hank. We won't be leaving together. Because whatever this was—" *though it had felt like the love of a lifetime* "—is over."

Her heart breaking, Ally turned on her heel and walked inside. She got her purse, her coat, and walked back out, to call a cab. Looking every bit as disappointed and disillusioned as she felt, Hank made no move to stop her.

"I figured you'd show up here sooner or later," Jeb McCabe said.

If anyone could understand the mess he found himself in, Hank figured it was his oldest brother. "Can I bunk here tonight?"

Jeb beckoned him in. "Ally kick you out?"

"No."

Jeb ambled into the kitchen and broke out the beer. "She sure left the open house in a huff."

Hank removed the cap on his and took a long drink. He tensed at the memory. "You saw that, huh?"

"See, that's why I'm married to my ranch." Jeb rummaged around and brought out a hunk of summer sausage, too. "Women are just too much trouble."

Hank pulled up a chair. "You wouldn't believe that if you'd spent the last two weeks under the same roof with Ally Garrett."

Jeb smirked. "While pursuing Lulu Sanderson on the side."

Not his brother, too! "For the last time, there's nothing romantic going on between me and Lulu!"

"Then why is Ally so jealous?" Jeb opened a can of

nuts and tossed a handful in his mouth. "'Cause I saw the way Lulu was looking at you and the way Ally was looking at Lulu. Not good, little bro. Not good at all."

Hank felt like a man who was fast coming to the end of his rope. "Lulu and I have a business deal in the works," he explained for what felt like the millionth time. "One I'm not at liberty to discuss. And won't be until the final details are set."

Jeb shrugged. "So tell Ally that."

Hank munched glumly on a slice of sausage. "I did…sort of. It didn't help. She feels excluded."

Jeb took another pull of beer. "Then call off the business deal."

Hank rolled his eyes. "I can't. Not if I want to buy Mesquite Ridge." And he did.

Jeb smiled like the carefree bachelor he was. "Sure you can. Just accept Dad's offer."

Hank froze. Was there no end to his humiliation tonight? "You know about that?"

His brother sighed. "For the record, I told Dad not to do it. That you'd only be insulted."

Obviously, their father had not listened. "As would you have been," Hank muttered, still fuming over having been treated like a snot-nosed kid who couldn't put a business deal together if he tried.

"True." Jeb leaned forward in his chair. "Although maybe Mom and Dad wouldn't hover over you so much if you talked to them more, let 'em know what's on your mind. And the same goes for Ally. 'Cause you can't be really close to someone unless you can confide in 'em."

Enough with the greeting card sentiment! "You

sound like Ally," Hank grumbled, downing the rest of his beer.

"So?"

A goading silence fell. "It's not that easy." Hank returned his brother's level gaze. *Not for me anyway. I don't like showing weakness. Don't like being forced to open up.*

"I know that." Jeb stood and clapped a fraternal hand on Hank's shoulder. "I also know if you want to feel understood by family and/or the woman in your life, you're going to have to start disclosing one hell of a lot more than you have been."

Ally was astounded to see Hank's little sister on her doorstep at nine the next morning, a gaily wrapped basket of baked goods in her hands.

"May I come in?" Emily asked.

Ally hesitated. "If you're here to talk about Hank…" She'd already spent a sleepless night crying her eyes out. She didn't want to start sobbing all over again, and she was fairly certain it wouldn't take much to set her off. Perhaps the mere mention of the scoundrel's name…

Emily walked in. "And Christmas."

Ally blinked. Now that she and Hank were no longer hooking up, she did not expect to be included in the McCabes' yuletide celebrations. Unable to help herself, Ally grumbled, "What does the holiday have to do with anything?"

"I know what Christmas means to Hank—celebrating the end of one chapter of your life and moving on to the next, with hope and joy in your heart."

Ally had planned to do just that…before the dirt had hit the fan. When she'd overheard Hank's argument with his father, she'd realized that Hank could have gotten the money to purchase the ranch from Shane all along—he just hadn't wanted to do it that way. Even if it meant aligning his fortunes with another woman, and shutting out the woman he seemed to love…

"But to me," Emily continued gently, "Christmas is all about giving—even when you feel you can't. It's about finding the courage to make that leap of faith that will transform your life." She paused, letting her words sink in for a moment, then pleaded softly, "Don't go back to Houston just yet. Stay another day or two and give your own Christmas miracle a chance to happen."

Ally thought about what Emily had said for the rest of the morning.

By noon, she knew what she had to do.

She left the silent, lonely ranch house and drove to town.

Luck was with her. Lulu Sanderson was standing at the cash register at Sonny's Barbecue, looking gorgeous as ever as she rang up preordered smoked hams and turkeys.

Lulu smiled at Ally. "If you're looking for Hank…"

That, she thought nervously, would come later. She swallowed and looked the other woman in the eye. "I wanted to speak to you first."

Lulu murmured something to her dad, and another employee, then stepped out from behind the counter. She escorted Ally through the restaurant and kitchen, then out the service entrance. The delicious scent of mesquite-smoked meat emanated from the giant iron smokers located behind the building.

Suddenly all business, Lulu said, "Look, I know the time I've been spending with Hank has caused some trouble between the two of you, but he's been helping me on a really important business deal."

"Just as you've been helping him."

"Yes." Lulu sobered. "I wanted to speak to you about what was going on, but Hank asked me not to. You see, there were reasons we had to keep everything between us quiet."

Trust me, Hank had said… *Believe I can find a way to purchase the ranch.*

The only question was, did Ally still *want* to sell the ranch to Hank? Or anyone else?

Oblivious to the conflicted nature of Ally's thoughts, Lulu paused. "As of nine this morning, that's no longer the case."

Here was her chance, Ally thought. She could get Lulu to tell her everything Hank wouldn't, and stop feeling excluded. Or she could demonstrate the faith she had in Hank and his integrity.…

Ally held up her palm. "That's not going to be neces-sary."

Lulu leaned forward anxiously. "Are you sure? Because in retrospect, *especially* after last night, I realize how this all must have looked.…"

And still looked, in fact. The only thing different was Ally's attitude.

"Hank will tell me what he wants me to know when he wants me to know it." *In the meantime, I'm going to draw on all the patience I possess and wait for that to happen.*

She drew a deep breath and extended her hand in the age-old gesture of peace. "Right now, I just want to offer my sincere apology. I haven't been very friendly to you and I'm sorry."

Lulu shook her hand warmly. "Apology accepted, and one given in return."

And just that quickly they were on their way to being what Ally had never dreamed they could be in a million years—friends.

Hank thought about the things Ally and his brother Jeb had said all night. By morning, he knew they were right. Ally had every reason to be upset with him. So did his parents.

If there was ever going to be a change for the better, it had to start with him. He called his parents and asked to meet them at their ranch.

"I know you've been worried about me," he began, as the three of them sat down to talk. "And a lot of it is my fault. In my efforts to be the kind of stand-up, I-can-handle-anything sort of guy I was raised to be, I haven't been very forthcoming about a lot of things." He paused, looking them both in the eye. "I realize that has to change."

His parents welcomed his confession. "We're at fault, too," Greta said quietly, reaching out to take her husband's hand. "In our efforts to protect and help you, your father and I realize we've been in your business a little too much."

Shane nodded. "We should have trusted that you

are capable of starting a ranch and running your own life—without our interference."

Hank didn't want to appear ungrateful. "I know you're both here for me, in whatever way I need, whenever I need it. And I appreciate it."

"We just don't want to let you down," Greta said.

Shane concurred. "Not ever again."

Hank grimaced. "About that." He knew it was past time he took his parents step by step through the decisions he had made. To his relief, his parents were equally candid. By the time they had finished their heartfelt discussion, Hank understood his parents as well as they understood him. The tension between them was gone.

They promised to maintain their transparency, then hugged and said goodbye.

Relieved that it had gone so well, Hank headed for his next destination. He turned into the driveway leading to the Mesquite Ranch just in time to see Graham Penderson come out of the house. The agent shook hands with Ally as if they were sealing a business deal, then got into his car.

Hoping that didn't mean what it looked like, Hank returned the other man's wave of acknowledgment and then parked in front of the ranch house.

Ally was still on the porch, looking radiant in a cranberry-red dress and black suede boots. His heart in his throat, Hank approached. "Do you have time to talk to me?" he asked.

She nodded, looking as reserved as he felt. "Come on in."

In the foyer was a case of champagne, with a gift

card that said "Merry Christmas from Corporate Farms." Beside it was a manila folder holding what looked like legal papers.

Had she sold the ranch? At the end of the day, did it matter?

Ally waved a hand. "I haven't sold Mesquite Ridge, if that's what you're wondering."

Relief mixed with the anxiety he felt about their future. "But Corporate Farms is putting the pressure on," Hank guessed, following her into the living room. At once, his eyes were drawn to the angel atop the beautifully decorated tree. It was as lovely and delicate as the woman who had put it there.

Ally reached out and took his hand. "They presented me with yet another bid, two percent higher than the last one."

Hank's throat closed. He looked at her with all the hope his heart could hold. "And?"

Ally's green eyes were steady, but her lower lip trembled. "I told them I was no longer interested in selling the house and the barn."

Which meant she hadn't changed her mind—she was keeping her link to Laramie County.

"Graham said both had to be part of the deal," Ally continued in a rusty-sounding voice. "I said, 'No way.'"

Hank clasped her fingers tightly. "So it's over?"

Ally regarded him shrewdly. "He'll be back, just like you said, until the land is sold. Then he'll look elsewhere."

Here was his chance to show her what she meant to him. What he cared about, and what he didn't.

And most important of all, to say what he should have said when she had been upset the evening before. "First off, I want to apologize because you were right. I *should* have talked to you earlier about my plans, even if they weren't completely formed…."

Ally matched his steady gaze, with obvious regrets of her own. "And I should have trusted you—even without detailed explanations," she said softly.

She meant that, Hank realized with gratitude. His spirits began to soar. Suddenly, the future was looking a lot brighter. Once everything that had kept them apart was out of the way, that was. Knowing a lot more than a simple apology was required to completely fix things here, he pushed on, "Second—about Mesquite Ridge…and the way you feel…"

Again, she cut him off, this time by going up on tiptoe and pressing her index finger against his lips. Ally looked him right in the eye. "I've talked to Lulu," she said softly. "Whatever the two of you want to do in terms of business is fine with me."

Hank eyed her in surprise. "You're serious."

Ally released his hand. "You need a partner."

"Yes," Hank agreed, catching her about the waist and pulling her flush against him, "I do." He looked down at her tenderly. "And that partner is you."

Ally splayed her hands across his chest. "I don't understand." But for the first time, she seemed willing and ready to listen, with a completely open mind and heart. Encouraged, Hank continued.

"Lulu plans to expand her father's barbecue place into a state-wide chain. She's already selected the locations and she's got venture capital lined up, to begin construction immediately."

Ally's eyes widened. "You're part of that?"

Proud of what he had negotiated, he explained, "I'm supplying the mesquite to fuel the smokers. Hopefully, it will come from your ranch. That is, if you agree to lease me the timber rights to the property." Hank pulled papers from his pocket. "That way the land will be cleared at no charge or bother to you. And I'll get enough money from the harvesting of the mesquite to provide the down payment I need to make a serious bid on the ranch and/or the timber rights." He locked eyes with her. "But if you don't want to do that, then Lulu plans to make a deal with you directly. In either case, you'll have the option to do a controlled burn and get rid of the mesquite permanently, hence increasing the value of the land for ranching or keeping it producing indefinitely, for harvesting."

Ally listened intently to everything he was saying, but he couldn't quite read her expression. "In the meantime," he continued, "you'll have a buyer for your wood, a steady stream of income and a way to pay the mortgage and the taxes on Mesquite Ridge for as long as you want to stay." He handed her the proposal he had meticulously drawn up, down to the last penny. He hoped it was enough. "It's all here, in black and white."

Ally stared at the numbers as if he had just given her the best gift she had ever received in her life. "This is very generous of you."

And selfish. "I want you to be happy and safe and free from financial worry," Hank said sincerely. And most of all, he wanted her to stay....

Ally looked at the papers and began to laugh. "You're not going to believe this," she admitted ruefully. "I've got a proposal all printed out, too."

She went to get it, came back and thrust it into his hands, her cheeks flushed with excitement. "I was going to let you live here and run a herd of cattle for me, in exchange for land."

Sounded good, Hank thought. Very good. And generous, too.

"Every year, you and I would split the profits on the cattle, fifty-fifty. Instead of a salary, I'd pay you in acreage. At the end of thirty years, you'd own it all. Or sooner, if you could pull together the cash." Before he could express his delight, Ally added quickly, "Except for the ranch house, that is." Firmly, she continued, "I've decided I want to hold on to this. It's part of my heritage."

Hank stared at her in wonder. "You really have changed your view of Mesquite Ridge!" And maybe ranching in general.

She looked at him with the affection he'd been craving. "Although it often felt to me that the land meant more to my mom and dad than I did, you've shown me it doesn't always have to be that way. You can own a ranch and make it your home and still put the people you love first in your life."

"Agreed. But your idea is good, too. Maybe there's a way we can combine our two proposals, and come up with something even more solid. In the meantime…" Hank put both sets of papers aside. He wrapped his arms around her and pulled her close. "We have a few more things to discuss."

She sent him a glance that started a flood of memories, both tender and erotic. "I'm not going back to Houston. I resigned my position."

Hank gazed into her eyes. "You're sure?" he prodded, wanting more than anything for her to be happy—even if it meant he had to commute, via helicopter gigs, to see her.

Ally nodded. "My home isn't there anymore, Hank. It's here."

She couldn't have given him a better Christmas present if she'd tried. "Does that mean I'm getting kicked out?" he teased.

"Depends." Her green eyes went misty again. She moved closer still. "Do you want to share the space with me?"

Wary of asking for too much too soon again, Hank paused. Being roommates or live-in lovers wasn't what he wanted. Unless it was all she was ready for. "You're talking about living together?"

"A little more than that, actually. I love you, Hank. I love you with all my heart."

Hope for the future mixed with the joy he felt. "I love you, too," he told her, then paused for one long, sweet and tender kiss. He looked deep into her eyes. "More than I ever dreamed was possible..."

Ally grinned as contentment swept over them. "Which is why," she informed him as her take-charge nature reasserted itself once again, "when all this ranch business is done, I'd like us to make it official."

"You want to get married?" He grinned, triumphant.

Ally tilted her chin, stubborn as ever. "Got a problem with that, cowboy?"

"Not at all!" Hank laughed with delight. "I like a woman who knows what she wants and goes right after it."

Ally rose on tiptoe and kissed him sweetly. "I like the same kind of man."

"My answer to your proposal is yes then." Hank danced her backward, stopping under the mistletoe. Clinging together, they made up for lost time with long, lingering kisses.

"I can't believe it," Ally murmured finally, when at last they drew apart and turned to admire their tree. "It's not technically even Christmas for a few more hours, and I've already got everything I ever wanted. Except..." she gave a heart-wrenching sigh "...one thing."

Hank listened in the silence of the ranch house and read her wistful expression and knew immediately what it would take to make life in the ranch complete.

"A dog of our very own," they said in unison.

Epilogue

Seven weeks later...

Ally was in the ranch house kitchen, trying to decide what to make for dinner, when Hank strolled in. His hands were full, a grin as wide as Texas on his face.

She gave him a facetious once-over and propped her hands on her denim-clad hips. Unable to completely stifle a laugh, she chided with mock censure, "Seriously? The mistletoe and Santa hat again? It's almost Valentine's Day!"

Hank waggled his brows and closed the distance between them in three lazy strides. He set the hat on her hair, lifted the sprig of greenery above her head, and paused to deliver a long, sensual kiss that robbed her of breath and warmed her heart.

Her toes curled in her boots.

With a look of pure male satisfaction on his handsome face, he drew back and drawled, "Cupid won't be here with his bow and arrow for another week. But you're right." He bent and kissed her again, ever so tenderly this time. "That is something to anticipate. We'll have to put our stamp on that holiday, too. In the meantime—" Hank blazed a steamy trail from her ear to her throat "—every day is Christmas, with you by my side."

Hank was right about that, Ally thought, as she clung to him lovingly.

Finally, he drew back, his midnight-blue eyes serious now. He put the mistletoe aside and clasped her in his arms. "Besides, if this is the only thing we ever disagree about, we're in pretty good shape, wouldn't you say?"

Ally nodded, and stated unequivocally, "We're a very good team."

After confessing their love, and pledging their commitment to one another, they had easily forged a deal regarding the ranch that implemented both their ideas and benefited them each, from a business and financial perspective. Hank had helped Ally set up an office in town, where she could give others financial advice. He had cleared more land, sold the mesquite and used the proceeds to buy two hundred head more cattle.

Most important of all, they'd agreed on a wedding venue and date, and had married a week ago in a private ceremony on the ranch, with family and close friends as witness.

"Except for one tiny thing," Ally added after a moment.

An inscrutable look came into Hank's eyes. "A dog."

"I want an older one," she reiterated the discussion

they had been having nearly every day in some form or another since Duchess and the puppies had gone home with Talia Brannamore.

Hank exhaled, no more willing to budge on this particular issue than she was. "And I think we need a puppy," he said firmly.

They squared off, both silent and yet unable to stop smiling. "Does it really matter what age the dog is," Ally asked finally, "as long as the one we adopt as ours is sweet and lovable?"

Hank winked. "And fluffy and golden..."

Ally laughed. She lifted a hand in a gesture of peace. "Okay, so we do agree on a breed."

"It's definitely got to be a golden retriever," Hank said firmly, then looked at his watch. "What do you know?" he drawled, as a familiar pickup truck turned up the lane toward the ranch house. He peered out the window. "It's time."

Time for what? Ally wondered, but didn't ask. Hearing scratching noises on the floor above them, Ally pushed Hank toward the door. "Better go see who that is," she said hurriedly.

He shot her a perplexed look over his broad shoulder. "I already know who it is. It's my cousin Kurt."

Probably here on some vet business regarding Hank's cattle, Ally thought. "Still..." Hearing another sound, she gave her husband a nudge.

No sooner was Hank through the portal than she raced upstairs.

Into the sewing room.

Where her "gift" was on her feet, sticking her nose out the window.

Ally adjusted the big red bow around her neck and patted her head. "Come on, honey. It's showtime!"

Together, they headed down the stairs.

Before they reached the bottom, Ally heard the truck start up again and drive off.

Seconds later, Hank walked in.

His jaw dropped as he saw who was standing at Ally's side.

"Duchess?" he said hoarsely.

Ally could have sworn there were tears in his eyes.

She gaped at the bundle of fluff with the big red bow in Hank's arms. "And Gracie!" she cried ecstatically.

The nine-week-old puppy squirmed and jumped free. She ran to her mother, gave Duchess a quick greeting, then made a beeline for Ally.

Ally dropped to her knees, and the adorable puppy leaped into her arms, burrowing close.

Duchess rushed toward Hank. He hunkered down on the floor to give her a proper greeting, and the mama dog climbed into his lap so enthusiastically she practically knocked him over. Whimpering eagerly, she licked him under the chin.

Gracie did the same to Ally, while the two humans laughed and cried in unison. Finally, the pup and her mama climbed off them. When Gracie started to circle, Hank jumped to his feet and scooped her up in his arms. "Oh no, you don't, sweetheart. We're taking this outside."

Ally looked at him in confusion as he shepherded all four of them out the front door to the yard.

He set Gracie down on the grass. She circled again and got down to business.

"Oh!" Ally said.

"House-training," Hank explained with a grin. "We'll get the hang of it."

She smiled and went to stand next to him as mother and pup romped together in the grass.

"Wow, she has grown so much!" Ally noted jubilantly. "From less than a pound at birth…"

"To nearly nine pounds now," Hank said.

Ally turned to him. She clasped his forearms and searched his face, aware that this truly was a miracle, one she never had thought would be possible. "How did you manage to get her? I thought Gracie was already spoken for."

"She was," Hank admitted, sobering. "But after a lot of begging and pleading I managed to convince her would-be owner to take another golden, from another championship litter, in Gracie's place."

"Good move! This is my best present ever."

"I'm so glad." Hank paused. "How did you get Duchess? Because I tried to buy her, too, but was told by the breeder in no uncertain terms that she was not up for adoption."

"I knew how much you loved each other, so I called Talia the day after she was here. She told me this was Duchess's second litter and that she was retiring—since it's not healthy for a golden to have more than two litters in a lifetime. So I arranged for her to come here. Only Duchess couldn't leave until all her puppies were weaned and old enough to go to their new homes."

"Which was today," Hank murmured.

Ally nodded. "That explains where I was this morning."

"And where I was this afternoon. I picked Gracie up,

took her over to the vet clinic for a checkup and her second round of vaccinations. Kurt wanted to keep her for a short while—just to make sure there was no reaction, and to let the techs in the office play with her a bit...."

Ally beamed. "Because she's so adorable!"

"Absolutely. Just like you." Hank kissed Ally again. "And then he followed me out to the ranch and kept Gracie in his truck at the top of the lane, while I came in to make sure you were ready for your surprise."

Ally watched the pup and her mother nestle together contentedly on the lawn. She shook her head, marveling at their many blessings. "So now we have two dogs."

Hank grinned, still looking a little stunned by their belated Christmas miracle. He wrapped his arms around Ally and hugged her close. "Looks like."

She rested her cheek on his shoulder. "I couldn't be happier."

He stroked a hand lovingly up and down her spine. "Me, either, Mrs. McCabe."

Ally grinned and drew back to look up into his face. "You really have made all my dreams come true," she told him seriously. The ranch that had been the bane of her youth was now the source of all her joy.

"For now," Hank stated, the fierce affection he felt for her reflected in his eyes. "There will be plenty more fulfilled wishes to come."

Brimming with hope and joy, Ally knew that anything was possible. She looked at Hank with all the love she possessed. "And plenty more Christmases to celebrate."

* * * * *

Two-time RITA® Award–nominated author **Linda Warren** has written over forty books for Harlequin. A native Texan, she's a member of Romance Writers of America and the RWA West Houston chapter. Drawing upon her years of growing up on a ranch, she writes about some of her favorite things: Western-style romance, cowboys and country life. She married her high school sweetheart and they live on a lake in central Texas. He fishes and she writes. Works perfect.

Visit the Author Profile page
at Harlequin.com for more titles.

THE CHRISTMAS CRADLE

Linda Warren

To Paula Eykelhof,
who gave this book a second chance,
and
to Beth Sobczak. Without your loving generosity,
this book would never have been published. Thanks.

Acknowledgments

Thanks to Carolyn Lightsey and Brenda Mott
for sharing your knowledge of horses and the rodeo.
And to Amy Landry, pediatric nurse,
for the crash course on childbirth.
Any errors are strictly mine.

Chapter 1

Dear Santa,

I've been real good this year, but could you please send Daddy and me a mommy for Christmas? Someone who's nice and pretty and likes dogs and horses. That's all I want for Christmas.

Love,

Ellie Kincaid

Ellie was stuffing the letter into an envelope and licking the flap as Colter Kincaid walked into the room.

"What are you doing, angelface?"

"I wrote a letter to Santa. Could you mail it for me, please?" Her bright green eyes waited for an answer.

A knot formed in Colter's stomach. He knew what she'd written because this was the same letter his daughter wrote every year—asking Santa for a mother.

He'd helped her when she was three and four, but after that she'd printed them herself.

She was seven now, a mother was all she ever thought about. Instead of enjoying her childhood, Ellie spent her time thinking of ways to get a mother; she'd landed him in a few embarrassing situations by asking women out to the ranch.

He didn't have the heart to tell her he'd never fall in love again and that she'd never have the mother she wanted. Life was cruel and love was painful, but he wouldn't tell his daughter that. She'd learn soon enough.

"First thing in the morning," he replied, taking the letter from her. "Now it's time for bed."

Ellie made a face. "Why do I have to go to bed at nine? I don't have school tomorrow 'cause it's Saturday. We're going shopping with Aunt Becky in Dallas."

"Because we have rules around here."

"Tulley doesn't obey the rules. He goes to bed when he wants to."

Colter pulled back the covers. "When you're Tulley's age, you can go to bed when you please."

"Oh boy." Ellie crawled into bed. Her dog, Sooner, jumped up beside her. "How old is Tulley? How long do I have to wait?"

"Tulley's seventy. You do the math."

Her face fell again. "I'll never be that old."

Colter gathered her in his arms. "Yes, you will, but you'll always be my little girl."

"I love you, Daddy." She gave him several loud kisses.

He kissed her soft cheek. "I love you, too, angel-face."

No matter what happened in his life, this child would always be the center of it, and he would do everything in his power to ensure her happiness.

And that meant he couldn't tell her the truth about her mother.

Marisa Preston sat at her desk and wondered what she was doing in her Dallas office on a Saturday afternoon. She didn't usually come in on weekends, but today she had to stay busy, to keep from thinking. She got up and headed down to the busy hub of Dalton's Department Store. The firm she'd hired to do the Christmas decorations had done an outstanding job, or so her secretary and father had informed her. Maybe looking at the decorations would inspire a little Christmas spirit. This time of year always left her with a lonely, empty feeling that was hard to shake.

She found herself in the gift section full of special items they'd gotten in for the holidays. Her eyes went to it immediately—the Christmas Cradle. They had one every year. A man who lived in Austin designed and crafted them, and each one was made from a single block of wood. He didn't use a single screw or hinge. His wife sewed the delicate bedding of white silk and lace. It was an antique design, and the wood was stained, not painted. All the intricate designs carved on the cradle denoted "The Twelve Days of Christmas," making it one of a kind.

Unable to stop herself, she walked over and touched the beautiful cradle. As it rocked gently, she suddenly felt suffocated. Closing her eyes, she drew several deep breaths, but she couldn't block out the sound—the sound of her baby crying.

She was powerless to halt the memories. This was the day she'd met *him*. She remembered it vividly; her friends, Stacy and Rhonda, had wanted her to go on an adventure to Las Vegas early in December. Back then, she'd lived in a New York penthouse with her mother and adhered to a strict regimen of training to be a concert pianist. While her mother was away in Europe, she had the opportunity to escape. She'd yearned for fun and freedom.

The National Rodeo Finals were taking place, and Stacy and Rhonda wanted to attend some of the events, to get a glimpse of a real cowboy. Once they were sitting in the audience, all of Marisa's attention was on one cowboy. He wasn't bigger or taller than any of the others, but he rode with such self-assurance and confidence, and he seemed to have a genuine respect for the animal he was riding.

He was the best and they all knew it. Not only had the announcer said he was the top rider in the country, he had numerous awards to prove it.

He'd been very impressive to a young girl from New York. She hadn't been able to take her eyes off him. Once, when he'd finished a ride, the pickup riders let him down right in front of where she was sitting. He'd bent to retrieve his hat and as he straightened and slapped his hat against the side of his leg, he'd looked directly at her.

He had the most unusual green eyes. They were light green, the color of grapes in summer. She remembered that first stirring of desire she'd experienced gazing into those eyes, and she'd known he would be far more stimulating than any nectar grapes could produce.

And he was. He was a true-blue Texas cowboy, with a brooding look that could make a young girl's heart flutter. He was handsome, exciting and very much a man. She'd fallen in love with him instantly.

If her mother… She exhaled a painful breath as other emotions crowded in—the shock, the heartache that followed. But those were only minor compared to the pain of her son's birth and his death. She still wasn't over it, and she believed a woman never got over losing a child. She hadn't. The memory of her son was always with her.

That was why at Christmastime she always managed to find her way to the cradle. It would soon be sold to a lucky expectant mother, but for a moment she could imagine… *No, no, don't.*

Shoving the memories away, she glanced around the large store, its merchandise and salespeople upscale and the very best. Dalton's was important to her and her family. Her grandfather, her mother's father, had started the business in the 1930s, and today it was one of the most successful family-owned chains in Texas. This was her heritage and she was proud of it.

She just wished she felt more enjoyment, more pleasure in her work. What she actually felt was trapped. As senior vice-president, she should have more responsibility for making decisions, but her father, Richard Preston, was the driving force behind Dalton's and nothing was ever done without his approval.

The decorations were perfect, she thought, studying the beautiful gold and silver bells and garlands and the red accents that seemed to reflect the cheer and enthusiasm of the busy shoppers.

Several of the employees watched her, but none spoke. She hated her father's rules: no fraternizing with the staff and vice versa. She'd been reprimanded more than once for speaking to employees while on the floor. If she had something to say, her father had told her, she was to summon that person to her office. Since her best friend worked on the floor, it was hard to follow the rules, but then, her father didn't need to know every little detail of her life. Although she resented his rigidity and control, she'd always be grateful to him because he'd been there when she'd really needed someone. Her mother she refused to think about—especially today.

She stopped abruptly as she caught sight of a man standing by the gift-wrap counter. *No.* Her breath congealed in her throat. *It can't be. It can't be* him! *Not today.*

Was she hallucinating? Thinking about him too much? The tall lean figure had to be a trick of her imagination. But as she took in the long legs in tight-fitting Wranglers, the silver buckle, the cowboy boots, the brown leather jacket, she knew this was real. *He* was real—as real as he'd been eight years ago.

Colter Kincaid, the man she'd loved so passionately and promised to marry when she was seventeen, the father of her son, was standing a few feet away.

She hadn't seen him even once since that morning in the motel, but she would've known him anywhere: the proud way he held his head, the sharp lines of his face, those broad shoulders. All these things were the same and yet he seemed so different. It was as if time and maturity had added another dimension that she knew nothing about. What was he doing here? Marisa fought an unwelcome surge of excitement as she trembled with an awareness she thought she'd long forgotten.

She felt that awareness like a raw wound, deep in her heart. Her first encounter with love had almost destroyed her. That all-consuming passion had controlled her mind, body and soul, and she never wanted to experience it again.

Yet she couldn't look away, couldn't move, was unable to do anything but stare at him. The years had enhanced his appeal, not dimmed it, but there was a hardness around his eyes that she didn't remember. She had waited so long for this meeting, for a chance to explain about the past. But the words wouldn't come and she felt as tongue-tied as the first time she'd met him.

Colter glanced impatiently at his watch. How long could it possibly take to wrap three packages? God, he hated shopping. That was part of being a parent, though. He did a lot of things he didn't really enjoy. Like having a multitude of little girls over for a slumber party and listening to them giggle all night, not to mention listening to music that could easily break the sound barrier. But when his daughter put her arms around his neck and said, "You're the best daddy in the whole world," it was all worth it. He sighed, checking his watch again.

His impatience vanished as an eerie feeling came over him. He could actually feel the hair on the back of his neck standing up, as if his body sensed danger. Raising his head, he received a jolt that he would remember for a long time. He felt winded and gasped, struggling for breath. It couldn't be. It couldn't be *her*. But he knew it was as he looked into the brown eyes of a woman he'd hoped never to see again.

They stood there silently, staring at each other, and against every conscious objection on his part, the years rolled back. He remembered that time in Las Vegas, the love they'd shared, the days and nights of sensual magic only their bodies could create. The happiness and pleasure of those weeks flashed through him, only to be overshadowed by the pain left in its aftermath.

Colter's first instinct was to turn his back on her and walk away. He didn't want to acknowledge her presence, but a force deep inside moved him forward until he was standing in front of her.

From a distance he could tell she'd changed, but he wasn't prepared for the impact of seeing her face-to-face. The young girl he remembered had matured into a beautiful woman. His eyes made a quick, thorough assessment of her, taking in the ash-blond hair around her oval face, the dark eyes that shimmered like brown satin, the delicately carved facial bones and the soft curve of her mouth. His appraisal missed nothing, not the beige linen dress and matching jacket, nor the way she nervously pushed her hair behind her ear. A provocative gesture he remembered well.

She was beautiful; he'd thought that years ago, too. Bitterness quickly filled his mind, reminding him what a fool he'd been—a stupid, infatuated fool. Her beauty was only a facade. She was not beautiful on the inside.

"Marisa Preston?" Her name erupted from his lips and came out as a question, and he couldn't imagine why, because he definitely knew who she was.

* * *

"Yes," she answered with a quaver in her voice, feeling as if her knees were going to buckle. "It's been a long time. Do you live in Dallas now?"

His eyes narrowed. "Why do you ask?"

She shrugged, not knowing how to answer. She'd only been trying to make the best of an awkward situation.

"What are you doing here?" he asked.

The bluntness of the question took her by surprise, but she answered without a pause. "I work here."

He frowned. "Work? Here?" He made no attempt to hide the incredulity in his voice as his eyes slid over her again.

"In the executive office," she amended.

"The executive office?" The frown deepened. "I assumed you'd be playing in concert halls all over the world by now. Isn't that what your mother planned for you?"

"You know I never wanted to do that," she answered almost inaudibly, wondering if that was what he'd believed—that she'd left him to pursue her career as a concert pianist.

"I never knew what you wanted," he said in a harsh tone. "I never knew you at all."

Her stomach tightened. She hadn't expected him to be so cold, so angry. After all these years, she'd expected idle curiosity about why she'd left him, but he didn't seem too concerned with her reasons for leaving. Her head began to throb and she lightly touched her temple to ease the ache.

His eyes caught the small gesture. "What's the matter? Do thoughts of the past upset you?"

If he only knew. Feelings of guilt mounted inside her. "Some thoughts," she acknowledged, forcing herself to meet his eyes. "But that was a long time ago, and I was very young." The statement sounded inane even to her own ears, so she tried again. "I made a lot of bad choices that I'm not proud of, but I've managed to put them behind me."

"How convenient for you," he muttered, urging himself to walk away. He couldn't do it, though. What was wrong with him? *Why* couldn't he just leave? It had to be the shock of seeing her, of knowing what she'd done to his life. She'd ruined him for other women. After her, he couldn't trust a woman again. He'd tried, but he couldn't, and he couldn't fully love again, either—the way a man should love a woman. Not even for his daughter had he been able to do that. All because of *this* woman.

She called it a bad choice, said she'd been young. Was he supposed to accept that and now have a pleasant conversation with her? Her gall was unbelievable! He mentally shook himself, fighting to keep his emotions under control.

Marisa had imagined this meeting a thousand times, but she was unprepared for this hostile stranger, especially since he'd married Shannon four months after Marisa had left him. Her mother was glad to tell her the details. So why would he still be so angry with a young girl who'd broken her promise of marriage?

She blinked nervously under his hard stare, unable

to stop herself from asking, "Don't you think you're overreacting? After all, it was a long time ago."

"Overreacting!" he repeated, his voice sharp as a whiplash. He jammed his hands into the pockets of his jacket. "Doesn't it ever bother *you?*"

How dare he ask her that? He was a married man. He had no right to judge her without knowing the truth. *The truth.* She suddenly knew she had to tell him that truth, the truth that had tortured her for years.

"Yes, it bothered me for a while," she began, lifting her chin, meeting his icy gaze as she struggled for the right words. "But as I said, I was young and—"

"Oh, please," he cut in. "Spare me your pretty speech. Why don't you just admit that you were a spoiled rich girl who couldn't handle responsibility or commitment, so you ran home to mother?"

"It wasn't like that," she denied, hating the picture he held of her in his mind.

"It was just like that. Tulley warned me. Shannon warned me, but—"

"Please," she begged, her head beginning to ache in earnest. "You don't understand."

"No. I'll never understand."

"If you'd just listen, I can explain."

"It may surprise you, but I'm not interested in anything you have to say—now or ever. I've moved on."

"I didn't mean to hurt you," she said, hoping for a weakening in his implacable attitude. He quickly disillusioned her.

"No, of course not," he replied in a scornful voice. "You never thought about me or my feelings. You just left."

"Please, listen—"

"I told you I'm not interested in anything you have to say. I had a feeling you were trouble the first moment I met you, but you seemed so different from the other girls who hung around the rodeos—or so I thought. You had me wrapped so tight around your little finger, I couldn't see the real woman behind the beautiful face." His eyes slid over her, sending a tiny shiver through her body. "It's hard to imagine I ever considered myself in love...with you."

"Mr. Kincaid, your packages are ready," a woman called from the gift-wrap counter.

Colter whirled toward her.

"Daddy," a little girl shouted, running up to him with a pair of low-rise jeans in her hands. Rhinestones glittered on the pockets and around the hem. "Can I have these? I really like them."

Colter grabbed his packages and turned to face the child. "You're too young for jeans like that."

"But all the girls in my class are wearing them."

"Ellie—"

He and Shannon had a daughter—a beautiful little girl with blond hair and green eyes. The Kincaid green eyes. She appeared to be around six or seven, and Marisa couldn't look away. Through the panic rising in her, she realized Colter and Shannon had started a family very soon after she'd left.

Before she could assimilate this piece of information, another child with blond hair came running up.

"Daddy said I can't have them," the girl called Ellie told the other one.

Marisa's stomach tensed in pain. *Colter has two daughters.*

"Go put the jeans back," Colter said.

"Aw, Daddy."

"Ellie."

"Okay, c'mon, Lori, we'll find something else."

They ran off and Colter followed. He didn't give Marisa a second glance.

Colter stopped and put his arm around a woman who had her back to Marisa. Marisa couldn't see the woman clearly, but it had to be Shannon Wells—Colter's wife.

Almost in slow motion, Marisa walked to the executive elevators. Once the doors closed, she jabbed the stop button and the elevator stalled. She sank to the floor, wrapped her arms around her trembling body and began to cry. Tears rolled down her cheeks and she didn't bother to wipe them away as pain encompassed every part of her. *Why today?* Why did she have to see him and his perfect family today?

And why, after so many years, did it still hurt so much?

"Ms. Preston? Ms. Preston? Are you stuck in the elevator?"

Marisa heard the man's voice over the intercom and rose slowly to her feet. She hit Talk and released the stop button. "I'm fine, thank you. The elevator's moving now."

When it reached the executive floor, the maintenance man was waiting. "Ms. Preston—"

"I'm fine," she murmured again, brushing past him and hurrying to her office, not wanting him to see she'd been crying. The news would quickly get back to her father, and she couldn't deal with that right now.

She went over to the window that overlooked down-town Dallas. She didn't see anything except Colter's angry face. So many years she'd waited to tell him about their son, yet she couldn't even bring herself to utter the words in his presence. *We had a son. He died.* How could she say that to him? Oh God, she had to talk to someone.

She picked up her phone. "Send Cari Michaels to my office, please."

"Yes, ma'am," her secretary responded.

Marisa wrapped her arms around her waist again to still her agitated nerves, and waited, staring out the window. Within minutes, Cari came through the door. Petite with dark eyes and hair, Cari had started working at Dalton's as a salesclerk. Today she was head of staff and, even though she had an office, she spent a lot of time on the floor making sure the store ran smoothly. Marisa had met her the first year she'd returned to Texas and they'd become fast friends, best friends. Cari knew all of Marisa's secrets.

"You're going to get me in trouble," Cari teased. "You keep forgetting I'm not allowed on the executive floor."

The executive floor was for the Preston family. Her father had a large suite of offices, as did she and her brother, Reed.

Marisa turned from the window.

"What's wrong?" Cari asked immediately.

"I saw him."

Cari frowned. "Him? Who?"

"Him," Marisa emphasized.

"Oh, no." Cari understood now, and Marisa blurted out what happened.

"He was awful and I… I don't understand." Marisa was trembling visibly, and Cari quickly got her a glass of water.

"Here—" Cari handed her the glass. "Sit down before you collapse."

Marisa sank into her chair and took a sip.

"Are you okay?"

Marisa nodded. "Seeing him was such a shock and he was so hateful, not at all like the man I once knew. It brought back so many memories. I wanted to tell him about our son, but he wouldn't listen. I wanted to tell him how sorry I was. I wanted him to know—" Her voice wavered as emotion closed her throat.

Cari knelt beside her. "Marisa, don't do this to yourself. You were so young, and you did the best you could under the circumstances."

"Did I?" Marisa jerked to her feet and began to pace. "I don't think so. I was weak and I let my mother control my life."

Cari stood, too. "Marisa, what good will it do to—"

"My mother has these priceless crystal eggs that have figurines in them. I feel like one of those figurines, encased in glass, sheltered from the world, not allowed to live or make my own choices. That's how both my parents treat me—like a piece of crystal."

Cari didn't say anything.

"Everyone knows my father created this job for me. I'm nothing but a figurehead. I'm allowed to decorate the store. That's rich. That's a joke."

"Marisa, please—"

"But not anymore, Cari," she said with renewed vigor. "No one's going to treat me like that—including Colter Kincaid."

"What are you going to do?"

"I have to see him again and tell him what really happened. That's the only way I'll have any peace." She drew a deep breath. "But I don't know where he lives. I never knew, even when we were together."

"Do you really not know?"

Marisa swung to face her friend. "What?"

"I guess it was inevitable that you'd run into him one day."

"What do you mean?"

A look of momentary discomfort crossed Cari's face. "He has a large horse ranch somewhere outside Mesquite."

"How do you know?" Marisa asked, pushing hair from her face.

"A couple of years ago, he was featured in *Texas* magazine. The story talked about his success as a horse rancher—and in the western wear business. His name's on everything from boots to belt buckles."

"What?" she whispered. "He was just a cowboy when I met him. And now he…"

"Marisa." Cari's eyes filled with compassion. "I never said anything because I didn't want to upset you—and what good could it possibly have done? You've come too far to let this get the better of you."

Marisa licked her dry lips. "Where's his ranch?"

Cari shook her head. "I've just read about it, that's all."

"Please, Cari, I need his address." Marisa stared into her friend's eyes with a silent plea.

Cari sighed. "Marisa, I have this feeling you're going to get hurt."

"More than I'm hurting right now? I don't think that's possible."

Cari flung up her hands. "Okay, let's try the Dallas and Mesquite phone books."

Marisa opened a drawer and pulled out the directories. Colter wasn't listed, but his company had a Dallas address.

"That doesn't help," Marisa said. "And I'm sure his company won't divulge his home address."

"Your father has a lot of contacts," Cari suggested. "I'm sure he could find the address in no time."

"I don't want my father involved in this," Marisa replied, her tone abrupt.

Cari shrugged. "Just an idea. Now, let's think. There must be a lot of people who know him." Cari grew thoughtful. "Wait a minute. Why didn't I think of this before? My sister's husband works for one of those large feed-supply places. Colter has horses, so maybe he buys feed from them."

"Call him, Cari, please."

As Cari punched out a number, Marisa's nerves were taut. She knew she should just forget about Colter and get on with her life. He had, so why couldn't she? She didn't have an answer. All she knew was that she had to find him.

Cari haggled with her brother-in-law; it was clear he didn't want to give out the information. Finally Cari scribbled something on a pad and Marisa's heartbeat accelerated.

Cari hung up, then handed her the paper. "I had to use a little family blackmail, but there it is."

Marisa hugged her. "Thanks, Cari. Thank you so much."

"Just don't tell anyone where you got the address, or Charlie could lose his job."

"I won't breathe a word. I promise." She grabbed her purse and coat.

"You're going now?" Cari asked, sounding dismayed.

"Yes. I need to do this and I need to do it now."

"But sleet's in the forecast. Why don't you wait until tomorrow?"

"No, I can't," Marisa said. "I'll be back before the weather turns bad. Mesquite is only about fifteen minutes from Dallas, and the ranch can't be much farther."

"Marisa—"

A tap on the door interrupted Cari. Reed Preston, Marisa's brother, walked in and shook his head at Cari. "You know you're not supposed to be on this floor," he said.

Cari didn't bat an eye at Reed's censure. "Don't worry, junior, I was just leaving."

"Don't call me that."

Cari lifted an eyebrow, then glanced at Marisa. "Call me later." She sauntered out the door.

"I don't appreciate it when you talk to my friends like that," Marisa said once the other woman had left.

"Cari? She's tough as nails, and if I didn't reprimand her, she'd think I was ill."

"Still, she's my friend and I invited her here."

"Point taken." Reed grinned at her.

He was five years older than Marisa and a younger version of their father, very tall and handsome with a disarming smile. She was four years old when she and her mother moved to New York, and nine-year-old Reed had stayed with their father in Dallas. It was well known that Harold Dalton had arranged the marriage of his only daughter, Vanessa, to Richard Preston. His daughter didn't have much interest in the stores, and her grandfather wanted a man who could control her and control the empire he'd built.

The marriage had been a disaster from the start, but they'd stuck it out until Harold Dalton passed away. Then they'd received a shock. Harold had left half his estate to Vanessa and the other half to Richard. If they divorced, they'd lose everything. Her grandfather had sentenced them to a life together. But her parents figured out a way around it—living separate lives without a divorce, and in the process making their children's lives a nightmare.

"I stopped by to see if you wanted to go with me to the airport to pick up Mother."

"Oh, no, sorry. I have other plans." She couldn't believe her mother's visit had completely slipped her mind. She'd been dreading it for days. Now other, more important, matters took precedence.

Reed watched her for a moment. "Are you okay?"

"Sure, why?"

"You seem a little nervous."

"It's nothing."

"I know you and Mother have had problems, but that's all in the past, isn't it?"

"Yes."

In her youth, her mother's complete domination of her life had turned her into a shy, insecure teenager. Vanessa had dreams and plans for Marisa—dreams Marisa didn't share. She'd rebelled only once, when she'd run away to Vegas, and that had been the happiest and yet most debilitating part of her life. She had thought she'd never recover, but after the death of her son, her father had brought her back to Texas. With his love and support, she'd stood up to her mother and refused to return to New York. For the first time in her life, she made her own plans. She went to university and earned a degree in business and then began working for Dalton's Department Stores, much to her father's delight.

She'd grown confident and stronger and was now able to cope with her mother on an adult level. She still had difficulty sorting out her feelings about Vanessa, but she did love her, although at times she found it impossible to like her.

"I really have to go," she said, brushing past Reed.

"Where are you going?"

"I'll be home in time for dinner." She threw the words over her shoulder.

As she drove out of Dallas, her nerve began to falter, especially when she thought about Colter's wife. Shannon had been crazy about him back then and she hadn't liked it when Colter took an interest in Marisa. Colter had said they were just friends, but Marisa knew it was far more for Shannon. In the end, Shannon had won. Colter had married her. That hurt, even now, but she didn't want to cause any problems in Colter's marriage. However, she had to tell him the truth, for her own peace of mind, her sanity. She couldn't live with the guilt any longer, and there was only one solution. To see Colter—and to tell him about their son.

Chapter 2

Colter sat at his kitchen table clutching a cup of coffee, unable to get *her* out of his mind. What was she doing in Dallas? Working, she'd said, but somehow that didn't fit the Marisa he'd known. She'd lived in New York with her mother who was wealthy, and Marisa was a daughter of that environment. She was so far out of his realm that he didn't understand why he'd gotten involved with her in the first place.

He shifted uneasily. What did she expect from him? She was the one who'd left. What did she hope to gain by trying to make amends?

He squeezed his eyes shut. He'd somehow known that someday they'd meet again. But she would not make a fool of him again—not now that he had his daughter. Ellie was his top priority, and ever since her mother had decided she didn't want to be a mother, he had devoted his life to her, making sure she had roots, stability and a home. He didn't bring other women into their lives and he realized that had probably been a bad decision. He'd thought his sisters would fill that void in Ellie's life, but they hadn't.

Ellie's quest reminded him of the mistakes he'd made after Marisa had disappeared from his life. Marrying Shannon had been one of them. He hadn't loved her the way he had Marisa, but he'd honestly believed they could make it work and raise a family.

Early on, it became clear he couldn't get Marisa out of his head, and Shannon had reacted in anger. After a heated argument, she left and went home to Wyoming. She never called or asked about Ellie, which bothered him. He'd received divorce papers in the mail. Shannon didn't want a thing and didn't even ask for visitation rights. She'd severed all ties.

He should have taken Ellie and gone to Wyoming to talk things out. Once she saw Ellie, she might have changed her mind. He couldn't do it, though. Shannon was as miserable as he was in the marriage, and staying together for Ellie's sake wasn't the solution. But he'd thought Shannon would make some effort to see Ellie. When she didn't, he'd decided to raise his daughter alone.

Ellie was the best part of his life, and he didn't want Marisa anywhere near her. That might be a little extreme, but it was the way he felt.

A familiar anger welled up in him. Seeing her, listening to her rekindled that pain of rejection, and he knew that he hadn't learned to control his feelings for her.

And he didn't know if he ever would.

* * *

As Marisa drove, memories of Colter wrapped around her. In the early days, thoughts of him had been painful, but time had eased the pain and she could now think calmly about the past. Or some aspects of the past, she reminded herself. Not her baby...

She'd first seen him at the rodeo, then later at one of the parties given for the cowboys. She'd never met anyone like Colter, and without knowing how, she'd realized he was going to change her life.

He had made her feel so special, so alive, so much a woman, and when he'd asked her to marry him, she had happily agreed. They loved each other and nothing else seemed important. The stupidity of youth still astonished her. Why had she ever thought—?

She inhaled deeply, but it didn't stop the memories. When her mother had returned home and found her gone, she'd called Stacy, who was then back in New York, and got the whole story—that Marisa had decided to stay in Nevada and was getting married. Announcing the news was like putting a match to gasoline, and the scenes that had followed were not pleasant. It had been the beginning of Marisa's nightmare.

A sob left her throat and she forced herself to look at the directions in her hand. She turned off the highway onto a blacktop country road. As she did, she noticed the dark thunderclouds. A storm was brewing, as Cari had said, but she'd be back in Dallas before it broke. Dinner with her mother would be an ironic ending to the task ahead of her.

Tulley came through the back door, removed his hat and folded himself into a chair opposite Colter. Jackson

Tulley was like a father to him. Everything Colter knew about riding, Tulley had taught him. He'd been there for every win and every loss. He also understood every hurt and pain Colter suffered, because he suffered them, too.

Tulley and Colter's father, James Kincaid, had been best friends, riding the rodeo circuit in their off time. James died when Colter was ten, and Tulley nurtured the boy's rodeo interest with his mother's approval. Looking back, Colter didn't know what he would've done without Tulley in his life.

"You still brooding about seeing her today?" Tulley asked, watching Colter's dark expression.

Colter tightened the hold on the cup. "I can't get it out of my mind. I turned around and there she was. I couldn't make myself walk away from her. I wanted to say so many things, but I'm not sure what I actually said. I just don't know what she was doing there."

Tulley ran one hand through his thinning gray hair. "Think about it, boy."

Colter raised his head. "What?"

"Marisa Preston."

"Yeah. What are you getting at?"

"Either you're getting dense or you have a mental block."

"What the hell are you talking about, Tulley?"

"Richard Preston, owner of Dalton's Department Stores. Marisa Preston. There has to be a connection."

"God, I never put it together." Colter ran both hands over his face. "She said her father lived in Texas, but she never mentioned what he did."

"Back then you two didn't do much talking."

Colter thought they had, but in reality Tulley was

right. They had hardly known each other. He couldn't understand why his memories of her were still so strong.

"So what are you going to do?"

"Nothing," Colter replied. "She's obviously working for her father now. What happened to the pianist career I don't know, nor do I care. She's not going to get her hooks into me again."

Tulley's eyebrows shot up. "Did she show any interest?"

"No, not really. She wanted to tell me something about the past and I didn't want to hear it." He ran his hands over his face again. "God, Tulley, why can't I forget her? It's been years and yet—"

"You know the answer to that."

"Yeah." Colter gazed out the window, his eyes matching the dark clouds gathering outside. "When I won at the finals in Vegas and she was there, I felt like king of the world. I spent a lot of my winnings on a ring, and when I got back to the motel room, she was gone. I hit the ground so hard, I've never recovered. No other woman ever made me feel like that. Not even Ellie's birth dimmed it."

Tulley just nodded. He'd heard the story before, and he cursed the young girl who had the power to hurt this man so much. Changing the subject seemed like the best thing to do.

"Becky got everything set for the stores in Austin?"

Colter took a long breath. "Yeah. She's worked nonstop to get Kincaid Boots into more western stores."

"That girl has a good head on her shoulders. Both girls do. You've done great with your sisters."

Colter's mother had died when he was eighteen and

he'd become solely responsible for his two younger sisters, Jennifer and Rebecca. Tulley and his wife, Cora, had moved in with them and Cora had stayed with the girls while the men were on the circuit. But his sisters had always been levelheaded and responsible and never given him any problems.

Becky and Jen had business degrees, and together they ran the Kincaid Boot Company. Colter put his expertise into the design of the boot, and Bart, Jen's husband, who had a marketing degree, had turned Kincaid Boots into a thriving enterprise. Thanks to Becky's drive, Jen's management skills and Bart's commercial savvy, a lot of western stores were carrying the Kincaid Boot. Accessories had recently been added.

Years ago they'd all lived in a small three-bedroom house, and when Colter had built this house he'd wanted it big, with enough room for everyone. But by then everyone was older and going off in different directions.

The girls were in college when Cora passed away. It had been a difficult time for all of them, but they'd had each other, and had adjusted. Jen was already dating Bart and soon married him. Becky lived in the house for a while, but then she became so involved in making Kincaid Boots a success that she was gone a lot. He'd encouraged her to rent an apartment in town because he didn't want her to feel honor-bound to stay because of Ellie.

Ellie was *his* responsibility, and Becky deserved her own life. After many discussions, she finally rented a place not far from the Kincaid offices, but he still kept a room for her and Jen to use whenever they wanted to come home. It was just the three of them there now—Ellie, Tulley and him.

Colter took a sip of coffee. "I'm very proud of them. They've done wonders with Kincaid Boots. Of course, Bart helped a lot, too."

"I think your name had a little something to do with it."

"Yeah, but they did all the work." He stared at his cup. "I was busy raising Ellie."

There was silence for a second.

Tulley cleared his throat. "Jen will probably spend less and less time on the business now that she and Bart are expecting."

"Jennifer's always been a homebody, and if she wants to stay home with her baby, then I'm all for that. A baby needs a mother."

Silence again.

"Dammit, Colt, boy," Tulley said, reading his mind. "Shorty's fine without a mother." That was what he called Ellie—and had since the first day he held her.

"I don't know. She has a dog that she insists talks to her and she writes all these letters to Santa. I've mailed four already this year. I'm at a loss as to how to deal with some of these problems."

"She's a little girl and she'll outgrow them. All I see is a happy, imaginative child—and so should you."

"Speaking of my child, where is she?"

"She's at the corral looking at that new horse you bought."

Colter jumped to his feet. "I don't want her anywhere near that horse. He's not broke."

Tulley shook his head. "Lordy, boy, you're jumpy.

Give Ellie some credit. She knows not to get in a pen with an unbroke horse. We taught her better than that."

Colter sank back into his chair with a groan. "I'm not thinking straight and I'm all keyed up."

Before Tulley could answer, Ellie and Sooner came charging through the back door. Ellie rarely walked; she was always in a run, her ponytail bouncing. She slid onto Colter's lap, and Colter held her tight, maybe a little too tight.

"That horse is real mean, Daddy," she told him. "He's pawing the ground, and Sooner growled at him. Sooner said he's not scared of him, but I think he's lying."

Sooner barked.

"Yes, you are, Sooner," Ellie said, and Colter closed his eyes briefly. He didn't want to have another conversation about whether or not she could hear Sooner talk, not today. He had to get rid of this restless energy.

"Let's go see just how mean that horse is."

Ellie's eyes grew big.

Tulley swallowed a curse word.

Colter got to his feet. "A good ride will calm him right down."

"Have you noticed the weather?" Tulley asked. "There's a storm coming and the temperature's dropping fast. This is no time to be breaking a horse."

"Getting soft?" Colter teased, but he knew he was about to do a stupid thing. It wouldn't be the first time, he told himself, but if he could obliterate Marisa's memory for those few minutes, it would be worth it.

Colter had a rural address, but it was easy to find. A couple of miles down the country road she came to a large brick entrance with a huge overhead sign in wrought-iron letters that read Circle K Ranch. She drove over the cattle guard onto a gravel road that led to a house.

Her eyes opened wide in appreciation of the scene that met her. The land was flat and a two-story brick colonial house nestled among huge oaks. Now bare, the trees stood proudly against the chilling wind, enhancing the beauty of the house with its white pillars and mullioned windows. Beyond the detached four-car garage were various barns, outbuildings and corrals, all neatly maintained. She couldn't help thinking that even her mother would be impressed.

Parking on the circular drive, she took a steadying breath, then ran up the paved walk to the front door. The wind bit through her clothes; it had definitely grown colder. She pulled her cashmere coat tighter around her and rang the doorbell.

There was no answer, so she rang it again. Still no answer. She felt a deep sense of disappointment. It'd been difficult to make the trip at all, and now that she was here, she hated to leave without seeing him. But it seemed she had no choice. It was after four, anyway, and she needed to return to Dallas for the dinner party her father had planned.

As she left the circular drive, a movement from one of the corrals caught her eye. A small child sat perched atop a fence, and Marisa drove in that direction. She stopped some distance away, got out and ran over, hoping she might find Colter.

The child, huddled in a winter coat with the hood pulled over her head, was too engrossed in what was going on inside the corral to notice Marisa. Following the child's gaze, she caught her breath at the sight of Colter astride a big red stallion.

The horse jumped and twisted, determined to dislodge his rider. Bending his head close to the ground, the horse struck out with his back legs, to no avail.

Marisa walked closer so she could see better. Too late, she realized her mistake. The child turned to look at her at the same time Colter did. As his concentration was diverted, the horse gave a wild kick that sent him flying against the fence.

Stunned, Marisa watched the horse run wild, his hooves threatening to trample Colter's inert body lying in the dirt. Without thinking, she hitched her skirt high and climbed over the fence. Someone yelled, "Stay back! Stay back!" but she didn't stop until she heard the sound of hooves close by.

She saw a man waving a rope above his head, trying to guide the horse into another pen. She felt a wave of panic as she realized she was in the corral with a wild horse. All those years ago, she'd been afraid of horses, and that hadn't changed. She held her breath as the horse thundered past her through a gate.

Her high heels hindered her progress over the loose dirt but nothing deterred her as she hurried to Colter's side. When she reached him, the child called Ellie was already there, holding Colter's head, crying, "Daddy, wake up! Please wake up."

Marisa squatted beside them, her hand gently brushing the brown hair from his face. He was completely motionless, and her whole body felt a chill that had nothing to do with the weather.

Ellie glanced up at Marisa, tears streaming down her face. "Is my daddy dead?"

"No, no," Marisa insisted, staring into green eyes so much like Colter's. She quickly looked back at Colter, feeling the cold hand of fear grip her heart as she stared at his eyelashes, so dark against the pallor of his skin. His broad chest moved slightly, and she sucked in a breath of frosty air.

Her eyes traveled down to his legs. "Oh, my God," she said. Something on the fence had ripped his jeans and blood was soaking through the denim.

The man came running over. "Is Colter okay?"

"He's cut his leg. Would you get me a clean cloth to stop the bleeding?" she asked him.

The man hesitated for a second, then walked off to the double doors that opened into the barn and came back with a small towel. She pulled the jeans away and saw a gash about three inches long. It wasn't deep. That was good, anyway. She pressed the towel against the wound and gave a sigh of relief as the bleeding slowed.

Colter's eyelids fluttered open.

"Daddy, Daddy," Ellie cried, kissing his face.

"Ooh," he groaned, his eyes blinking. "What happened?"

"That mean old horse threw you," Ellie told him.

"Damn." He sat up, and as his hand went to his head, his eyes caught hers. "What are—?"

"You cut your leg on the fence," she broke in.

Colter's dazed eyes focused on her.

"Please leave," he muttered in a thick voice.

"Colter, you're hurt and…" Her voice trailed away as he struggled to his feet.

Marisa and Tulley immediately tried to help him. Colter shook off Marisa's arm.

"Who are you?" Ellie asked, staring at her.

"Uh—I'm Marisa Preston, a friend of your dad's. I knew him a long time ago." Silence followed.

"Lots of people know my daddy," Ellie declared a moment later. "He's a famous rodeo rider."

The two men walked slowly to the house, Ellie and a grayish brown dog running ahead. There was no invitation for Marisa to come in, but she hesitated only a fraction of a second before trailing after them. She had to talk to Colter.

As they walked to a covered walkway, a light sleet began to fall and the cold wind tugged at their clothes. Shivering, she followed the others through the door and down a hallway—there was a laundry room to the right and a closet on the left. They entered a spacious breakfast nook and a kitchen decorated in a lovely country style. Touches of cobalt-blue and white milk glass were here and there, and the white-and-blue tiled floor only added to the feeling of warmth.

Marisa looked around for Shannon but didn't see her. It suddenly dawned on her that this was inappropriate. She shouldn't be here interrupting his family life. She should have called and arranged a meeting—that would've been the proper thing to do. Since confronting him in the store, though, she hadn't been thinking too clearly.

"Ellie, turn up the heat. It's getting cold," Colter said, and slumped into a chair.

Ellie disappeared, and the man knelt in front of Colter with a first-aid kit and began to clean the jagged cut.

"Can I help?" she asked.

"I've been fixing his cuts, bruises and broken bones for more years than I care to remember," the man replied. "So, no, I don't need any help."

That voice finally jogged her memory. "I'm sorry, Tulley, I didn't recognize you."

Tulley slit Colter's jeans slightly to bandage the cut, then rose and faced her. "It's been a long time, Marisa, and under the circumstances I think it'd be best if you left."

Marisa bit her lip for fear it would start to quiver. This man had been kind to her once, but now kindness was not extended. She should leave; she'd already acknowledged that, but for some reason she couldn't make herself go. The urge to talk to Colter was still strong, overriding good manners and common sense, and it kept her rooted to the spot.

"Daddy, what's all that noise?" Ellie asked, running into the kitchen.

The adults had been so involved with one another that they hadn't noticed it was sleeting in earnest now and that the wind howled.

"It's just sleet, angelface."

"Oh boy! Is it gonna snow, Daddy?"

"I don't think so."

"C'mon, Sooner, let's go see," Ellie shouted, and rushed out the door with the dog behind her.

"Ellie…"

"I'll get her," Tulley offered, glancing from Colter to Marisa. Colter nodded and Tulley left.

"I apologize for the intrusion," she said as his eyes

bore into her. "I shouldn't have interrupted your life
with Shannon and your daughters, and I..."

Colter looked confused. "What are you talking
about?"

"I just saw Shannon from a distance in the store and
I assumed the other little girl was yours, too."

"If you saw Shannon, you have very good eyesight.
She lives in Wyoming. The other little girl is Lori,
my daughter's best friend. The woman was my sister,
Becky. It's just Ellie and me now."

"Oh." Marisa didn't know quite what to say. She'd
pictured a perfect, happy marriage for him, and she
wasn't sure how to deal with the situation now that she
knew differently. Leaving would be the best course of
action. But she couldn't go without telling him about
their son. It was now or never.

"After seeing you today, I felt I needed to explain
about the past," she plunged in.

He shook his head. "Marisa, I thought I made this
clear, but evidently you didn't understand. I'm not interested in anything you have to say. We had a brief
time together. It was over years ago. Nothing you say
can change a thing, and I don't care about your excuses
anymore. It just doesn't matter."

It just doesn't matter. Their son didn't matter. She
swallowed hard, trying to accept that, but nobody, not
even Colter, could ever make her believe the short time
their son was alive inside her didn't matter. Their son
had changed her life, and her perception of life in general. Losing him had given her the strength to stand up
to her mother. She was still struggling to find herself,
to find her niche in the world, but that had been a start.

It just doesn't matter, he'd said. Maybe to him it didn't. He had a new life, a new child, and Marisa was the only one not able to accept the past and move on. Suddenly she could see that Colter was right; telling him wouldn't change a thing except maybe to cause him more hurt. And what would that accomplish? Nothing.

Losing their son was her own private pain and she had to deal with it on her own. Mistakenly she'd believed that sharing the truth about their baby with Colter would ease her heartache. But she was the only one who could overcome that grief.

"Please leave and don't come back." Colter's voice penetrated her thoughts. "There's nothing left to say."

They stared at each other like strangers, total strangers, and Marisa felt the numbness of that reality. She had to leave.

But before she could move her feet, Ellie burst through the back door, followed by the big dog.

"Daddy, you should see," Ellie shouted, pushing back the hood of her coat. "Ice is everywhere. It's like a big skating ring, and Sooner says it's gonna snow, too."

Momentarily diverted, Marisa patted the dog's head. "Sooner?" she repeated.

"Yeah, he's part German shepherd and we don't know what else, and Daddy named him Sooner 'cause he'd sooner eat and sleep than do anything else." Ellie gave the dog a big hug. "Daddy, Sooner says he's not going back outside 'cause it's too cold."

"Ellie, that dog does not talk."

"Does, too." Ellie pouted. "You just can't hear him."

"Ellie." There was a note of warning in Colter's

voice. "We've been through this before. Sooner does not talk."

Marisa didn't understand how Colter could be so harsh. Lots of kids had imaginary friends, especially the lonely ones like her. She'd talked to a doll when she was about Ellie's age, and she'd outgrown it, as would Ellie. She could offer Colter some reassurance, but she knew it wouldn't be welcomed.

Ellie wriggled onto Colter's lap and put her arms around his neck. "Does your leg hurt, Daddy?"

"Naw," Colter answered, kissing her cheek.

Clearly Colter had a good relationship with his daughter. She couldn't help thinking that while she'd been lying in a New York clinic in labor with their child, he'd already married someone else, started a new life, a family. A pang of jealousy pierced her as she realized he'd gotten over her with remarkable ease.

She wondered about his marriage. Were he and Shannon separated? Divorced? She couldn't imagine Shannon ever leaving Colter or their child. What had happened?

Ellie didn't look much like Colter, she thought, but the green eyes were definitely his. They'd said her son's eyes were blue. Most babies were born with blue eyes, though. Later, would he have had the Kincaid green eyes or— *Stop it.* Her son was dead.

It was time to let go of the memories. It was time....

Chapter 3

Marisa turned to leave and just then, the electricity went out, shrouding the house in darkness. Outside the light was fading and nightfall wasn't far away. She should've left already.

"Oooh, Daddy, what's happening?" Ellie curled closer against Colter.

"The storm's probably taken down some power lines. The electricity's been out before, remember?"

Ellie raised her head to look at him. "Yeah, and we lit candles. I'll go get the candles." She jumped off his lap and ran to the cabinet, opened drawers.

"Top drawer on the left, angelface," Colter said, and Marisa noticed how gentle and reassuring he was.

He was a great father. She felt an ache deep inside her, in a private place kept only for her son, a son Colter would never know.

Tulley came into the room with a battery-operated radio, and Marisa switched her focus to him, unable to deal with all the emotions railing within her.

"The Dallas–Fort Worth area and Mesquite are under a weather advisory," Tulley said. "Some places, like here, don't have power, and people are being advised to stay off the roads because of the ice."

Ellie plopped several candles on the table, then handed Colter a box of matches. He absently lit a couple, and Marisa could see he was absorbing Tulley's news.

"I need to get back to Dallas," she said.

Tulley shook his head. "Not tonight."

Colter's eyes darkened in the glow of the candle-light. "Are you sure?"

Tulley set the radio on the table and turned it on. Through the static they heard, *"...Do not drive unless it's an emergency. Road conditions are hazardous..."* The warning faded away into silence.

"Daddy, aren't you gonna light another candle?" Ellie piped up.

Colter stared into Marisa's eyes, trying to accept that she was here for the duration, trying to accept that he had to deal with her presence and, above all, trying not to lose his temper.

Ellie tugged at his arm. "Daddy?"

"Uh." His gaze swung to his daughter. "Okay." He lit several more candles.

"I'll take one to the den," Ellie offered.

Colter grabbed her before she got too far. "Walk, don't run, and be careful."

"Okay." Ellie slowly walked to the den with the candle held tightly in both hands, Sooner at her heels.

Colter stood, his eyes holding Marisa's. "I don't want your death on my conscience, so it seems I have no choice but to let you stay here."

"I'm sorry," she said, feeling a need to apologize.

"I don't think you are. You barge into my life, my home, without any regard for my feelings. I fail to understand how something that happened more than eight years ago could be so damn important. Say what you have to say and then get the hell out of my life."

She gritted her teeth, the words stalled in her throat. She couldn't tell him like this—not when he was so angry.

"Nothing to say, huh?" he asked, his words loaded with sarcasm.

"No." She stiffened her backbone, tired of being the recipient of his insults. "And I will not apologize again. You don't deserve it."

His eyes narrowed to mere slits, but before he could vent his rage, Tulley stepped in. "Calm down. Ellie's in the next room."

Colter swerved around her and grabbed a big coat off the peg of a closet door. "Ellie, let's go," he called.

Ellie came running, with Sooner, as usual, right behind. "Where we going?"

"We'll check on the horses and make sure they have enough feed and water to outlast the storm, then we have to bring in more wood for the fireplace. It might be the only heat we have for a while."

Tulley spoke up. "I can do that. You should rest your leg. You were knocked out for a bit, too."

"It's just a scratch." Colter dismissed Tulley's warning. "And I've been knocked out so many times I've lost track."

"All the more reason—"

Colter cut him off. "Let's go."

Ellie secured the hood of her coat over her head, glancing at Marisa. "Aren't you coming?"

"No. Ms. Preston is not coming," Colter said before she could find her voice. He quickly ushered Ellie out the door.

Tulley stared at her with a sad expression.

"I'm sorry. I shouldn't have come." Colter might not deserve an apology, but she felt Tulley did.

"Not sure why you did."

"I'm wondering that myself."

Tulley removed his worn hat and scratched his head. "When you left, it was worse than when that horse trampled him in Cheyenne. He recovered from those bruises, but he's never fully recovered from what you did to his pride, his heart."

For the first time she realized how much she must have hurt him. But he obviously didn't suffer long. She gestured at the darkened room. "He seems to have moved on rather easily." Colter's dream had been to own a horse ranch. He'd already bought the land and was saving to build a house when he retired from the rodeo circuit. After meeting her, he'd decided it was time to quit and settle down, and she'd wanted so desperately to be part of his dream. But she never had the chance....

"Not so easily," Tulley said dryly. "I thought he'd

kill himself with the drinking and the partying, then something happened that turned him around."

She raised her eyes to his. "Ellie?"

"Yeah. When he found out about her, it changed his whole life. Her…her mother decided she couldn't be a mother, and Colter took full responsibility."

To say Marisa was shocked was putting it mildly. She couldn't imagine Shannon not wanting their child. Shannon had been crazy about Colter and they had shared the same interests—horses and the rodeo. What had gone wrong?

She swallowed. "Colter's a good father."

"Does that bother you?"

"A little," she admitted reluctantly. *A lot* would have been closer to the truth. Colter should know he'd had a son, too.

Tulley crammed his hat back on his head. "That little girl is the center of Colter's world. Everything he does, he does for her. Please don't come between them."

"Oh, Tulley, I would never do that."

He nodded. "I'm glad. And for good measure I'm asking you not to hurt him again. He didn't deserve it eight years ago, and he certainly doesn't deserve it now."

"Tul—" But Tulley was gone and all she heard was the slamming of the door.

She watched the candles on the table, her emotions flickering and wavering like the glow of the flames. One minute she wanted to tell Colter the truth, the next she didn't. She took a deep breath, recognizing that her actions were thoughtless and inconsiderate. She'd only been thinking about herself. Maybe Colter was right that she hadn't changed. Maybe her mother— Oh God, her mother! Her parents were probably waiting for her this very minute to sit down to dinner. She had to call.

Through the dimness she saw a phone on the kitchen wall. She reached for it, but the line was dead. Now what? Her cell phone might work. Looking around for her purse, she realized it was still in her car at the corral. She'd have to go herself, because she certainly wasn't asking Colter for any favors.

She opened the back door, then immediately closed it. The temperature was freezing, and she needed a heavier coat. Her eyes settled on the closet full of coats—surely Colter wouldn't mind? She rummaged until she found a heavy navy windbreaker with a hood. Holding the jacket to her face, she breathed in the leather and musk scent—Colter. She remembered that tantalizing fragrance, and for a moment she was lost in its magic.

She slipped on the jacket, which was rather large but would do. She zipped it up and tucked her hair beneath the hood.

Outside she stopped as the frigid air took her breath away. It was bitterly cold—the temperature had dropped at least twenty degrees. Light sleet fell to the ground. Icicles hung from the roof and the trees, and the wind added to the chill factor. She had to get her phone in a hurry.

There was no ice under the covered walkway, but as soon as her heels touched the grass, it crunched beneath her feet. Suede heels were not the ideal footwear for this weather. They'd be ruined, but she didn't particularly care. Her goal was to reach her car without breaking her neck.

She judged each step carefully, but a few yards from her car her feet slid out from under her and she landed on her butt with a thud that jarred her whole body. Sleet peppered her head, and her face, hands and feet were numb. Tears weren't far away. Everything seemed to close in on her at once.

What am I doing here? What am I doing here?

Sitting there, miserable, she felt her life become as clear as the chill in her bones. She'd believed she'd grown stronger and more confident, but in reality she hadn't. That was why she was so dissatisfied with her work. She'd traded living with her mother for living with her father, and he was just as domineering and controlling. Yet she clung to that security. Why? At almost twenty-six, she should be making a life for herself. She was a pampered little rich girl, just as Colter had said, unable to stand on her own two feet.

At the moment, that was the actual truth. Her body shook with cold, and she made a promise, a vow to herself. She was going to change her life completely—get away from her parents. Now if she could just get to her feet...

Colter dumped fifty pounds of feed into a trough under the eaves of the barn. He turned—and saw Marisa as she fell. He dropped the bag and ran for the gate. She wasn't getting up. Was she hurt? His feet slowed as he realized what he was doing—going to her aid. The past came full circle, and so many feelings were choking him, he fought to breathe. *I don't care about her. I don't.* He'd help anyone who needed help. *I don't care about her. I don't.* Over and over, he repeated the words, but he never stopped in his movement toward her.

"Are you hurt?"

Marisa glanced at him, squinting against the sleet. "No. Just my pride."

"Well, get up. It's freezing out here."

"I've tried, but my feet keep slipping out from under me."

Without a word, he held out his leather-gloved hands.

She placed her cold hands in his and he pulled her to her feet. When she slid into him, he caught her, holding her steady. He hadn't touched her in eight years and the sensation radiated a warmth that dispelled the cold. It brought back so many wonderful memories of touching her, loving her, until the warmth became a blazing flame. He hated the fact that he could remember those emotions so clearly.

"Were you trying to leave?" he asked, suddenly releasing her.

She brushed sleet from her nose. "I was trying to reach my car to get my cell phone. I need to call my parents, and the phone at the house is dead."

At the mention of her parents, he stepped away from her. "Mommy still keeping tabs on you?" he asked, unable to disguise his sarcasm.

She stuck out her chin in defiance. "I live with my father in Dallas."

"I don't—" He stopped and sucked air into his lungs. "Get in your car and drive into the garage and call whoever the hell you have to." Saying that, he strolled back to the barn.

Marisa shoved away the pain of his words and quickly drove her car into the garage. Not because he'd told her to, but because it was the sensible thing to do. She let the motor run, hoping the interior would soon warm up. She found her cell phone, but when she tried to call, there was nothing but static.

The clock on the dash told her it was seven o'clock. Dinner was at six, so by now they would be wondering where she was. Lamar Norris and his son, Adam, were dinner guests, and her father was not going to be happy she wasn't there. He'd been trying for the past few months to arrange a date between her and Adam. She had stoically refused. She was not attracted to Adam. He didn't wear cowboy boots or a Stetson hat or have green eyes. Every man she met she compared to Colter, and they all came up short. She'd never admitted that to herself before. She hadn't moved on at all. She continued to wallow in the emotions of the past.

The man in question didn't want her anywhere near him or his daughter. He'd made that very plain. Yet here she was, stuck for the night.

She wondered if her mother had arrived safely. If she had any idea where Marisa was, she'd have a fit. Cari was the only one who knew. She hoped her parents assumed she'd sought shelter from the storm. They'd be worried, but there was nothing she could do about that.

Hearing voices, she turned the motor off and climbed out. She grabbed her purse, then followed Colter, Ellie and Sooner into the house. Colter carried an armload of wood and Ellie held the door for him. Tulley was outside piling more wood on the patio.

Colter had a roaring fire going in a matter of minutes, and Marisa realized she had a problem: her clothes were dirty and wet. But she wasn't going to mention it. She'd caused enough trouble. She huddled closer to the fire.

Tulley came through the patio doors with a couple of flashlights. "Ah, it feels better in here already."

"Ellie, take the flashlight and see if you can find Ms. Preston some dry clothes in Becky's room." Colter spoke from the doorway, and she could feel his eyes on her.

"Are you wet?" Ellie asked, still wrapped in her big coat.

"Yes. I went out to my car."

"You have to walk fast. That way you don't get wet."

"I'll remember that," she replied with a grin.

"Ellie, the clothes," Colter said in an impatient voice.

"Okay. Okay." Ellie took the flashlight from Tulley and headed for the stairs.

"I'll go with you," Marisa offered.

"There's no need," Colter snapped.

"She has to put them on, Daddy," Ellie said, as if she were talking to a child.

There was a long pause. "Okay, but hurry. It's cold up there."

Marisa trailed Ellie and Sooner up the stairs onto a balcony overlooking the den. She could see the fire blazing and Colter and Tulley silhouetted against it.

They were talking—probably about her—and she wished this night was over.

Ellie found her a pair of jeans, a T-shirt, a sweat-shirt, wool socks and a corduroy jacket. The jeans were a tad big in the waist, but everything else fit fine. Her cashmere coat was ruined, as were her shoes.

Ellie shone the light on her high heels. "Wow. Can I try them on?"

"Sure, but let's take them downstairs. It's warmer there."

"Okay." Ellie took off running with the heels, and Marisa followed more slowly.

In the den, Colter and Tulley had made a pallet with blankets and quilts, and there were more quilts on the sofa.

"Oh boy," Ellie cried, falling down on the pallet, the heels forgotten. "We're having a slumber party."

"It's not a party," Colter said, his voice stern.

"Is, too," Ellie insisted.

Colter sighed. "Tulley's put out some cold cuts, fruit and soft drinks, so eat, and then we'll all get some sleep."

They sat on the floor around the coffee table. Colter ate sitting on the sofa, and she noticed a telltale grimace when he leaned over to reach for the mustard. His leg must be hurting, but he'd never admit it.

Marisa wasn't aware of what she was eating. The fire was warm and cozy and the candlelight flickered hypnotically. She felt as if she'd slipped into another time, another place, where she should've been eight years ago—here with Colter… She stopped those thoughts immediately.

Tulley gathered up the leftovers. "I'll throw this in the trash, then I'm off to my featherbed."

Ellie ran and gave him a kiss. "'Night, Tulley."

"'Night, shorty."

"Tulley's tough," Ellie told her. "He grew up in the— What did he grow up in, Daddy?"

"The Depression."

"Yeah, and sometimes all he had to eat was bread and water. He didn't have any shoes, either, and he had to walk ten miles to school."

"Tulley's pretty impressive." She smiled.

"He also tells impressive stories," Colter said under his breath.

"'Night, everyone," Tulley called, and Marisa could hear the laughter in his voice.

Colter stood. "You take the sofa." He didn't call her by name, but she knew he was talking to her.

"No. I'll sleep on the floor."

"You'll sleep on the sofa." His words were final.

"Let her sleep with me, Daddy, please," Ellie begged. "We're having a slumber party."

"Ellie." He groaned in frustration.

Ellie quickly removed her coat and crawled beneath the covers, Marisa did the same before Colter could object.

"'Night, Daddy," Ellie said.

Marisa heard a long, irritated sigh, then the squeak of the sofa. He was giving in, and she felt as if she'd achieved a small victory.

"Oh, oh." Ellie jumped up and ran to Colter. "I forgot to kiss you."

In a moment she was back. "I kiss Daddy every

morning and every night. He can't live without my sugar—ain't that right, Daddy?"

"Isn't that right?" Colter corrected.

"Yeah. It is."

Marisa smiled as Ellie crawled beneath the covers again. Sooner nuzzled his way beside her. How could any woman give up this child? She was adorable.

"Do you have kids?" Ellie asked.

"No—" she answered with a catch in her voice.

"Are you married?"

"Ellie." Colter's voice rang out.

"Daddy's kind of grouchy," Ellie whispered to her.

"Go to sleep," Colter said.

"It's too early."

"I'm not in a mood to argue about that tonight. Just go to sleep."

"He's *real* grouchy," Ellie amended.

Colter closed his eyes, hardly able to believe that Marisa Preston was here in his house, talking to his child, and there was nothing he could do about it. This was going to be the longest night of his life.

He knew Ellie wouldn't stop asking her questions. She did that with every woman she thought might be a mother candidate. He wasn't sure how to tell her that Marisa wasn't the motherly type, that there was no way in hell he'd ever get involved with her again.

No way. Under no circumstances.

Chapter 4

"Where the hell is she?"

Richard Preston paced back and forth in the library of the Dalton mansion in Highland Park. Vanessa Preston and Reed watched him.

"The police haven't been able to find her car, so she's not stranded on any of the highways. Where could she be? It took me forever to get Lamar and Adam here, and she does a disappearing act. This isn't like her." Richard turned to Reed. "She didn't say where she was going?"

"I've already told you, Father. She said she had somewhere to go and that she'd be back for dinner."

"Why the hell did you allow her to go out in this weather?"

Reed's eyebrows darted up. "Allow?"

"She's not strong like you. She needs protection."

"I—"

"Lay off Reed, Richard." Medium height with blond good looks, Vanessa Preston crossed her legs and smoothed her silk skirt over her knees. "You're missing the obvious, as usual."

Richard glared at her. "What are you talking about?"

"Me, Richard. She's avoiding me."

"That's absurd. Marisa's gotten over the past."

"Mother might be right," Reed said. "Marisa was very nervous about something, and Cari…" He snapped his fingers. "That's it. I interrupted Cari and Marisa talking, so she's either with Cari or Cari knows where she is."

"Call her," Richard ordered.

Reed dialed Cari's number and she answered on the second ring. "Cari, this is Reed Preston."

"Hi, junior, what can I do for you?"

Reed's mouth tightened. "I'm looking for Marisa."

"Isn't she at home?"

"No, and it's late and we're getting worried."

"Oh, no."

"What? Where's Marisa?"

"I'm not telling you anything, junior."

Reed took a deep breath. "In this weather she could be stranded somewhere, maybe needing medical attention. Please tell us where she went so we can check on her."

Reed listened for a few seconds, then said a curt goodbye and hung up. He stared at his parents.

"What?" Richard demanded. "Where is she?"

"She…she went to see Colter Kincaid."

Silence.

"Oh, my God," Vanessa muttered.

"No, no." Richard shook his head. "She wouldn't do that, not after what he did to her life."

Reed shrugged. "That's what Cari said."

"Richard, do something." Vanessa twisted the pearls around her neck.

"I will," Richard said. "I'll make sure that man never hurts my daughter again."

The fire burned brightly, enclosing the room in its inviting warmth. Marisa stared into the darkness, listening to the howl of the wind and the icy refrain of the storm, but she wasn't afraid. Oddly, she experienced a peacefulness that was comforting.

"Are you asleep?" Ellie whispered so Colter wouldn't hear.

"No," Marisa whispered back.

"Me, neither." Ellie scooted closer. "Are you married?"

Marisa smiled. Ellie remembered she hadn't responded to that question earlier, and it seemed Ellie needed an answer.

"No. I'm not married."

"Daddy's not, either." A slight pause. "He's handsome, don't you think?"

At seventeen, she'd thought Colter the handsomest man she'd ever met. Her opinion hadn't changed. "Yes. I suppose."

"Did Santa Claus send you?"

"Excuse me?"

"Well, you see, I wrote Santa for a mommy, and

you appeared out of nowhere, so I figured he answered my letter."

Marisa hated to disappoint Ellie, but she couldn't lie. "No, sweetie. Santa didn't send me."

"Oh, gee, that's not fair. Why *can't* I have a mommy?"

"You have your father," Marisa reminded her, not sure how to handle this conversation.

"Yeah, and he's the best daddy in the whole world, but he doesn't know any girl things."

"Like what?"

"Well, my friend Lori has a sister. Her name's Ashley, and she started her period. Lori and me didn't know what that was, so her mom explained. When I got home I told Daddy, and his ears turned red. He said I was still too young, but it happened to all girls and when it did I was supposed to tell him and we'd buy what I need. That's gross, though. Aunt Becky said she'd come and help me, and Lori's mom offered to help, too. But I don't want Aunt Becky or Lori's mom. I want my own mommy. She'd know all about things like that."

"I'm sure she would." Poor Ellie. Clearly she wanted a mother any way she could get one. "But you have to leave that up to your father."

"Oh, no. My mother broke his heart and he's never falling in love again, but I'm not giving up."

Colter had been in love with Shannon. She couldn't believe how much that hurt—and it shouldn't. She'd left him, so he had had every right to get on with his life. How she wished she'd been able to do the same.

"Lori and me heard Santa's coming to Dalton's Department Store, and I'm going to see him. I want to ask him why he hasn't sent me a mommy. I've asked a bunch of times. Lori says Santa Claus isn't real, but I believe in him. Do you believe, Ms. Preston?"

Ellie's words danced in her head with childish candor. "Yes. I believe." She believed in anything that made another person happy, and believing in Santa made Ellie happy—that was obvious.

"Since I work at Dalton's, I'll make sure you get a private sitting with Santa. How's that?" Colter wouldn't like her interfering, but she couldn't help herself. She certainly wasn't telling Ellie there wasn't a Santa Claus.

"You do?" Ellie sat up, her voice excited. "That's awesome."

Colter lay listening to the conversation, biting his tongue and clamping his jaw so tightly his head hurt. If he stopped Ellie, she'd just start again with the questions. They'd been through this many times, and Ellie never gave up. He didn't understand her strong desire for a mother. He'd done everything he could to fill that gap, but he'd failed. And he had never felt that more than he did at this moment.

The menstrual cycle talk had caught him off guard. Considering the nature of the subject, he thought he'd done a good job. Clearly he hadn't. He wasn't even aware his ears had turned red.

Ellie needed a woman to discuss things with, that was very plain now. However, Marisa Preston was the last woman he wanted Ellie talking to.

"Are you *sure* Santa didn't send you?"

"Ellie Kincaid, go to sleep this instant." Colter's

voice shot through the darkness, and Ellie dived beneath the covers.

"I gotta go to sleep before Daddy has a coronary," she said. "That means a heart attack—Tulley told me." Then she whispered in Marisa's ear. "I'll be at Dalton's." Ellie snuggled against Sooner and silence prevailed.

Marisa stared into the glow of the fire with so many questions running through her mind. Why hadn't Colter remarried? Ellie had said he'd loved Shannon. Maybe he still did.

She'd thought the love she and Colter had shared was special—a once-in-a-lifetime love. She saw now that as a naive young girl, she'd been in love with love. She also saw that she'd needed to come here—to see Colter and his family. It was cathartic. This was what she needed to bury the past and get on with her life.

And she prayed she could.

Colter tossed and turned so much that his leg started to throb. Dammit. Would this night never end? At least Ellie had fallen asleep, and the quiet outside signaled that the storm had stopped.

He sat up, grabbed a flashlight and made his way to the bathroom near the laundry room. A couple of Tylenols would help. He got a bottle of water, swallowed two pills and headed back to the den. As he did, the lights came on. Thank God. Looking at his watch he saw it was 5:00 a.m.

The heat came on, but he stoked the fire and threw on a couple of logs. He glanced down at Marisa and Ellie sleeping on the floor. His eyes centered on

Marisa, her blond hair disheveled, her features serene. She had that same appeal, that same look of innocence and beauty she'd had back then. He drew a deep breath. She wasn't innocent or beautiful. Try as he might, though, he found himself wishing she could've been Ellie's mother. The pain of that stabbed him.

Marisa stirred and sat up, pushing her hair behind her ears.

His stomach tightened at the gesture, and he remembered mornings like this when she'd wake and smile at him and the world became a brighter place. It had all been a lie, though. At the first sign of trouble, she'd given in to her mother and left him behind without even saying goodbye.

"The lights are on," she said in a sleepy voice.

"Yeah. They just came on." He walked to the sofa and sat on the arm, gazing down at her. He had to do this, so he might as well get it over with. "You came here to tell me something. What?"

She blinked, unable to believe what she was hearing. He wanted to listen, and she welcomed this opportunity. She'd decided it would be better for him not to know, but suddenly she changed her mind—maybe because his voice wasn't so angry anymore.

Searching for the right words, she glanced at Ellie, unsure of whether to talk in front of her.

Colter followed her eyes. "She's sound asleep and she doesn't wake up until about seven."

Marisa swallowed. "I wanted to tell you why I left."

"Does it make a difference?"

She looked him in the eye. "Yes—to me."

He shrugged. "You let your mother force you into

leaving, and that pretty much said how you felt about me and the future we'd planned. What can you add to that?"

"Have you ever wondered *how* she forced me?"

"From what you said about her, she wielded immense power over you and your life. When she showed up, you caved and went home like the dutiful daughter."

Marisa shook her head. "No, it didn't happen like that. I refused to go with her."

His eyes narrowed. "But you went."

"She didn't leave me much choice. When I refused, she said she'd have you charged with statutory rape."

"What!"

"There was a policeman waiting outside, and I knew she meant what she'd said."

"You were twenty-one."

She locked her fingers together. "I lied. I was only seventeen, a month from my eighteenth birthday."

He stood and jammed both hands through his hair. "*Seventeen?* I was ten years older than you. You were seventeen?"

"Yes. My friend Stacy had a friend who knew someone who made fake IDs. We just wanted to have some fun, and that was the only way we could get into the casinos."

"You never said anything."

"You never asked."

"I just assumed— God, you were seventeen."

"Yes." A flush of guilt stained her cheeks. "I couldn't let you go to jail, so I went with my mother. As soon as I reached New York, I called the motel, but you'd checked out. I was devastated. You didn't give me an address or a phone number, and I didn't know how to get in touch. I kept trying for weeks, then I hired a private investigator."

Colter's gaze sharpened. "Evidently he didn't find me."

"I made the mistake of writing him a check. My mother had access to my account, and she contacted him. She was furious at what I'd done and we had a big scene. In the end she gave me the information the investigator had found out—that you'd already married someone else."

"I wasn't married then," he said in a controlled voice.

The fire crackled behind her, and daylight peeped through the blinds, but she was only aware of his words. They didn't make sense. "What?"

"I married Shannon after Ellie was born."

"Oh."

His eyes flared. "Your mother lied to you."

It took a moment to assimilate this, to believe her mother would do that to her. But then, her mother would've done anything to keep her away from Colter. That little lie was supposed to make Marisa forget all about him. It had done just the opposite. Every day she'd carried their son she had thought about Colter constantly, and over the years he'd never been far from her mind.

"Let's stop playing games, Marisa. The decision you made years ago, under whatever circumstances, is final. The past is over and it's been over for so long that I don't even care anymore. Ellie's birth may not have been the way I wanted it, but that's something I'm honest about. I don't think you even know what the word means." He swallowed visibly. "As soon as the ice melts, I want you out of here."

She paled at the cruelty of his words. The anger was back, and his eyes blazed as hot as the fire. Before she could retaliate, someone rang the doorbell, then knocked loudly at the front door.

"What the hell?" Colter hurried to answer it.

Marisa got to her feet and realized she was shaking. She wrapped her arms around her waist to still that reaction. After a moment, she heard raised voices and moved toward the foyer, surprised the racket hadn't awakened Ellie.

"I'm sorry, Colter. I have orders," a man was saying. "I have a warrant to search your house. Richard Preston says you kidnapped his daughter, and he has the Dallas Police Department in an uproar. The sheriff wants me to check it out before they call in the FBI."

"Search away," Colter replied. "But you might want to ask the woman herself what she's doing here."

Marisa stood in the doorway, her eyes big and troubled.

"Ms. Marisa Preston?" the man asked.

"Yes," she answered in a weak voice.

The man stepped forward. "I'm Deputy Jimmy Walsh. Are you being held against your will?"

"Of course not! Why on earth would you think that?"

"Your family believes Mr. Kincaid kidnapped you and they're very worried."

Mother. She wasn't going to stop...until Marisa

stopped her. The only person who'd ever kidnapped her was her mother. She'd taken away her childhood and now she was trying to destroy what little peace Marisa had managed to find. A white rage filled her.

"Mr. Kincaid doesn't even want me here. I came of my own free will, and you can tell my mother—"

The deputy held up his hand. "I've only spoken with your father, so if you'll get your things, I'll take you back to Dallas and your family."

Her mother could manipulate her father into doing anything. This time she wasn't giving in. She was fighting back.

"Are the roads passable?" she asked.

"The highway department's been working all night and I managed to get here without too much of a problem."

"Then I'll follow you in my car."

"It'd be better if you came with me."

"Am I under arrest?"

His face turned slightly red. "No, ma'am."

"Good. Then it's settled. I'll drive my own car." She whirled toward the den.

"Sorry for the intrusion, Colter," she heard the deputy say.

She sank onto the pallet, where she found the corduroy jacket and slipped it on. Ellie stirred and sat up, rubbing her eyes.

"The lights are on," she said.

"Yes," Marisa answered, looking around for her shoes.

"Are you leaving?" Ellie asked.

"Yes. I have to go."

"Then Santa didn't send you." The forlorn voice bothered Marisa.

"No. Santa didn't send me, but here's an early Christmas present." She handed her the high heels.

"Cool."

Marisa stood. "Goodbye, Ellie."

"'Bye. You sure you don't need your shoes? It's cold."

"I have wool socks on, so don't worry about it."

"Okay." She stroked Sooner. "Can I still come and see Santa?"

Marisa could feel Colter's eyes boring into her, but she wasn't going to disappoint Ellie. She didn't care how angry he got. "Sure. Anytime you want."

Ellie smiled. "Thanks."

Marisa picked up her purse and walked toward the back door. Tulley was in the kitchen drinking coffee. "'Bye, Tulley," she said, but didn't stop. She had to get away.

Colter caught her at the door. "Let's be clear about one thing."

She'd had all she could take from him. "No," she snapped. "I'm not listening to any more of your nastiness or your insults. I made some bad choices—very bad choices—but I had my reasons. Reasons I thought were valid at the time. If you could stop thinking about your pride for one tiny second, you might want to hear those reasons. Until then, I have nothing to say to you."

Chapter 5

Colter walked into the kitchen and flopped down into a chair. Tulley placed a cup of coffee in front of him, but he barely saw it. All he could see was Marisa's angry face.

Ellie tottered in on the high heels.

"Take those shoes off," he said, more sharply than he'd intended. "We're sending them back to Ms. Preston."

Ellie stuck out her lip. "She gave them to me."

"They're going back."

Ellie stepped out of the shoes, picked them up and ran to her room, slamming the door. Sooner barked. The door opened and then slammed again.

Tulley sat down. "You were a bit rough on her."

"I'll apologize in a minute—after I cool off." He looked at Tulley. "She lied to me."

"About what?"

"She said she was seventeen in Vegas, not twenty-one."

"Yep, that's a whopper, but I told you she looked too young and inexperienced for Vegas. Back then you weren't listening to much I had to say."

"I wore rose-colored glasses where she was concerned, but they were brutally ripped away and I can see her for the woman she really is."

"Are you sure?"

"What do you mean?"

"The young Marisa was weak, but this Marisa seems strong. Remember the time you scratched your arm riding Diablo at the rodeo in Vegas? She almost passed out when I changed the bandage. But yesterday she climbed over the fence, with the horse running wild, to get to you. She even stopped the bleeding. The young Marisa wouldn't have gone anywhere near that horse and she certainly couldn't have attended to your leg."

"So she's matured. That doesn't change anything."

"Guess not."

"What does she expect from me?"

"Forgiveness."

"No." He shook his head. "I can't ever forgive her—yet last night, when she fell on the ice, I ran to her without thinking. I could feel her pulling me in with those soft eyes and that sweet smile—just like in Vegas. She was sitting with all those people and the only one I could see was her. That connection was there, and it wouldn't have mattered if she was seventeen or twenty-one."

"Nope. Probably not."

Colter took a gulp of coffee, hearing the truth of his words but not wanting to face it. "I can't believe any of this. Her parents sending the cops out here was the last straw, and it seemed to be for her, too. She was furious when she left, but I hope they convince her to stay away."

"That would be best."

Colter got to his feet. "I'd better go soothe Ellie's ruffled feathers."

"What would it hurt if she kept the shoes?" Tulley asked. "She's a little girl, but she's starting to like big-girl things."

"Yeah." Colter glanced toward Ellie's room. "She's growing up too fast and I'm lost when it comes to this girl stuff."

"Yep. Ellie's reminded you of that on more than one occasion."

"I thought I could be everything to my daughter, and it hurts that I can't. She still keeps asking for a mother...."

"Then let her keep the shoes." Tulley stood and grabbed his hat. "She'll feel like a big girl. What harm can it do? That's my two cents. I'll check on the horses and be back to fix breakfast."

Colter watched him go with a bitter taste in his mouth. He didn't want any reminders of Marisa in his house—not even a pair of damaged shoes. But it was a little late for such thinking. Marisa had invaded his carefully built world in more ways than he cared to think about.

* * *

As Marisa followed the deputy, her anger mounted. How dare her parents treat her like a child! That was what she'd always been to them—a child who needed protection, guidance and supervision. When her parents separated, the agreement had been that her father would raise Reed and her mother agreed to raise Marisa, and they would do so without interference from each other.

It had worked, more or less, until her father had come to New York for a visit and found her an emotional wreck. She'd just lost her son and she couldn't bring herself back from that dark place of grief and intolerable sadness. When her father learned what had happened, he and Vanessa had argued bitterly, but he had ignored Vanessa's threats and brought Marisa home to Texas to heal.

She'd had a strained relationship with her mother after that, but they'd reached a degree of understanding. Vanessa was not to meddle again. But Marisa had never been in control of her own life; one or both of her parents had. That was going to change. She'd been thinking about this earlier and now she had to put it into action.

The deputy didn't stop at the outskirts of Dallas. He obviously had orders to deliver her, like an expensive package, to her father. The drive had taken twice as long because of the icy roads, but soon he pulled up to the security gate of the Dalton mansion.

When he got out and came to her window, she pushed a button to lower it.

"I've been instructed to take you to your father. Could you open the gate, please?"

"Yes," she answered with deceptive calm, and punched the code into her remote control. The gates swung open and the deputy ran back to his car.

She parked behind him in front of the palatial home that had belonged to her grandfather. Normally, she'd drive to the garage, but today she wasn't planning on staying that long.

Before the deputy could ring the bell, the door opened and her father stood there. His eyes went immediately to Marisa. "Oh, sweetheart, you're okay." He tried to put his arms around her, but she sidestepped him and walked through the foyer into the living room.

Vanessa ran to her. "Darling, thank God you're home." She tried to hug Marisa, but again Marisa moved away.

They walked into the library and Marisa turned on them.

"How dare you humiliate me like this. How dare you treat me like a child."

"Now, Marisa, we only did what we thought was best for you," Richard said.

"Best for me!" She laughed, unable to keep the hysteria out of her voice. "That's a joke. You've never thought about me or my feelings. It's always what both of you want."

"Calm down, sweetheart, and we'll talk about this rationally," Richard urged.

"I'm not calming down or listening to anything else you have to say."

"Okay. Okay." Richard was trying to pacify her. "But, sweetheart, why would you go see that man?"

Marisa took a step closer to Vanessa and stared her straight in the eye. "Because I wanted to tell him about our son. He has a right to know."

Vanessa lifted her chin. "What did he say?"

"I never had a chance, with the storm and the electricity going out."

"So you never told him?" her father asked.

"No, but it's just a matter of time. Unless, of course, you have the police tail me everywhere I go."

"Doesn't he have a wife and a little girl?" Vanessa asked as if she hadn't spoken.

"He has a little girl, but the wife isn't there anymore. You probably know that, though, don't you?"

Vanessa's expression barely changed.

"He wasn't married when you told me he was. He married Shannon later. You only told me that so I'd get on with the wonderful life you had planned for me."

Vanessa lifted her chin again. "Yes, I lied. But the detective said Kincaid was involved with her. That didn't sound like a man deeply in love. I'd do it again to protect you."

"Protect me? From the man I love?"

Vanessa was obviously shocked.

"Don't worry, Mother. I'm so mixed up I don't know *what* I feel. But Colter hates me and he doesn't want me anywhere near his little girl. That should make you happy."

"What happened to his wife?"

"I'm not sure."

"But he has his daughter?"

"Yes, and she's adorable, bright and spunky—everything a child should be. So you see, Colter already has a child and he's not interested in hearing about the one we lost, but for my own peace of mind I have to tell him."

Richard spoke up. "Sweetheart, that's not wise. I thought you'd let the past go, but you're still clinging to unreal fantasies about this man."

Before Marisa could answer, Reed came in from the kitchen holding a cup of coffee. "Marisa, you're back," he said, coming over to her. "You okay?" he asked in a low voice.

"Yes, I am."

He gestured at her feet. "Where are your shoes?"

"I ruined them in the sleet." She wasn't telling them anything else.

"Other than that, you look fine." Reed took a sip of coffee.

"No, she isn't." Richard picked up the phone. "I'm calling a therapist and setting up some counseling sessions so you can get this man out of your system. Now, go upstairs and get some rest, and we'll discuss this again when you're in a better frame of mind."

Marisa was dumbstruck. They hadn't heard a word she'd said. This was the pattern of her life. They ordered and she obeyed. But not anymore. Not one minute more.

She raised her head, knowing her eyes were as dark as the secrets in her soul. "I'm going upstairs, but I'm not resting. I'm packing a few things, then I'm leaving for good."

Vanessa gasped.

Richard slammed down the receiver. "What are you talking about? This is your home."

"This is my prison," she said, her eyes not wavering for a second. "And everything here is for show, especially me. I'm a glorified puppet. You pull my strings, Father, and I entertain your business associates, decorate your stores and wear a made-up title. You parade eligible bachelors in front of me, in hopes that a marriage could benefit Dalton's. As a dutiful daughter, I keep trying to please, but you and Mother have broken me. I don't even know who I am anymore." She took a calming breath. "I have to find me."

"You're just upset," her mother said. "A lot of that's probably my fault, but Marisa, I'll be leaving tomorrow for a Christmas cruise to the Greek Isles on Niko's yacht. Please don't do anything drastic because you're angry with me."

"I was very angry," Marisa admitted. "Now I just want some peace, and I have to find that on my own. I hope you'll both try to understand." She turned toward the stairs, then stopped. "Have a good trip, Mother."

"I forbid this, Marisa," Richard said, his voice rising.

"Forbid all you want. I'm leaving." She ran up the stairs feeling light-headed.

Richard frowned at Reed. "Talk her out of this."

"How am I supposed to do that?"

"Any way you can. She's not leaving this house."

"I told you this would happen if you brought her back to Texas," Vanessa railed. "But no, you wouldn't listen. You wanted control of both our children, and now you've lost her. How does it feel, Richard?"

"Shut up, Vanessa."

"No, I won't." Vanessa pointed a finger at him. "*You're* the cause of this. If she'd just stayed in New York, like our separation stated, none of this would be happening."

"She was a zombie, and I wasn't leaving her in that condition."

"She'd just lost a child," Vanessa shouted. "That's a normal reaction for a woman. If you'd left her alone, she would have gone back to her career."

"Get out of my face, Vanessa, because I'm not listening to this."

"Both of you, take a deep breath," Reed said, intervening. "I'll go up and talk to Marisa, but only if you stop shouting."

Richard stormed off to his study, and Vanessa sat on the sofa, her lips tight.

Reed headed upstairs.

Colter opened Ellie's door and walked into her room. She was lying on the bed, the shoes in her hand, Sooner at her feet.

He sat beside her, his back against the headboard. "We need to talk, angelface."

Ellie rose to her knees, her eyes red. "Why don't you like her, Daddy? She's nice and pretty and—"

"And what?"

Ellie fiddled with the shoes. "Nothing."

"And Santa might have sent her?"

Her eyes flew to his. "You know?"

"Yes." He touched her cheek. "Ellie, baby, you do understand that there's only one way you're going to have a new mother?"

"You have to get married." She hung her head.

"That's it, and I'm not doing that until I fall in love again."

"Like you were with my mother?"

"Yes."

"But you're getting old and it might not happen."

He suppressed a laugh. "Well, then, is it so bad with just you, Tulley and me?"

"No."

"Are you unhappy?"

"No. I'm happy all the time."

"So why do you want a mother?"

Ellie shrugged. "I could talk to her about things—girl things."

He'd heard some of this last night when she'd been whispering to Marisa. "You can talk to me about anything. You do know that, don't you?"

"Yeah. But sometimes it's embarrassing."

"If we talk about it, then it won't be embarrassing."

She smiled and dived into his arms. "I love you, Daddy."

"I love you, too, angelface." He kissed the top of her head. "I'll do the looking for a mother, okay?"

Ellie nodded against his chest. "I don't know why I want a mommy so much. I think about it all the time and I can't stop. Why do I do that, Daddy?"

"Oh, baby." He held her tight, his heart breaking. "I think it's normal for little girls who don't have mothers. And there's a club for kids who only have one parent. It's called Big Brothers and Big Sisters. How'd you like a Big Sister?"

A teacher at Ellie's school had told him about the program after Ellie had gotten several of her classmates involved in her matchmaking schemes. He'd told the teacher he'd think about it, but he hadn't—until now.

Ellie lifted her head. "But you said we didn't need to join."

"I've changed my mind."

"Cool! I'd like a Big Sister."

"Then we'll do it. Now, let's go have some breakfast."

Ellie stared at the shoes with a gloomy expression.

Colter's chest tightened. "You can keep the shoes."

Ellie threw her arms around his neck. "Thank you, Daddy, and I'm gonna give you lots of sugar this morning."

She kissed his face, and Colter knew he'd do whatever it took to keep her happy. Whatever.

Marisa grabbed a suitcase and gathered an assortment of clothes, not knowing what she'd need. She didn't stop to think. She packed quickly before her parents could do something to prevent her from leaving.

Reed stood in the doorway. "You're determined about this?"

She paused for a moment to glance at her brother. "Yes."

Reed walked inside. "I've been sent to talk you out of it."

"I figured that." She zipped up the suitcase.

"They love you. They're just a little overprotective."

She set the case on the floor. "I don't feel loved," she told him. "They're smothering me and sometimes I can barely breathe. I don't want to live like that anymore. I'm going to get a job. I have to find out if I can survive in this world, away from the support of my parents."

"Get a job?" Reed echoed. "That's absurd. You have a trust fund and you can do whatever you want. Travel, do charity work, help the poor—but there's no need to join the workforce."

"You sound like Father." She pushed her hair back.

"Oh, God," Reed groaned, but quickly shook off the comparison.

"Marisa… You've been obsessed with this man, and now that you've seen him again, you're not thinking rationally. I'll admit Father went over the top calling the police, but we were all very worried. Please don't do something you'll regret."

She drew a long breath. "I haven't been 'obsessed' with Colter. I've been obsessed with the loss of our child. You've never experienced that, so you don't know the emptiness, the loneliness that never goes away. When I saw Colter again, I thought if I told him about our son, that feeling would leave. But he's not interested in anything I have to say. It made me realize, though, that he's moved on, and I have to do the same. I can't do that under the watchful eyes of our parents. I need time, space and my freedom. Please, Reed, help me."

He wavered, but not for long. "Go out the back and I'll stall them."

She kissed his cheek and grabbed her suitcase and clothes bag. "Thanks, Reed."

"Call and let me know you're okay."

"I will," she promised, and ran down the hall to the back stairs.

* * *

Richard paced his study, downing whiskey. He heard a noise and walked to the window in time to see Marisa driving away.

"Goddammit." He ran for the control panel to the gate.

Reed stood in front of it. "Let her go, Father."

"Get the hell out of my way." He pushed Reed aside and hurriedly punched in some numbers. He and Reed stood at the window and watched as the gate closed behind Marisa's car.

"Goddammit, Reed! Look what you've done. A split second more and the gate would've locked and she would've had to stay here, where she belongs."

"And what? Lock her in her room? She's not seventeen anymore."

"You don't know what the hell you're talking about," Richard yelled. "She's going straight to him and he'll destroy her—again."

"What's going on?" Vanessa asked, coming into the room. "Why are you yelling?"

"Marisa's gone and your son helped her leave."

Vanessa glared at Reed. "Why would you do that?"

"Because she needs some time and she needs her freedom. I see nothing wrong with that. You two act insane when it comes to Marisa. Let her live her own life, for a change." He stalked out of the room.

Vanessa stared at Richard. "She'll see him again. You know she will."

Richard nodded. "Yeah."

"Stop it before she gets hurt."

Richard reached for his whiskey. "I plan to."

Chapter 6

The weather had cleared and the ice had all melted, leaving the streets wet and slippery. Marisa drove very carefully. She knew that in a matter of minutes her father could have someone following her, so she had to think fast. She wouldn't let herself be brought back like a disobedient child. It didn't take her long to figure out a plan. She headed for Dalton's and parked in her usual spot, then called a cab using her cell phone. Once the driver had dropped her at a small café, she phoned Cari.

Marisa walked into the restaurant with her suitcase, clothes bag and purse, and found a booth in a corner facing the entrance. She ordered coffee, which she drank while she waited. Maybe she shouldn't have called Cari, but she desperately needed a friend right now.

Ten minutes later, Cari came through the door

and hurried toward her. She wore jeans and a heavy sweater, although her dark hair was still damp. She'd obviously just showered.

"I'm sorry," Marisa apologized, getting up and hugging her. "But I need to talk."

"No problem."

"Has my father called?"

"Oh, yes, and I have strict orders to call him the instant you show up. What on earth is going on?"

Marisa heaved a sigh. "It's a long story."

"Where are your shoes?" Cari asked, staring down at Marisa's feet in her heavy socks.

In her haste to leave, she'd forgotten to put on shoes and hadn't even noticed. "Ah." Marisa smiled. "I gave them to the sweetest little girl you'd ever want to meet."

"You gave your shoes away?"

"Yes. I did."

Cari frowned. "Are you okay? You're acting a little…strange."

"I *feel* a little strange."

"Let me get some coffee, and you can tell me this long story. Do you want some more?"

"No, thanks." Marisa resumed her seat.

Cari signaled a waitress, ordered coffee and slid into the booth.

For the next thirty minutes, Marisa told Cari everything that had happened since she'd left Dalton's yesterday.

"Oh, my. Your father sent the police out there. That's unbelievable."

"The deputy arrived, and I never got the chance to tell Colter about our son."

"So all of this was for nothing?"

Marisa fingered her cup. "No, not really. It made me see that I have to change my life. My parents control me like the proverbial puppet—they always have and I've let them. I'm finally breaking free. I'm quitting Dalton's and finding my own place to live, and next week I'll be looking for a job."

"A job?" Cari asked in disbelief. "Your family's wealthy and you have what everyone thinks of as the American dream. You don't have to work."

"The American dream, I believe, is making it on your own in this land of opportunity, and that's what I plan to do."

Cari shook her head. "I don't understand. I've had to struggle for everything I've gotten and sometimes the struggle's exhausting."

"But you feel good about succeeding by yourself— you've told me many times."

"Yeah. I only have a high school education but I took some business courses. I was determined to be more than a salesclerk."

"I want the same thing. To be a productive human being."

"So what's the plan?"

"I have to find a place to live."

"You can stay with me," Cari offered.

"If I did, you'd lose your job—the one you've worked so hard for."

"Hmm." Cari sipped her coffee.

"When you get back to your apartment, call my father. Tell him you saw me and that I refused to tell you where I was going." She smiled at her friend. "Because I'm not telling you. That way you won't have to lie."

"Marisa…"

"Sorry, no exceptions."

"But…"

"No," Marisa said, refusing to budge on that decision.

"Okay. You will call me from time to time to let me know how you're doing?"

Marisa nodded. "I'll do that."

Cari watched her for a moment. "So you gave your heels to Colter's daughter?"

"Yes. She's just a delight."

"You didn't feel any resentment toward her?"

"Not for a second. She has nothing to do with the past."

"Did you resent Colter?"

She gripped the cup more tightly. "At first I did. He and Shannon got married so quickly, and that hurt, but I have to take some responsibility there. That's what healing's about—admitting fault and taking responsibility." She pushed her cup away. "I'd better go before my father shows up."

"Marisa…"

"I'll be fine. Don't worry."

Marisa called a cab and left. She switched cabs several times, in case her father checked with the companies, then she bought a paper and checked into a motel. She didn't plan on being found too easily. After taking a shower, she scanned the want ads, looking for a place to stay. There were lots of apartments, but she felt the rents were too high. She wanted something she could afford on a working girl's salary. She was about to give up when she noticed a section describing rooms for rent. That would fit her requirement more closely; she wouldn't have to worry about furniture, and the rent would be lower.

She talked to a couple of the homeowners, but they didn't sound very appealing. The third one seemed pleasant, so she decided to have a look. The room was in an old Victorian house in an older part of Dallas. Getting out of the cab, she studied the house, which was attractive and well kept. The grounds, too, were nicely maintained, and the whole place had a warm, homey air.

She met Hazel Hackleberry, the owner, a short, plump friendly older woman whom Marisa liked the moment she shook her hand. Within minutes, Marisa had become her boarder. The room itself was white and pink with a lot of frills and lace, but Marisa didn't care. It would be her home for now.

The next day she moved in, and bought a used car because she couldn't continue to spend money on cabs. On Monday, she began searching for a job. She spent the entire week submitting applications and attending interviews, with no luck. She had a business degree, but once a firm became aware of her connection to Richard Preston, she was no longer considered a viable employee. Her father had put the word out— don't hire her.

Meanwhile she settled comfortably into Mrs. Hackleberry's house. Hazel was the motherly type, and although she'd told Marisa that meals weren't provided, she invited her to dinner almost every night. Hazel's only son had been killed in Vietnam and her sister lived next door. Other than that she had little family, and Marisa knew she was lonely.

There was a large Steinway in the living room. Every time Marisa passed it she itched to play. One evening, without really thinking about it, she sat down on the piano bench and ran her fingers across the keys. She hadn't touched a piano since her son's death. It felt so natural, though. So right. She played a Chopin piece, but the piano needed tuning. Still, she was lost in the music.

"Oh, my dear," Mrs. Hackleberry said, listening. "You play beautifully."

She turned on the bench. "Thank you. Do you play?"

Hazel shook her head. "Good Lord, no. My aunt left me the piano. Why, I don't know. I never played a day in my life."

"Do you mind if I play while I'm here?" Marisa couldn't believe the words coming out of her mouth. For years, she had ignored her training and avoided anything to do with music, but now she felt liberated. Maybe it was seeing Colter again. Maybe it was her bid for freedom. Or maybe she was finally letting go of the past.

"No. I'd enjoy it."

"Do you mind if I get it tuned?" she asked, then quickly added, "I'll pay for it."

"Go ahead," Hazel replied. "It's time someone used that old thing."

The next day Marisa had the piano tuned. On impulse, she stopped by the Dallas Symphony Orchestra. She was almost high with excitement when the conductor granted her an interview and then an audition. He seemed pleased with her work and said he'd be in touch after the winter season. She intended to pursue her music—her way this time. But now she had to find a job.

That night after dinner, Marisa played for Hazel, then sat at the table going through the want ads again, searching for a job.

"You can't find a job?" Hazel asked.

"No. My father's pretty well closed most doors." When she'd rented the room, she'd told Hazel some of the reasons she needed it. Later, she'd confided more. Hazel was easy to talk to, and Marisa felt she was lucky to find this place.

"I wish I could help, but I used to be a seamstress and that's all I know."

"Oh. Who did you work for?"

"Madame Hélèna."

Marisa's head jerked up. "You worked for Madame Hélèna, the designer?"

"Yes. Do you know her?"

"Just her work. She's very famous."

"We dressed some of the most important people in the world," Hazel said with pride. "When Hélèna first started, it was just the two of us sewing, but now she has factories full of workers turning out her designs."

"I love her work," Marisa said. "Her line is sleek yet simple."

"Would you like to meet her?"

"Oh, Hazel, no. I wasn't fishing for an invitation."

"It's not an invitation. It's an offer. Hélèna's always looking for good help."

"That would be wonderful. Do you think she's hiring?"

"I'll give her a call and find out."

Marisa waited, her heart in her throat, hardly able to believe her luck. She needed this. She needed a break.

Hazel wrote something on a piece of paper and laid it in front of Marisa. "That's the address. Be there at nine and don't be late. Hélèna likes a responsible person."

"I won't—and thank you." Marisa got up and hugged her. Marisa had trouble hugging her own mother, but with Hazel it was so easy. She knew the healing process had started now, and sometime soon she might be able to talk to her parents again. They had left her alone, which she found rather suspicious, but she was grateful for it. Marisa supposed they were waiting for her to fall on her face. She wouldn't, though. She was going to make it.

She *had* to get this job.

Later, she picked out clothes for the interview, took a shower, then crawled into bed. Excitement trickled through her and, try as she might, she couldn't keep thoughts of Colter at bay. All week she'd tried not to think about him and his little girl. At times she succeeded and at others she didn't. She'd had his sister's clothes cleaned, packaged and mailed to him, with a note that said simply, "Thanks for lending me these." No signature. Her own clothes were still at his place, and she was sure he'd probably thrown them out.

She turned over in bed and smiled, imagining Ellie

in her heels. She hoped Colter let her keep them. Flipping onto her back, she wondered if Ellie was still searching for a mother; she'd never know, because she'd never see them again. Her excitement turned to sadness but she fought it. She had to. There was no other choice.

Marisa was at Madame Hélèna's office at 8:45 a.m., and she couldn't believe how nervous she was. She straightened the jacket of her dark green suit three times before she forced herself to stop.

Madame Hélèna walked in promptly at 9:00 a.m. Marisa had only seen pictures of her and was surprised she was so petite. Barely five feet, she was slim and elegant, with auburn hair worn in a knot.

She stared at Marisa. "So you're Marisa Preston?" She spoke with a slight accent.

"Yes, ma'am," Marisa answered, and shook her hand.

Bracelets dangled from Hélèna's wrist, and she wore a beaded choker that complemented the sleek raw silk dress with its V-neck. Marisa recognized the style as one of Madame Hélèna's.

"Have a seat." Hélèna sat, too, putting on a pair of glasses, and looked through some papers on her desk. "Hazel says you're looking for a job."

"Yes."

Hélèna leaned back. "Why, *chérie?* Your father is rich."

"I've been pampered and smothered all my life. I need freedom and I need to make it on my own." Marisa tried to be as honest as she could.

"I understand that. I was born in Paris and I met an American GI and fell in love. He brought me to Dallas and I thought I was in hell. I hated it here, but I loved the man more. I gave birth to a son and became very domesticated—and then my husband died. I didn't know what to do. I could sew, so I started sewing for people—anything to feed my son and me. Dallas women were willing to spend extra money for an original dress. I tapped into that. Word got around and soon my business was flourishing. But there were a lot of people who tried to stop me." She paused. "Richard Preston was one of those people."

Marisa swallowed. "Oh."

"He resented that I was taking business away from Dalton's, but I stuck it out, and today I have shops here, in New York, Los Angeles and in my beloved Paris."

Marisa was unsure of how to respond, so she nodded. "Yes, I know. Your designs are very popular."

"Ten years ago, I would've hired you in a second to settle that score with Richard, but I don't have time for revenge anymore."

Marisa's heart sank. "Are you saying you're not hiring me?"

"I'm saying I won't indulge your whim to get back at your father."

Marisa slid forward, perching on the edge of her chair. "Madame Hélèna, this isn't about getting back at my father. It's about my independence. I have to work to pay my bills and, before you ask, I'm not taking money from my father. I have to find out who I am— All I'm asking for is a chance."

Hélèna studied her for a moment, then leaned forward. "What do you know about fashion?"

"I know what I like."

Hélèna stood. "Come with me." They went through a door into a large studio crowded with easels, rolls and rolls of fabric, mannequins and everything else a designer might need. Hélèna went to a drawing board. "This is a dress I'm working on. What do you think?"

Marisa looked over her shoulder at the drawing— a straight black dress with long sleeves and, again, a modified V-neck. "Very nice," she murmured. "Simple but classy—something that could be worn to almost any formal occasion. And that neckline works for practically every woman."

Hélèna picked up a pencil. "Yes. I'm debating whether to put the slit up the back of the skirt or on the side."

"The side. It shows off the leg and is more attractive." When she realized what she'd done, she immediately apologized. "I'm sorry—"

Hélèna turned to her. "Never be afraid to voice your opinion, *chérie*. You have good instincts about fashion. The slit up the side *is* better—makes a woman feel sexy, and we need that every once in a while." She laid the pencil down. "If you want a job," she said abruptly, "you've got it. Just be prepared to do whatever is asked of you. You might run errands, wait on customers, answer the phone, check in freight, whatever."

"Yes, ma'am. I'm willing to do anything."

"You'll start on Monday and I'll give you a week's trial run. If it works out, we'll talk about something permanent."

"Thank you, Madame Hélèna. Thank you so much."

Marisa left walking about six feet off the ground. She had a job and a place to live; things could only get better from here on.

She called Cari and told her the good news. Cari was genuinely happy for her, and said Richard had stopped pressuring her for information. Surely that meant he and her mother were finally going to let her live her life. She and Cari talked for a while, and Marisa told her where she was living, since it seemed her parents weren't going to bother Cari anymore.

Before she could end the call, Cari said, "I wanted to tell you the cradle's been sold."

"Oh." She felt a moment of sadness, as she did every year when it went. But some lucky couple had purchased it for their baby and that was the way it should be.

"Marisa?"

"Hmm?"

"I don't know why you don't buy it yourself. You love it."

"The cradle is meant for a couple waiting for the birth of their child."

"Marisa—"

"I'm all right," she said before Cari could ask. "I'm glad it has a home."

They talked for a few more minutes, then Marisa said goodbye and hung up. She stared at the phone, wondering why she was so attached to that cradle. But she knew. It represented all the happiness a baby was supposed to bring, and it spoke about the true meaning and joy of Christmas. She'd wanted all of that for her son and, yes, she'd wanted it for herself, too. But some things weren't meant to be.

She started to call Reed, but she'd talked to him yesterday and told him she was fine. That was all he needed to know. She didn't want to put him in the middle again.

Marisa went to bed feeling good about herself and her life. She was determined to work very hard for Madame Hélèna and she'd practice her music at night. For the first time in ages she looked forward to tomorrow.

Colter received the package of clothes from Marisa and went upstairs to put them in Becky's closet. He stopped short as he entered the room. Marisa's clothes were strewn across the bed. He hadn't even been up here since that night, and he'd forgotten about them. What was he supposed to do with her things?

He laid the package on the dresser, then picked up the linen dress. A faint scent of lilac drifted to his nostrils. She'd worn the same fragrance in Vegas, and it wrapped him in captivating memories.

No, no, no. He wouldn't do this to himself. Throwing the dress onto the bed, he left. He couldn't let himself get caught in that maelstrom of emotion. The whole week had been nerve-racking as he waited for a second impromptu visit, but she'd stayed away. He suspected her parents had something to do with that. He was just glad she wasn't going to disrupt his life again.

As he reached the bottom of the stairs, the phone rang. It was his sister, Becky.

"I've got bad news," she said without preamble. "Jen's having a problem with the pregnancy and the doctor's ordered complete bed rest."

"Is she okay? Is the baby okay?"

"Yes. The doctor said she and the baby are fine, but she has to stay off her feet until the delivery. The baby's due in February, so this makes it a little harder for Bart and me. Bart and I have the McKinney Western Stores on our schedule for next week. As you know, they'll be carrying your boots in their outlets in Austin, and I have it all set up for you to visit each store. The newspaper ads have all gone out."

"We'll just cancel. Jen and the baby are more important."

"No way are we canceling, big brother. It took Bart and me a year to arrange this. We're working out a routine with Jen. Bart's mom's going to help out while we're in Austin, then I'm taking two weeks off and Bart's taking two weeks at Christmas."

"Sounds as if you've got it all figured out."

"Not everything. Christmas does present a problem. We've always spent it together at the ranch, but since Jen can't travel, we were hoping that you, Ellie and Tulley would come to Jen's house."

"I don't know, Bec. Ellie's never been away from home at Christmas."

"Just think about it and we'll talk again."

"Okay. I'll give Jen a call, too."

Colter hung up, hoping Jen and the baby were okay. She and Bart had been trying for years to conceive, and he didn't want anything to go wrong. He wanted only happiness for both his sisters. The three of them had been so close since their mother's death, and then, when Shannon had left, his sisters had helped him with Ellie. Ellie was barely three months old at the time, and he'd hoped Shannon would come back, but when he got the divorce papers he knew that wasn't happening. He'd decided he would tell Ellie very little about Shannon. Maybe that had been a mistake. Maybe—

He yanked up the phone and called Jen. She seemed in good spirits, so he felt immeasurably better.

As he finished the call, Ellie and Sooner bounded into the room. Tulley followed at a leisurely pace.

"Hey, Daddy." Ellie propped her elbows on the table, her face in her hands, staring at him, and his pulse accelerated at the love he felt for his child. "You should've seen me! Dandy goes around the barrels so fast Tulley says all he sees is a streak. She's the best barrel racer we've ever had and I don't even have to guide her. She knows what to do. She's awesome."

He smiled. "*You're* awesome—and you're out of breath."

Ellie gulped in air. "I know. Dandy goes so fast."

Tulley removed his hat and sat down. "Shorty's right. Dandy's a good barrel-racing horse. Sassy's, too."

"When can I ride in the rodeo, Daddy? When?"

"When you're old enough."

"When's that?"

"When I say so." He'd ridden in rodeos, so Ellie wanted to do the same thing, but he tried to deter her in every way he could. He wanted a better life for her, one that included a good education, but she loved horses and she got that from him. She was good at it, too. And it didn't help that Tulley encouraged her. Or that Shannon had been a championship barrel racer.

"Aw, you always say that."

He changed the subject. "Aunt Becky just called."

Ellie's eyes grew big. "Is she coming here today?"

"No." Then he told them what Becky had said.

A sad expression came over Ellie's face and she crawled into Colter's lap. "Is the baby gonna be okay?"

"Sure, angelface, the baby's fine," he reassured her. "But Becky wanted to know if we'd come to Jen's for Christmas, because Jen can't travel."

Ellie jumped up, shaking her head. "No! We can't do that."

Colter frowned, not sure what this was about. "Why?"

"'Cause I *can't* leave. Santa knows where I live and I have to be here. If I go to Aunt Jen's, he won't know where I'm at and I won't get my wish."

"Ellie…"

"We can't go, Daddy," she said, turning and running to her room. Sooner sprinted after her.

Colter sighed in frustration. "I'm getting tired of this mother-Santa thing. I should just go in there and tell her there's no damn Santa Claus. What do you think?"

Tulley scratched his head. "I think I'm not going to be the one to break her heart."

"Dammit, Tulley. She doesn't want to leave because she's waiting for her mother to come back."

"Well, if you're going to tell her there's no Santa, then you'll have to tell her the truth about her mother. Are you ready to do that?"

"No," he replied in a wooden voice. He'd never be ready to do that. He'd never be ready to tell Ellie her mother didn't want her.

Not ever.

Chapter 7

The week passed quickly for Marisa. She was at Madame Hélèna's early every day, and she stayed late. At first, she did everything from answering the phone to waiting on customers. Then Hélèna asked her to work in her private office, and she ran errands, reminded her of appointments, answered her mail and tried to calm her when she became enraged at a store or supplier. Marisa didn't mind any of it; she enjoyed the excitement and the challenge. It became very clear that the famous designer had a temper and none of her staff wanted to risk her ire.

On Thursday, as Marisa was getting ready to leave, Madame Hélèna asked to speak with her. It was after nine and Marisa was tired, but she didn't complain. This was what being in the workforce was like—long days, tired muscles and aching bones. She'd never felt like this in her life and she was exhilarated. Cari said she was crazy, but all the work and effort meant freedom and independence to Marisa.

"I know you're anxious to go home," Hélèna said, frowning over a sketch.

"Not if you need something." Marisa liked the fact that she could help someone instead of being waited on.

Hélèna took off her glasses. "I told you I'd give you a week's trial."

Marisa's stomach tensed. "Yes."

"I thought I'd tell you my decision tonight instead of waiting until tomorrow."

Marisa held her breath.

"You have a permanent job here and—"

"Oh, thank you!"

Hélèna held up a hand. "Let me finish. The job will be as my personal assistant. Very few people can work with me on a day-to-day basis. I'm told I have a temper and that I'm not nice sometimes, but you seem to take all my idiosyncrasies in stride. Besides, you have an eye for fashion and I appreciate that and the number of hours you're willing to put in. So what do you say?"

Marisa smiled. "I say yes."

"Good." Hélèna scribbled something on a piece of paper and handed it to her. "That will be your monthly salary, and you'll be paid every two weeks."

Marisa stared at the figure. "This is very generous."

"You'll earn every dime of it," Hélèna said. "Richard's a fool not to recognize your potential." Hélèna reached for her glasses. "My son, who's also my business manager, tells me it's not wise to hire Richard

Preston's daughter, but I've always been a good judge of people—it's one of the assets that got me where I am today—and I trust you implicitly, Marisa."

"Oh, yes, ma'am, I know that everything is confidential."

Hélèna nodded. "All the information you see or hear in this office is extremely private and not to be discussed with anyone."

"I would never—"

"I know, *chérie,*" Hélèna cut in, "and I wish you were going to be with me for a very long time."

Marisa frowned slightly. "Why wouldn't I be?"

"Like I said, I can read people, and you're searching for yourself, your place in the world. I hope it's here, but I feel your heart is somewhere else."

Colter's face flashed into her mind. Tears welled up in her eyes, and she was unable to stop them.

Hélèna got up and put an arm around her. "*Chérie,* what is it?"

In a few sentences, Marisa blurted out everything about Colter, their child and the past. She hadn't meant to but Hélèna's sympathy was her undoing.

Hélèna led her to a small settee and urged her to sit down. "Now I understand the sadness in your eyes," she said quietly.

Marisa wiped at the tears on her cheeks. "I'm sorry. I shouldn't be bothering you with this."

"*Chérie,* affairs of the heart can be so painful. I lost the love of my life and I never found anyone to replace him, so I threw myself into my work. That's what you're trying to do—lose yourself in something."

'That deep pain is always there, though."

"Ah, *chérie,* you have to face those demons from the past, and you've made a great start by striking out on your own. You've said you don't know who you are, but I do."

Marisa blinked away tears. "You do?"

"Yes, you're a warm, compassionate woman. A sweet woman. As a matter of fact, you're so sweet, I'm sure you bleed honey."

"Thank you." Marisa smiled.

"Now, go to Hazel's and you don't have to come in so early tomorrow morning."

"Oh, no. I'll be here at my usual time."

Hélèna smiled. "I failed to mention responsible, loyal and dedicated."

Marisa gave her a quick hug—she'd never done that before, but it felt completely natural. Then she drove home.

When she reached the house, Hazel came hurrying from the den.

"You're back. I was getting worried," she said.

"Hazel, you're not to worry about me," Marisa scolded in a gentle tone.

"I know, but you're so young and inexperienced and—"

She raised an eyebrow, and Hazel backpedaled. "Have you had anything to eat?"

Marisa held up the bag in her hand. "I bought something at a deli."

"I'll get you some tea."

"No." Marisa shook her head. "I'll get my own tea. You go to bed. It's past your bedtime."

"Okay. I am getting a little tired."

"Good night, Hazel—and, oh, I almost forgot. Madame Héléna hired me as her personal assistant."

"That's wonderful. I'm so happy." Hazel smiled, then yawned. "I'd better go to bed. 'Night."

"'Night," she called.

Marisa was exhausted, and she could barely stay awake to eat her dinner. The exhaustion was very satisfying, though. She went to bed soon after, but dreams of Colter kept her tossing and turning.

Colter spent the week driving back and forth to Dallas to check on Jen, whose good spirits had turned to boredom because she had to stay in bed. She and Bart lived close to the office and the factory that made Kincaid Boots. He tried to cheer her up with talk of Christmas, although they still hadn't made a decision about where to have their get-together. Jen's focus was now on the baby.

He hadn't spoken to Ellie about Christmas again, because he didn't want to trigger a scene. But he'd have to broach the subject, and soon. In his view, her obsession with Santa Claus was out of control.

On Friday, Becky had him scheduled to put in appearances at the stores in Austin that would be carrying Kincaid Boots. Ellie's last day of school was Thursday, so he had decided to take her with him. To his surprise, that plan was met with resistance.

"I can't, Daddy. I have to go to Lori's birthday party. She's my best friend."

He rubbed his temple. "I forgot about that." This presented a quandary. He didn't like leaving Ellie anywhere, but now that she was older it was getting increasingly harder to avoid.

"I can stay at Lori's. Her mommy said so."

"Tulley and I are flying to Austin. Aunt Becky and Uncle Bart are already there. You like meeting people and you've even signed a few autographs." He was trying to cajole her; he couldn't help himself. He wanted Ellie with him.

"I know." She twisted her feet, inner turmoil evident on her face, and he cursed himself for making her feel guilty.

He pulled her onto his lap, kissing her quickly. "Okay, Ellie. You go to Lori's, and I'll pick you up when I get back."

She covered his face with kisses. "Thank you, Daddy."

Ellie ran to her room, and he sighed. He didn't understand why he felt so reluctant about this. He just didn't like being away from her.

Ellie sat on the floor in her room, rubbing Sooner's head. "We gotta have a plan," she said.

Sooner barked. "I *know* Daddy's gonna be mad, but I hafta do this. We might be going to Aunt Jen's for Christmas and I hafta see Santa. I really do."

Ellie thought for a minute. "We need money." She got up and opened a drawer and counted her savings. "Twelve dollars and fifty-two cents. That's not enough."

Sooner whined. "Okay, but I'm telling Daddy you told me to do it." She walked to the door and looked in the hall. "Bark if you see Daddy."

She hurried to her father's room. She knew where he kept extra cash—inside his sock drawer. Opening the drawer, she slipped her hand beneath the socks and pulled out a hundred-dollar bill. "That should do it," she murmured, stuffing it in her pocket. "Daddy, please don't be mad at me. I *hafta* do this."

The next morning Colter dropped Ellie at Lori's house. Ellie insisted on taking Sooner, which puzzled him, but Ellie said she'd promised Sooner he could go to the party. He called Gail, Lori's mom, to make sure it was okay; she told him it was fine, that all the kids loved the dog.

Colter still had misgivings, although he couldn't explain exactly what they were. Ellie was nervous and excited, and that was the way she should be, he told himself. She was going to a birthday party for her best friend.

But something wasn't right. He felt it in his gut.

He hugged Ellie tightly, hoping his fatherly instincts were wrong. On the drive to the airport and the flight into Austin, he kept thinking about it. He finally put it down to overprotectiveness. Ellie was growing up, and he had to let her—and he had to stop analyzing all her moods.

Their lives had been fine until Marisa showed up. Now he was on edge all the time. Why did he go to Dalton's that day? Why did he see her? And why couldn't he stop thinking about her?

That Friday, Marisa had a busy day. Madame Hélèna was flying to her New York office, and Marisa had a list of things to do before she left. Her son was picking her up in an hour. Marisa packed the designs and swatches of fabric Hélèna had requested. In another case were various reports and sales figures she wanted to share with her New York staff.

Marisa had just finished when the phone rang. She picked it up as Hélèna walked into the room.

"Marisa, it's Cari. I have a problem."

Marisa glanced at Hélèna, hoping she didn't mind a personal call. "What is it?" Marisa felt sure it concerned her father, and she braced herself.

"I have someone here who wants to see you."

"Who?"

"Ellie Kincaid."

Marisa almost dropped the phone. "What...what's she doing there?"

"She said you promised her she could talk to Santa Claus."

"Oh, yes, I did, but I never dreamed Colter would bring her."

"I haven't seen him—just Ellie and a big dog who caused a scene downstairs. That's why they called me. I have her and the dog in my office. I think you need to get over here."

Marisa glanced at Hélèna again. She didn't want to jeopardize her job, but she'd made a promise to Ellie and she had to keep it.

"I'll get there as soon as I can."

"Your father's not in this afternoon, so you don't have to worry about running into him."

"Thanks, Cari."

She hung up, wondering how to explain this to

Hélèna. Before she could find the words, Hélèna spoke up. "Where do you have to go, *chérie?*"

Marisa told her about Ellie and her promise.

"I see." Hélèna rummaged through the mail on her desk. "Have you finished everything I asked you to do today?"

"Yes, ma'am, and your son should be here in about thirty minutes."

"Then go." Hélèna waved a hand. "Everyone should believe in Santa Claus."

Marisa grabbed her coat. "Thank you. I'll come in early tomorrow."

'Tomorrow is Saturday, *chérie,* so take the weekend off. I'll expect you back first thing Monday."

"Yes, ma'am," Marisa said. "Have a good trip," she added, hurrying out the door.

She parked in the customers' parking lot of Dalton's and went into the store, taking the escalator to Cari's office.

Opening the door slightly, she saw Ellie sitting in a chair, feet dangling. Sooner lay on the floor watching her. She didn't see Colter. *Where was he?*

When she stepped into the room, Ellie leaped up. "Ms. Preston, it's me! I came to see Santa Claus."

"Hi, Ellie."

"I'll wait outside," Cari said.

"Thanks," Marisa answered. "But could I speak with you first?"

"Sure."

"I'll be right back," she said to Ellie, following Cari into the hall. "What happened?"

"Like I said, I got a call from downstairs that a

girl and a dog were in the children's department. The dog was barking his head off, and the little girl kept saying she had to see Ms. Preston. I brought them up here. Could've knocked me over with a feather when she told me her name. I paged Colter on the intercom and got no response."

"So he's not in the store?"

Cari shrugged. "He never answered the page."

Marisa nodded, frowning. "I wonder how she got here—and if Colter knows where she is."

"I'll let you find that out while I go get the man I hired to play Santa."

"Thanks, Cari."

Marisa went back into the room.

"Is he coming?" Ellie asked, her voice excited.

Marisa sat beside her. "Where's your father?"

"I can't tell you." Ellie stuck out her chin.

"I see," she said, knowing she'd have to be tough to get anything out of Ellie. "You can't see Santa until you tell me."

"Oh." Ellie's eyes widened.

"Where's your father?" Marisa asked again. If Colter didn't know where Ellie was, he must be extremely worried, and she had to notify him.

Marisa's serious tone obviously made an impact on Ellie, because she started talking. "He's in Austin."

"Austin!"

"Yeah. Some western stores are carrying Daddy's boots, and he goes there to meet people and sign autographs. I wanted to go, but I couldn't. I had to see Santa, and this was my only chance 'cause Daddy wouldn't let me come if he was home." Ellie looked at Marisa. "He doesn't like you."

"How did you get here?" she asked, trying not to show how those words affected her. Colter couldn't hide his hostility even from his child.

"My best friend had a birthday party, and her mom said Sooner and me could spend the day. When the party was over, Lori and I called a cab—we found it in the phone book—and it brought me here."

"Where's your friend now?"

"She didn't come. She was scared she'd get punished. Just Sooner and me came."

"Does your friend live in Dallas?"

"No. In Mesquite."

"You took a cab from Mesquite to Dallas?" She couldn't keep the shock out of her voice.

"Yeah, and I don't have any money left to get back to Lori's. The man said it was extra for Sooner."

"Where'd you get the money?"

The child squirmed.

"Ellie?"

"I took it out of Daddy's extra cash."

"Oh, Ellie."

"I know I did a bad thing and I'll probably be grounded for the rest of my life, but I *hafta* see Santa."

"Why is it so important that you see Santa?"

"Well, I wrote him a bunch of times asking for a mommy. I do that every Christmas, but I never got one. This year he could be sending me a mommy, and I have to tell him I might not be home for Christmas. I hafta be there when she comes." Her eyes searched Marisa's. "You *will* let me see him, won't you?"

Marisa's heart ached for this little girl who wanted a mother so badly, and she couldn't deny her wish. "Yes, but you have to give me your father's and Lori's phone numbers."

Marisa got a pencil and paper, and Ellie rattled off the numbers, along with Colter's cell.

"What's Lori's mother's name?"

"Gail Freeman."

Marisa called Colter's cell phone first, but there was no answer. She got Gail, who didn't even realize Ellie wasn't there. Lori and Ellie were supposed to be playing in Lori's room. She became agitated when she found out what Ellie and Lori had done. Marisa assured her Ellie was fine and that she'd continue to try to reach Colter.

Gail said that they were going to her mother's for Lori's family celebration in a little while, but she would come and get Ellie. Marisa told her there was no need, that she'd take Ellie home. Gail gave in reluctantly. Marisa hung up, wondering if she'd done the right thing. Colter was not going to appreciate her coming to his home again.

"Is she really mad?" Ellie asked, her face puckered in a frown.

Marisa sat beside her again. "Worried is more like it, and I have to continue trying to call your father."

"Okay," Ellie said in a quiet voice.

Marisa turned to her. "It was so dangerous to take a cab from Mesquite to Dallas by yourself."

"I know. Daddy talked to me about strangers, but I took Sooner. He protects me. Except when we got in the store, he got scared."

Sooner barked.

"You *were* scared, Sooner. So don't say you weren't."

Sooner barked more loudly.

"Be quiet." Ellie put a finger to her lips.

Marisa suppressed a smile. This was a serious situation, but it was delightful to be around Ellie and Sooner.

"Ellie." Marisa got her attention. "Promise you won't ever do anything like this again."

Ellie's face creased in thought. "You have to keep a promise, right?"

"Right."

Ellie shook her head. "Then I can't promise."

Marisa was stunned, and she couldn't hide her reaction.

"Daddy says not to lie and I don't want to lie," the child explained. "He says I think about a mommy too much, but I can't help it. Around Christmas it's all I think about. I knew coming today was wrong, but I *had* to. My mommy might come this Christmas, and I have to let her know I want her to. Santa will make it happen 'cause I believe."

Marisa's throat closed up. That was it. That was what Ellie's obsession was really about—wanting her mother to come home. Subconsciously, it had probably always been her desire, which was understandable in a child her age. She wondered if Shannon knew how much her daughter wanted her. Or if Colter had even told Shannon.

"Ellie, are you hoping your mother will come home?"

The child fidgeted in her chair. "Maybe I just want a mommy."

"Oh, Ellie." Marisa's heart broke and she wanted to comfort the little girl and— No! That was Colter's job. Still…

She didn't have time to consider that now, because there was a tap at the door. She opened the door to a man dressed completely in white: suit, shoes, shirt, tie—even his long hair and beard were white.

"I'm here to see Ellie Kincaid," he said, then added in a low voice, "I'm Santa Claus."

Marisa just stared at him. He was in his seventies and he fit the Santa persona to a tee, including the rounded stomach and red cheeks, except he didn't have on a red costume. But that was minor. Cari had done a great job in hiring someone so authentic.

She stepped aside, and as he entered the room, Ellie got to her feet. "Are you Santa?"

He nodded. "Yes. I'm Santa Claus."

"Where's your red suit?"

"I only wear it when I'm seeing children in the stores or riding in my sleigh. This is the suit I wear at home—and for seeing special little girls."

"Oh."

He sat in a chair and Ellie climbed onto his knee. "What did you want to see me about, little angel?"

"I wrote you a lot of letters asking for a mommy, and you never sent me one. This year we might have to go to my aunt Jen's for Christmas so I had to tell you I might not be at home. I didn't want you to send her if I'm not there."

"Don't worry. I know where you are at all times."

"You do?" Ellie's eyes grew enormous.

"Yes, and I'm not happy about what you did today. You're not ever to do that again."

"Yes, sir," Ellie answered, hanging her head.

For a moment, Marisa was perplexed. How did he know what Ellie had done? Oh, Cari must've told him. She'd almost believed he was the real thing.

"Am I ever gonna get my mommy?" Ellie twisted her hands.

"Don't fret, little one," he said. "You'll have your mommy before Christmas."

Ellie's head jerked up. "I will?"

"Yes. Now I have to go. I have lots to do before the twenty-fifth."

Ellie threw her arms around his neck. "Thank you." She leaned back and tugged on his beard.

"Why'd you do that?"

"My friend Lori says you're not real and that your beard is fake, but it *is* real, just like I told her."

He stood, setting Ellie on her feet. "Yes, little one, I'm real. Never be afraid to believe—belief is a very powerful thing."

"I won't," Ellie promised.

The man walked to the door and then stopped. He touched the back of his hand to Marisa's face. "You're never too old to believe, Marisa."

She was so surprised by his touch, and the sincerity in his eyes, that words eluded her.

"She believes," Ellie told him.

He exited the room and Marisa stared after him, feeling even more perplexed. *What did he mean? And how did he know my name?*

Chapter 8

Marisa called Colter again in case he hadn't received the first message, then she took Ellie and Sooner home. Cari had a meeting, so she didn't have a chance to talk to her about the Santa Claus, which she planned to do later.

Today the weather was much nicer than the last time she'd made the trip out to the ranch. The temperature was in the fifties and a pale sun shone. Ellie sat in the front seat, Sooner in the back, and Ellie chatted nonstop. She was in a very good mood, thanks to Santa, but Marisa felt sure Colter would change all that the minute he got home.

Ellie knew where the key was and let them into the house. Sooner whined plaintively.

"Okay. Okay," Ellie said, and ran into the kitchen. "I gotta feed Sooner."

Marisa took a seat at the table, wondering why Colter hadn't called.

* * *

Colter hurried to his truck at the airport, cursing that he'd left his cell phone inside. He always kept it with him when he was away from Ellie, but this morning he'd been in such a state over leaving that he'd placed it on the seat and forgotten it.

He'd called Gail once from a store and she had said everything was fine. When he tried again, he didn't get an answer. That worried him.

In the truck, he picked up the phone. "Dammit."

"What?" Tulley asked, closing the door.

"There are two messages from Gail and two from Marisa."

"Marisa?" Tulley's eyebrow shot up.

"There's only one way she could have gotten my cell number."

"Ellie," they said in unison.

"What the hell's going on?"

"Listen to the messages," Tulley suggested.

All of them were the same: *call as soon as possible*. He called Gail's cell first and his blood ran cold at the story she told him. As he relayed it to Tulley, he gripped the steering wheel until his knuckles turned white.

"She took a cab from Lori's to see Santa?" Tulley asked in a horrified tone. "What in the world possessed her to do such a thing?"

"Marisa," Colter said from between clenched teeth. "She told Ellie she could have a private sitting with him."

"Lordy, lordy, this is getting out of hand."

"I'm putting a stop to it once and for all." He punched in Marisa's cell number.

He heard her soft, tantalizing voice and it made him that much angrier. "Where's my daughter?"

"I brought her home to the ranch," Marisa answered.

"You're at my house?" he asked, taken aback.

"Yes. I didn't know where else to take her."

"This is all your fault." He couldn't stop the angry words. "If you hadn't encouraged her, none of this would've happened."

"I didn't—"

"Listen," he snapped. "Stay with her until I get there. Don't you dare leave her by herself."

"I would never do such a thing."

"Yeah, right." He clicked off before his anger completely overtook him.

Once again Marisa felt the brunt of his anger, but she tried not to let it upset her. Turning to Ellie, she noticed the little girl had removed her coat and was standing on a chair pulled up to the cabinet, busily applying butter to a pile of toast.

"What are you doing?" she asked as she watched her continue to toast bread, four slices at a time, butter it and stack the toast higher.

"This is for Sooner."

"You're making toast for the *dog?*"

"Yep," she said, jumping down from the chair. "Sooner's real mad at me 'cause I got him in trouble. So I'm making his favorite food. When he eats all this toast, he won't be mad at me anymore."

"Oh," Marisa said for lack of anything better to reply. Somehow she felt that Colter would not approve.

"Is Daddy mad?" Ellie asked.

Mad was a mild word for Colter's reaction, and she hoped he'd be patient and understanding with Ellie.

"Let's just say he's not happy," Marisa replied.

Ellie's face crumpled, and she picked up the plate of toast and quickly ran out the back door, Sooner whining at her heels.

Marisa was caught in the middle and she didn't understand how that had happened. Colter had said it was her fault. Maybe it was, maybe she'd been too eager to help Ellie see Santa Claus. She'd made such a mistake in coming here that first day, but it was a little late to change that. It was too late to change anything.

Ellie came back and settled in a chair. "I'm sorry I upset everybody."

"You scared me by taking such a risk, and I'm sure your father feels the same way. I'm just happy you're all right."

"You're nice. You're pretty, too," Ellie said, studying Marisa's face.

The compliment took Marisa by surprise, but she smiled. "Thank you. And you're a very pretty little girl."

"Daddy says I'm going to be beautiful, just like my mother."

Colter thought Shannon was beautiful. She experienced a pang of jealousy and forcefully pushed it away. Why hadn't they stayed together? Why hadn't they made a home for Ellie?

"Of course, I've never seen her, so I don't know

what she looks like." Ellie's words cut through her thoughts.

"You've never seen your mother?" The words charged out of their own volition.

Ellie shook her head. "No, she left after I was born."

Marisa could hear the wistfulness in the tiny voice and felt an intense dislike for Shannon. How could she do this to Ellie?

As if reading her mind, the girl murmured, "Daddy said she left 'cause she was unhappy. It wasn't 'cause she didn't love me. She lives way off on a ranch and she's a champion barrel racer. I'm gonna be one, too."

Ellie was silent for a moment, and Marisa was unsure of what to say.

Ellie squirmed in her chair. "Santa's sending my mommy."

"Please don't get your hopes up." Marisa had to say it. She would also have a talk with Cari about Mr. Santa promising children things he couldn't deliver.

Ellie looked into her eyes. "I believe, Ms. Preston. Don't you?"

"Call me Marisa," she invited, hoping Colter wouldn't mind.

"Okay," Ellie said. "She'll come back. I know it."

"Ellie—"

The sound of a truck stopped her.

"Uh-oh. Daddy's home."

Tulley caught Colter's arm before he could get out. "Take a deep breath and calm down."

He exhaled deeply. "I am so angry."

"I know, and anger never solves anything. Ellie's a

little girl searching for answers and it's time you told her the truth about her mother. That's the only way all of this is going to stop."

"None of this would've started if Marisa hadn't put ideas in her head."

"Stop blaming Marisa for everything," Tulley said. "Ellie had these ideas before Marisa ever showed up."

Colter glared at him. "You're taking *her* side?"

"I'm stoutly on your side—always have been—always will be, but it's time to lay the past on the table and sort through all the painful stuff. You blame Marisa for everything that happened to you after she left, so tell her. Tell her the whole damn story. That's the only way you're ever going to get over your feelings for her."

Colter began to speak, but Tulley held up his hand. "Don't say you feel nothing for her. I see it in your eyes every time you look at her and I see it in her eyes, too. You have Ellie, and she and Marisa seem to have a connection. So tell Marisa about Ellie and Shannon, and take it from there."

"You're asking the impossible," Colter muttered, but his anger was easing.

"Maybe. You do best, though, when the odds are stacked against you."

Colter got out of the truck without another word. On the walk into the house, Tulley added, "Go easy on Ellie. And you might think about going easy on Marisa."

Colter appeared in the doorway dressed in jeans, boots and a leather jacket. Marisa's stomach tightened.

His eyes were worried and rimmed with shadows of resentment.

Ellie got out of her chair and stood facing her father. Colter removed his hat, placed it on the table. He was taking his time, making Ellie sweat, and it was working. Ellie shifted from one foot to the other.

"Are you gonna spank me, Daddy?"

Tulley cleared his throat and walked into the den.

All of Colter's anger evaporated with those nervous words. He didn't want Ellie to be afraid of him under any circumstances. "Have I ever spanked you?"

"No, sir, but I did something really bad, and Lori said when you're really bad you get spanked. So I'm ready for my spanking."

Colter reached down and picked Ellie up, held her tightly in his arms.

Ellie started to cry. "I'm sorry, Daddy. I'm sorry."

He smoothed her hair. "I know, baby. Now go to your room while I talk to Ms. Preston."

Ellie slid to the floor. "Don't be mad at her. She didn't know what I was doing, and she was real nice and helped me."

"Wait in your room and think about what you did. I'll be there in a little bit and we'll discuss it thoroughly."

"Yes, sir," Ellie muttered, her head bent as she went toward the back door.

"No." Colter stopped her. "Go to your room without Sooner."

Ellie's bottom lip trembled and she ran toward the hall. Marisa noticed that Tulley quickly followed.

Ellie had been spared her father's wrath, but from

the glitter in his eyes Marisa had a feeling she wasn't going to fare as well.

Her nerves were stretched to the breaking point as she watched him. His dark hair curled against the collar of his leather jacket and his expression was resentful. She waited.

"What happened?" he asked in a voice so low she could barely hear him.

Marisa did a double take. Those weren't the words she was expecting and she could see he had a tight rein on his temper. But he was willing to listen—that was the important thing.

"I got a call at Madame Hélèna's that Ellie was at Dalton's asking for me."

His eyes swept over her in the slim-fitting champagne-silk Madame Hélèna's creation. Hélèna insisted that her staff wear her clothes to show them off to customers. Marisa was glad to do so; the dresses were fabulous and offered at a considerable discount.

"You buy your clothes at Madame Hélèna's?" he asked in disbelief.

"Yes. I work there."

He shook his head. "You said you worked at Dalton's."

"I did until my father sent the police out here. I knew then that my parents were still controlling my life, so I left. I found a place to live and I got a job with Madame Hélèna. I'm out on my own, which I should've done years ago."

He shook his head again. "We're getting off track. Tell me about Ellie."

She told him what Ellie had told her, and Colter sank into a chair.

"God, I get cold chills every time I think about her taking a cab by herself. Anything could have happened...."

"But she found me and I brought her home. She's okay."

His eyes flashed. "Why did you have to come back into my life?"

She chewed on the inside of her lip. This might not be the time or place, but she had to do it. She knew that now beyond any doubt. "I came here to tell you something—something important. But you wouldn't listen."

He sighed with fatigue. "I'm tired, upset, my head's pounding and I'm not in a mood to listen to any more lies."

"I haven't lied to you."

He stared at her, his eyes matching the challenge she knew was blazing in hers. "Okay." He gave in with a hint of anger. "You've got five minutes."

She glanced toward Ellie's room.

"Don't worry," he said. "Tulley can't stand to see her cry and he'll pacify her for a while. You've already told me you were seventeen instead of twenty-one and your mother forced you to leave by threatening to have me arrested. What else is there?"

His tone offended her, but she had to follow through. She took a steadying breath. "When I left, I had plans to find you again, but that never happened. Then I discovered one fact that changed everything."

"What?"

She counted to three, then said, "I discovered I was pregnant."

Nothing. Not even a flicker of surprise. For a second she was thrown, but she quickly recovered. "I had to find you, so I hired the private investigator. Then my mother found out and everything came to a head. I told her I was pregnant and she told me what the PI had discovered—that you were married. I know that's a lie now, but back then I was devastated."

She paused, waiting. No response. Nothing. She went on. "Mother insisted I have an abortion, but I refused."

A distressed sound left his throat, but he didn't say anything.

"She then demanded I give up the baby for adoption and I still refused. I wanted my baby. The stress caused a lot of problems with the pregnancy, and Mother put me in a clinic in upstate New York. I didn't realize it was an adoption clinic until later. Then I became so upset that I went into early labor." She swallowed. "After thirty long hours, the baby was born dead."

His glare was chilling. "What did you say?"

She made herself repeat the words. "Our son was born dead."

"We had a son?" he asked.

"Yes. I never got to see him or hold him…but I heard him crying. Though the doctor said I only imagined it, because he was stillborn."

"You and I had a son?" he asked again.

"Yes," she replied. "That's why I came out here—to tell you about him. I wanted you to know he existed."

"Did you give him a name?"

"Yes. James Colter—after you."

Colter didn't react. "Where's he buried?"

"What?" She blinked in confusion.

"If he was full-term, then he'd be buried somewhere. All I'm asking is where."

She put a hand to her temple, which was beginning to throb painfully. "Mother took care of all that."

"You've never been to your son's grave?"

"No."

"Every year during the holidays, Ellie, Tulley and I put flowers on my parents' graves and Tulley's wife's grave. That's what you do when someone's important to you." His eyes narrowed. "Did you think I wouldn't ask?"

"I…uh…" Words jumbled in her head. She didn't know where her own son was buried. Her mother had said it would be too traumatic for her, and she'd been in such an emotional state that she'd adhered to her mother's wishes. Then her father brought her to Texas and she never went back to New York—never went back to her son…

Colter stood abruptly. "Get out of my home and don't come back."

She shivered at the cold hostility in his voice. She'd expected a lot of reactions, but not this rage. He was acting as if he didn't believe her. Did he think she hadn't wanted their child?

Fear made her feel shaky. *He didn't believe her.* The reality of that overwhelmed her and she had nothing to say, no words to defend herself. Callously she'd never asked to go to her son's gravesite. That made her an awful mother. Oh God, she had to get away from him.

But how could she get away from herself?

"The truth has your tongue tied?" he asked, his voice ripping through her. "Our child might be dead to you but not to me, and if you cared anything about that child you wouldn't sit there so selfishly and expect me to understand. Just leave and stay out of my life."

Despair, swift and strong, swept over her and she stood on legs that felt like rubber. She gripped the table for support, but Colter didn't offer any help. Numbly she grabbed her coat and purse and headed for the door.

Running to her car, she gulped in the chilly evening air, but it didn't cool the heated emotions churning through her. As she drove away, tears streamed down her face. For years she'd agonized over the death of her son—not able to really live again. She'd thought it had to do with Colter and his not knowing, but it had to do with *her* and a deep-seated guilt she hadn't even known was there. The guilt of never going to her son's grave.

Her mother had convinced her of the trauma of such an act, and she'd acquiesced—as always. Where was their child buried? That was the first thing Colter had wanted to know, as a good parent would. A sob left her throat. She had to find out what cemetery they'd put her son in, and she'd be on the first plane to New York.

Her mother was on a cruise, but her father would have information on how to reach her. Since they both owned Dalton's, it was imperative that they know each other's whereabouts.

She could be in New York by morning. And she'd touch her son's grave, feel his presence and apologize. Then maybe she could find that measure of peace she'd been searching for.

And she didn't need to see Colter again. Not ever.

Chapter 9

Her inner turmoil drove her thirty minutes later as she sped down the street leading to her father's home. The brown brick was a Greek Revival mansion with classic white columns that framed the front portico. Built by her grandfather, it boasted spiral staircases, hardwood floors and stone fireplaces, echoing Texas style both past and present.

Seeing the familiar house didn't make her feel better. She'd been a prisoner behind those wrought-iron gates and brick walls—sheltered, protected and suffocated. Coming back wasn't easy and facing her father wouldn't be easy, either. But she had to know where her son was buried.

Colter sat in a stupor, hardly able to believe what Marisa had told him. They had a son? *A son.* James Colter. He was still grappling with that.

"Colt, boy."

He jerked up his head to see Tulley staring at him.

"What's wrong?" Tulley glanced around. "Where's Marisa?"

"Gone—for good."

Tulley took a seat. "What happened?"

He jammed his hands through his hair. "You won't believe what she tried to tell me. Lies. Why does she keep lying to me? She stuck a knife in my heart eight years ago, and she keeps on twisting it."

"What did she say?"

Colter told him what Marisa had said.

Tulley frowned. "A son? She said you had a son?"

"She sat there, her voice so sincere, her eyes sad, and she was pulling me in like she always did. God, Tulley, I *wanted* to believe her—and that makes me the biggest fool that ever lived." He took a quick breath. "But you should've seen her face when I asked where he was buried. She was speechless and she could see that I knew she was lying."

"Colt, boy, I've said this before and I'll say it again. You two need to have an honest-to-God talk. Put the past on the table, call an ace an ace and a spade a spade. You have to get at the truth. Marisa doesn't seem the type to tell lies but then, I don't suppose either one of us really knew her."

"I sure didn't. But you're right. I thought I could let this go, but—"

The phone rang, interrupting him, and he got up to answer it.

"This is Cari Michaels with Dalton's Department Stores. I'm calling to check if Ellie made it home okay."

"Yes," he said. "Ellie's fine."

There was a pause.

"May I speak with Marisa? She left a message that she'd be there."

"She's left."

"Oh, well, I'm glad Ellie's okay. Thank you."

"Ms. Michaels," he said before she could hang up. He had to sort out the truth, and to do that he had to see Marisa again. "Could you please tell me where I can find Marisa? I'd like to speak with her."

This pause was longer. "Normally she'd be at home with her family in Highland Park, but she rented a room recently and that's probably where she'll be." She rattled off the address, and he scribbled it on a pad.

"Thank you," he said, hanging up and stuffing the paper into his shirt pocket.

"Before you blast out of here, you'd better talk to your daughter," Tulley informed him. "She's about to cry herself to sleep."

"I wouldn't go anywhere without talking to Ellie. She's my first priority and always will be."

He found Ellie lying on her bed clutching a pillow. Her hair had come out of its ponytail and her face was red from crying. His heart twisted at the sight, but he forced himself not to take her in his arms and say all was forgiven. They had rules and she'd broken a big one today. As a father he had to make her understand he loved her, but she still had to obey the rules—rules that existed for her benefit, whether she saw that or not.

He sat in the old wooden rocker that had belonged to his mother. Becky had put pink and white floral cushions on it to match Ellie's room. He'd rocked Ellie in this chair since she was a baby: when she had colic, when she was teething and when she was sick. Raising a child alone had been rough, but Ellie made it a pleasure. She was a smiling, happy baby and her bubbly personality had quickly surfaced. She took after her mother—a mother she wanted in her life. His heart twisted a little more.

Ellie sat up and wiped her eyes. "Are you mad at me, Daddy?"

"No, Ellie, I'm not mad," he told her. "I'm troubled. Troubled that you'd take such a risk. Troubled that you'd take money out of my drawer without permission. And troubled that you couldn't talk to me."

Her bottom lip quivered and she dived off the bed into his arms. He held her tight. "I'm sorry, Daddy."

He stroked her hair. "I know, baby. Tell me why you did it."

"You said…you said we might have to go to Aunt Jen's for Christmas, and I had to tell Santa Claus. He had to know where I'd be when he sends my mommy."

"Ellie." He tried not to show his frustration. "We've had this talk before, but obviously we're not communicating. Is all this Santa stuff about your real mother coming back?"

Ellie nodded against his shoulder.

"Oh, baby." How did he explain that her mother didn't want her?

She raised her head. "It's okay, Daddy. Santa said I'll have a mommy by Christmas, and he told me not to worry about being at Aunt Jen's. He knows where I'm all the time."

"Santa told you that you'd have a mommy by Christmas?" Why would the man tell her that? Now he had to undo the damage.

"Yep." Ellie nodded. "So all I have to do is wait."

"Ellie…"

She placed her fingers over his lips. "Don't say it, Daddy. I believe."

He could see that she did, and he just couldn't break her heart. He'd deal with it later. That was the coward's way out, but he couldn't hurt his daughter. Still, he had to talk about her trip to Dalton's.

"Do you understand that what you did today was very dangerous for someone your age?"

She hung her head. "Yes, sir."

"Promise me you won't ever do anything like that again."

She lifted her head, her eyes watery. "I promise, and you can spank me if you want."

He gently pinched her cheek. "Ellie, I've never spanked you and I never will. Hitting doesn't solve anything. However, you will not talk on the phone or watch TV for a week. And you will not get your allowance for a month."

"Okay." She clenched her hands. "Can Sooner come back in the house?"

It would hurt Ellie far more if he kept Sooner away from her, but he couldn't do that. He hesitated, though, just so she'd think it was a possibility.

"Yes. Sooner can come back in."

Her arms crept around his neck and she whispered, "I love you, Daddy."

He swallowed. "I love you, angelface." He held her

for an extra moment. "Daddy has to go out for a little while, so help Tulley feed the horses, take your bath and read one of the books you brought home from school."

"Okay. Can I go get Sooner now?"

"Yes. Go get Sooner."

Like a whirlwind she was gone. He drew a long breath at what lay ahead of him. He had to see Marisa, though; that was the only way to settle this.

He stopped at a gas station to buy a map of Dallas. He spread it out over the steering wheel and searched for the street Ms. Michaels had given him. The Highland Park area caught his eye. When he'd started his boot business, he, Tulley, Becky, Jen and Bart had dinner with a business lawyer who'd given them his advice. He was a man Becky had met in college and he lived in Highland Park.

Colter knew exactly where Richard Preston lived. He remembered the sprawling estate and the large security gates with the Dalton logo. Marisa was probably there at the time and he hadn't known. So close, yet...

He folded the map. If he wanted the truth, he'd have to get it from Richard and Vanessa Preston. They would know what Marisa was talking about.

Marisa parked in front and ran up the steps to the double doors. Instead of ringing the bell, she went in. Winston, the butler, was instantly at her side.

"Ms. Preston, it's so good to see you," he said in surprise. "I'll tell your father you're here."

"No." She stopped him. "There's no need."

"Yes, ma'am."

She made her way through the living room to the library. She heard loud voices and paused, frowning. *It can't be,* she told herself, as she listened to the high-pitched voice that sounded like her mother's. What was Vanessa doing here? She was supposed to be on a cruise.

She walked uneasily toward the closed doors. Yes, it was definitely her mother's voice—shouting angrily at her father.

"Leave her alone, Richard."

"She's working as Madame Hélèna's gopher and making us the laughingstock of Dallas. I won't have it."

"I can't take any more." Her mother's voice was no longer angry, just resigned.

"Then why the hell didn't you go on your cruise? I can take care of Marisa. I can take care of both my children."

"Marisa belongs to me." Vanessa's voice rose an octave. "That was in the agreement, Richard. You would raise Reed and I'd raise Marisa—without interference."

"You're the one who called me, Vanessa."

"I never should have listened to you. You said Marisa would come back to New York, but she hasn't."

"Texas is her home and this is where she belongs," her father bellowed. "If *he* hadn't shown up, everything would be fine."

"But he has, and now…"

There was a moment of silence, and the chill inside Marisa turned to an icy foreboding. Then she heard her mother's voice.

"Yes. We'll lose her. We will lose her forever."

What was her mother talking about? Marisa restrained herself from charging into the room. Her heart pounded painfully, and she tried to steady her erratic pulse as she waited for her mother's next words.

"It wasn't easy having full responsibility for Marisa when she was seventeen and pregnant. I handled things badly and I wish…"

Unable to stand still for one more minute, she opened the door. "You wished what?" she asked.

Her parents stared at her, shock on both their faces. Her mother was the first to recover. Dressed in a fashionable cream-colored suit, she rushed over to greet Marisa, giving her a quick hug. "Darling, you're back."

"What were you talking about?" she asked again.

Her mother looked nervously at her father, and it was clear that Vanessa didn't want to answer. Marisa was about to insist when her father spoke up.

"Your mother is dramatizing everything as usual."

It was more than that and, for a change, she was getting some straight answers. "Mother said she never should've let you talk her into something. What did she mean?"

Richard shoved his hands into the pockets of his suit slacks. "She was talking about our decision to call the police when you were stranded on *his* ranch. It was probably the wrong move, but I couldn't tolerate the thought of that man hurting you again. You almost didn't survive the last time, and when I think of the pain he put you through—well, I did what I figured was best."

Normally she would have accepted that explanation,

but not now—not after what she'd heard. "His name is Colter Kincaid, and it was *my* decision to go to his ranch. He didn't force me."

"Of course not, darling. We're just glad you're home," her mother put in.

"Yes," Richard added. "I'm very glad you're home. Your room's waiting for you and so is your job at Dalton's."

"I have a job, Father, and I get paid for the work I do, not for being Richard Preston's daughter."

Her father bristled. "You are a Dalton and a Preston, and you belong here and at Dalton's."

"Really?" She lifted an eyebrow as she remembered parts of the conversation she'd overheard. "I thought I belonged to Mother."

Her father was speechless, and suddenly she could see the past for what it was. "That's it, isn't it? You brought me to Texas to get me away from Mother. I'm like a prized object, and neither of you has ever thought about *my* feelings. It's just you and this tug-of-war for dominance of your children."

"Darling, please, let's not argue," her mother begged.

Marisa turned to Vanessa. "Why aren't you on your cruise?"

"I couldn't leave with you running off like that. I had to know you were okay."

"Surely Father's PI told you I was."

"All right, Marisa," Richard said, his words sharp. "This rebellion isn't like you, and I've had enough. It's time for you to come home."

In the past she'd always submitted to that tone of

voice, but not today. Not anymore. "Sorry, Father. I'm not seventeen and I've earned the right to live my life the way I choose."

"Fine, you want more control at Dalton's, you've got it. You want an apartment somewhere, you've got it. Just tell me what the hell you want."

"Peace, Father. That's what I want."

He scowled, looking perplexed. "What are you talking about?"

"I need peace about the past. I've never recovered from losing my son."

Richard's features softened. "Sweetheart, no woman ever truly recovers from something like that."

"I know what my problem is."

"What?" Richard asked.

She turned to her mother. "Where's he buried?"

Vanessa turned a pasty white. "Darling, why are you putting yourself through this?"

"Because a mother should know where her child is buried." She swallowed visibly. "When Colter asked me, I couldn't answer, and I realized that I left my baby behind and I never visited his grave. I was emotionally traumatized by his death, but—"

"You told Kincaid about the baby?" her father asked.

"Yes." She glanced at Vanessa. "Where did you bury him?"

Raised voices interrupted them, and Marisa turned to see Colter and Reed walk into the room.

What was Colter doing here? Had he followed her? A new hope lightened her heart. Was he ready to listen? Was he ready to hear about their son?

He looked tired and angry—just as he had earlier. He wasn't wearing a hat and his dark hair had been tumbled by the wind. There was a disturbing glint in his eyes.

Richard confronted Colter. "How did you get in here, Kincaid? You're not welcome— Winston!" he shouted.

"I let him in," Reed said. "He asked to see Marisa and I didn't see any harm in that."

"You know what this man did to your sister. Can't you use some common sense?"

"I am," Reed replied, undaunted by their father's temper. Then he looked at Marisa. "Do you want to see him?"

"Yes," she answered in a low voice.

Winston rushed into the room. "Yes, sir."

"Remove this man immediately," Richard ordered.

Colter stood almost six feet tall, broad shouldered and whipcord lean. Winston was five foot six, thin and almost effeminate. The thought of Winston bodily removing Colter was ludicrous.

"Come this way, sir," Winston said.

"I'm not going anywhere until I speak with Marisa."

"I'll call the police," Richard threatened.

"Go ahead," Colter said.

Richard stepped toward the phone.

"No," Marisa insisted. "Colter's here for the same reason I am. We want to know where our son is buried. Just tell us and we'll leave."

Colter stared at her blankly. "I deserve more than your lies," he said coldly.

Marisa stared back at him. Lies? What was he talking about? She'd been as open and honest as she could. What else did he want from her?

His gaze swung to her mother. "We meet again, Mrs. Preston."

Marisa's eyes widened in disbelief. "You've met my mother?"

"Of course," he answered, as if that should make sense.

"But how?" she asked, her voice like a film of ice that threatened to crack at any moment.

"Come on, Marisa, stop playing games," Colter warned.

"Games?" she choked out. "Do I look like I'm playing games? I feel I'm going insane and everyone around me is talking in riddles! I tried to tell you how much I wanted our son, how I fought to keep him, how he died before I could even hold him, but you wouldn't listen. Now, you're accusing me of lying. Please tell me what—" Her voice cracked as a sob rose up in her throat.

Colter took in the pallor of her skin, her harassed appearance and the desperate look in her brown eyes. She wasn't acting or lying. She *believed* everything she was saying. That realization fueled his anger and resentment, and he turned to face Vanessa Preston with a look bordering on suppressed violence.

"You didn't!" he demanded, begging to hear a denial.

Vanessa remained silent, studying her long pink fingernails.

Her refusal to speak gave Colter his answer. "OhmyGod, you did," he groaned. "OhmyGod."

His body stiffened and he clenched and unclenched his hands, fighting for control. "Tell her the truth, dammit—tell her!"

Chapter 10

Vanessa looked at her daughter, her eyes filled with torment, then she shook her head. "Don't do this, Mr. Kincaid," she begged. "It'll destroy her."

"There's no choice. She has to know."

A vein in her mother's neck jerked erratically. "I can't, I can't," she sobbed, wiping tears from her cheeks.

Marisa had never seen her mother cry. She was always so strong, so in control, and Marisa knew that her mother was confronting something she couldn't handle. The thought scorched her nerve endings, but could do nothing to stop the panic.

Richard grabbed Colter by the arm. "We'll take care of it from here. You can leave."

Colter pulled his arm away. "I'm not going anywhere until the truth is said out loud."

Vanessa appealed to Marisa. "Darling, please ask him to leave."

"Why?" she asked, more confused than ever. Vanessa didn't answer, and Marisa felt questions beating at her, but she wouldn't acknowledge them. She had one goal and she focused on that. "Just tell us where our son is buried." That was the only thing that made sense to her at the moment.

"Tell her!" Colter shouted. "Tell her, or I will."

Vanessa flinched. "You were so young and I didn't know what else to do. You had your whole life, a brilliant career, ahead of you, and I couldn't…couldn't let you throw it all away."

"What are you talking about?" Marisa asked, her voice sounding unfamiliar to her ears. "Tell me," she demanded.

Vanessa took a jagged breath, but before she could speak, Richard broke in. "Don't, Vanessa."

It was clear that her parents had some information she needed, and Colter knew what it was. She glanced at him. "What don't they want me to find out?"

He opened his mouth, but there was no sound. He tried again. "You…didn't have a…son."

The words ran through her head like the shrill of a whistle alerting her to danger, and she tried to rid herself of that sense of foreboding.

"Yes, I did," she said. "I carried him for almost nine months and I felt him kick and move and I talked to him. I named him James Colter, and he weighed five pounds, two ounces. He was stillborn."

Colter closed his eyes briefly. "Yes, except—"

"Except what?" she asked, wondering how he knew

all this. She had the urge to put her hands over her ears to block out his next words.

"Except your baby wasn't a boy and he wasn't still-born."

Marisa turned to her mother. "Tell him about my son, Mother. Please."

Vanessa hung her head, and Marisa turned to her father next—and what she saw in his eyes chilled her to the bone. "Father, you know what happened. Tell him."

Silence became a deafening sound that echoed through her heart.

She looked at Colter and braced herself for his next words.

"You had a daughter…and she was born alive."

"What!"

"It's true," he said.

"No, no, no." She flung her head from side to side. "Why are you saying that? Why are you lying to me?"

"It's true, Marisa," he repeated.

She stared at Vanessa, mouth dry. "Mother, please, tell me he's wrong."

Vanessa raised her head. "He's not," she said in a low, defeated voice. "Your baby didn't…didn't die at birth."

A black fog settled over Marisa. Her first reaction was to laugh, then cry, then scream, but of course, she did none of those things. Her mother's words rendered her immobile as the full implication drove into her.

She swallowed convulsively, and her body began to tremble. She was dangerously close to the breaking point and she tried to calm herself, but all she could do was continue to stare at her mother as if she was some diabolic stranger.

"You're lying! Why are you lying?" Marisa choked out. She closed her eyes against the shock, the truth, only to hear her baby cry once again. It was so clear, so real, just as it had been years ago. Everything began to fall into place: the crying, the dreams, Colter's hostility, her mother's nervousness. As her mind began to clear, she knew her mother wasn't lying. Not this time.

"Your daughter is alive," her mother said.

The words bounced in Marisa's head like lead marbles, each one making an indention she could feel. "How?" she breathed, not knowing if she had enough strength to face the truth.

Vanessa took a breath. "When you wouldn't sign the adoption papers, I didn't know what to do, so I called Richard."

Her eyes moved to her father. "You were there?"

"I came when your mother called, and we decided what was best for your future."

"*You* decided. *You* decided," she cried, almost hysterical. "I loved my baby and I wanted him—her, but you decided…you decided…" She had to take a breath before she could continue. "You took my baby from me! You told me he… I mean, she was dead and you let me live with that lie. How could you think *that* was best for me? I'll never forgive you for this. Never!"

A gasp of pain left her throat. Her baby was alive. Fast on that thought, a more agonizing one followed. *Where was she?*

She fought the fear rising in her. "Where's my daughter? Did you give her to strangers?"

"No," Vanessa said.

"No?" Marisa echoed. "What does that mean? Who did you give her to? I demand to know."

There was a slight pause, then her mother glanced at Colter and said slowly, "We gave…gave her to… her father."

A tense silence followed the announcement. Marisa turned to Colter as the truth began to sink in. That meant…that meant… She couldn't even formulate the thought that tortured her mind.

"Ellie is our daughter." Colter said the words for her.

"No!" she cried, her hands against her mouth. "No! She's Shannon's daughter." As she denied it, Ellie's face flashed before her eyes—the delicate features so like her own, the blond hair. Why hadn't she recognized her own daughter? "Oh God," she moaned. She didn't want to be the woman who'd given away that adorable child.

She could see how things had happened. Her mother had told her she'd had a son and that Colter had married—all lies to keep her away from him.

Colter took a step toward her, his face etched with pain. "Your parents found me and told me you didn't want the baby, so I gladly took her."

Another lie. Another deception.

Ellie wasn't Shannon's. Ellie was her daughter.

The reality was too much to endure, and she felt herself shattering into a million pieces. Through the pain and numbness, she held onto one fact. Ellie was her daughter…her precious baby. *She was alive!*

She backed away from her parents, muttering incoherently, "No, no, no." She knew she was shaking her head and the denial burned her throat, but she was only aware of grappling with the facts, striving desperately to comprehend and accept them. Backing into Reed, she clutched at him for support.

"Reed, is this real or am I dreaming?" she asked in a feeble voice.

"You're not dreaming," he said, his voice touching a chord of reality.

It was true, then. Colter had their daughter and had raised her for over seven years, since the day she was born. That was why he hated her so much—he believed she'd willingly given their baby away.

"Darling, listen," her mother appealed.

"No! I don't want to hear anything you have to say. Being my parents didn't give you the right to do this."

She could feel the pressure building inside her head, the sharp throbbing, and she sensed the walls closing in. She felt faint, but she fought back, needing to explain. She had to make Colter believe how much she'd wanted their baby.

"Colter, I..." she began to say in a shaky voice as the dizziness consumed her. The room swayed and blackness engulfed her—and two strong arms reached out to catch her as she crumpled to the floor.

Marisa awoke to a strange numbness, a numbness of mind, body and soul. It was several moments before she realized she was lying on the sofa in the library. The events of the last hours started to come back. Was it true? she asked herself. Was Ellie really her daughter? Yes, she was. The truth resounded in her head like chimes in the wind. Ellie... Ellie... Ellie.

With that name secure in her heart, she slowly sat

up, pushing her tumbled hair away from her face. She tried to calm her shakiness as her eyes strayed to Colter.

He sat in a chair, his lean body hunched forward, his elbows resting on his knees, hands clasped tightly together. He was white as a sheet, and his eyes reflected a sorrow that broke her heart.

What must he think of her? For years he'd believed that she hadn't wanted their child—that she'd given her away. And she'd thought he was being hostile for no reason, when all the time… A whimper left her throat.

At the pained sound, Colter glanced at her, his eyes full of worry and concern, but he didn't come to her. He watched her with a troubled gaze as if he didn't know what to say or do. He seemed disillusioned with the whole situation. She couldn't blame him.

She hadn't realized Reed was sitting beside her until he asked, "Sis, are you okay?"

"Yes," she muttered through dry, stiff lips, but she knew her answer belied the grief that must show in her face.

"Good," he said. "I know you're still shaken up, but Mother and Father have some things to say that you need to hear. It's important. Okay?" He patted her hands to reassure her.

"I have nothing to say to them."

"I empathize with the feeling, and after they're done, you and I will walk out of here and never come back."

Her eyes narrowed on his face. "You're leaving?"

"You and I will not be puppets anymore, but I feel you need to hear the details before you can completely accept what happened. Okay?"

She nodded. Everything in her rejected the idea, but she didn't have the strength to resist.

Colter got slowly to his feet. Their eyes met and intense emotions flowed between them, but neither said a word. They didn't need to. Their eyes were conversing in a way their voices never could. There were so many feelings written on his face, but the one that she saw most clearly was "I'm sorry," and she was sure the same message was written on hers.

Vanessa and Richard moved forward, and Marisa gripped her hands as they lay in her lap, waiting for the appeals and the pleading to start. But the silence stretched until she thought they weren't going to speak at all.

"I don't expect you to forgive us," Vanessa said. "I'm not sure I can forgive myself, but I hope you'll listen…and try to understand."

Understand? They wanted her to understand. No woman on earth could be that understanding.

"When I met your father, I had a promising career as a ballerina in front of me—a dream I'd had since I was a child. There was a strong sexual attraction between us and we had a brief, passionate affair while I was visiting my parents in Texas. I returned to New York to continue my dancing and then discovered I was pregnant. I was nineteen years old and faced with becoming a mother and losing everything I'd ever dreamed about." She paused.

"My parents forced me to marry your father. It was the only option for a young lady in those days. The marriage was a disaster, of course. I had to give up my dream of becoming a dancer, and I've regretted it every day since."

She'd always thought her parents had an arranged marriage. She didn't know her mother was pregnant at the time. Vanessa had never talked about that part of her life.

"Don't you see, Marisa?" her mother begged. "As much as I love you, I couldn't let history repeat itself. You deserved the career I never had. I didn't want anything to take that away from you."

Marisa got to her feet, surprised she could actually stand; something inside was giving her strength she hadn't known she possessed. She began to see her mother in a whole new light—a woman tormented by her own past, trying to protect her daughter from the same fate she'd suffered. She had allowed her own shattered dreams to become entwined with her daughter's. In effect, she'd done the very thing she had tried to prevent—she'd taken drastic measures to force Marisa onto the path she deemed best for her and had not considered Marisa's own desires.

"I never wanted that kind of career, Mother," she said, her voice weak but very clear. "*You* wanted it, but you can't live your life through me. I have feelings and dreams of my own. You never gave me a choice. You just demanded and manipulated until I gave in. And I was desperate to please you. I wanted your love."

Her mother closed her eyes as if she was in pain, then opened them again. "Oh, darling, I do love you. You've been my whole life since the day you were born. Reed was always so independent, your father's son, but you—you always seemed to need me."

Marisa realized that was true. She'd been very attached to her mother as a child. Leaving her father and brother had been a traumatic experience, and she had clung to her mother even more, afraid of losing her, too. She'd been eager to do everything her mother had asked of her, even playing the piano for long periods of time, trying to gain the expertise she needed to achieve the goals Vanessa had set for her. She'd never had the courage to tell her mother that those goals weren't hers.

She could see now that as a teenager looking for freedom, she'd probably used Colter as a means of escape. It didn't diminish the love she'd felt for him; it only helped explain how everything had gotten so out of control. If she'd been open and honest and able to talk to Vanessa, she would've saved everyone so much heartache.

Her mother thought she'd done the right thing. She had wanted Marisa to be happy and she'd believed that happiness was in her career. It showed just how little they knew each other.

Her eyes darkened. "I'll never understand that kind of love. The kind that hurts and destroys other people."

A spasm of pain crossed Vanessa's face. "I have a hard time understanding it myself. All I can say is that I wanted to save you from the mistakes I'd made. I was sure the infatuation you had for this man would burn itself out, and you were so young, so ill-equipped to raise a child on your own. Adoption seemed the only choice, but I couldn't get you to agree. I was at my wits' end and finally I called your father. He agreed that you were too young to be a mother." She looked down at her hands. "We decided the best solution was for the child to be with her father. We contacted Mr. Kincaid, and he came immediately and took the baby. Richard paid the doctor to lie to you. It was the perfect solution. The child would be with her natural father and you could get on with your wonderful life."

Wonderful life echoed through Marisa's mind, resounding in the hollow places of her heart left by the empty years.

"But your feelings went deeper than we ever imagined. You didn't get over losing the baby. You were close to a nervous breakdown and you seemed to use your father as a sort of lifeline to get away from me. By then I knew we'd made a terrible mistake, but I didn't know how to correct it."

"You could have told me the truth," she said with force.

"Don't you think I tried? As the months turned into years, you seemed determined not to come back to New York and your training, and I knew I should tell you. But I couldn't. I tried so many times, but I didn't want you to hate me."

"Now I've lost seven years of my daughter's life. Seven years I can never get back."

"I'm so sorry, my darling."

Marisa didn't respond to the heartfelt words, but she saw the past with much greater clarity. She'd been the focal point of her mother's life—a way to fulfill the dream she'd wanted so badly. And Marisa, in awe of her beautiful mother and wanting her approval, had been a willing victim. But not anymore.

New strength pumped through her veins. She could get through this. She wasn't going to sink down into that valley of despair. A younger Marisa might have, but not the adult Marisa. In her determination she felt as if she'd emerged from shadows into sunshine.

"When I overheard you and Father talking earlier, you said if I ever found out, you'd lose me forever. You were right. You have hurt me beyond belief, and no parent has the right to do that. I will never forgive you."

"Marisa, please," Richard begged. "You're a Dalton, a Preston. We're bound by blood—we're family."

She drew a deep breath. "Ellie's a Dalton, a Preston, and you gave her away like unwanted garbage."

Richard paled.

"You should see her, Father. She's bright, funny, adventurous, strong-willed—everything a Preston should be."

"Marisa…"

"You want me to understand, to forgive, but some things just aren't forgivable." She turned toward the door. "I'm leaving. Please don't try to contact me." She walked out, and Reed and Colter followed.

Outside, she leaned against her car, trembling severely.

"You can't drive in this condition," Reed said.

"Please take me to Cari's."

Cari's? Colter frowned, wondering why she didn't want to go to Ellie. That should be her first reaction. Maybe she needed time. He didn't want to judge her, but he had a little girl who desperately wanted her mommy.

He was still reeling from the impact of everything he'd heard tonight. Marisa was, too. He had to give her a chance to adjust. He didn't know what Marisa had in mind.

One thing he knew for certain, though: Ellie wasn't leaving the ranch or him. He'd lost Marisa, but he would not lose his daughter.

Chapter 11

"Please follow us in your car," Marisa said. "We have to talk."

Colter nodded. There wasn't much he could say. They would now decide what was best for Ellie, and his gut tightened at the thought of his daughter getting hurt. Marisa had been hurt too much, though, and she deserved to know their child. But he wasn't sure where that left him—somewhere in the middle, fighting for a future for Ellie…and himself.

He followed them through the busy Dallas traffic to an apartment complex and parked beside them. A dark-haired woman ran out to the car; this must be Cari, and obviously Marisa had called her. Colter took a moment to call Tulley. Ellie was in bed, and he told Tulley he'd get back as soon as he could. He'd tell him later about everything he'd learned tonight. It wasn't something he wanted to discuss on the phone. He grabbed his hat from the seat and made his way toward the group.

Marisa and Cari hugged while Reed stood some distance away. "My baby's alive, Cari. My baby's alive."

"This is so wonderful," Cari said, studying Marisa's face with a big smile.

"What?" Marisa asked, brushing away an errant tear.

"I'm just so relieved. I was afraid this last blow might be too much for you. But looking at you now, I know you're made of much stronger stuff. I also know you can handle anything—including Colter Kincaid."

"Oh, Cari, what am I going to say to him? He's lived with as many lies during the past few years as I have."

"Just tell him what's in your heart."

She tried to remember those words as he walked up, and they climbed the stairs to Cari's apartment with its stunning view of the Dallas skyline. No one was looking at it, though, or commenting on Cari's Christmas decorations. Marisa saw only Colter. His hat was in his hand, his eyes filmed with anguish.

She realized she'd never truly known this man. He had stirred her emotions, filled her heart with girlish fantasies and made her body yearn in a wanton fashion that had left her wanting more, but she'd never really known the person he was inside. How many men would give up so much to raise a child? He was probably more of a man than she'd ever meet again.

She moistened her dry lips with the tip of her tongue. "Colter." Her voice came out a mere whisper.

Uncertainty mingled with disbelief in his eyes. She

could see that he was having difficulty adjusting to the truth. Oh God, how were they ever going to get through this?

"Marisa," he murmured, taking a step toward her. "Are you all right?"

She took a stilted breath. "I don't think I'll ever be the same again."

Running a hand through his hair, he admitted, "I know what you mean. I feel as if I've been kicked in the gut and I'm still trying to catch my breath."

Silence took hold, and no one seemed inclined to speak.

Cari stepped forward and held out her hand to Colter. "Nice to meet you in person, Mr. Kincaid."

Colter shook her hand, dragging his eyes away from Marisa. "Thank you for taking care of Ellie today."

Cari smiled. "She wanted to see Marisa, and I found Marisa for her. She's a very determined little girl."

"Yeah. She can be headstrong."

She didn't get that from me, Marisa thought. She'd always been the dutiful daughter…until she met Colter.

Silence prevailed again.

"Junior," Cari said, "there's a nightclub around the corner. Why don't you buy me a drink?"

"I don't—"

"Sure you do." Cari grabbed her purse and linked her arm through Reed's. "We'll see you two later."

Cari pulled Reed out the door, but Marisa and Colter hardly noticed. His eyes held hers, and it was just the two of them, needing answers, reassurance and, most of all, forgiveness.

"Have a seat," Marisa invited, sitting on the sofa before her legs gave way.

He sat beside her.

"I—" They spoke at the same time.

She pushed her hair nervously behind her ear. "I'm not sure what to say to you. Words seem insufficient."

He placed his hat on the coffee table. "I feel the same way." He stared at his hands. "I'm so sorry for all the cruel things I've said to you."

"It doesn't matter now," she murmured. "I understand."

"I just keep thinking that if I'd demanded to see you the day Ellie was born, none of this would've happened." He paused. "When the PI gave me the address and I discovered the kind of clinic you were in, I felt like I'd been sucker punched. Not only did you not want *me*—you also didn't want our child."

As he talked, tears streamed down her cheeks. He turned to look at her, his eyes darkened by the emotions he was feeling.

"God, Marisa, why did you let your mother take you there?"

She felt a familiar stab of guilt. "I think I told you I had a lot of problems with the pregnancy. Mother suggested it would be easier for me in a private clinic, where I could get constant medical attention. I didn't object because I knew she was ashamed that her daughter was another statistic, an unwed pregnant teenager, and I also knew she wanted to get me away from her circle of friends and the impending gossip. But I didn't realize it was an adoption clinic until I arrived. By then I was very depressed that you'd married someone else. Nothing seemed to matter anymore. I just wanted peace and quiet." Her eyes held his. "I adamantly refused to sign any adoption papers. I intended to keep my baby. I…" A sob escaped her and she couldn't speak.

He waited, clenching and unclenching his fingers.

She quickly brushed the tears away with the back of her hand. "I yearned and prayed for you to be with me when he—I mean, she—was born. And all the time you were there, thinking…" She stopped, fighting for control, then added, "I wanted our baby."

"I know," he assured her. "Believe me, I know… now."

Struggling with her tears, she whispered, "Tell me about Ellie."

His eyes took on a soft glow. "Let's see, you know how much she weighed. She had these blond curls, and her eyes were a bluish green, and the first time I saw her she was crying at the top of her lungs."

Crying? She closed her eyes and she could hear the sound. It *had* been real; Ellie was real.

"I heard her crying," she said. "The labor was so long and they medicated me. I don't remember much afterward, but I do remember hearing a baby cry. Mother said it was my imagination. Afterward, I continued to hear that cry in my dreams. The sound has haunted me for years. Somehow, my subconscious must've known my baby wasn't dead."

After a pause he said, "Don't you think it's time Ellie met her mother?"

Yes instantly hovered in her throat, then fear consumed her. What was she going to say to Ellie? Could the child cope with the situation?

"Don't you?" he asked, obviously noticing her indecision.

"Yes." She gulped in air, trying to explain. "I want to be in control of my emotions when I see her so I can handle her reaction. I don't want her to hate me."

"You've met Ellie, and you're well aware of her desire for a mother."

"Everything in me wants to drive straight to the ranch and take her in my arms, hold her, tell her I'm her mother, but I'm afraid I'll fall apart if I do that. I have to—"

"I can't even imagine the pain you're going through, and when I think of your parents all I feel is anger. But I'm tired of all the anger and resentment, and it's time to focus on Ellie."

"Santa said she'd have a mother by Christmas and he was right. I just never dreamed it would be me." She took a deep breath. "How do we tell her what happened?"

"Very carefully—with the truth. And we need to do it together."

"Yes. But I need tonight to prepare myself."

"Okay," he said, and stood. "It won't be easy for you or for her, but it has to be done."

"I'll be there first thing in the morning," she replied, knowing she couldn't stay away any longer than that.

He moved to her side and gently stroked her cheek. A familiar flutter started in the pit of her stomach, making it difficult to think coherently. He slipped his arm around her waist and pulled her close to him.

Resting her head against his chest, she felt his heart beat out a message, a message she understood, a message of forgiveness. They stood there holding each other, letting the pain and misunderstandings of the past slowly ebb away.

"I've got to go," he murmured into her hair. "I don't like leaving Ellie this long."

She drew back, feeling deprived of his warmth, his closeness, but Ellie came first.

"Yes." She smiled through her tears. "Tomorrow her real mother's coming home."

Colter picked up his hat. "See you in the morning." He turned and left.

Almost on cue, Cari and Reed walked into the apartment.

"You okay?" Reed asked, giving her a hug.

"I'm better than I've been in the past eight years. I have a daughter, and tomorrow I'll see her as her mother for the first time."

"I'm proud of the way you're handling this."

"Me, too," Cari said. "Now, let's have some pizza."

Marisa noticed she had a big pizza carton in her hand. "I'm not very hungry."

"You're eating," Cari insisted. "You'll need your strength for tomorrow."

Marisa gave in, and as she nibbled on the food, Cari and Reed's bantering kept her amused. Then the three of them discussed sleeping arrangements. Marisa tried to talk Reed into going home, but he was adamant in his decision to leave Dalton's and their parents behind. Like her, he was tired of the manipulation and control.

In the end, they all slept in the den. They talked until the wee hours, then Reed fell asleep in a recliner and Cari on the sofa. Marisa curled up on the love seat with thoughts of Ellie...her baby.

She went over and over every detail of their short time together, especially the conversation about Ellie's mother. "She's very beautiful, and Daddy says I'm gonna look just like her." There was much more meaning behind those words now; Ellie hadn't been talking about Shannon, but about her. *Colter thought she was beautiful.* That was what he'd told Ellie—probably to satisfy her curiosity. She wasn't sure why Colter had married Shannon, but she would find out in the days ahead.

It must have been very painful for him to talk about Ellie's real mother, believing what he had. She was just grateful he hadn't poisoned Ellie's mind against her. But he wasn't that kind of man. He loved his daughter; he would never hurt her.

What was she going to say to Ellie? She pushed those troubling thoughts from her mind. For now, she'd just savor the knowledge that her baby was alive. If someone had asked her to draw a mental picture of her daughter, the child would have looked exactly like Ellie. She was perfect with her big green eyes and that enchanting smile. Marisa felt a deep sadness for all the years she'd missed, but she couldn't let herself dwell on that. The fact that Ellie was her daughter gave her the strength to face what lay ahead.

Colter walked through the back door feeling tired and drained. When he'd left here earlier, he'd just wanted answers. Now he was wondering if he could deal with everything he'd learned tonight.

Tulley was in the recliner watching TV, half asleep. When Colter sank onto the sofa, Tulley sat up straight, blinking.

"You've been gone a long time. What happened?"

Colter rubbed his hands over his face. "It's unbelievable and nothing like I imagined—nothing." He went on to tell him the events of the night.

"What! She didn't know Ellie was her daughter?"

He shook his head. "Thanks to her parents she thought her baby was dead…and Ellie was mine and Shannon's."

"Lordy, lordy, what kind of parents would do something like that?"

"I don't know, but you should've seen Marisa. Her pain was heart-wrenching and she actually passed out from the shock. But she came back with a strength that surprised me. She told them exactly how she felt and broke all ties with them. She's staying at a friend's."

"Why didn't she come here with you?"

He didn't have an answer, but Tulley had plenty to say. "*This* is where she belongs—with Ellie…and you."

"We can't just turn back the damn clock," he snapped. "Too much has happened and the good emotions have gotten lost in all the senseless pain. I'm not even sure how I feel about her anymore."

"Well, then, you need to buy yourself a mirror."

"What are you talking about?"

"Whenever you look at Marisa, all those good emotions are in your eyes for the world to see. They're not lost. They're right there inside you."

Colter jumped to his feet. "I'm not ready to talk about this."

Tulley rose more slowly. "You know how sometimes we put blinders on a horse to keep him from getting skittish?"

He didn't respond.

"Well, Colt, boy. You're wearing the blinders now."

"I'm checking on Ellie." He headed for the hall.

"Tripp called. Said he and Brodie would come by tomorrow to pick up those horses," Tulley called after him.

"Fine," he muttered.

He walked into Ellie's room, clearing his mind of everything but thoughts of his precious child. She lay on her stomach, arms and legs in all directions. Sooner was curled at her feet, and raised his head when Colter entered.

Colter patted Sooner and drew the covers over Ellie. As he did, she stirred and murmured, "Daddy?"

"Yes, angelface, it's Daddy."

"Hug me."

He gathered her in his arms and she laid her face on his shoulder. "I did something bad and I thought you weren't coming back. I waited and waited and…"

His throat closed for a second. "You can never do anything bad enough that I wouldn't come back. I will always be here for you. Always."

She rubbed her face against him. "I love you, Daddy, and I tried to stay awake so I could give you kisses. You can't sleep if I don't give you kisses."

"No, I can't. I have to have my angelface kisses."

She kissed his cheek and was asleep almost instantly. He held her for a moment longer, then gently put her down and pulled the blanket over her. He stared down at this little girl he loved more than life itself. For now it was just the two of them. Tomorrow would be different.

Tomorrow she'd meet her mother.

Tomorrow.

Marisa dozed on and off and woke before dawn, feeling an anticipation, an exhilaration she hadn't experienced in a long time. She was going to see her daughter, her baby, she told herself. A chorus of nervous jitters followed this, but nothing and no one would keep her away from Ellie.

Reed and Cari were sleeping soundly. They'd been up late comforting her, and she didn't wake them. She scribbled a quick note, which she placed on the table, then left. She knew Cari would drive Reed wherever he wanted to go.

Within minutes, she was at Mrs. Hackleberry's. It was 5:00 a.m. and, not surprisingly, the house was dark. Marisa let herself in and tiptoed up to her room. She quickly showered and changed.

She went through everything in her closet, unable to decide what to wear. Finally she chose rust-colored slacks and a matching jacket with a cream-colored silk blouse. It wasn't too dressy or casual; it was just right. Or was it? She wavered, then realized she was only procrastinating. She brushed her hair one final time, checked her makeup and hurried to the front door.

The kitchen light was on, so she stopped to speak with Hazel, who offered her a cup of coffee. The aroma alone gave her a jolt of energy, and Marisa happily accepted the cup Hazel handed her. She told Hazel about her daughter, and for the first time actually let herself feel an incredible joy.

"Oh, my dear." Hazel hugged her. "This is so unbelievable. And your baby's a girl instead of a boy?"

"Yes. My parents weren't taking any chances," she said, unable to keep the bitterness out of her voice. "If I ever met Colter again, they wanted to make sure I'd never suspect Ellie was mine. And I didn't."

Hazel clicked her tongue. "I don't understand how your parents could do such a thing."

"I'm having a hard time with that myself," she admitted. "But can't dwell on it. I have to go see my daughter." She slipped her purse over her shoulder. "I'm not sure when I'll be back, so don't worry about me."

"Oh, my dear, I don't think I can help doing that."

Marisa gave her a hug and left, her thoughts totally on Ellie…and Colter.

The drive out to the ranch was similar to the one she'd made yesterday. Had it only been yesterday? It seemed like decades ago. So much had changed; her whole life had changed.

Today she had a child—a daughter. It all felt so unreal, so ethereal, and she knew it would be quite a while before it became real to her.

Her nerves were taut by the time she reached the ranch. She drove to the back and parked beside a truck pulling a horse trailer with horses inside. Two men were standing by the truck talking to Colter. She rec-

ognized them immediately—Brodie Hayes and Tripp
Daniels. They were cowboys just like Colter and had
been in Vegas all those years ago.

She sat for a few moments, gathering strength, as she
stared out at the cold December day. There was a slight
breeze and the air seemed to crackle with excitement.

She took several deep breaths and finally climbed
out. She was nervous enough about seeing Ellie, and
she didn't want to have to make small talk with these
men. She had liked them years ago because they were
close friends of Colter's, but she hadn't expected to
see them today.

Colter came over to her, and her heart fluttered
anxiously at the sight of him. He was dressed in jeans
and a white shirt that emphasized the broadness of
his shoulders.

"Hi," she said, her voice husky.

"Hi," he replied.

She sensed a tension in him and knew that he was
nervous, too. It was there in the steady gaze of his brilliant eyes, in the vein that beat fitfully in his neck, and
in the way he shoved his hands into his pockets. They'd
been through so much, but they still had one hurdle to
get over, and it was clearly on both their minds.

Colter turned to his friends. "You remember Brodie and Tripp?"

"Yes," she replied with a slight smile. "Nice to see
you again."

Brodie removed his hat, revealing dark wavy hair.
"The pleasure's all ours. You're more beautiful than
ever, Marisa." Brodie was a born flirt and a charmer,
and Marisa never knew quite how to take him. He

and Colter had been friends for a long time, so she merely smiled.

"That goes for me, too," Tripp put in.

So many memories came back at the sound of his voice. Tripp didn't talk much, but she remembered when he'd told her about his estrangement from his family; there was a sadness in him she could identify with. She liked Tripp. He and Colter had been the best of friends, competing together, and Marisa was glad they'd remained friends over the years. This wasn't the day to reminisce, though.

The message must have gotten through, because Brodie said, "Catch you later, Colt." Tripp tipped his hat and they climbed into the pickup.

She and Colter walked into the house. "Sit down," he invited as they entered the den.

She was glad of the invitation, fearful her legs wouldn't support her much longer.

Tulley stood in the doorway to the kitchen. "Good morning, Marisa."

"Good morning." She tried to smile and failed miserably.

"I'm so sorry, girl. Colter and I never dreamed anything like this had happened."

"I know." She sat on the sofa. "Colter thought I didn't want our baby."

"Yep." Tulley nodded. "That pretty much sums it up." He grabbed his hat. "I'll mosey outside before the person in question makes an appearance."

"Where is Ellie?" she asked, gripping her hands. She wanted to see her daughter so badly that the anticipation was almost unbearable.

"She's not up yet," Colter said, sitting down in a recliner.

"Have you told her anything?"

"No," he replied. "She was half-asleep last night when I got home. In any case, we agreed to tell her together."

"Yes," she muttered, trying to control the spasmodic trembling within her.

He eyed her strangely. "You're not having second thoughts, are you?"

"Of course not," she said. "I'm scared. I don't know how she's going to react."

"Just relax and everything will be fine," he told her, his voice softening.

She was starting to relax, but her whole body tensed at his next words.

"We haven't discussed Ellie yet, but she's been my whole world for the last seven years and her home is here on the ranch. I want her to stay here."

He was worried she might try to take Ellie away from him; she could see it in his eyes and hear it in his voice. She had to reassure him.

"I would never do anything to disrupt Ellie's life. I'm just hoping you'll allow me to be a part of it."

They stared at each other. Colter started to speak, then stopped when he heard Ellie calling, "Daddy, where are you?"

"In the den, angelface," Colter called, his eyes holding Marisa's.

Everything in Marisa seemed to tighten, and she had trouble breathing as she waited for her daughter to enter the room.

Chapter 12

Ellie came racing into the room in her pajamas, Sooner behind her. She slid to a halt when she saw Marisa. "You're back," she exclaimed, and climbed onto Colter's lap. She wrapped her arms around his neck and gave him several loud kisses.

Marisa's breath solidified in her throat as she watched her daughter. This was the baby she'd created in her womb, the baby she'd nourished for almost nine months. She remembered the joy of hearing her first heartbeat and of feeling that first kick. Her hand strayed to her stomach, and she remembered the months she'd lovingly stroked her swelling abdomen, talked to her baby. The baby was now in front of her. *Ellie.*

She'd given Ellie life, fought for thirty long hours to bring her into the world—but did that make her a mother? A mother's title was earned by getting up in the middle of the night, walking the floor during bouts of colic, changing diapers, being there to hear the first sound, the first laugh and to applaud the first step. She'd missed all that, and at that thought, an intense pain filled her heart.

"Did you come to see me?" Ellie asked Marisa, resting against Colter.

"Yes." Marisa clenched her hands until her nails dug into her palms, but she didn't feel it. All she felt was the anxiety in her stomach.

Noticing her difficulty, Colter came to her aid. "Angelface, I want to talk to you."

Ellie swung her gaze to her father's, eyes wary, as if she knew what was on his mind. Raising her hands in a palms-up gesture, she declared, "I won't be bad anymore, Daddy."

"This isn't about yesterday," Colter said calmly. "This is about something else."

"Okay." Ellie gave Colter a little smile.

She was so adorable, it took every ounce of strength Marisa had not to grab her and cover her pixie face with kisses. Instead, she bit her lip and watched as Ellie looked up at Colter with trusting eyes.

"You've been wanting a mother…"

"Yep." Ellie nodded. "Santa said she'd be here by Christmas."

He swallowed, glanced at Marisa, and said, "She's here now."

Ellie sat up, clapping her hands in excitement. "Here at our house?"

"Yes."

Ellie bounced off his lap like a rubber ball, jumping up and down at his feet. "Is she outside with Tulley? Is she? Is she?"

Colter was a bit taken aback by the quick response, but didn't falter in his answer. "No. She's in this room."

"Where?" Ellie looked around as if she expected her mother to pop up from some hiding place. Then her eyes settled on Marisa. "There's nobody here but Marisa."

Colter cleared his throat. "Marisa's your mother... your real mother."

"No, she isn't." Ellie leaned against Colter's knee. "Why are you saying that, Daddy?"

"Because she is."

"No," Ellie said adamantly. "My mommy raced barrels. I heard Brodie say so."

Colter's heart kicked against his ribs. "That was Shannon—your stepmother. Marisa is your real mother."

Ellie stared at Marisa as if she were seeing her for the first time. A sense of inadequacy swept over her as Ellie inspected her from the top of her blond head down to her shoes. She didn't miss a thing, her eyes finally resting on Marisa's face. Marisa wondered what she was thinking, but all she could see in the child's expression was a deep curiosity. Then her face puckered into a frown.

"How come you didn't tell me you were my mommy?"

Marisa tried to speak, but the words were trapped in her throat.

Ellie's pucker deepened. "You lied to me. I don't

want a mommy who lies. And I don't want you." Saying that, she ran for the bedroom.

"Ellie," Colter shouted, but she didn't stop. She kept running.

Marisa bit her hand to keep from crying out. Her worst fears had come true. Ellie had rejected her. She felt as if she'd been hit by an eighteen wheeler and there was nothing left of her. Nothing.

She wasn't even aware of Colter sitting down beside her until he took her into his arms. Her arms went convulsively around his waist, and she found herself clinging to him, needing his support and comfort more than she'd ever needed anything in her life.

He held her, gently rocking her. "She didn't mean it, Marisa. We'll give her a minute, then talk to her again. She's just a child. She'll change her mind. I promise."

"No, she won't," she sobbed against his chest. "She hates me. I knew it. Somehow I knew it. That's why I was so afraid."

His hand idly caressed the nape of her neck, his breath on her hair. "She's just upset right now. In a few minutes it'll be a completely different story. She's wanted a mommy for so long, and at the moment she's angry that you didn't tell her immediately. Ellie doesn't stay angry for long, though. Trust me."

His voice soothed and caressed her, lulling her fears and her pain. Her body began to react to him, and she became aware of other sensations, like the hardness of his chest pressed against hers, the muscles in his back, the clean tangy scent that emanated from him. Desire began to curl in her stomach, sending her emotions off in an entirely different direction.

Those feelings consumed her and she drew back to look at him. His eyes were glazed, and his head came down, his lips lightly touching hers. It was a comforting, soothing kiss. He pulled her closer, and she formed herself against him, enjoying the feel of his body. She didn't know when the kiss changed, but her lips opened under the sensual pressure of his, returning an ardor she'd almost forgotten. The blood that had lain lifeless in her body started to pump hard through her veins.

It felt good and right, and one kind of tension was replaced with another. But this *wasn't* right. They should be thinking about Ellie.

Pushing herself away from him, she self-consciously brushed her hair back from her face. "Please, let's not cloud the issue."

He studied her, his face unreadable. "Yes. I'm sorry."

Marisa didn't want an apology. She wanted…she couldn't put into words what she wanted from Colter. What she'd felt in his arms was only a remnant of the past and it was simply a result of their heightened emotions. She certainly didn't want to complicate things by getting involved with Colter. Ellie was her only concern.

Before she could think of a suitable reply, Tulley came in. "What's wrong with Ellie?"

Colter got to his feet. "Why?"

"I was checking to make sure all the gates were closed after Brodie and Tripp left and I saw her running toward the creek in nothing but her pajamas. It's forty degrees outside. I hollered at her but she wouldn't stop."

"Damn. She must've sneaked out," Colter said. "We told her and she didn't take the news well. I'll go get her. First, I'd better get her some clothes." He hurried away to Ellie's bedroom.

Tulley squinted. "I don't understand this. She's wanted a mother ever since she realized other kids had mommies and she didn't."

Marisa stood on unsteady legs. "She thinks I lied to her."

"Oh."

Colter came back with a jacket, socks and slippers, and they went outside into the cool December morning.

"Aries is saddled if you want to take him," Tulley said.

"Thanks." Colter looked at Marisa. "I'll bring Ellie back and we'll talk this through. Don't worry."

That wasn't so easily done, but she concentrated on Ellie and not on the pain in her heart. Colter ran toward the barn, and she watched as he led a horse outside and swung effortlessly into the saddle. She remembered that about him; he was magnificent on a horse.

"Why don't you go inside where it's warmer?" Tulley suggested.

"I'm not going anywhere until I know my—" she wiped away a tear "—daughter is okay." The word was so new to her that she had a hard time saying it, believing it.

She caught Tulley's worried expression. "I'm not going to fall apart," she told him. "I'm not the weak young girl I used to be."

"I can see that." He folded his arms across his chest.

"I've hated you a lot of years for what you did to him and to Ellie. Now I'm not sure what to say to you."

"Just be understanding. That's all I ask."

"I can do that," he answered, buttoning his jacket. "Why don't I get you a chair."

"No, I'm fine. Thanks," she replied. "I couldn't sit anyway. I'm standing right here until I see her again."

"Then I'm standing with you."

They stood together, waiting, and Marisa wrapped both arms around her waist to still her nerves. Ellie *had* to forgive her. How could she explain to a seven-year-old child what had happened? How could she expect a child to understand? Those questions tore at her, but she was confident that Colter would have the answers. He knew Ellie better than anyone, and she'd listen to him.

Ellie, baby, please listen to your daddy.

Colter saw her not far from the barn, sitting in the winter grass by a small creek that ran through the property. Her arms were tight around Sooner, her face buried against him. His heart lurched at the sight, and he dismounted and walked over to her, searching for the words to ease her pain. He squatted beside her and handed her the socks and fuzzy slippers.

She grabbed them. "Sooner and me are running away," she announced, shoving a foot into a sock. "Don't try to stop us."

He laid her jacket in her lap. "Where are you going?"

"Don't know." She poked her arms into the sleeves. "We might live in the woods. Tulley said you can live on berries, bark and other stuff, but I forget." She shrugged. "Doesn't matter. Sooner and me will figure it out."

"I see." He sat on the grass and drew his knees up. "That makes me very sad. Who's going to give me angelface kisses?"

There was silence for a moment, then her bottom lip trembled and she flew into Colter's arms. "I will, Daddy. I will," she cried against his face. "Why did she lie to me? Didn't she want me?"

He smoothed her hair with a shaky hand, praying for strength to tell her the truth without hurting her. "She didn't lie to you, baby."

Ellie stuck out her chin. "Yes, she did. She knew she was my mommy and she didn't tell me. She even let me talk to Santa and she *knew*."

Colter settled her in the crook of his arm. "I'm going to tell you a story and I want you to listen carefully."

"Okay." She held his hand tightly.

"When I met your mother, she was seventeen, shy and very beautiful. The moment our eyes met, it was like—" he thought for a second "—like spontaneous combustion. Do you know what that means?"

"No."

How could he explain so she could understand? "We fell in love instantly, and we spent every moment we could together."

"Oh," Ellie said. "It was real love, Daddy?"

"Hmm." He'd believed it was, hoped it was. Now he wasn't sure. He wasn't sure about anything.

"What happened next?" she asked, playing with his fingers.

"We were so busy being in love that we ignored the problems in our relationship."

"What problems?"

"Remember how when you asked about your mother, I told you she left because she was unhappy?"

Ellie nodded.

"That was partly true. Marisa lived in New York and was a gifted pianist, and it was her mother's dream that one day Marisa would be a world-renowned musician. But that wasn't Marisa's dream. She was tired of the long hours of training. That's why she and some of her friends came to Vegas that year for the National Rodeo Finals. Her mother was away and she wanted some freedom, some fun. But when she told me she loved me as much as I loved her, I asked her to marry me and she said yes."

Ellie was quiet, so he continued. "The next morning, I rushed out to buy her a ring. When I got back, she was gone."

"Where did she go?"

"Her mother found out where she was and came after her and made her leave."

"Why?"

"Marisa was only seventeen, and her mother had control of her. She was still considered a minor."

"Like you have control of me?"

"Yes. Like I have control of you." He rested his chin on the top of her head and prayed for strength to finish the story. "Back in New York, your mother soon realized she was pregnant, but she didn't know how to get in touch with me. I hadn't told her exactly where I lived when I wasn't riding on the circuit. So she hired a private investigator to find me, and he told her I was already married to someone else."

"Oh." Ellie looked up at him. "Were you, Daddy?"

"Not then, but later I married Shannon," he said. "The detective was paid to lie to her, and Marisa became very upset and started having problems with the pregnancy. The problems became so severe, her mother put her in a clinic."

Ellie was absorbing every word, and he was glad she didn't ask who'd paid the detective.

He had to finish the story. His courage wavered for a second, then he resumed. "Marisa's mother felt Marisa was too young to be a mommy and planned to put the baby up for adoption, but Marisa refused to sign the papers. She wanted her baby, and she intended to keep you."

"Did she really want me, Daddy?"

"Oh, yes, she wanted you." He was certain of that now.

"What happened?"

"Her parents decided that you belonged with your father, so they contacted me and I went to New York to get you. They told me Marisa didn't want the baby and she didn't want to see me."

"No, Daddy, no," Ellie whimpered, squeezing his hand.

"They were wrong about that, but I didn't know it then." His arm tightened around her. "Three days later, I flew back to Texas with my brand-new daughter."

"What happened to Marisa?"

He noticed she couldn't say "Mommy" just yet, and he took a long breath. The next part would be hard, but he had to tell her. "Your mother was under a lot of medication for the delivery, so she doesn't remember too much. She heard a baby crying, though, and she's been haunted by that sound for the past seven years." He turned her face up to his. "You see, baby, they told her you were stillborn."

"What does that mean?"

He breathed in deeply. "That you were born dead."

She shook her head. "No, I wasn't."

"I know, but your mother's believed that for all these years. She's been very sad. That's the reason she came out here the first day, when we had the storm. She wanted to tell me about you—that you were born—but I was so angry because I still believed she'd given you away."

"But she didn't?"

"No, baby. She didn't even know you were alive until last night. It's been quite a shock to her."

Ellie threw her arms around his neck.

"You've been wanting a mommy and she's been grieving for her baby. Both of you have been searching for the same thing—each other. She loves you, angelface. Give her a chance."

"I want my mommy," she sniffled into his shoulder.

He stood with her in his arms. "Let's go tell her that."

He placed her in the saddle, then mounted behind her. It had been a while since they'd ridden like this. Ellie was fiercely independent, and by the age of three she was riding by herself. People changed, just like the seasons, and he hoped he was ready for the changes that were about to occur in his life and Ellie's.

* * *

They rode up to the barn and Ellie swung her leg over the saddle horn and slid to the ground. Marisa stood in the spot where Colter had left her. Her arms were wrapped around her waist as if to brace herself. He dismounted and watched Ellie.

Marisa watched her, too. She held her breath as she waited for her daughter's next move. Ellie's hair was disheveled and she looked a sight in the fuzzy pink slippers and heavy jacket—the best sight Marisa had ever seen.

Forgive me. Forgive me. Forgive me echoed back through the years, through all the pain, all the heartache. And everything came down to this child's reaction, her understanding and acceptance.

Ellie kept staring at her.

Marisa licked parched lips. "Remember when we were waiting to see Santa, you told me your mommy wanted to come home and you had to let her know you wanted her to. That's why you had to see Santa. That's why you believe." She dragged in a breath. "You were right. I'm here, Ellie. I'm your mother."

Ellie flung out her arms and sprinted toward Marisa. The pain inside Marisa abated and she ran to meet her daughter. She lifted her up in her arms, holding her in a fierce grip.

"I'm sorry, Mommy," Ellie cried against her neck.

The sound of that word tripped every emotional breaker in her, and she struggled for composure. "No, baby, no." Marisa caressed her hair, her face. "You have nothing to be sorry for."

"Mommy, Mommy, Mommy" was Ellie's sad refrain.

The emotional current took its toll and Marisa sank to her knees under the impact. Tears flowed unheeded and she held tight to her daughter, kissing her face over and over.

Colter watched from a distance, his stomach churning with the same emotions.

Tulley walked up to him. "I can't take this. I'll unsaddle Aries."

Colter couldn't take it, either, but he had to. Mother and daughter had found each other. He was happy about that, but deep inside a worry stabbed at him. It had been just the two of them, he and Ellie, for so long. Where did this leave him? He had no desire to question or to deny Marisa's right to Ellie. He just wished he knew her plans for the future. At this point, he suspected she didn't have any. Later, though, it would be different. *How* different was what he wondered.

He remembered the way they'd kissed earlier. The fire, the passion was still there for him. For Marisa he wasn't sure. She'd responded, but seemed to hate herself for that reaction. He shouldn't have kissed her in the first place. It was spontaneous, as he'd told Ellie—like it always had been between them.

He had never been more aware of the differences in their two worlds than he was today. She was imported wine and vacations on the Riviera. He was beer and a drive to the lake. How did he ever think two such different people could make a marriage work? They had nothing in common except a simmering passion, and they'd both learned the hard way that it wasn't enough.

Where did they go from here? *To an uncertain future* was his only answer. He'd take it one day at a time and make this transition as easy as possible for Marisa and Ellie…and pray that he wouldn't get his heart broken again. Hell, it had never even been repaired after the last time, so the best he could hope for was a friendship with Marisa to build a stable future for Ellie.

It wouldn't be easy being friends with a woman he'd loved and hated more than anyone in his life, but he had to find some kind of compromise with Marisa— for all of them.

Chapter 13

Colter walked over and clasped Marisa by the elbows, lifting her to her feet. He tried to take Ellie from her, but her arms tightened around the girl.

"Let's go into the house," he suggested. "It's much warmer."

He went ahead and held the door open. Marisa followed him, then settled on the sofa with Ellie on her lap. She helped Ellie off with her coat and cupped her face in both hands. "I love you," she said in a hoarse voice. "I have always loved you."

"I know. Daddy told me."

Marisa glanced at Colter, sending him a silent thank-you. He sat beside her, his leg brushing against hers.

"I told her the whole story. The time for lies and secrets is over."

"I don't like your mommy," Ellie said. "Why didn't she want me?"

Marisa stroked her face. "Oh, baby. It wasn't that." She kissed Ellie's cheek. "She just thought I was too young to be a mother."

It seemed odd to be defending her mother, but she had to protect Ellie to ensure she didn't grow up with any hatred or bitterness. Ellie deserved complete happiness. For a paralyzing moment she wondered if her mother had experienced those same feelings about her.

"Daddy said you play the piano really good."

"Yes," she admitted, surprised he'd told Ellie that.

"I take piano lessons, and my teacher says I'm really good, too."

This time she couldn't hide her surprise, and she looked at Colter for confirmation.

"I thought it might be something she'd enjoy," he explained.

She stared at him, seeing a different side to this man she'd once loved so deeply. Back then, their relationship had been mostly physical. Now she was getting a glimpse of the loving, caring man he really was.

"I do," Ellie said, "but I like riding better. I race barrels, and Tulley says I'm getting faster. You got to be fast to win and I'm gonna be a winner like my daddy."

Marisa stroked Ellie's face again, loving the confidence in that tiny voice. She'd never been that way, and she envied that strong spirit. "There's no doubt in my mind you will be."

"I can play the piano, too," Ellie told her again.

Marisa sensed that Ellie wanted to please her, and she had to make something clear. "You never have to do anything to please me. I love you just the way you are." She wouldn't pressure Ellie or set goals for her that weren't her own.

"Okay, but I can play sometimes, except Sooner said it hurts his ears."

Marisa smiled, hardly able to believe this adorable child was hers—and Colter's. She held Ellie's face. "Do you know how many times I've wondered what you looked like?"

"Bunches?"

"Yes, bunches, and in all my wondering you had those beautiful green eyes." In her dreams her baby was a boy, and she realized Colter hadn't told Ellie that part of the story. She was glad—it would only confuse the child more.

"Daddy's eyes."

"Oh, yes, you have your daddy's eyes. I wish I'd seen you as a baby, as a toddler, as a—" Her voice cracked and she had to stop.

"But you can see me now," Ellie said, her eyes bright.

"Yes. I can see you now, and I'm so grateful for that. I meant when you were first born."

"Me, too." She jumped off Marisa's lap and pointed to the built-in entertainment center, its rows of book-shelves filled with videos. "Daddy took tons of videos of me. Let's show her, Daddy."

Colter got to his feet and joined Ellie.

"Get the first one," Ellie instructed. "The very first one."

"Okay, angelface," Colter said. "Have a seat and I'll pop it in the VCR."

Ellie ran back to Marisa and sat on her lap. Colter got the remote and clicked it on, then returned to his seat by Marisa.

Soon images flashed on the screen and Marisa caught her breath. There was Colter, a younger Colter, the man she'd known, and he was holding a baby wrapped in a pink blanket.

"I'd like to introduce Ellen Kincaid." Colter's voice came from the TV. "I named her after my mother, but I think I'll call her Ellie. With that angel face, she looks like an Ellie to me." The camera zoomed in on the precious little face. Ellie was asleep, and her features were perfect—bow mouth, pert nose and blond hair with a pink ribbon in it. Marisa's arms ached to hold that baby. Instead she hugged the little girl in her arms.

"There's Tulley, Aunt Becky and Aunt Jen." Ellie pointed out the people hovering around the newborn. "There's Brodie and Tripp and a friend of Daddy's."

It was Shannon Wells—the woman Colter had married, the woman who had taken her place. She wondered about that relationship, but she didn't have time to speculate on it as she watched her child.

She was mesmerized by the videos. Her baby grew right before her eyes; she heard the first gurgles. She saw her smile, roll over, rock on all fours and then crawl. Ellie pulled herself up on furniture and took tottering steps toward Colter. He was there to catch her when she fell, just like he'd been since the day she was born.

Marisa didn't even realize she was crying until Colter thrust a wad of tissues into her hands. She wiped at her eyes, unable to take them from the screen. *Dada* was Ellie's first word and she said it over and over, trailing behind Colter. Every birthday, holiday and special occasion was there for Marisa to see, and her heart broke a little more at each one she'd missed.

Tulley made sandwiches for lunch, and they continued to watch Ellie's life. There were so many videos, but Marisa never grew tired of them. She needed to see them all, and Ellie was excited to show her everything.

Marisa lost track of the time. She was enthralled with the wonderful gift she'd been given—the gift of her daughter's life. They ate supper around the TV, and her eyes didn't move from the screen as Ellie got ready for her first day of school. In the video Colter was trying to reassure her, but it was clear that Colter was the one who was nervous, not Ellie. Later she saw Ellie lose her first tooth and wake up to find money from the tooth fairy under her pillow. The last video was of this past Thanksgiving with the Kincaid family; she could clearly see that Ellie was the center of attention in a loving home.

The screen went blank; the videos were over and Ellie was asleep in her arms.

She looked at Colter. "What time is it?"

"Almost midnight." He stood. "Let me take Ellie. I'll put her to bed."

"No." Her arms tightened around the child. "Please, let me do it."

"Okay." As he stepped back, Marisa rose to her feet with Ellie and carried her to her room. Colter pulled the covers back and she gently laid her down. Ellie still had her pajamas on.

"Should we change her pajamas?" Marisa asked.

"No, she's fine." He tucked her in.

Ellie squirmed. "Daddy?"

"Yes, angelface?"

"Gotta...gotta give you kisses," she mumbled.

He bent down to kiss her, and Marisa wondered if Ellie would ever need her the way she needed her father. Anger threatened to overwhelm her—anger at her mother, her father, at what had been taken from her—but those were emotions that could destroy her. She wouldn't let them. She had too much to be happy about and that was what she'd concentrate on.

"Mommy," Ellie whimpered, and hearing that one word made all the grief and rage disappear.

"I'm right here, baby," she answered, kissing her softly. She rearranged the covers around her, and Sooner jumped on the bed. "'Night," she whispered as she and Colter left the room.

In the hallway she asked Colter, "Do you mind if I stay the night? I'd like to be here when she wakes up."

"No," he replied. "It'll save me answering a million questions in the morning."

She wanted to hug or touch him, but she didn't. "Thank you," she said instead.

"You can use Becky's room. Take whatever clothes you need."

"Thank you," she said again. "And thanks for explaining everything to Ellie."

He nodded and she could feel a tension building between them, an unbearable tension that neither knew how to end.

He turned toward his room, then swung back. "Tulley said your friend Cari called. He told her you were watching videos of Ellie and she said not to disturb you. She asked if you were okay, so you might want to give her a call."

"I will, thanks."

"Good night."

"'Night," she called as he walked down the hall.

She hurried upstairs to Becky's room and picked up the phone. It was twelve-fifteen, but since it was a Saturday, Cari was probably still awake.

"Cari, it's me," Marisa said when she answered.

"Marisa, are you okay? What's going on?"

She told her about Ellie and what they'd done that day.

"Wow. So you're spending the night?"

"Yes, and I don't want ever to leave my daughter."

"Maybe Colter will let you stay there for a while."

"I don't know." She hesitated. "He's been very kind under the circumstances, but I can feel the distance he keeps between us. I'm not sure I want it any other way."

"Marisa, you're kidding yourself," Cari said. "You've been in love with him ever since I've known you. You can't just turn off that kind of love."

She drew a jagged breath. "But that kind of love hurts, and I don't want to experience it again. All I want is my daughter."

"Are you saying you're going to try and get custody of Ellie?"

"God, no. I'd never do that to Ellie or Colter. But I intend to be a part of her life."

"Well, Marisa, you may not have noticed, but they come as a package deal."

"Yes," she mumbled, suddenly feeling tired. She had to ask Cari a question, though. "Where did you find the Santa with the white suit and beard who talked to Ellie?"

There was a slight pause. "I didn't hire anyone like that."

"Sure you did. He came to your office and spoke with Ellie."

"Oh, good. I'm glad he finally made it. I rushed all over the place and never could find the Santa who was scheduled that day. They said he was taking a break, and I told everyone to send him to my office, so I guess he got the message."

"Cari, this man was round, with red cheeks and his long hair and beard were white and obviously real."

"I didn't hire anyone who looked remotely like that."

"Did you tell Santa about Ellie or me?"

"No. I never had a chance to speak with him, but as I said, I left messages all over the place."

"That's so weird," Marisa mused. "He knew Ellie had taken a cab to Dalton's and he also knew my name."

"Maybe it *was* Santa Claus," Cari teased.

"At this point I'd believe just about anything—the toy shop, flying reindeer, the works."

Cari laughed. "I'll ask around to see if anyone's seen this man."

"Please do. I'm very curious now, since he told Ellie she'd have a mother by Christmas." She paused, then asked, "Do you know where Reed is?"

"He checked into a hotel." Cari gave her the number.

"I'll call him tomorrow."

"Marisa, are you okay?"

"No, I'm not." She didn't lie. "I'm worried and scared, yet I feel a strength I've never felt before. I'm not sure about the future, but one thing I do know—I will not let go of my daughter again."

Another long pause. "Your father's called several times."

"Please, Cari, I can't talk about them. I'll call you later. Bye."

Overpowering feelings returned in full force. "No," she said aloud to stop the turmoil inside her. She wouldn't think about them today—not today, when she had all these wonderful new memories of Ellie.

She took a quick shower and found an oversize T-shirt to sleep in. The lonely bed wasn't all that appealing. She was too far away from Ellie…and Colter. She grabbed a terry-cloth robe and went downstairs, intending to sleep with Ellie. That was the only way she'd get any rest tonight.

As she walked down the hall, she noticed Colter's light was on, and without thinking, went toward his room. He was sitting on the side of the bed, his face in his hands, his shoulders stooped, as if the weight of the world had crashed down upon him. In that moment, she realized how all of this had affected him. She had broken his heart once before and now she was doing it again by disrupting everything he'd built with Ellie. She wasn't sure how to make any of this right—there probably *wasn't* a way—but she had to talk to him.

"Colter."

His head jerked up. "I thought you were in bed."

"I came down to sleep with Ellie."

"She has a twin bed," he told her.

"Doesn't matter. I just need to be near her." Her eyes held his. "You do understand that, don't you?"

"Yes, Marisa, I understand that." His voice was cool, belying those words.

She sat on the bed beside him. "Could we talk?"

"Sure." He moved a space away from her, which didn't escape her notice.

"I feel as if I should apologize, but I'm not sure for what. Maybe for being young, stupid and gullible."

"Do you regret what happened between us?"

"No," she admitted in a strangled voice. "I just regret what happened afterward."

"But that wasn't your fault."

She linked her fingers. "It was. Don't you see? I was looking for freedom...and excitement. I found all of that with you, and I never considered any consequences. And later when I discovered I was pregnant, I was too scared and weak to stand up to my mother. I let her make all the decisions for me, just like she always had." There, she'd said the words that had tormented her during the long hours of the previous night.

"You didn't sign the adoption papers," he reminded her. "That took strength."

"But look what happened. I kept thinking I heard Ellie crying, and yet I believed everything I was told. If I'd just—"

"Marisa, you can't live your life on *ifs*. It happened, and we can't go back and change a thing. We have to move forward."

"I know, but I just feel so responsible, so helpless."

"Don't you think I've been feeling the same way? I lay awake last night wondering how I could've let this happen. I was old enough—and experienced enough—to think about the consequences, but when I was with you all rational thought went right out of my head. Placing blame isn't going to help either of us, though."

It wasn't that she wanted to place blame. She just had to voice these feelings that were clamoring inside her—and she had to know how he really felt about her.

"What comes next?" she asked. "For us, I mean."

"What do you expect me to tell you?"

"The truth," she said.

"I don't want to hurt you. You've been hurt enough."

His poignant words touched her, and for a moment she hesitated. Maybe she should let him keep his feelings to himself, but she couldn't. They had to be honest with each other to get through this.

"Don't worry about me. I can take care of myself," she told him with more confidence than she felt.

He glanced at her. "You've changed in so many ways."

"Yes," she agreed.

"But I can't help wondering if maybe everything worked out for the best."

Color drained from her face. "How can you say that?"

"I don't mean about Ellie," he hastened to explain. "You and she will never get back those lost years. I'm talking about you and me."

"What *about* us?" she asked, suspecting she wouldn't really like the answer.

"I don't think we were ever meant to be together."

To Marisa each word was like a blow.

"Looking back, can you honestly see yourself traveling the country in a small trailer? The rodeo life was stressful for you. The animals frightened you, and you were uncomfortable with the crowds, the injuries, the day-to-day existence. Within a month, the gypsy lifestyle would've gotten to you and you would've gone back to New York, to your mother."

The truth of his words lay between them, and as much as she wanted to, she couldn't deny what he'd said. "Maybe," she had to admit. "I was so young, so out of touch with reality, but I... I really loved you."

"You were seventeen years old. You knew nothing about love. I was the first man you'd ever slept with."

"Does that diminish my feelings?"

"No, of course not, but—"

"I was unsure about a lot of things back then, but not of that. I loved you."

He swallowed. "I loved you more than I'll ever love anyone again."

"So what happened to all that love?"

He took a deep breath. "It's like ashes after a fire. It's too late to revive the flames."

She gripped her fingers until they were numb. "I probably would've made you a terrible wife anyway." She'd meant to be lighthearted, but the words came out sounding hurt.

"We'll never know, will we?" was his only reply.

"No," she said, feeling an acute pain for losing more than seven years of her daughter's life.

"We're two totally different people. In certain ways, you're still that young girl whose life is so completely unlike mine." He ran a hand through his hair. "Your life is the city, your career, your family. My life is here on this ranch, tending to my horses, looking after my daughter. My idea of a good time is saddling up and camping out under the stars. Your idea of a good time is going to New York—shopping, dining out and spending the evening at the opera."

She remembered telling him how much she loved the opera, and she did love New York. But that was so many years ago, a lifetime ago, and it wasn't who she was today.

"I'm *not* that same girl." She tightened the belt of her robe. "I'm estranged from my family and I have a nine-to-five job. I can't even remember the last time I went to the opera."

His eyes clung to hers. "Yes, you've changed— you've matured, but…" His voice trailed off, leaving them with visions of a life they were never going to share.

"Did you love Shannon?" The words emerged before she could stop them. He and Shannon shared the same kind of life, the same interests, but their marriage had failed, and she was curious—very curious.

He got up and shoved his hands into his pockets. "Not the way I loved you."

"Then why did you marry her?"

For a second, she thought he wasn't going to answer, then his words came.

"After you left, I tried to lose your memory in a bottle. I took risks I shouldn't have and got several cracked ribs and a broken collarbone. Tulley talked until he was blue in the face, but I wasn't listening. I was set on a course of self-destruction. Shannon made me her own personal cause, and eventually I started to listen to her. I saw her differently than I had in all the years I'd known her. She was an attractive, caring woman. I knew she wanted us to have a future, but I couldn't do that until I got you out of my system."

He sucked air into his lungs. "Neither one of us was prepared for the shock of finding out about Ellie. Shannon said it didn't matter—that she wanted to try and be Ellie's mother. *Try* was the operative word. Ellie was my baby and I wanted to do everything for her and, in truth, I never really gave Shannon much of a chance. I regret that, but after a few months we both knew the marriage was over. She returned to Wyoming, then filed for divorce. She continued to ride the circuit and I stayed in Texas to raise my daughter."

"I see," she murmured, staring down at her white knuckles. So much heartache and pain, and a little girl caught in the middle.

"I apologize for kissing you earlier. I was entirely out of line."

Her eyes flew to his.

"As much as we might want to, we can't rekindle feelings from the past. Those ashes have been scattered to hell and back, and there's nothing left. Right now our concern is Ellie and her future, and that should be our total focus. She's at the age where she needs her mother."

Tears stung her eyes. She willed herself not to cry. He was only echoing her feelings. Then why did his words hurt so much?

"She's out of school for the holidays, and it's only

seven days before Christmas, so why don't you plan on spending that time with her."

Her pulse quickened. "You mean stay here?"

"Yes. I think it's what Ellie needs."

"I need it, too," she said, getting to her feet. Still, she had the impression that it was the last thing Colter wanted. She wasn't questioning his reasons, though.

"You can use Becky's room. She won't be here for the holidays. In her off time, she's helping our sister Jennifer, who's having a difficult pregnancy."

"Thank you. I appreciate that, but I have a job with Madame Hélèna and I'll have to check with her about my schedule."

His lips thinned. "When you can fit Ellie into your schedule, let me know."

He began to walk past her and she grabbed his arm. All the years of being manipulated and controlled came down to this moment, and strength born from the lessons learned surged through her.

"How dare you!" she said fiercely. "Everything else has been taken away from me, but you're not taking my pride. Madame Hélèna was gracious enough to give me a job when no one else would. Out of respect, I feel I owe her an explanation. On Monday I plan to tell her about Ellie and I'm hoping she'll give me the time I need. If not, I'll have to quit. My daughter comes first."

He removed her hand from his arm and his touch sent pinpoints of warmth along her skin.

"Let's be clear on one thing. As I said before, Ellie stays here with me. This is her home."

"What are you saying?"

"I'm saying Ellie's not to go *anywhere* without my permission."

"Oh," she whispered, seeing fear in his eyes and recognizing it for what it was. He was afraid she'd try to leave with Ellie and never come back.

"Let *me* be clear on one thing," she said, her anger subsiding. "I will never hurt Ellie or take her away from you. If you want me to ask permission to go places with her, then I will—to set your mind at ease."

He seemed dumbstruck. Finally he said, "Thank you."

"You're welcome. All I'm asking is that you not judge me as the weak young girl I used to be. Judge me for the woman I am today and trust me a little."

"I'll try," he muttered, but she could see that she'd have to earn that trust. And she would.

She stalked toward the door. "Now I'm going to my daughter."

Ellie was sprawled across the bed, and Marisa stood there for a moment, watching her. Then she pulled back the covers and crawled in. Sooner whined in protest and moved to the foot of the bed. She gathered Ellie in her arms.

She didn't know how she and Colter had arrived at such an angry standoff, but she knew their difficult situation would invoke many disagreements, possibly even arguments. She just hoped they could continue to talk them out.

She drifted into a beautiful dream, and she held the dream in her arms.

Colter walked into his closet, pushing back clothes to reveal a safe. He turned the knob to the correct numbers and opened it. He took out three objects—a small box, a certificate and a piece of paper—and carried them into the bedroom. Sitting on the bed again, he opened the box. A diamond ring sparkled up at him, as bright as all the lights in Vegas. He'd bought it for Marisa and he still had it. Why? He wasn't sure. He just hadn't been able to get rid of it.

Picking up Ellie's birth certificate, he stared at the name: *Marisa Ellen Kincaid.* He and Tulley were the only ones who knew he'd put Marisa's name on it. At the time, he wasn't sure why he'd done that, either. He just wanted Ellie to have something of her mother's.

Later he'd regretted that impulse. He didn't want Ellie to have *anything* of Marisa's, so he told everyone her name was just Ellen. No one ever questioned him, not even when he registered her for school.

He reached for the single sheet of paper and forced himself to read the words on it: Colter, I've changed my mind. I can't marry a rodeo rider. Our worlds are too different. I'm sorry. Marisa.

He'd told Marisa their love was like ashes after a fire. Then why did these three objects have such power over him?

Quickly, he left the house and headed for the corrals. Within minutes, he'd saddled up and headed out into the cold December night. He spurred the horse on, feeling as if demons were chasing him, knowing that the only way to escape them was to ride hard and long until exhaustion overtook him.

Chapter 14

Colter woke up the next morning and quickly dressed. He wasn't sure what this day was going to bring, but as long as Ellie was happy, that was all that mattered to him. He stopped at her doorway, glancing in. Ellie was cradled in Marisa's arms and both their faces looked content. *You have your mother, baby girl. And Daddy's feeling a lot of conflicting emotions.*

He'd been hard on Marisa last night, but she'd asked what he was thinking and feeling. A lot of his inner turmoil had spilled out, and he'd said things he hadn't meant to.

The sight of the two of them was mesmerizing. They'd kicked the covers away, and Marisa's T-shirt had ridden up to reveal her long, slim legs. An unwelcome jolt of awareness centered in his lower abdomen. She was a restless sleeper. He remembered that about her—and so many other things that continued to haunt him.

Tearing his eyes away, he went to the kitchen. Tulley was sitting at the table drinking coffee and reading the paper.

"Morning," he said, pouring himself a cup.

"Morning, boy." Tulley put down the paper. "Marisa's car is still here. Is she in Becky's room?"

"No." He sat across from Tulley. "She slept with Ellie."

"Should've guessed that." Tulley peered at him. "Why are you so down in the mouth?"

He shook his head. "I'm not sure. I'm glad we finally know the truth. Ellie has her mother and Marisa has her daughter, but I keep wondering where we go from here."

"To the future...together," Tulley answered without hesitation.

"I wish it was that simple."

"Why isn't it?"

"Because it isn't," he snapped. "Marisa's life has been torn apart and she's not sure *what* she wants."

"Her daughter," Tulley replied. "She wants her daughter."

"Yeah." He shifted uncomfortably.

"What are you worried about?"

He gripped the cup. "This is Ellie's home, I want her to stay here, but as she gets to know her mother she might feel differently."

"You mean she might prefer to live with her mother."

"Yeah and...and that would kill me." He took a big swallow of coffee.

Tulley clicked his tongue.

"What?" he asked when Tulley didn't say anything.

"Colt, boy, you have to trust Marisa to do the right thing."

"I don't think I can ever trust her completely again."

"That's the problem," Tulley said. "You're hiding behind the past and all the pain—pain you don't want to feel a second time. But you're going to have to step forward now and see Marisa for the woman she is today. The woman I see would never hurt Ellie—or you. So give her a chance. For Ellie, give her a chance."

Marisa had said almost the same words last night. He gazed out the window, knowing Tulley was right, but that trust would not come easy. "I invited her to stay here during the holidays."

"That's good. I'm proud of you."

His eyes slid to Tulley. "How long do you think she'll hang around the ranch? It's not what she's used to."

"I don't think she cares where she is as long as she's with Ellie—and you."

"No. I'm not even in the picture."

Tulley clicked his tongue again, and it irritated him.

"Will you stop that?"

"Now we're getting to the crux of what's really bothering you. It has nothing to do with how long she'll stay here or if she'll take Ellie away. It's how she feels about you."

"That's nonsense. What we had is over—has been for a very long time."

"Has it?" Tulley raised an eyebrow.

Colter glared at him and opened his mouth to speak, but then they heard voices and he knew Marisa and Ellie were awake. His concentration was now on them.

Tulley got to his feet. "I'll start feeding the horses."

"I'm going to Dallas to tell Becky and Jen about Marisa, so I'll be gone most of the day."

"Leaving the wicked mother alone with your child, huh?"

Colter stood. "That's not funny."

"Lighten up, boy, or you're gonna explode with all those emotions inside you."

He took a deep breath. "Just keep an eye on them while I'm out."

"Okay. Tell everyone hi." He reached for his hat and ambled out the door.

"Daddy, Daddy, Daddy," Ellie called, racing into the room with Marisa and Sooner behind her. She flew into Colter's arms and he held her tight. "Daddy." Ellie smothered his face with kisses. "When I woke up, Mommy was in my bed."

"Really?" He met Marisa's eyes.

"Yeah. That's cool, huh?"

"Very cool."

He sat with Ellie on his lap and watched Marisa pour a cup of coffee. He should've asked if she wanted some, but when he was around her his brain didn't function too well.

"Listen up, angelface." He pushed back Ellie's hair. "Daddy's going to Aunt Jen's, so you and your mother are on your own today."

"Okay. I'll show her my horses and how good I can ride."

He tweaked her nose. "No showing off."

Ellie made a face.

He stroked her hair, needing to hold her for a moment longer. "We have to get a Christmas tree. We've never left it this late."

"When can we, Daddy? When?"

He rose and stood her on her feet. "Maybe tomorrow. You be good for your mother, okay?"

"I will," Ellie chirped.

His eyes met Marisa's again. "She usually has cereal and fruit for breakfast."

"I'll fix whatever she wants."

He grimaced. "Please don't say that. She'll have you jumping through hoops."

"What's that mean, Daddy?" Ellie asked.

"It means, don't take advantage of your mother."

"Okay." She pulled a chair up to the cabinet. "I'll fix toast. Sooner likes toast."

"Ellie…"

"Don't worry," Marisa said. "I'll make sure she doesn't give Sooner a loaf of bread."

"You're beginning to know her." They stared at each other for endless seconds, then Colter turned away and grabbed his hat. "I'll see you both later."

Outside he drew a couple of deep breaths. He hadn't planned to leave this early, but he had to get away to sort through what he was feeling.

The day was one of the happiest of Marisa's life. She was grateful to Colter for giving her this time with Ellie, although she wished he hadn't felt he had to leave. After last night she wasn't sure where she stood with him. He didn't trust her—that was very clear. In the days and weeks ahead she resolved to regain his trust. *And his love.* Those words hovered in her mind and she pushed them away. She couldn't be in love with Colter after all these years. But sometimes, in her weaker moments, she wondered if she'd ever fallen *out* of love with him. Colter was right, though; their love was like ashes after a fire, never to be rekindled again. Today she chose to believe that.

After breakfast, Ellie took a bath and they got dressed, then Ellie showed her every nook and cranny of the house. Marisa hadn't really looked at Colter's home before. It was quite large, with three bedrooms upstairs and three downstairs. Tulley's room was off the kitchen. She loved the country charm, the baby grand piano and especially the attention lavished on Ellie's room.

The room that really caught her eye, though, was Colter's study. It suggested masculinity, from the dark mahogany walls to the oversize desk. Large windows gave a breathtaking view of the ranch, but that scene wasn't what really held her. It was the trophies, belt buckles, hats, pictures and memorabilia from his rodeo days. There were so many things, even a silver saddle, that she could hardly take them in.

Later they went to the barn. Ellie wanted to show her how well she could ride. Marisa sat on the fence, her heart in her throat, as Ellie raced around the barrels, but the little girl handled her horse magnificently. Just like her father...

"Did I do good?" Ellie asked Tulley, who was timing her.

He nodded. "Gettin' better."

"You were marvelous." Marisa clapped from the fence.

Ellie rode up, dismounted and gave the horse some sugar cubes. "Wanna pet her?"

Marisa's pulse quickened, but she slid to the ground, trying to hide her fear.

"She won't hurt you, see?" Ellie patted the horse's head, sensing Marisa's nervousness. "Touch her," she said, as if instructing a child, and Marisa reached out and stroked the reddish brown face. If Ellie had asked her to walk on hot coals, she probably would've done that, too.

"Her name is Dandelion, but I call her Dandy."

"Hi, Dandy." Marisa smiled and the horse nuzzled her. Her whole body froze.

"She just wants sugar," Ellie said, handing her a couple of cubes. "Usually I give her carrots 'cause Daddy says it's better, but Dandy loves sugar." Marisa relaxed and held the cubes out to the horse. She gobbled them up.

Surprising herself, Marisa stroked Dandy's neck. It was so easy. The horse was gentle and affectionate, and she responded to that.

"Time to feed Dandy," Tulley said.

"Okay," Ellie answered, and Marisa followed them into the barn.

Ellie unsaddled the horse with the ease of someone much older and then led Dandy to a pasture, where she removed the bridle. She hurried back for a bucket of feed and dumped it in a trough.

Marisa noticed a red stallion, the horse that had thrown Colter, in another corral, pawing the ground in anger.

"That's Red Devil," Ellie told her. "He's a mean old horse, but when Daddy gets through training him he won't be so mean. Daddy knows all about horses."

There was pride in every word, and it reinforced what Marisa already knew—how much Ellie loved her father. Marisa had no intention of changing that.

They sat on a wooden swing on the patio, and Ellie talked about her friends, her school and the ranch. Marisa listened avidly. She soaked up every nuance of her daughter's life and personality, and for the first time in years she felt at peace.

When Colter returned, they had a quiet supper. He seemed distant, and she wondered what his sisters had said about her. He announced that everyone was fine and looking forward to Christmas, with no further comment or details.

Later Marisa explained to Ellie that she'd be gone in the morning, assuring the child she'd be back as soon as she could.

"You *will* come back?" Ellie asked with a tremor in her voice.

Marisa cupped her face. "Now that I know about you, I'll always come back. No matter what, you can count on that."

"Okay." Ellie shuffled her feet, and Marisa wanted to call Madame Hélèna and quit on the spot.

She couldn't do that, though. She had to be a responsible adult and she had to set an example for Ellie.

"When I get back, maybe we can talk your dad into getting that Christmas tree."

"Oh boy." Ellie brightened. "A big one?"

"Yes," Marisa said with a grin. "A really big one."

"Time for bath and bed," Colter interrupted.

"Aw, Daddy."

"Ellie." There was a note of warning in his voice.

Ellie stomped off to her room. "When I get big, I'm *never* going to bed."

As Ellie left the room, Marisa glanced at Colter and noticed something in his eyes she couldn't describe. Was it sadness? No, it couldn't be. He had no reason to feel sad unless…unless he was regretting his decision to invite her for the holidays.

Marisa and Colter tucked Ellie into bed, and Marisa assured her again that she'd be back. They made their way to the den. Tulley had already gone to bed. Marisa sat staring into a roaring fire, watching the flames dueling with each other, just as her emotions were. She was intensely happy, yet deeply saddened by all that had happened. The child she'd thought dead had been returned to her. What more could she ask? Why was there still a void deep inside? She had to admit there was a place in her that Ellie couldn't reach.

She looked over at Colter, recognizing that he was the reason for the void. Until he forgave her and trusted her, she would never have complete peace.

"I can't believe she accepted me so easily," she said, studying him closely. "I expected it would take weeks, months even."

He smiled. "She's been wanting her mother for a long time."

That smile leaped out at her, touched her.... No, she couldn't.... It would only complicate things. She forced her thoughts down a less dangerous path.

"It must've been hard for you with a small baby," she said, thinking that Ellie had probably changed his life drastically.

"It wasn't easy," he said, easing into his recliner. "The first week of her life, I sat by her bassinet just to make sure she was still breathing. I was paranoid about her—Shannon pointed that out to me numerous times. I tried to continue riding the circuit, but found that she required all my attention, especially when Shannon left. Luckily, I was at a point in my career where I could retire and concentrate on the business end. Becky and Jen were already here, handling the construction of the house. Ellie, Tulley and I lived in a trailer until the house was finished. Becky had all these business ideas and we worked on them. I designed a boot like the one I'd specially made for myself, and the girls and Bart, Jen's husband, did all the rest. Kincaid Boots is a corporation of five people— Tulley, Becky, Jen, Bart and me."

"I'm glad it all worked out for you," she said. "You've done very well, and you have a beautiful home."

"Thank you. I had a lot of help with the business end, but Ellie was solely my responsibility. That was a big problem between Shannon and me. I diapered her, fed her, took her everywhere with me. Shannon was very fond of Ellie, and I should've let her step into the role of mother, but—well, I handled it badly."

She closed her eyes, listening, having no difficulty envisioning a younger Colter being fiercely protective of his child. He was that type of person. She couldn't even bring herself to imagine Shannon as Ellie's mother. That would hurt too much.

Opening her eyes, she dispelled the image. "You've done a great job. She's energetic, spirited and caring, and not in the least spoiled. She's very special."

He raised an eyebrow. "And you might be slightly prejudiced."

When he looked at her like that, it did crazy things to her and she remembered how he'd held and kissed her yesterday. So many emotions struggled for dominance. Emotions she wasn't ready to face.

"I'd better get some sleep." She got unsteadily to her feet. "I plan to leave before dawn." Taking a step, she turned back. "You haven't mentioned what your sisters said." It was none of her business, but she couldn't leave it alone.

"Like everyone else, they were shocked," he said. "Being women, they're trying to see this from your point of view, but it might take them a while."

She swallowed, knowing Colter's family had a right to dislike her, but she hoped they wouldn't judge her too harshly.

"Tulley, Ellie and I will be spending Christmas Day with my family at Jen's house. You're welcome to come, but that's up to you."

She nodded. "Thanks, but I wouldn't want to intrude." That was how she felt—like an intruder. She hurried from the room before tears defeated her.

Her abrupt departure left his mind in turmoil—once again. He'd hurt her, and he didn't like that, but he couldn't seem to stop. He was still struggling to accept this situation.

Tulley was right. He was bound to the pain of the past; it was easier. It was safer. Opening himself up to more heartache seemed too much of a risk. And that was the coward in him. A man who'd ridden wild bucking horses was a coward. He'd never seen himself that way until now, and he hated the feeling.

He trudged to his room and went to sleep, still seeing the pain in her brown eyes.

Marisa curled up in Becky's bed, unable to get Colter out of her mind. He'd been so gracious, allowing her time with Ellie, but why did he have to be wary of her? Why did he continue to hurt her? At times she could feel a softening, but almost instantly his guard would go back up, as if he needed to protect himself. Why? She'd never hurt him again. Didn't he believe that? Couldn't he see how much she'd changed?

The next morning, Marisa was up and dressed at 5:00 a.m. She tiptoed into Ellie's room and gave her a kiss, then headed for Dallas. Forty-five minutes later, she arrived at Mrs. Hackleberry's, where she quickly packed her clothes. With her suitcases in the hall, she went to the kitchen to tell Hazel about her plans. The older woman was very understanding, as Marisa had known she'd be.

She got to Madame Hélèna's before seven. When

she unlocked the door, she noticed the lights already on and was surprised to find Hélèna at her desk.

She glanced up as Marisa entered. "You're very early."

Marisa sat in a chair opposite the desk. "Yes. I need to talk to you."

Hélèna nodded, removing her glasses. "I've already spoken with your father."

"What!"

"There were three messages on my machine from him. He finally got me last night, wanting news of you."

"I'm so sorry, Madame Hélèna. He had no right to bother you." Why couldn't her father stay out of her life?

"Yes, and I told him that." She picked up a swatch of fabric from her desk. "But he's used to getting his own way and at the moment he wants to talk to you."

She shook her head. "No. I'm not ready to see my parents." She looked directly at Hélèna. "Did he tell you the whole story?"

"Yes, *chérie,* and I'm so happy you have your daughter."

"Thank you."

"I suppose you're here to quit your job."

"Not exactly," she said. "It's presumptuous of me after working here for such a short while, but I was hoping you'd let me have the holidays to spend with my daughter."

Hélèna caressed the fabric. "Yes, that's presumptuous."

"I need this time, but I also need this job."

Hélèna laid the fabric down and stared at Marisa. "The reason I'm here so early is that my son and I have decided to spend Christmas in Paris, and we're leaving tomorrow."

"Oh."

"So take the time you need, but when I return after New Year's I expect you back in this office."

"Oh, yes, ma'am. Thank you!"

"Under other circumstances, I would fire you."

Marisa stood. "Thank you for understanding."

"*Chérie,* I see a lot more than you do, and as I've said before, your heart is not in this job. You're good at it, but your future is not in fashion."

"Do you read tarot cards or something?"

Hélèna waved a hand. "Go be with your daughter and find the happiness you deserve."

"Why are you being so kind?" She had to ask.

Hélèna leaned forward. "It's not kindness, *chérie.* That's what you don't see." Her smile was flimsy. "I've waited a lot of years to stick it to Richard Preston, if you will forgive the vulgarity, and this is about as sweet as it gets."

Marisa stiffened. "You said you didn't have time for revenge."

"Sometimes an opportunity's too good to pass up."

Marisa couldn't keep the disappointment from showing on her face.

"I like you. I have from the beginning, but old hurts are hard to forget."

Marisa knew someone else who felt like that. Colter couldn't forget, either.

"I like working with you, and I appreciate your letting me keep my job. I'll see you in January."

"Ah, *chérie,* don't sound so wounded."

She slipped her purse over her shoulder. "I guess I'm naive about the business world."

"No. You just don't have that cutthroat instinct."

She didn't see that kind of instinct as a plus. She saw it as deceitful and conniving, and she knew her father's world and Hélèna's wasn't a place she wanted to live in. It was a world where they took innocent babies from their mothers and—

"Have a wonderful Christmas, Madame Hélèna."

"You, too, *chérie.*"

She walked away, feeling thoroughly inducted into the world of business. She didn't like it—but she had a job. Suddenly she didn't see that as a plus, either. Her parents were still controlling her life behind the scenes. Right now, though, her focus was on Ellie.

As she drove back to the ranch, she called Cari and then Reed.

"Marisa, I'm glad you phoned," Reed said as soon as he heard her voice. "How are things going?"

She told him about Ellie.

"That's great. And I'm glad Colter asked you to stay."

He paused, then said, "I saw our parents yesterday."

"Oh?"

"I felt I had to make my position clear. I told them I was disgusted with what they'd done to your life and said I'd no longer be working for Dalton's."

"Reed, your whole life is Dalton's! You've been trained to take over one day. Think about it."

"I have."

"Don't do this out of some misguided loyalty to me. This is your *life*."

"That's what I've finally figured out," he said. "I'm almost thirty-one years old and my father still dictates my decisions—but not anymore. I'm going away for the holidays, but I'll call every now and then."

"Reed…"

"Be happy, Marisa. You deserve it, and maybe one of these days, I'll find happiness, too."

"Merry Christmas, Reed." She hung up, feeling lonely and alone. Then she saw the sign for the Kincaid Ranch and her spirits lifted. Ellie was waiting—and maybe Colter was, too.

Chapter 15

As she drove up, she saw Ellie and Sooner sitting on the front step. Her heart lodged in her throat. She hadn't expected this.

She pulled up to the garages and they both came running. Marisa opened the door and got out, catching Ellie as she flew into her arms.

"You came back," Ellie cried. "You came back."

Marisa kissed her face. "Baby, I will always come back. Remember? I told you."

"I know," Ellie said, resting her face on Marisa's shoulder. Marisa felt so vulnerable, so… She held on to Ellie, fighting tears. But she was tired of crying. It was time for smiling, laughing and happiness.

"Want to help me get my things out of the car?"

Ellie raised her head. "Sure. Sooner and me can help. Can't we, Sooner?"

Sooner barked.

"That's very thoughtful." Marisa smiled, trying to act normal when what she felt was ecstatic, excited.

Marisa handed Ellie a small suitcase and took the larger one and a clothes bag herself. Together they made their way into the house.

Inside Sooner whined, then barked several times.

"He wants to stay outside," Ellie told her. "Okay, okay," she said to Sooner. He trotted to the back door and disappeared through the doggie flap.

Marisa smiled inwardly. Maybe they did understand each other on a level that only they knew.

Dragging the bag upstairs, Ellie said, "You can stay in the same room." She talked as if Marisa had stayed there many times before.

As Ellie helped her to unpack, Marisa wondered where Colter was, but didn't ask. She enjoyed having Ellie to herself.

"Wanda, the cleaning lady, put the clothes you left in the closet," Ellie said.

"That's fine," Marisa replied, realizing she'd forgotten all about them.

Ellie picked up a pair of high-heeled shoes. "How do you walk in these?"

"Very carefully." She laughed.

"Can I try?" Ellie asked. "I still got the ones you gave me, but I keep falling."

"Sure. Just walk slowly."

Ellie was sitting down to take off her sneakers when they heard Colter calling, "Ellie, where are you?"

Ellie jumped up, ran to the door. "Upstairs, Daddy."

A few seconds later, Colter appeared in the doorway. "Sooner is chasing Mr. Squirrel again," he said to Ellie.

"Oh no, that bad dog," Ellie cried, running from the room, completely forgetting about the high-heeled shoes.

"Mr. Squirrel?" Marisa lifted an eyebrow.

"He's a squirrel that lives in the backyard. Ellie feeds him, so he's become more or less a pet. But Sooner's jealous and chases him every chance he gets."

"She loves animals, doesn't she."

"She takes after me in that," he said, walking into the room.

As he drew near, her stomach fluttered nervously. Looking away, she put some clothes in a drawer, hoping her face had revealed nothing.

She turned around. "Ellie was waiting for me when I got here."

"She's been waiting out there ever since breakfast. I think she was afraid you wouldn't be coming back."

Her heart ached with a new pain—the pain of knowing Ellie felt insecure about her. She sank onto the bed. "How do I make her understand that I'm never going to leave her again?"

He shoved his hands into the pockets of his jeans. "By loving her and never letting her down."

Her eyes met his. "I won't."

"That's all she wants. To be able to trust you."

A message hovered behind the words and she didn't miss it. *I want to trust you, too.* She'd have to prove herself; that was the only way to show them she was sincere.

"I promised Ellie we'd get the Christmas tree," he

said, breaking into her thoughts. "So if you're ready, we'll go."

"Yes." She'd finish unpacking later. "Where do you buy trees?"

"We go to a tree farm not far away."

She remembered Christmases past. A decorator did the trees in her mother's home and in her father's. She had never had anything to do with it, not even as a child. The tree was just there, beautifully decorated, but that personal touch was lacking.

"This will be a new experience for me," she said, then added without thinking, "I seem to experience a lot of firsts when I'm with you."

As soon as the words left her mouth, she wished them back. Colter knew exactly what she'd meant. She could see it in his eyes. He was remembering their first night together; she'd been a virgin.

"Something else you lied about." His words weren't harsh. He was just stating a fact.

"I didn't lie—you never asked me," she said defending herself. She had tried to appear experienced, like the other women he'd known. She'd wanted to be with him so much, but that omission *was* the same as a lie.

"You let me assume you had experience, and later, well...it was much too late."

She hung the clothes bag in the closet. Yes, it had been too late. She remembered that night as if it were yesterday. She'd been so naive. Everything she knew about sex she'd learned from books and from the other girls. She'd always heard that the first time would hurt. But Colter had been so gentle and had carried her to such heights of pleasure that there'd been very little pain.

Later, his eyes had blazed with anger at her lie about her virginity, but using feminine instincts she hadn't known she possessed, she'd been able to coax him into a better mood. Their second time had been even more satisfying. Her body had come alive under his tutelage.

From then on, a look, a touch, a caress could send their bodies up in flames. They had lived in their own private world, full of intimacy and sensual delight. But outside, the real world had been waiting.

"I don't see any point in rehashing the past," she said, steeling herself against the onslaught of memories.

He observed her closely. "Does it make you uncomfortable to talk about that night?"

She shut the closet door. "Of course not. As I told you, I just regret what happened afterward."

"We keep coming back to that," he retorted.

"Yes, and it's something that will always haunt me."

He stared at her, seeing the young girl she'd been at seventeen, completely dominated by her mother. The fact that she'd ignored her mother's wishes and gone out with him, made love with him, agreed to marry him, must mean that she'd felt something for him at the time. He desperately needed to believe she hadn't used him merely as a means of escape.

He saw the sadness that touched her face and wanted to ease her pain. "Let's go get that tree with Ellie."

"Okay." She smiled slightly.

They walked out the door, but Marisa suddenly

stopped. "Oh, I forgot my jacket," she told him. "I'll be right with you." She hurried back into her room.

"We'll be waiting outside," he said.

She grabbed her jacket, slipping into it as she ran down the stairs. She found Colter leaning against a pillar on the patio, smiling at Ellie. He was wearing a sheepskin coat and a Stetson. He stirred her senses. She quickly followed his gaze to Ellie, trying to forget how he made her feel.

Ellie had Sooner by the collar and was leading him to his doghouse. "Naughty, naughty dog," she scolded. "You have to stay in your house until you learn you can't eat Mr. Squirrel." Tucking his tail between his legs, Sooner ran into his house in disgrace.

Colter looked at Marisa, then wished he hadn't. His muscles tightened with a sexual need that shocked him as his eyes roamed over her tight-fitting jeans and settled on the blond hair that hung around her face. Her brown eyes were so deep, so sensual, so—oh God, where was his strength? This woman could wreck his whole life; he had to remember that.

They stared at each other in silence for several seconds before he forced himself to break the contact and shifted his attention to Ellie. "Come on, angelface. Let's go get the Christmas tree."

They started for the garage, with Ellie marching ahead. A woeful whining stopped them in their tracks. All three turned simultaneously to see Sooner's pitiful face peeking out from the doghouse.

Ellie glanced up at her father, and Colter nodded.

"Okay, you can come," Ellie called, and Sooner bounded out of his house. He ran to her, jumping up to put both paws on her shoulders while licking her face, nearly knocking her over in the process. Ellie gave him a big hug, laughing. "You crazy dog."

Colter rolled his eyes, and Marisa smiled.

They got into a silver four-door pickup. Ellie and Sooner climbed into the back, while Colter and Marisa sat in front. They traveled several miles from the ranch to the tree farm and, not surprisingly, the place was busy.

Ellie had to personally inspect each and every tree, occasionally asking for their opinion—and Sooner's. Every time Sooner barked, Ellie shook her head and moved on to another tree.

"Remind me to strangle that dog," Colter whispered to Marisa.

Although she laughed, his low voice and the warmth of his breath caused a tremor of excitement to course through her.

After much deliberation, Ellie decided on the right tree. Colter looked up at the tall Virginia pine. "That's about twelve feet. It's going to touch the ceiling."

"I don't care," Ellie said, looking defiantly at Marisa. "Do you care, Mommy?"

"Not in the slightest," she answered, and received a frown from Colter. But he accepted defeat graciously.

A man at the farm helped cut the tree down, and within minutes they had it in the bed of the truck. As they headed for home, Ellie kept a watchful eye on it through the back window.

Decorating a Christmas tree with Ellie was unlike anything Marisa had experienced. She'd thought the tree had to be perfect, with the ornaments and decorations coordinated like they'd been in her parents' homes. Ellie, however, had a very different view. Everything had to be done with the greatest speed, using as many bright colors as possible. Marisa followed Ellie's lead until it came to the icicles. Ellie made short work of those by throwing them all on at once.

Marisa glanced at Colter, smiling, and he returned the smile, amused at the antics of their child. The sincerity of his smile flowed through her like good wine, soothing and relaxing.

"Oh, Daddy, we forgot the star," Ellie cried, rummaging in a box and lifting the ornament into the air.

Colter placed the star on the tree, which required a ladder, since the top brushed the ceiling. Everything completed, Ellie stood back admiringly.

"Oh, it's the most beautiful tree in the whole world," she exclaimed, walking over and putting her arms around Marisa's waist. "I'm glad you're here, Mommy."

At those precious words and the tiny arms around her, Marisa fought back tears. Ellie had called her Mommy several times, but suddenly she *felt* it—felt it deeply. She bent down and held her child. She was a mother. Ellie's mother.

"I didn't mean it when I said I didn't want you for a mommy," Ellie mumbled into her neck.

Marisa stroked her hair. "I know, baby. I know."

Colter had a lump in his throat. Mother and daughter were forming a bond. He only hoped Marisa would live up to Ellie's expectations.

The days before Christmas were busy and happy. Every morning Marisa found Ellie sitting on her bed, waiting for her to wake up. As soon as Marisa opened her eyes, Ellie would start chattering, planning their day.

Colter was cool and distant at times; at others, he was warm and friendly. He obviously still had doubts, but he'd put them aside for Ellie. Both were determined to make this a special time. But she wondered if Colter was ever going to see her as the woman she was now, if he'd ever trust her with his daughter's heart—or his own.

As Christmas drew near, Ellie could hardly contain herself. Her excitement was infectious, and Marisa was looking forward to Christmas in a way she never had before.

Every day Ellie thought of something new that had to go on the tree. Today it was popcorn, so that evening, Marisa and Ellie sat on the den floor, stringing strands of popcorn.

Tulley was half asleep in his chair, while Colter lazed on the sofa with his legs stretched out in front of him, eating popcorn.

Colter was in a good mood as he observed Marisa with Ellie. Her eyes sparkled, her skin glowed, and there was an air of anticipation about her that he remembered from long ago. An excitement that charged his senses—which was something he would do well to forget.

Ellie giggled, and moved closer to her mother. It seemed as if they'd known each other all their lives, and that was how it should be. A girl needed her mother. There were so many things that Marisa could share with Ellie that he couldn't—makeup, boys and feminine things he hadn't a clue about.

He felt as if Ellie was slowly taking steps away from him. He shouldn't think like that, but he couldn't keep the doubts from torturing him. *He had to trust Marisa. He had to trust her. He had to trust her.*

"Daddy, you're eating the decorations," Ellie scolded, shaking him out of his reverie.

"Well, pardon me." He pretended to be affronted. "I'm just trying to help. If you put anything else on that tree, it's going to collapse." Some branches were actually beginning to sag.

"The tree's *supposed* to look like that," Ellie informed him.

"Oh, excuse me, I didn't know." Colter grinned. His amused glance swung to Marisa, and when she smiled back at him he couldn't look away. *Admit it,* he challenged himself. *You want to make love to her as badly as you did eight years ago.* His gaze slid over the tight jeans, her breasts pressing against her blouse and the soft blond hair. She was beautiful. More beautiful than ever. She was a mature woman now, and he wondered what it would be like to make love to her....

Although Colter tried to stop his thoughts, he couldn't. He had to acknowledge that she fit into his household well. He'd expected the city lady to be completely out of place when it came to the everyday routine of a working ranch. And yet the other day he'd found her helping Tulley feed the horses in the corral. Of course, Ellie was there helping, too, but it shocked him to see Marisa handling the feed. And then he'd seen her making supper alongside Tulley, which was another shock to his system. He would've sworn she didn't even know what a stove was. Maybe she *had* changed. She certainly seemed able to take care of herself these days.

She'd become strong and independent, but he had to wonder how deep that strength went. Years ago, she hadn't been strong enough to fight for their love, but now he felt she was capable of fighting for whatever she wanted. And she wanted Ellie....

Colter's penetrating gaze heated Marisa's skin and she immediately looked away. One glance from him had the power to make her feel giddy and breathless, like that seventeen-year-old who'd fallen in love with him. But there wasn't any chance of that happening again. His feelings toward her had hardened, and the only reason he tolerated her presence was Ellie.

She knew he'd been watching her, judging her actions, making sure she had Ellie's best interests at heart. At times it made her angry, and at other times she understood, but she wished he didn't feel as if he had to protect Ellie from her.

It would make things a lot easier if she wasn't so *aware* of him. Even knowing the way he felt about her, she was still intensely attracted to him. Her pulse pounded as her eyes found the taut muscles of his legs and the dark curls of hair that peeped out from the V of his shirt. She could remember winding her fingers through them and tugging gently, initiating a response that ended with them making slow, passionate love. Why was she torturing herself by recalling every detail, especially when the man in question seemed to distrust her.

Marisa and Ellie hung the strands of popcorn on the tree. "Gosh, that looks great, huh, Mommy?"

"Just great," Marisa answered.

"Wanna hear me play the piano?" Ellie asked eagerly.

"Sure."

Ellie and Sooner charged off to the living room where the piano was, and Marisa followed more slowly. Ellie ran her fingers across the keys and Marisa sat beside her on the bench. She could see herself at that age, and felt a bitter sadness for all the tireless hours she'd spent on a piano bench.

Ellie played through a chorus of "Jingle Bells" and "Frosty The Snowman." Marisa thought she was brilliant.

As the last note died away, Ellie said, "Now you play."

After her baby's birth, she hadn't been able to bring herself to play, no matter how much pressure her mother had applied. It'd been so easy at Mrs. Hackleberry's, though—and Marisa felt she knew why. She'd met Ellie, and subconsciously must have known that this child was her baby.

Lightly she touched the keys, and her fingers moved as if of their own volition. She played Rimsky-Korsakov's "Flight of the Bumble Bee," then went into a spirited Chopin piece and ended with Gershwin's "Rhapsody in Blue." The lovely sounds consumed her, and she was unaware of anything but the music.

When her fingers stopped, the room became very quiet.

"Golly," Ellie said, her eyes round. "I never heard music like that. That's awesome."

"I agree," Colter said from the doorway. "I'd never heard you play before."

Marisa looked at him and realized again how little they'd known about each other back then. They only knew they were in love, but there was so much more to a relationship. Things like responsibility and commitment, which were concepts that had been virtually unfamiliar to her as a teenager.

Colter stood transfixed, suddenly understanding just how talented she was. And she'd been willing to give it all up for him. That was a sobering thought.

If Ellie had that kind of talent, he wasn't sure what he'd do. Would he pressure her like Vanessa had pressured Marisa? And if Ellie got pregnant at seventeen, what measures would he take to ensure that she reached her full potential? He didn't have an answer, but he had a very chilling look at the other side of Marisa's life.

"Time for bed," he said to Ellie.

"Daddy," Ellie groaned.

"Christmas is still three days away," he reminded her.

Ellie pulled a face, but obediently slid off the bench. "Remember to come and tuck me in," she called, running from the room. Sooner barked as he loped behind her.

Marisa stared down at the piano keys.

He noticed her tearful brown eyes and he wanted to take her in his arms and kiss her, to feel the softness of her lips against his. Instead he sat down beside her.

She clenched her hands in her lap and he wondered if his nearness bothered her.

"I never realized your great talent," he said, needing to tell her that.

'Thank you," she replied, head down. "It feels good to actually be playing again. I just couldn't play after I lost my child. I didn't have the drive anymore. The lady I live with in Dallas has an old piano, and I've been playing it. I even stopped by the Dallas Symphony Orchestra to try out."

"Do you regret giving up your music?"

"No. But I have missed it." She looked at him. "I plan to continue playing."

"With a talent like yours, I think you have to."

"Thank you," she said, her eyes holding his.

"As I was listening to you, I wondered what I'd do if Ellie had that kind of talent."

She frowned. "What do you mean?"

"I mean—would I force her to play?"

"Oh."

"And more important, I wondered what I'd do if she got pregnant at seventeen."

The question gnawed at her, and she was unable to answer.

"This isn't easy for me to say—but if I'm completely honest—I know I'd want to kill the boy who did that to her—to her future."

"But you'd listen to Ellie, wouldn't you?"

"I hope I would, but I'd probably be so angry I couldn't say that for sure."

She had no response, and silence fell between them.

"I never imagined I'd see this from your parents' point of view."

"Me, neither," she said in a quiet voice.

"Sometimes it's easier to hate than to understand and forgive."

She pushed back her hair with a trembling hand.

"I didn't mean to upset you."

"You haven't," she assured him. "I'm just staggered by the view I'm seeing as a parent. It's one I never considered before."

"Yeah," he murmured.

She got to her feet. "We'd better tuck Ellie in."

Later, as she lay in bed, Colter's words returned to her. She had thought she'd never forgive her parents and she wasn't sure she could. But now she was able to see the reasons behind their actions. They did what they believed was best for her, as any parent would. As she'd do for Ellie.

Some of the sadness in her eased, and she was grateful to Colter for opening her eyes. Now she wondered if he'd ever forgive her.

And if she could forgive herself.

Chapter 16

The next day Marisa and Colter went Christmas shopping. Since Ellie wasn't grounded anymore, they dropped her off at Lori's so the girls could exchange presents.

Ellie wanted a red bicycle and they searched until they found the perfect one in a large sporting goods store.

Marisa told Colter she'd like to give Ellie the jeans she'd wanted that day in Dalton's. He said that was fine, so she called Cari and met her in the children's department. She knew she wouldn't run into her father; he was never on the floor unless it was a special occasion.

Colter browsed in the store while she shopped with Cari, and she tried to hurry because she didn't want him to wait too long. She bought Ellie a complete

outfit—jeans, a matching jacket, blouse, socks and
headband. Then she found something for Colter and
Tulley, and a pen-and-pencil set for the brother-in-law.
Shopping for Colter's sisters was more difficult. She
decided on a purse mirror that folded into a decorative
case for Becky and a photo album for Jen.

"So, how are you?" Cari asked as they waited for
the items to be gift-wrapped.

"Great." She smiled.

"I can see that."

"I wanted to wish you a Merry Christmas because I
won't see you on Christmas Day." Marisa hugged her.
Colter had left it up to her, and she didn't want to be
away from Ellie, so she'd decided to spend Christmas
with Colter's family.

She handed Cari an envelope.

"What's this?"

"It's your Christmas present—a day at the spa. The
works, from a facial to a massage to a pedicure."

"Marisa! You didn't have to do that."

"Yes. I did. You're my best friend."

"Thank you. Wait right here," Cari said, hurrying over to a counter. She came back with a package,
which she gave to Marisa.

Marisa opened it then and there. It was a small,
beautifully produced book on the Christmas Cradle
and how it was made and it included the illustrations
of the Twelve Days of Christmas that were etched on
the cradle itself.

"Oh, Cari. Thank you."

"In the back is the man's name and address, in case
you'd like one of your own."

Marisa hugged her again. "My baby is seven years old, so I don't think I'll need one, but I love the book and I've always loved that cradle." Over Cari's shoulder, she saw Santa Claus handing out candy to children, and it jogged her memory about the Santa in the white suit. She drew back. "Any news on the Santa who spoke with Ellie?"

"Yes. I've been meaning to call you. My assistant talked with him, and he was an older gentleman filling out an application in her office, which is across the hall. I called him and he said he'd heard everything that was going on between you and Ellie, and he decided to play Santa. So he told Ellie everything she wanted to hear. I informed him that we like our Santas to use a little more discretion and not promise children things that are unrealistic."

"What did he say?"

"He apologized and said he hoped there was a happy ending. He also said anyone who believes that strongly should get his or her wish."

"I knew there had to be a reasonable explanation," Marisa murmured.

Cari lifted an eyebrow. "You sound disappointed."

"Maybe, like my daughter, I want to believe." And she did. Not in Santa Claus, but in the power of love.

"Well, then, believe." Cari laughed. "It's Christmas, after all."

"Have a wonderful one." She hugged Cari once more and soon joined Colter, who'd been wandering through the store.

They'd been gone two hours, and Marisa couldn't wait to see her daughter. She met Lori and her mother when they collected Ellie. The child bounced up and down with excitement, and that excitement lasted all the way home. Ellie couldn't stop talking.

Colter grinned at Marisa. "I think she's had too many sweets."

Marisa smiled, feeling truly a part of this family for the first time.

Christmas Eve dawned bright and sunny, but cold. Brodie and Tripp came by to bring presents for Ellie, and she proudly introduced Marisa as her mother. Brodie and Tripp were both friendly, and she enjoyed visiting with them.

The men saddled up and galloped to the pasture to look at a horse Tripp wanted to buy from Colter, and Marisa and Ellie fed Dandy. Walking back to the barn, Marisa noticed a young Mexican man holding something in his arms. He was one of several ranch hands, but she hadn't met any of them.

"Let's go see what José's got," Ellie said, running toward him, Marisa close behind.

"It's a baby deer," Ellie cried as José carried the animal into the barn and laid it on some loose hay.

The little animal was limp and trembling and had sores all over its body. Ellie touched it gently, and Marisa wanted to grab her hand, afraid she might catch something.

"Where's Tulley and the boss?" José asked.

"They're looking at a horse with Brodie and Tripp," Ellie said.

"Ain't nothin' the boss don't know about animals. He fix this little one up in no time."

A moment later, they heard the clatter of hooves as Tulley and Colter rode in. Colter swung out of the saddle in one easy movement, then handed the reins to Tulley, who guided the horses through the barn into the corral. Obviously Brodie and Tripp had left.

"Look what I found, boss." José pointed to the bundle in the hay. "I was feeding in the south pasture and there it was. Thought it was dead, but no, it's still alive."

Colter knelt down in the hay and ran his hands over the small animal. "Fire ants almost got her. She's weak and dehydrated. Her mother must've been killed or she'd never have left her alone."

"Killed," Marisa breathed, unable to keep the horror out of her voice.

Three pairs of eyes turned to her. "Yeah," Colter answered, "it's deer season around here."

"But surely it's not legal to kill a mother!"

"'fraid so, ma'am," José said.

"That's terrible! How could someone kill a mother?"

Colter pushed back his hat, noting the painful emotions on her face. "Does are plentiful, so permits are issued every year. Most of the time it's sport, but a lot of people hunt to feed their families."

"Still—" Her eyes flashed with outrage. "It's not right."

Colter got up and went into the stockroom, and soon he was back with two syringes, a bottle, some ointment and rubber gloves.

He handed Ellie the bottle and gloves. "Start cleaning the sores with peroxide, then rub ointment into them."

"Okay, Daddy," Ellie said, slipping on a glove.

Goose bumps rose on Marisa's skin as Colter gave the animal two injections in its hip. Ellie meticulously cleaned the wounds, then rubbed the ointment into them. Marisa didn't think this was a job for a small child and she wanted to tell Colter so, but the words stuck in her throat.

"Keep at it, angelface. I'll fix some milk." Colter and José disappeared into the stockroom, and Marisa watched as Ellie worked. The animal made a whimpering sound, and Marisa realized that the little thing was in pain. She didn't know what it was—the thought of the pain or the thought of this small animal without a mother—but she found herself sinking down into the hay, reaching for a glove. In silence, she and Ellie cleaned and medicated every wound.

Colter came back and stopped as he saw Marisa helping Ellie. This was something he hadn't expected and the sight was a little unnerving. He could've sworn Marisa wouldn't touch the animal, but he was wrong.

"We're through, Daddy." Ellie's voice interrupted his musing.

"Good. The milk's ready." He knelt down and tried to get the fawn to suck from a bottle, but the little creature didn't respond. She just lay limp, stretched out on the hay as if she was ready to die.

"José, bring me the force feeder," Colter said.

He poured the milk into a bottle with a long tube that had a sort of squeeze pump. He opened the fawn's mouth and pushed the tube down her throat. As he squeezed the pump, gently, the milk flowed into her throat to her stomach. The fawn's throat convulsed, and Marisa had to look away.

"There, that should do it," she heard Colter say, and she turned back. The poor thing was still trembling, and the sight was more than Marisa could stand.

"Can't you stop her from shaking like that?" she asked Colter.

"I've given her an antibiotic and an anti-inflammatory. The pain will ease as soon as the medicine takes effect."

Marisa didn't want to wait that long. She got to her feet and found a horse blanket, then covered the small body, hoping the warmth would stop the quaking.

Colter watched her with a strange expression on his face, but he didn't say anything.

"Daddy, is she gonna live?" Ellie asked anxiously.

"I don't know. We'll keep an eye on her and feed her again this evening. That's about all we can do."

Marisa checked on the animal several times that afternoon. She couldn't seem to stay away. She wanted to do something to ease the fawn's pain, and that thought was as startling to her as it was to everyone around her. Whenever she headed for the barn, she could feel Colter's eyes on her.

When they went to feed her that evening, Marisa rushed over, hardly able to believe her eyes. "Look, Colter! She's not trembling anymore. That means she's out of pain, doesn't it?"

He stared into her eager eyes. Clearing his throat, he answered, "Yes. Now let's see if we can get her to suck."

The little fawn still didn't respond, so Colter

squeezed more milk into her stomach. Marisa's heart sank. She'd felt sure the animal was improving.

She kept thinking about the fawn, but she soon got caught up in Ellie's exuberance about Christmas. They made oatmeal cookies for Santa, under Tulley's guidance, while Colter sat at the kitchen table drinking spicy apple cider.

"They have to be real good, Tulley," Ellie said, "so don't forget anything."

"Are you saying I'm forgetful?"

"No, yes, maybe." Ellie giggled.

Marisa laughed, a soft happy sound, and Colter reflected that this was what it would be like if they were married. He didn't push the thought away as he normally would, and realized he was finally seeing Marisa for the woman she'd become. He liked what he saw—a warm, giving, loving person.

Tulley closed the oven door. "The timer's set, so all you have to do is take 'em out when it dings."

"I can handle that," Marisa told him. "And I'll clean up the kitchen."

Tulley removed his apron. "Thanks, and ladies, this is about as much fun as I can stand for one night. I hear my bed calling."

"He always hears his bed calling," Ellie whispered to Marisa.

"I heard that," Tulley said as he walked toward his room.

"I love you." Ellie ran over and gave him a kiss.

"Aw, shorty, that makes everything okay. 'Night, everyone."

Marisa began to load the dishwasher and wipe counters, and Colter helped. They worked side by side in comfortable silence. Just as she turned the dishwasher on, the oven dinged. She removed the cookies and set them on the stove to cool.

Ellie pulled a chair to the cabinet and got down a plate with a Santa face on it.

"This is Santa's plate." She jumped down, then handed it to Marisa, who placed several cookies on it. Ellie carried the plate to the table and rushed back to the refrigerator to pour a glass of milk.

"Santa's gonna love these," she said, munching on a cookie. "Tulley didn't forget a thing."

Marisa took a bite of one and agreed—they *were* good. She should've written the recipe down, but she could always ask Tulley. She became still as she envisioned herself always here—with Ellie. And Colter.

"Bedtime, angelface," Colter said.

"Okay, Daddy, but first I have to do something." She raced to her room. For once, Sooner didn't follow. He was busy eating a piece of cookie Ellie had given him.

Colter looked at Marisa. "What's she up to?"

"I have no idea."

A few minutes later, she was back and set a piece of paper by the plate. "*Now* I'm going to bed." In a whirlwind she and Sooner were gone.

Marisa and Colter walked to the table and glanced down at the paper. In bold letters Ellie had printed:

Dear Santa,
Thank you for sending me my mommy for Christmas.
Love,
Ellie Kincaid

Tears rolled down Marisa's cheeks. At the sight, Colter's stomach seemed to tie itself in knots and he drew her into his arms. With one hand, he caressed the tears from her face. She looked up at him, and unable to stop himself, he kissed her. At first he kept his touch gentle, but then she whimpered deep in her throat, her hands sliding up his arms to his neck. At her response, he deepened the kiss. Rational thought was impossible as heated passion, too long denied, took over.

He had only meant to comfort her, but the touch of her soft skin, the feel of her in his arms, was his undoing. God, he wanted her. Eight years of hate, bitterness and love had fueled a flame so intense that both were oblivious to everything but the passion consuming them.

"Daddy, Mommy," Ellie called, shattering the moment. Marisa pulled away instantly and went to Ellie.

Colter stood for a moment, trying to get his emotions under control, but all he could feel was Marisa. He didn't have the strength to continue fighting a battle he was losing.

Slowly he made his way to Ellie's room, feeling as if he'd just been thrown from the meanest, baddest horse in Texas.

They put their gifts under the tree. Then Marisa climbed the stairs to her room, while Colter talked to Becky on the phone. Marisa showered, then called Hazel to wish her a Merry Christmas. She'd sent her former landlady and friend a holiday flower arrangement, which Hazel had loved. Marisa promised to visit after Christmas.

She crawled into bed with thoughts of Colter. He'd kissed her with a passion she remembered from the past, and she wondered if he could kiss her like that without loving her. Love and sex went hand in hand for her, and she finally had to admit she loved him as much as she ever had—the years, the heartache and separation hadn't changed a thing.

But how did he feel about *her?* He desired her; she knew that. This time, though, she wanted it all—love, home and a family. And she wanted it with Colter.

The wind wailed outside and the temperature had dropped to the low thirties. With the cold, she wondered if the fawn was trembling again. She sat up in bed, holding her hands to her face. Why was she so deeply concerned about this small animal? Was she somehow comparing her and Ellie's situation to the fawn's? She didn't know. All she knew was that she had to check on her once more.

She quickly slipped on her clothes and headed downstairs, grabbing her coat from the hall closet. As soon as she opened the back door, she heard a howling in the distance and the blackness of the moonless night seemed to engulf her. Thoughts of wild animals ran through her mind, but she walked stoically toward the barn.

Opening the door, she flipped on the light. The fawn was where they'd left her, stretched unmoving on the hay. Marisa knelt and tucked the blanket tightly around her. The little thing wasn't shaking, so that had to be good.

She stroked her face. "You *have* to live, little one," she whispered. "I know you don't have a mother, but

I'll be your mother. I'll take care of you. I don't know anything about deer, but Colter does and I'm sure he'll help me."

Everyone should have a mother, every living creature. She thought about her own mother, and Marisa recognized that Vanessa was probably in pain at losing her. A sob left her throat, as she gazed toward the ceiling. "If you let the fawn live, I promise to talk to my parents and maybe I can find a measure of forgiveness." Suddenly she felt a sense of peace.

"What are you doing?"

Her head swiveled around. "Colter?"

He squatted beside her. "What are you doing?" he repeated.

"I had to check on her one more time." She rubbed the fawn's head.

"What is it with you and this baby deer?" he asked, his voice low.

"I can't explain it. I just don't want her to be in pain and alone."

"Is that how you felt?"

She let her eyes cling to his, knowing exactly what he meant. "Yes," she said hoarsely. "After losing my baby, the pain was so bad I didn't think I'd survive, and at times I didn't want to."

He swallowed hard. "I'm sorry for all you've been through."

There, in the quiet of the barn, the past came full circle and slid into the present. He knew that all he had to do was reach for her to obliterate the remaining sadness.

Instead, he helped her to her feet. "Let's go back to the house. It's cold out here."

She stared at the deer. "Will she live?"

"Maybe. Maybe not. We'll know by morning."

He took her hand, then flipped off the light and they stepped into the darkness, the wind whipping fiercely around them. They could hear howling in the distance. Marisa instinctively moved closer to Colter and he squeezed her hand.

"It's only a coyote foraging for food. They don't come near the ranch."

His touch and his words warmed her against the chilly night.

As they walked into the house, he asked, "Now can you get to sleep?"

"Yes," she answered, taking off her coat. "Thank you."

He watched the light in her eyes, then touched her cheek with his fingers.

The unexpected touch made Marisa catch her breath. Her eyes flew to his and she saw an emotion that stole her breath. *He wanted her.* His hand curved around her neck and she swayed toward him. "Colter," she whispered a moment before his mouth covered hers. Her lips parted eagerly as longing enveloped her. His tongue moved into her mouth, to taste, to probe, and a fire coursed through her. She quivered uncontrollably.

"Marisa," he groaned, his body trembling. He pulled her closer, kissing her hard and furiously. They strained together, lips touching lips, heart on heart, striving to say with their bodies what they hadn't been able to say with words. Marisa's hands traveled hungrily over his face, as if she were trying to imprint the feel of him on her fingertips. Colter kissed her again and again.

He felt himself exploding with all the emotions he'd kept inside, and he gave them full rein. He didn't want to think. He just wanted to *feel*—to feel all those wonderful sensations that were a part of her. Nothing else mattered, not their differences, not the past—just this moment, this feeling.

As he slid a hand beneath her blouse and caressed her heated skin, she couldn't control the whimpering deep in her throat. She wanted him, plain and simple, and she couldn't hide it. She returned his kisses with equal fervor, each taking and giving until nothing existed but the two of them. Finally, he rested his forehead against hers.

"Marisa..."

She placed her fingers over his lips. "Please don't apologize. Please..."

They stared at each other, both realizing that their anger was gone. Hers had faded into nothingness, and she could tell his had, too.

"I'm not." He drew a ragged breath and released her. "But we should slow down."

"Yes," she said, knowing he was right. This time they had to be clear about what they wanted. She gave him a brief smile. "It's Christmas Eve—Santa's going to be here soon."

He grinned. "You've been listening to Ellie too long."

She ran for the stairs singing, "You'd better watch out, you'd better not pout, you'd better not…"

Falling into bed, she felt young and very much in love. She touched her lips, still tender from his kisses. She loved him and wanted to be with him, but she couldn't make love with him unless she knew he loved her just as much. Maybe she was wishing for the impossible. Maybe the forever kind of love didn't exist in real life. Like Ellie, though, she believed.

And it was Christmas.

Christmas morning came very early and Ellie's excited shouts echoed through the house. She tore into her gifts like a hurricane, hardly giving Marisa and Colter time to fully wake up.

Pulling out the rhinestone studded jeans, she screeched, "Oh boy. Oh boy." Then she immediately slipped them on over her pajamas.

"Ellie." Colter sighed, but Ellie wasn't listening. She proceeded to dress completely in the outfit, whirling around for everyone to see.

"Don't I look cool, Tulley?"

"You're so cool I'm about to get frostbite," Tulley joked, working the video camera.

"My mommy gave them to me." She hugged Marisa, and Marisa held her tight, her eyes meeting Colter's. Their first Christmas…

Marisa could hardly breathe as she opened Ellie's gift. It was a plaster of Paris imprint of two hands, with Ellie's name and the date written beneath it. "That's my hand," Ellie said, as if she needed to explain. "I made it in kindergarten for Daddy, but he said I could give it to you. And I got you this, too." It was a school photo of Ellie in a silver frame. "You can put it on your nightstand and see me all the time."

"Thank you, baby. I love them."

A feeling of anticipation flowed through her as she watched Colter open his gift from her. She'd been torn with indecision about what to get him on such short notice. A sigh of relief escaped her when he seemed pleased with the green pullover sweater she'd finally chosen. And Tulley liked the leather gloves she'd given him.

Colter handed her a large box and she quickly unwrapped it. A pair of dark brown cowboy boots lay inside. "Oh, my," she whispered.

"I had them specially made at our factory. I got your shoe size from your heels."

She kicked off her slippers and pulled on the boots. Then she stood up and whirled around. "What do you think?"

"Cool, Mommy—just like a cowgirl," Ellie said. "Except you probably need to wear jeans instead of a bathrobe."

Marisa made a face.

Colter couldn't take his eyes off her, but forced himself to reach for another gift. And these—" he gave her the package "—are for when you're mucking around in the corrals with Ellie."

She removed a pair of black rubber boots from the box. "Thank you." She smiled and leaned over to kiss his cheek.

"You're welcome," he said, looking into her eyes.

"Daddy, Mommy," Ellie shouted, interrupting

their silent communication. "Come on! I gotta ride my bike."

They spent the next hour teaching their daughter to ride her new bicycle. With Colter on one side and Marisa on the other, Ellie was soon off on her own, Sooner barking and racing after her. As she circled the driveway, the darkness of the night faded into another Texas winter morning. The wind whistled through the trees and the dew glistened on the grass like happy tears. It was going to be a chilly yet beautiful day.

"Becky's on the phone," Tulley called from the foyer.

Colter went inside, and Marisa continued to supervise Ellie's cycling. The child pedaled up the walk and Marisa caught the bicycle because Ellie hadn't learned to brake yet.

A few minutes later, Colter came running out. "They had to take Jen to the emergency room and the doctor admitted her. They were able to stop her labor, thank God. She's doing fine, but the doctor wants to keep an eye on her." He took a breath. "That now means we'll be staying home for Christmas."

"I'll see what I can rustle up for lunch," Tulley said.

"Are we going to the hospital, Daddy?"

"This afternoon we'll all go." He glanced at Marisa. "Is that okay?"

"Yes," she answered, touched that he was including her.

Before breakfast, they went to check on the deer. When Colter opened the door, a surprise met them— the fawn was holding her head up, gazing around with wide-open eyes!

Ellie dashed over to her. "Look, Daddy! She's better." The fawn started to lick Ellie's hand. "And she's hungry."

This time she sucked her bottle readily as Marisa and Ellie hovered over her. "Isn't she beautiful?" Marisa gently stroked the little head, examining the white spotted body.

"Let's call her Beauty," Ellie suggested.

"Wait a minute." Colter held up a hand. "When she's healthy again, I'll call the game warden and—"

"No, Daddy! No," Ellie cried. "He'll take her away. Why can't we keep her? I'll take care of her."

"And I'll help," Marisa said, her dark eyes holding his.

Colter stared at Marisa, then at Ellie and then back at Marisa. "Okay." He gave in with a frown. "But just remember. When she gets old enough, we have to let her go. She's a wild animal and needs to be free. It would be inhuman to keep her penned up."

Marisa felt a moment of pure joy. His acquiescence meant he accepted her presence here in the future. The thought gave her hope—hope that one day he'd love and trust her again.

A warm glow lit her heart, and the holiday spirit seemed to embrace them in a world all their own.

Chapter 17

They all pitched in to help Tulley with dinner. He had a chicken roasting and had made corn bread for the dressing. Green beans and yams waited on the counter. It was plain that he had everything under control.

Marisa and Ellie set the table in the dining room, and Colter prepared iced tea and apple cider. They were happily absorbed in their tasks, and Marisa soaked up the atmosphere and that sense of family, something she'd never felt before. Most of all she just watched Ellie, and she had to resist the impulse to hug Ellie every few seconds.

The phone rang, interrupting the silence. Colter answered it and talked for a few minutes; he hung up, saying, "That was Becky. She's on her way over with dessert. She said she's not going to miss seeing Ellie at Christmas."

"Oh boy. Oh boy." Ellie jumped up and down. "Now you can meet my Aunt Becky. She's real nice."

Marisa couldn't believe how nervous she was at the prospect of meeting this woman who probably hated her. She busied herself picking up discarded Christmas paper and straightening the den. Turning, she bumped into Colter.

He took the paper from her. "Relax. Becky won't do anything to spoil Ellie's day."

"I guess I needed to hear that."

"Becky's here, Becky's here, Becky's here," Ellie shrieked, running through the house with Sooner on her heels.

"Guess Becky's here," Colter said. "I'd better help her get things out of the car." He took a step, then turned back. "Do you want to come?"

She shook her head. "No, thank you. I need a moment."

"Okay." He gave her a sympathetic smile and walked out.

Taking a deep breath, she looked down at her clothes—jeans and a cream-colored silk blouse with her new boots, which she found very comfortable. She was fine…if only the tenseness in her stomach would go away. Maybe a little lipstick. No, she didn't have time. She could already hear Ellie's chatter.

Ellie was pulling a brown-haired woman with Kincaid green eyes into the room. She was the same height as Marisa and about the same size—the reason Marisa could wear her clothes.

"This is my mommy." Ellie pointed to Marisa. "Her

name is Marisa and she's gonna stay with Daddy and me forever."

Complete silence followed that statement.

Ellie glanced at Colter and back at Marisa. "Why's everyone looking so funny?"

"Your mother is here for the holidays, angelface," Colter said. "We haven't discussed anything beyond that."

Ellie stared at Marisa. "You're gonna leave?" Her bottom lip trembled, and Marisa hurried over to gather the child into her arms.

"I'm never leaving you again, baby. I promise."

What about me? Colter stood there, somehow needing an answer to that question. But he didn't get one. All he felt was the empty hole in his chest. Trying to conceal his sudden grief, he quickly carried the desserts into the kitchen.

"Nice to meet you." Marisa shook Becky's hand.

"Me, too. You're all Ellie's been talking about."

"Santa sent me my *real* mommy," Ellie said, her earlier distress forgotten.

"That's because you're special." Becky kissed her cheek.

"I'll get the presents out of the car." Colter headed for the door.

"I brought the poinsettias that were delivered to the office. I knew you'd want them today."

"Thanks, Beck."

Ellie ran after him, shouting, "I'll help, Daddy."

Marisa's throat felt tight and she was glad Becky walked into the kitchen just then and hugged Tulley. "How you doing?" she asked him.

"Fine. How's Jen?"

"Great. When I left, she and Bart were both sleeping."

"Just glad everyone's okay," Tulley said.

"Yeah, but when my sister's feeling better, I think I might kill her. She ruined my beautiful Christmas dinner. For once I was going to outshine her in the kitchen, but what does she do? Have premature labor pains and scare Bart and me to death. The doctor wants to monitor her to make sure it doesn't happen again."

"We're planning on going to the hospital this afternoon. Hope it's okay."

"Yeah. Jen will be heartbroken if she can't see Ellie on Christmas."

Marisa listened attentively; it was clear how much Tulley loved Colter and his sisters and how much they loved him. He was the only father they'd known, and she envied that closeness.

But she was still reeling from Ellie's announcement. She wouldn't leave Ellie—she was sure of that. It was Colter who worried her; he apparently felt some need to point out that she was leaving after the holidays. She had a week to change his mind—and she intended to do just that.

"Look what else Aunt Becky brought," Ellie said, placing a pie carefully on the table.

"I made homemade apple pie just like Mama and Cora used to, plus Colter's favorite four-layer cake."

"You did good, girl." Tulley patted her shoulder.

"Hmm." Colter laid packages under the tree. "Better wait until we taste it."

"Colter Kincaid!" Becky rested her hands on her hips.

The rest of the day Marisa listened to their easy banter, and if she expected animosity from Becky, she didn't get any. Becky was lively and energetic, with an irrepressible sense of humor, and Marisa suspected that Ellie had inherited some of her aunt's exuberance. By the middle of the afternoon, Marisa and Becky were talking like old friends. Becky reminded her a lot of Cari in her zest for life.

After dinner, they opened presents. Becky liked the mirror and said it was definitely something she would use. She handed Marisa a large package. "This is from Jen, Bart and me."

Marisa unwrapped it carefully and gasped when she saw what it was—a framed collage of photographs showing Ellie from infancy to the present. Tears trickled down Marisa's cheeks. Hugging Becky, she whispered, "Thank you. I love it."

Afterward they got ready to go to the hospital. Ellie wanted to wear her new clothes and she asked Marisa to do her hair in a French braid with a pink ribbon.

Becky took her own car, since she wasn't coming back to the ranch. Colter, Tulley, Marisa and Ellie rode in Colter's truck, but not before Ellie had given Sooner a long talk about why he couldn't go. They left him in the backyard.

Marisa wasn't nervous. She'd weathered one Kincaid, so she figured the rest couldn't be so bad. And she was right.

Colter helped Ellie carry in one of the big poinsettias. Jen's eyes lit up, and she welcomed Marisa warmly. Jennifer was an older version of Becky, but much more serious. Marisa thanked her for the photo collage, and Jen accepted her gifts, smiling serenely.

Bart's brother, Ted, and his wife, Susan, and son, Jarred, arrived soon after, and they all crowded into Jen's room. She was half sitting in the raised hospital bed, wearing a bright red robe with holly on the collar and cuffs.

Ellie introduced the boy. "This is Jarred. He's in my class at school."

"Hi, Jarred." Marisa smiled, pleased to meet Ellie's classmates.

He raised a hand in greeting and sidled closer to his father, obviously embarrassed by Ellie's attention.

"I'm sorry, big brother," Jen said. "I ruined Christmas."

"There's no way you could ruin Christmas. Just take care of yourself and the baby."

"Golly, your stomach's big," Ellie said, staring at her wide-eyed.

"Ellie—"

"Yes," Jen interrupted Colter. "My stomach's big. I feel like a bloated cow."

Ellie looked at Marisa. "Did you have a big stomach with me?"

"Enormous. I didn't think I was ever going to see my feet again." She couldn't believe it was so easy to talk about—especially in front of Colter and his family.

Colter glanced at her, and for a brief moment she remembered those months, being pregnant and feeling miserable. There were so many things about that time she wanted to share with him, good *and* bad.

"Daddy, can Jarred and me go look at the babies?" Ellie asked.

"Yes, but come right back," Colter replied, sitting next to Marisa.

Ellie and Jarred flew out the door, and the adults continued to talk about Christmas, babies, horses and business. They included Marisa, who was grateful they made her feel like part of the family.

"Thank you for being so nice." She felt she had to say that as she gathered up her purse and coat at the end of the visit.

"You're welcome," Jen said. "I admire your strength in dealing with everything you went through. I think I'd lose my mind if someone took my baby." She rubbed her stomach as she was talking.

"I was close to it when I found out the truth, but seeing Ellie saved me." She got to her feet. "She's been gone for a while, so I should check on her. And thanks again, everyone." She moved toward the door.

"I'll go with you," Colter said. "We should be heading home. You probably shouldn't have a lot of company, but we couldn't let this day pass without seeing you." He kissed Jen and Becky and followed Marisa out. Tulley was still saying his goodbyes.

In the hallway, Marisa hardly recognized her child. Her clothes were askew and her hair straggled out of its braid. She held the crumpled ribbon in one hand.

Marisa ran to her, pushing the blond hair from her heated face. "Baby, what *happened?* Are you all right?"

Ellie shrugged her shoulders. "Sure."

"What happened to your clothes and hair?"

"Are we going home?" Ellie asked instead of answering, evidently trying to change the subject.

"Ellie." There was a stern note in Colter's voice.

Jarred darted into Jen's room, but Marisa barely noticed. Her eyes were on Ellie.

"What happened?" Colter asked.

Ellie shuffled her feet.

"Ellie."

"Jarred pulled my hair and said I looked like a girl, and I hit him and he hit me back, then I pushed him and he pushed me." She shrugged again. "I guess we got into a fight."

"Jarred *hit* you?" Marisa was aghast, unable to believe someone would do this to her child.

"Don't overreact," Colter warned, obviously seeing the anger that filled her eyes.

Ted stepped into the hall holding Jarred's hand. Jarred stared at his shoes. He pulled the boy forward.

"I'm sorry," Jarred mumbled. For the first time Marisa looked at him; his hair was disheveled, his shirt hanging out of his jeans, and a sleeve was ripped at the seam.

"It's okay," Ellie said, hanging her head.

Colter cleared his throat.

"I'm sorry, too," Ellie added quickly.

Colter and Ted talked for a minute, and then they left. Marisa was still in a state of shock. She didn't want anyone hitting her child and she didn't want Ellie in school with someone who'd do such a thing.

On the way home, they stopped at the cemetery

to put the flowers on Colter's parents' graves and on Tulley's wife's.

When they got back to the ranch, Tulley fixed a light supper while they fed Beauty. The fawn was standing up now, so Colter put her in a horse stall.

These activities, and her pleasure over the fawn's recovery, eased Marisa's tension over Ellie somewhat.

Later, Marisa played some Christmas songs Ellie wanted to hear, followed by "Ave Maria" and "O Holy Night," ending with parts of Tchaikovsky's "Nutcracker Suite." The day had come to an end, but she wanted to hang on to every second. Ellie nodded sleepily beside her.

Marisa kissed her. "Time for your bath."

"Okay." Ellie slid off the bench and went to her room, Sooner behind her.

"That was beautiful," Tulley said, pushing out of his chair. "Now I hear my bed calling."

"'Night, Tulley. And Merry Christmas."

"'Night," he called. "And same to you."

She turned to Colter, who was sitting on the sofa looking relaxed. "I'm having a hard time with Jarred hitting Ellie," she admitted.

"She hit him first," he said.

"He was baiting her. He said she looked like a girl."

One dark eyebrow rose. "She *is* a girl."

She shook her head. "That's beside the point. He only said it to taunt her."

"Marisa…"

"No." She refused to be put off. "I will not have someone hitting her. I think we should talk to her teacher and have her removed from that class. I don't want her anywhere near Jarred."

Colter leaned forward and rubbed his hands. "Have you asked Ellie how she feels about this?"

"No, of course not. She's just a child. She doesn't know what's best for her." An eerie calm came over her as the words resounded in her head. She'd heard them before, many times, but they'd been spoken about her. For a moment she was paralyzed as she fought for control over the emotions that gripped her.

Ellie came racing into the room in pink-and-white flannel pajamas, Sooner obediently by her side. "I'm ready for bed." She smiled at them.

"Angelface, your mother's upset because Jarred hit you. She wants to take you out of Jarred's class. How do you feel about that?"

Ellie's face crumpled. "No! Don't do that," she cried, staring at Marisa.

"Tell us why you feel that way," Colter said.

"Well." She twisted on her bare feet. "I like him and I think he likes me, too. That's why he was teasing me. If you move me to another class, I'll never see him again. *Please* don't do that."

Marisa could hear her own voice saying almost those same words when she was seventeen. *Please, I love him. If you make me go, I'll never see him again. Please.* But her mother hadn't listened to her. She was considered a child, her feelings and opinions inconsequential. Fear overwhelmed her as she realized she was treating Ellie the way her mother had always treated her.

Kneeling on the floor, she gathered Ellie into her

arms. "Don't worry, baby." She smoothed her hair. "I won't do anything that'll upset you. I'm just overreacting. I'm new at this mother thing. You have to be patient with me." She kissed the tip of her nose. "But I still don't like anyone hitting you."

"It was just a tap," Ellie assured her.

"We'll discuss this 'tapping' later," Colter said. "Now off to bed."

"Gosh," Ellie grumbled, heading for her room, Sooner trailing behind her. "Does anyone love me enough to tuck me in?" Her voice echoed from the hall.

"We'll see," Colter called.

"Parents" they heard faintly.

Colter raised an eyebrow. "I guess you're included in that."

"It's not one of the ways I was looking forward to being included." She rose to her feet. "I'm sorry. I got carried away."

"If I thought for one minute that he'd hurt her or intended to hurt her, I would've been the first to box his ears. But they were just playing, and I seriously suspect Ellie was trying to get his attention." At her confused look, he added, "She has a crush on him."

"I should've known you had everything under control. I just—" She tried to explain and couldn't. Instead she said in a rushed voice, "We'd better say good-night before she thinks we've forgotten about her."

As soon as Ellie went to sleep, Marisa made a quick exit.

She grabbed her coat, exchanged her shoes for the new rubber boots and hurried out to the barn. The night sounds no longer bothered her. She had to get away, to sort out these new emotions that were tearing her apart. And she wanted to make sure Beauty was comfortable.

She opened the barn door and turned on the light, then entered the stall. Beauty was curled in one corner, blinking up at her in the sudden brightness. Marisa sank onto the hay and leaned back on her heels, stroking the fawn's soft body. Beauty licked Marisa's fingers.

"Hi, Beauty," she cooed. "Are you okay? Did you have a nice Christmas? Do you miss your mommy?"

A bubble of laughter escaped her. Here she was sitting in a barn, talking to a deer. And it felt…right. This New York City girl liked living on a ranch—because her daughter was here…and so was the man she loved. No, it was more than that. She *wanted* to be here and she was beginning to feel a connection with the animals. She couldn't explain what had happened. Maybe she'd grown up. But something still tormented her, a deep-seated pain she had to face.

"Marisa."

Her head jerked toward Colter's soft voice.

He walked in and knelt beside her. "Why didn't you tell me you were coming out here? I would've come with you."

"I just wanted to be by myself and think."

"Are you still worried about Jarred?"

"No." She sighed heavily, feeling all those buried emotions gathering force inside her. She couldn't stop the tears that filled her eyes. Quickly, she tried to brush them away, hating that she couldn't control this weakness.

He caught her hand. "It's all right to cry."

"I thought you didn't like it when I cried," she mumbled, remembering that from Vegas when it didn't take much to make her tearful.

Tenderly, he brushed the tears away with his thumb, his gentleness threatening to open a floodgate. "Sometimes you try to be too strong," he answered. "So, what are the tears about?"

"It's just…" She had a hard time finding the words, but she knew she could share anything with him. That was how it had always been. He was probably the only person who'd understand what she was feeling. "Tonight I saw my mother in me. She treated me like a child without feelings, she never asked what I wanted or how I felt, and I was doing the same thing to Ellie. I've always thought I was nothing like my mother, but—" She choked back a sob.

His hand curved around the nape of her neck and she rubbed her cheek softly against his arm, feeling warmth and comfort.

"You are nothing like your mother," he said, his voice husky. "She was manipulative, driven and deceitful. You are a loving, caring woman, and you don't have a deceitful bone in your body."

She wanted to believe his words, but she wasn't sure she could. She pulled away from his hand. "Don't say that just to pacify me."

"I'm not. I mean it."

"No, you don't," she replied. "If you meant it, you wouldn't keep this distance between us. Today when Ellie said she wanted me to live here forever, you looked as if you'd been kicked in the stomach."

"Marisa. Let it drop."

"No, I won't," she snapped. "What is it? Why can't you let the past go? Why can't you trust me?"

"It's nothing, really," he murmured, obviously trying to put her off.

"No, it's something, and I want to know what it is."

There was a moment of hesitation. "In all the time you've been here and all the times we've talked, not once have you mentioned the note."

She frowned. "What note?"

"God." His jaw clenched. "How could you write something like that and not even remember it?"

"What are you talking about?"

He reached in his back pocket and took out his wallet. Flipping through it, he removed a piece of paper and handed it to her. She unfolded the worn sheet and quickly scanned the contents.

"No." She shook her head as each word pierced her. Her mother had done this, had left Colter this awful note. A cold shiver spread through her as all her bitter feelings toward Vanessa began to surface. But she knew, with everything in her, that her mother had done this because she loved her. Vanessa had wanted what she considered best for her daughter. She had done all the wrong things for the right reasons.

She stared at the note, wishing her mother had known Colter the way she did, but those doors to the past had been irrevocably closed.

Why had he kept this terrible note all these years? The answer came swiftly—because he thought she'd written it. And this was the reason he wouldn't admit he felt anything for her. He couldn't trust her feelings.

"I didn't write it," she told him in a shaky voice. "Surely you know I never felt that way about you and never will."

"You…didn't write it."

"No. I was crying so hard I couldn't write a word. I planned to get in touch with you later—remember, I told you? I guess Mother decided to leave the note to ensure that you wouldn't come after me."

For a moment his body went still, then he reached for the note, crushing it in his hand. "Another damn lie, another deception," he said in anger.

Marisa had to get away. So much pain, so much suffering, and it still wasn't over. This last blow brought all her hopes and dreams crashing down around her. She couldn't fight the inevitable anymore.

"I was hoping that in time we could put the past behind us, but I can see that's never going to happen. If you can believe I ever felt that way about you, then there's no future for us." She stood. It was too late. Nothing could help them now. She walked from the stall on heavy feet.

He let her go.

Chapter 18

"Marisa."

She stopped. Had he called her name? No, she'd just imagined it. She told herself to keep walking. Tears stung her eyes and her stomach churned with a sick feeling, but her feet wouldn't move.

"Please don't ever leave me again."

This time the voice was faint, but she heard it. His words were full of pain and entreaty and seemed to come from somewhere deep within him. Or was she hearing things? Still, she couldn't walk away. Slowly she turned around. He stood, a solitary figure with his shoulders slightly hunched. Her heart contracted as she saw the tears glistening on his cheeks. She took a couple of steps toward him.

"What are you saying?" she asked, her voice trembling.

He gave a harsh laugh, a desolate sound that seem to echo between them. "I'm afraid," he admitted. "Big, fearless Colter Kincaid is afraid. I've tamed wild horses, but I'm afraid of the emotions I feel for you. Help me, Marisa. Because everything I believed about you is lies. I don't know what to think or feel anymore, but I'm certain of one thing. I'm tired of fighting you, I'm tired of fighting myself, but most of all, I'm tired of fighting all these emotions inside me."

"What emotions?" she asked, not daring to breathe.

"I've tried to hate you, to forget about you, but I've never succeeded. Even when you came back and we learned the truth about Ellie's birth, I still couldn't accept you in my life. I told you our love was like ashes and could never be rekindled. That was just another lie to protect me from the way I knew I'd feel when you tired of that rodeo rider who'd fathered your child. When you left me for the second time."

She whimpered in protest, but he didn't seem to hear as he continued. "So I tried to keep a distance between us because I knew I couldn't survive you leaving me again."

She took a step closer to him. "I've never really left you."

"What?" His eyes centered on her face.

"Eight years ago, my mother took me away, but you were always here—" she placed a hand over her breast "—in my heart, and you always will be. No one can take that from me—not even you."

"Marisa—"

He blinked back tears, and she could see that the

battle within him was raging, but this time, she was winning.

"I need you," he whispered.

"I need you, too," she whispered back, wanting to throw herself into his arms, but she couldn't. He hadn't said the words she wanted to hear, and she didn't know if he ever would. "But needing isn't loving," she added. "And I need you to love and trust me. Without that we have nothing."

"I trust you with our child. Doesn't that tell you how I feel?"

"No, that only tells me how you feel about Ellie and me. I have to know how you feel about *you* and me."

He drew a ragged breath and placed a hand over his heart. "Even after all the times I've denied it, and all the times I've hurt you, this heart beats only with love for you." They stared at each other for endless seconds, both absorbing the truth. Then, with a muffled exclamation, he reached for her, gathering her into his arms. "Can't you feel how much I love you? My life has been so lonely and empty without you."

"I love you, too," she said with a tremor in her voice. It seemed as if she'd waited forever to hear those words, and she gave a sigh of pure happiness. "Say it again."

"I love you," he breathed against her face a moment before his lips covered hers, his arms molding her against the hardness of his body.

Her lips softened voluntarily, her hands curling into his hair. At her submission, he deepened the kiss, his tongue probing, tasting the sweetness of her. The kiss went on and on. They didn't seem to need to breathe.

Their lips, tongues and hearts gave them the sustenance they needed.

He rested his forehead against hers. "Now do you believe me?"

Breathing heavily, she had trouble thinking above the hammering of her heart. But she knew with certainty that the wounds of the past had finally healed.

"Yes," she cried, her arms tight around his neck.

"Marisa," he groaned, gathering her closer. "I love you. I've always loved you. Even when I hated you, I loved you."

She touched his cheek gently and they swayed together like two drifting leaves in the wind. They stood for minutes just holding each other, both needing the comfort and reassurance that only touching could bring. Finally, Colter stared into her dark eyes, seeing all the love he would ever need.

"God, I love you," he murmured, kissing her deeply. "It feels so good to be able to say that."

"I know," she said, realizing how hard it had been for him. Tilting her head, she looked at him with dreamy, love-filled eyes. "I wish you'd mentioned the note earlier."

"I was waiting for you to bring it up, and when you didn't, I assumed you wanted to forget about it."

She tasted the tears on his face. "But *you* never forgot it. I'm so sorry for the pain that note caused you. In Mother's eyes, you were wrong for me, and she stopped at nothing to keep us apart. I've had all this anger and bitterness inside me. I couldn't understand how she could do that to me, how she could hurt me like that. But tonight with Ellie, for a brief moment,

I got a glimpse into her motives. Everything she did, she did because she loved me. For my sanity, I have to believe that."

"You're very forgiving" was all he said.

She cradled his face in her hands, staring into his eyes. "When I was seventeen and I looked at you, I got this wonderful feeling inside. I've never felt anything like it before or since. I felt it the day I met you again, although I didn't want to admit it, and I feel it every time I look at you now. I can't describe it, but I know it's love and I know I'll never feel it for any other man. I want to spend the rest of my life with you, more than anything in the world."

"Oh, Marisa." He buried his face in the warmth of her neck.

She understood that he'd opened his heart to her and allowed her to see his vulnerability, his uncertainty and fear. All his defenses were down, showing her just how much he trusted her. How much he loved her. That love flowed through her body.

"I'm so happy." Her fingers caressed his neck.

Slowly, her lips replaced her fingers, her tongue gently stroking the pulsing nerve at the base of his throat. Urgently turning his head, his mouth captured hers with a mindless, burning need that left her limbs trembling, her senses spinning, and her body aching for the ecstasy that only he could give.

Fighting for restraint, she drew back slightly, wanting to be sure. "Does this mean we're going to be a family now?"

He grabbed her hand and headed for the house.

"Colter, where are we going?"

"Shh." He put a finger to his lips.

She followed him to the house through the back door and to his study. "Colter?"

"Shh," he said again. "We don't want to wake our daughter."

He closed the door, and Marisa stood transfixed, staring at an object in the corner. The Christmas Cradle was there, and for a moment she couldn't believe her eyes. She blinked, but it was still there. She walked over and touched it lovingly. "Where did this come from?" she whispered.

Colter was busy getting something out of a drawer and he swung to face her. "What? Oh, the cradle?"

"Yes. Where did it come from?"

He set something on the desk and came to her. "I bought it that day I met you in Dalton's. I thought it was beautiful and would make a great gift for Jen. They delivered it to the office. I brought it home the other day and stored it in here."

"Do you know it's called a Christmas Cradle?"

He shook his head. "No. It just caught my eye. The saleslady wanted to explain, but I didn't have time."

She pointed to the figures carved in the wood. "These depict The Twelve Days of Christmas and it's all carved by a craftsman in Austin. His wife is from England and she sews the lovely bedding. See, the song starts here at the head of the cradle with a partridge in a pear tree, two turtle doves, three French hens and so on. You can see the song depicted along the sides of the cradle and at the base. On the rockers are eleven pipers piping and twelve drummers drumming." She smiled mistily. "Dalton's orders one every year. The cradle takes a long time to carve and the craftsman only makes a few. See? It's made from one block of wood and is unique in its design. I love just looking at it and I looked at it that very same day and—and…it was something I always had to do. Every year. I could almost see my baby in it. I could…"

He slipped his arms around her waist from behind.

"I was wondering that same day who would buy it." She rested her head against his chest. "And you did. I would never have guessed. Jen will love it."

"I don't think so."

She turned in his arms. "What do you mean?"

"I'd never give that cradle to anyone but you. I can hear the love in your voice when you talk about it."

"No. You bought it for Jen."

"Not really," he said. "I think I must've bought it for myself—call it fate or whatever. I don't usually believe in those things, but subconsciously I must've sensed your interest in it. Becky told me Jen didn't need it— she's using Bart's bassinet from when he was a baby. I bought it anyway."

"Oh, Colter." She wrapped her arms around his neck. "Thank you."

"You're welcome." He kissed her briefly and reached for something on the desk.

Puzzled, she watched as he opened a small velvet box. Her heart skyrocketed as she stared at a diamond ring.

"I was going to give this to you the day you left." A wistfulness entered his voice. "Afterward, I planned to return it, but I never did. Later, I decided to keep it for

Ellie. But now—" he looked deep into her eyes "—I think the woman I purchased it for should wear it."

"Oh, Colter, it's beautiful!"

He slid the ring onto her trembling finger, saying, "Marisa Preston, will you marry me?"

"Yes, yes, yes." She threw her arms around his neck.

He kissed the side of her face and picked up a document on the desk, which he handed to her.

It was Ellie's birth certificate.

Tears gathered in her eyes as she saw Ellie's birth name. "You named her Marisa Ellen."

"Yes. I wanted her to have a small part of you. Later, I regretted that impulse and I never told Ellie. Tulley's the only one who knows."

"I'm not sure what to say."

"Say you love me," he said in a hoarse voice.

Her eyes sparkled. "I love you, forever and always."

His arms tightened around her and he let his lips travel from her mouth, to her cheek, to her hair. "Oh God, Marisa, I love you so much it's killing me. These last few days, every time you responded to me you seemed to hate yourself and me afterward." She smoothed his dark hair and he breathed a kiss behind her ear. "When I saw you in Dalton's, I was so angry. Then you came here to the ranch and the moment I saw you beside Ellie, I knew you weren't out of my system."

"You were thrown from that horse and got hurt." Her finger touched the quivering muscle in his jaw. "I don't think I ever told you how sorry I was about that."

"It wasn't your fault," he told her. "The first thing

a rodeo rider learns is concentration, total concentration. Lose that for even a second and, well…you saw what happened."

His voice grew weaker and weaker as her lips touched his jaw. He turned his head, his mouth covering hers once again with a driving need. She reveled in the mastery of his kiss, her senses spinning, her body aching.

"Marisa," he groaned into her throat. "I want you so badly that I'm burning up with it."

"Me, too." She left a trail of moist kisses from his jaw to his ear. His body quivered, and she slowly began to unbutton his shirt, then splayed her hands across his chest. She took his hand, then led him toward the hall.

They ran up the stairs like two excited teenagers. As soon as the door closed, they were locked in each other's arms. She clung to him, her blood raging like a river, sweeping her along with a passion her body remembered well.

Within minutes, their clothes were a heap on the floor. Colter paused to slip off his boots and his jeans, his eyes lingering on the silken smoothness of her body. Her skin tingled at his dark gaze.

"You're more beautiful than ever," he murmured, swinging her up into his arms and placing her on the bed. His fingers skimmed her heated flesh. "I've dreamed of this moment so many times, but the fantasy is nothing compared with the reality."

He pressed his lips to every inch of her skin. Tiny flames ignited in the pit of her stomach, but before the flames consumed her, she wanted to tell him.

"Colter," she managed to say between gasps of air.

"Mmm?"

He kissed one breast and then the other, and she forgot what was so important—but only for a second. "It's...it's been a long time."

"I know." His tongue explored one rosy nipple, and all rational thought was fast leaving her.

"No. I mean it's really been a long time for me." She spoke in a rush. "There...there hasn't been anyone since you."

He raised his head, his eyes glazed. "My God, why not?"

"After losing my baby, I lost interest in everything, including men. When I did start dating, I was careful not to let my emotions get involved. I didn't want to be hurt again." She smiled tentatively. "I'm telling you this because in Vegas I neglected to tell you I was a virgin. I want everything to be right this time."

His eyes clouded for a second. "That means you're not on the pill?"

"No..."

"I don't have any condoms, and we should be adults about this. Responsible."

"We were the last time, and look what happened."

"I know, but..."

She caressed his face. "I see this as a commitment to our life, our future."

"Then you wouldn't mind another child?"

"I've been given a beautiful cradle, so what do you think?"

His sweet smile and loving kiss evoked a response deep within her. They made love to each other as they had years ago. Everything came just as naturally as it had before, but it was all so much better. Their responses were stronger, more ardent, because they knew all those secret little joys that brought each other pleasure. They gave of themselves without holding back. When the ecstasy came, it came with a fierce abandonment that left them both sated, content, wrapped in the arms of love.

Later, his head lay possessively on her shoulder and her hand lazily stroked the muscles in his back.

"Colter?"

"Mmm?" His lips nuzzled the curve of her neck.

"Merry Christmas."

He raised his head. "Ah, you're the best Christmas gift I've ever been given."

She ran her fingers over the stubble that was beginning to show. "I've changed, haven't I?"

He rolled away, pushing up against the headboard, and pulled her into his arms. "The younger Marisa was insecure, afraid of a lot of things and dominated by her mother. I loved her anyway. The older Marisa's independent, making it on her own and stronger than I ever thought she could be. When you learned about Ellie, I thought you'd fall apart, but you didn't. And I loved you even more."

They shared a long deep kiss. "You gave up so much to raise our daughter," she said. "You're a very special father, Mr. Kincaid. I hope I can be as good a mother."

"You will be. Ellie adores you already."

She remembered a time when she'd adored her own mother.

"What is it?" Colter asked, seeing her sad expression.

"I was thinking about my parents—especially my mother."

His arms tightened around her. "Our future's together, but what kind of future can we build on bitterness and resentment? I want more for Ellie."

"Me, too." She idly caressed the firm muscles in his arms. "I never thought I'd see the past from my mother's point of view. But I've had these insightful moments ever since that night you wondered what you'd do if Ellie had my talent and got pregnant at seventeen. I couldn't really answer. And tonight the incident with Jarred opened my eyes even more. She did the things she did because she loved me. She just didn't *know* me. I don't want to make that mistake with Ellie."

She snuggled close to his body and a comfortable silence enveloped them both.

The future was so bright she could almost touch it. But as Colter had said, what kind of future could they build if she continued to harbor bitterness and resentment toward her parents? She knew what she had to do, and it wouldn't be easy.

He kissed the top of her head. "You can do it."

She looked up at him. "How did you know what I was thinking?"

"Because I'm thinking the same thing. You've been through hell, but you're not going to be completely happy until you talk to your parents." His lips took hers again, and they forgot everything but each other.

Sometime toward morning, Colter placed a gentle kiss on her lips and slid from the bed.

"Colter," she murmured sleepily.

He tucked the covers around her. "Go back to sleep.

I'm going to my own room so Ellie won't find me here."

"I love you."

"Love you, too." He found his clothes and quickly left.

Marisa turned over, feeling lonely without his warmth. She glanced at the clock—5:00 a.m. Soon Ellie would be bouncing on her bed. Soon they'd tell her they were getting married. Soon they'd be a real family.

First, though, she had to see her parents. Without forgiveness, there could be no happiness, and she wanted true happiness for Ellie, Colter and herself.

But could she actually forgive them for taking her child?

Chapter 19

"Mommy, wake up! Mommy."

The precious voice tugged at her brain and Marisa slowly opened her eyes. "Morning, baby."

"Morning, Mommy," Ellie said, and crawled in beside her; predictably, Sooner, too, jumped onto the bed, and Marisa stroked his sleek fur. "Did you sleep good?"

Better than I've slept in years. Colter's touch, his kiss, was still with her.

She pulled Ellie into her arms. "Yes, and how about you?"

Ellie shrugged. "I don't know. I fall asleep and I don't remember anything. I just wake up."

Marisa kissed her good-morning. "Is your father awake?"

"Yeah. He and Tulley are drinking coffee."

"Then let's join them."

"Okay." Ellie scrambled off the bed.

Marisa reached for her robe. She didn't want to take time to dress, she just wanted to see Colter.

They hurried downstairs and she paused in the kitchen doorway, her eyes on Colter. He was smiling as he noticed her, and she was, too. They couldn't seem to stop.

Ellie slid onto Colter's lap.

"What do you want for breakfast?" he asked Ellie, his eyes never leaving Marisa.

"I don't…"

As Marisa pushed her hair behind her ears, her diamond ring caught the light—and Ellie's attention.

"What's that, Mommy?" Ellie pointed.

"Yeah, what's that?" Tulley asked, grinning.

Marisa and Colter exchanged a secret smile. "Well, you see, angelface, last night I asked your mother to marry me and she said yes."

Ellie's mouth fell open and then she jumped off Colter's lap, shouting, "Oh boy, oh boy, oh boy, this is big—bigger than Christmas. I gotta call Aunt Becky, Aunt Jen and Lori. Golly, this is the best Christmas *ever*." Sooner barked in a frenzied manner as Ellie bounced around the room.

Colter finally grabbed her by the arm. "Okay, baby girl, calm down."

"I can't, Daddy. I'm too excited. My mommy's gonna live here forever. I'll never be without a mommy again."

She ran to Marisa and threw both arms around her

waist. Colter came to stand beside them, sliding an arm around her shoulder.

"I believe in Santa Claus—don't you, Mommy? Daddy?"

"Ellie." Colter sighed.

Marisa smoothed Ellie's hair, gazing into Colter's eyes. "Oh, yes, I believe."

Looking at her, he believed in the unbelievable, the impossible. "Daddy believes, too," he said.

Tulley stood and scooped up his hat. "If that don't beat all. I'm beginning to believe myself."

Ellie giggled as Tulley ambled out the door.

They ate breakfast with Ellie asking a million questions. She couldn't sit still for one second—up and down, up and down, until Colter said it was time to feed Beauty. Marisa and Ellie changed into jeans and boots and headed for the barn. Colter tagged along, unable to stay away from them.

Marisa prepared the milk and poured it into the bottle. Beauty was walking around in her stall, hardly resembling the fawn of two days ago. Ellie fed her the bottle, and Marisa knelt in the hay applying ointment to the sores still evident on the small body. Happy and content, Beauty curled up on the hay and went to sleep.

Marisa then helped Ellie tend to her horses. They filled buckets with horse and mule feed and carried them to the long troughs in the pasture. Dandy and Sassy immediately galloped toward them. Marisa pulled a chunk of carrot from her pocket, which Dandy ate from her hand.

Colter observed all this with a sense of wonder. She seemed at home here on the ranch and with the animals. She was nothing like the frightened young girl of eight years ago, but she had the same big heart, the same innocence and beauty he'd never forgotten. And never would. This time she was in his life to stay.

But he saw the sadness that lingered in her eyes. He'd thought he would never forgive Richard and Vanessa Preston, but love had miraculous healing powers. Now Marisa had to find the strength to do the same, and he would be right beside her.

"Mommy." He heard Ellie talking. "I'm gonna put on my new outfit and ride Dandy. Please fix my hair in a French braid with a red ribbon. I'll look so cool."

Marisa sat on a bale of hay and pulled Ellie to her side. "Mommy has to go into Dallas for a little while."

"Why?"

"I'd like to go see my father."

"Oh." Ellie twisted on her boots. "When will you be back?"

Marisa caught her hands. "About lunchtime, and then I'll fix your hair and watch you ride Dandy."

"Okay," Ellie said, but she didn't look up, and Marisa knew something was bothering her.

"Mommy?"

"What, baby?"

"Is your daddy gonna be mean to you?"

"Oh, baby, no." She gathered her child in her arms. "He loves me."

As she said the words, she knew they were true. For days she'd been telling herself that her parents had to love her to do what they'd done, but she hadn't fully believed it until now. She'd grasped it intellectually but not emotionally. Until now. She knew her parents would never intentionally hurt her. They'd sheltered and protected her from the world; and at seventeen she'd had no clear idea of what was out there. Their decisions had been wrong for Marisa. They'd had no way of knowing that, though, because communication was not a strong suit in their family.

Thank you, baby. It took her child to make her fully understand—and accept—the past.

Within the hour she was dressed and ready. Colter walked her to the car holding her hand. Ellie was riding her bicycle, completely competent at stopping and turning after her Christmas Day lesson and this morning's practice.

"If you wanted me to, I'd go with you," Colter said, "but I know you have to do this by yourself."

She touched his face, loving him all the more for realizing that. "Yes, I do." She went into his arms and he held her for a second, then she got in the car and drove toward Dallas.

Colter watched until the car was out of sight. He felt as though the sun had just stopped shining in his world. It wouldn't shine again until she was back.

Hurry home, Marisa.

Marisa tried not to think about the meeting ahead. She didn't even know if her father was home. Her mother had gone on a cruise, and she didn't have a clue to where Reed was. He had said he'd call over the holidays, but so far he hadn't.

She picked up her cell phone and called Cari. They talked until she turned in to Highland Park. Cari was thrilled to hear that she and Colter were getting married, and Marisa could hardly contain her own excitement. But as she pulled up to the gates, all she felt was apprehension.

She punched in the code and thought that maybe she should've called, after all. With the upheaval in the family, her father might have gone away for the holidays. If so, she'd go back to Colter and Ellie and wait until after New Year's. She knew she had to do this.

As she drew closer to the house, she noticed Reed's sports car parked in front. Had he been in Dallas all along? Why hadn't he called her? Maybe he'd reconciled with their father and didn't know how to tell her. She got out and ran to the front door and rang the bell.

Winston opened it immediately. "Miss Marisa, how nice to see you."

"Thank you, Winston. Is my father home?"

Winston stepped aside. "Yes, ma'am. They're in the library."

"They?" She walked into the foyer.

"Mr. Reed and Mrs. Preston are here, as well."

"Oh. My mother's back from her cruise?" She could see both her parents at the same time; she hadn't expected this.

"She cancelled her holiday plans," Winston replied. "She spent Christmas with Mr. Preston."

"Really?" It was hard to keep the shock out of her voice. For years she and Reed were the only thing that had kept her parents civil. Had they actually managed to spend time together without tearing each other apart?

Marisa walked toward the library, her mind whirling. Her mother was still here; apparently she'd never left. And Reed was here, too. What was going on? As she reached the library, she heard raised voices. She didn't want to eavesdrop, but she didn't want to interrupt, either.

"Those are my conditions, take them or leave them." That was Reed and he sounded angry.

"I don't like ultimatums, son," her father warned.

"And I don't like how you've controlled and manipulated my life. You've been grooming me for years to take over Dalton's, but I'm nothing more than a figurehead. I have no real responsibility or power. Marisa felt the same way."

"Have you seen your sister?"

"No. I've given her the time she needs with Colter and their child."

"I thought she'd call over the holidays," Richard said plaintively.

"Why would she do that?" Reed asked with a touch of sarcasm. "You and Mother have treated her like a porcelain doll, unable to live her own life because of her great talent. Well, you've finally shattered her life into so many pieces, I'm not sure she'll ever be the same."

"I'm fine, Reed," she said, stepping into the room.

All three looked at her. "Oh, my darling, you're home," Vanessa said. She was standing by the fireplace drinking a cup of tea. Putting the cup down, she hurried toward Marisa, but halted abruptly a few feet from her.

Her father seemed unable to speak.

Reed came and hugged her, smiling broadly. "How are you doing? You look great."

"I am great." She smiled back. "I have my daughter."

"I'm glad you're home," her father finally said.

"I'm not home." She wanted to make that point clear. "I just came to tell you I'm getting married."

"Oh." Vanessa blinked.

"So you're marrying him?" was Richard's response.

"Yes. I've never stopped loving him." She looked directly at her mother. "I think you know that."

"After I told you the baby was stillborn and you sank into such a deep depression, I felt we'd done the wrong thing. But when you refused to play the piano, I knew for sure that we had. I just didn't know how to make it right without hurting you even more."

"I thought I'd never recover," she said, wanting to be completely honest. "But Colter and Ellie have made me see things in a new way—well—I'm playing the piano again."

"Oh, darling, that's wonderful." Vanessa clapped her hands together.

"Colter had never heard me play and he said he hadn't realized I was so talented. He wondered what he'd do if Ellie had that kind of talent and got pregnant at seventeen. I really couldn't answer until yesterday. Ellie was playing with a friend from school and they got into a disagreement and he hit her. I was furious. I wanted Ellie removed from that class. I wanted to get her away from him—that was all I could think of." She took a breath. "Colter asked me if I'd asked Ellie what *she* wanted, and I told him she was a child and didn't know what was best. And I began to understand that was exactly how you felt about me. I was young, so young."

"Yes, darling, you were."

"Today when I told Ellie I was coming here, she was afraid you might hurt me."

A strangled sob left Vanessa's throat, but Marisa continued. "I knew then that you didn't intentionally hurt me. You've loved and protected me all my life, yet you've never really known me. I hated the long hours of practice and I wanted to be like other girls—having fun. In rebellion I made some bad choices, but I will never regret loving Colter."

There was silence for a moment.

"I want to thank you for giving my child to Colter," she said quietly. "He's done a great job with Ellie."

Vanessa twisted the pearls around her neck. "He kept demanding to see you. I had to tell him another lie—that you didn't want anything to do with him or the baby. I could see how much that hurt him."

"Yes," Marisa said, staring down at her hands. "He's been hurting for a lot of years."

"Just like you," Reed put in.

"Yes, just like me." She looked at her father. "Why didn't you tell me you were there when Ellie was born?"

His eyes didn't waver from hers. "I didn't want you to know," he said with more honesty than she'd expected. "When Vanessa called, I saw it as a way to get what I wanted—you, back in Texas. I told her I'd help if she didn't pressure you to stay in New York. She kept her word, and you came home with me." He drew a long breath. "That doesn't make me look very good, but you're being honest and I have to do the same. I've always been angry at Vanessa for taking you away, and I saw this as my chance to have both my children with me. But giving up your baby was not an easy thing to do."

After another long silence, he resumed. "I grew up poor, as you know. My parents died when I was small and I lived with an aunt and her family. I started working when I was twelve, mowing yards and helping people in the neighborhood, but there was never enough money to go around. I studied hard and got a university scholarship. I was determined to have a better life. I worked in the men's department at Dalton's while I went to college. When I graduated, I applied for a management job at Dalton's and was hired as an assistant to the vice-president of sales." He walked to the fireplace and stared into the fire.

"I knew what I wanted, but I wasn't sure how to get it—until I met Vanessa. Her father doted on her and I set out to marry her. She was my stepping-stone to the big time. She was home for the holidays, and by New Year's we were heavily involved. But Vanessa had no plans to marry me. She went back to New York and her career." He picked up a poker and stoked the fire. "Fate intervened, though. When her parents discovered Vanessa was pregnant, I was called in to Mr. Dalton's office. He said, 'Buy a tux, boy, you're marrying my daughter.' And that was it. Vanessa and I did the right thing, but we fought all the time. She blamed me for everything that had happened. However, Mr. Dalton took me under his wing and taught me everything he knew—and I learned fast. I had what I wanted. My kids wouldn't have to work a day in their lives."

He turned to look at Reed and Marisa. "I did everything for you, and both of you complain that you don't have any responsibility. With responsibility come long hours and hard work. I didn't want that for you. I wanted you to enjoy life—and I was wrong. You have to learn, to grow. You have to experience pain in order to be strong. I tried to spare you all that, but I made a mistake. You have to experience the losses as well as the rewards. That's what creates character, and Marisa, I've never been prouder of you than I am today. I'm sorry for the pain I've caused you. I wish you nothing but happiness in your marriage." His voice wavered on the last word.

She'd never seen her father so humble and sincere, and she knew he meant what he'd said. "Thank you, Father."

Richard turned to Vanessa. "I'm sorry for the years I wouldn't listen to how you felt, but I'm not very good at sharing and I'm afraid I don't hear anyone's viewpoint but my own."

Vanessa brushed away a tear.

"And, Reed, I agree to all your conditions. By the time you're forty you will be CEO of Dalton's, and in the meantime, I will gradually ease into retirement."

"Thank you, Father," Reed said. "And maybe *you* should try to enjoy the life you've built."

"I'm going to try." Richard glanced at Vanessa. "Your mother and I are going to New York for New Year's and she's going to show me her city."

Marisa and Reed were speechless. Their parents hadn't gone anywhere together that Marisa could recall. She felt as if she'd stepped into some fantasy realm where fact and fiction were closely entwined.

But this was completely real. She could look at her parents and see how they'd changed. Ultimately the tragedy had changed all their lives—for the better.

"Marisa," her father said. "There will always be a place for you at Dalton's."

"I'm not sure what direction my life will take, but I do know I'll be a wife and mother and I will continue with my music."

"Oh, darling," Vanessa whispered through her tears.

"Then you're not going back to Madame Hélèna's?" Richard asked in a controlled voice.

"Hélèna helped me when no one else would, and I will fulfill my commitment to her—even though I suspect she only hired me to get back at you."

"She's a spiteful old witch."

"She's a brilliant designer and her clothes should be in Dalton's."

Richard smiled. "Then make it happen."

She smiled back, admiring his cleverness. "It's not that easy, Father. My life is now with Colter and our child. I'll leave the business deals to Reed. I had to tell you I've forgiven you, but it'll take me a while to forget—if ever."

"Thank you, darling." Vanessa stepped forward and hugged her, and Marisa hugged her back.

She couldn't go into the future with one foot in the past. She found she could make the transition easily now because so much was waiting for her.

"I'd better go. I don't want to stay away from Ellie too long." Marisa saw fresh tears in her mother's eyes, and if she felt any residue of resentment, it completely dissipated at the sight.

"Do you…do you think you might one day allow us to see Ellie?"

Marisa swallowed. "That'll be up to Ellie and, of course, Colter."

"Tell us about her," Reed invited.

She nodded readily. "Ellie's the most wonderful little girl. She's bright, funny and she never walks, she's always running. She has a dog named Sooner who she swears talks to her, and she's not afraid of anything. She has two horses named Dandy and Sassy, and she rides almost as well as her father."

"I can't wait to meet her," Reed said.

"Maybe soon," she replied. "Now I have to go."

"Goodbye, Marisa." Richard embraced her. "Just be happy."

"I am," she said, fighting tears.

She quickly left and ran to her car, then headed for home—her home, the place she'd been searching for. She'd done the right thing in seeing her parents. Now she could love Colter completely.

Colter checked his watch again. It was just after twelve. Marisa should've been home by now. A farrier was shoeing a couple of his horses; Ellie was watching closely, which kept her occupied. She knew her mother loved her and would be back. He knew the same thing, but he didn't want Marisa hurt or upset. He checked the time again.

"If you look at that watch once more, you're going to burn a hole through it." Tulley leaned on the fence beside him.

"I wish I knew what was happening."

"She'll tell you all about it when she gets back."

Colter jammed his hands into his coat pockets. "Yeah. I'm just nervous for her and—"

They both saw the car coming down the road, and Colter raced for the gate. Marisa parked by the garage, then got out and ran toward Colter. He met her halfway, caught her and swung her around and around. He set her on her feet, kissing her deeply. Finally he held her face with both hands.

"How'd it go?"

"Better than I ever dreamed. In some ways it's as if they've become different people. They're feeling a lot of pain over their actions, but I've forgiven them. It felt so good to be able to do that. By letting go of the heartache, I'm free to live a whole new life with you and Ellie."

"I love you," he whispered, running his fingers through her long blond hair.

She held his gaze. "I will love you forever."

"Mommy, Mommy, Mommy," Ellie shouted, racing toward them.

"Later," she whispered.

Ellie wrapped her arms around Marisa's waist. "I missed you."

"I missed you, too." She kissed the top of Ellie's head.

"Guess what, Mommy?"

"What?"

"Mr. Harvey is shoeing some horses and his son is gonna build Beauty a pen. Daddy asked him to."

"Really?" Marisa looked at Colter.

"We can't continue to keep her in the barn. She

needs to be outside. I'll have Rod make a shelter for her to get under when the weather's bad. But eventually we have to let her go."

"You're so wonderful." She gave him another slow kiss.

"Are y'all going to be doing that a lot?" Ellie asked, frowning at them.

"Yep, a whole lot," Colter said.

"Then Mommy's going to give you kisses in the morning and at night, too?"

"Yep." He grinned. "I've got two beautiful ladies. I'm one lucky man."

"Yes, you are." Ellie nodded.

Colter picked her up and groaned. "You're getting heavy."

"No, I'm not. You're just getting old."

"Old! I'll show you old." He tickled her rib cage and she giggled, squirming and squealing. Sooner barked agitatedly trying to reach her, and Marisa laughed.

"Help me, Mommy," she squealed more loudly.

"Oh, no, you got yourself into that one."

Ellie slid to the ground amid a fit of childish laughter. Sooner eagerly licked her face.

Colter slipped an arm around Marisa's waist, and she rested her head on his shoulder. They had weathered the storm, and now laughter and sunshine would fill their days. When other storms came, they would face them as a family.

Epilogue

Colter knew Marisa was miserable, but he didn't know what more to do. He'd rubbed her back, her legs, her neck until his arms ached. At nine months pregnant, nothing helped much. She'd had contractions earlier, and they kept waiting for them to start again, but they hadn't.

He listened to her steady breathing. Finally she seemed to be drifting into sleep. That was what he'd been hoping for—that she could get a good night's rest. Both families were coming for Christmas dinner; so were Cari and Hazel. He didn't think it was such a good idea, since the baby was due on the twenty-ninth, but it had been a year of forgiveness, change and acceptance, and Marisa wanted it—so he gave in. He found he couldn't refuse her anything.

Holding Marisa, his thoughts drifted back over the past year. His wife was awesome, as Ellie called her. She'd worked at Madame Hélèna's until they discovered she was pregnant, then Hélèna had said she should go home and enjoy her family. Marisa was ready to do that because she was involved with Ellie's school. The teachers were grateful for the help she provided with parties and outings, and for the music programs she arranged.

After she left Madame Hélèna's, Reed had talked her into taking a seat on the board of Dalton's. Colter and Marisa discussed it for a long time, and in the end she accepted out of respect for Reed and the new ideas he was bringing to the company. Colter knew she'd made the right decision.

He marveled at her energy and her talent. Between her and Reed, they'd made a deal with Madame Hélèna and, come spring, her line of clothes would be carried at Dalton's for the first time. It was a major coup for the company, and Marisa had been the driving force behind it.

Not only that—Marisa and Reed had put their heads together with Becky and Bart, and Dalton's would now carry the Kincaid Boot. The boots would be in the stores in early March. Marisa and Reed were energized by the new ventures, and Dalton's was flourishing, reaching a younger clientele while continuing to satisfy their older customers.

Richard was still head of the board and CEO, but he kept a low profile. Vanessa had moved from New York to Texas and had taken an active seat on the board, but both Richard and Vanessa acquiesced to the ideas of their children. Vanessa now lived with Richard again, and although Marisa and Reed weren't sure about the relationship, their parents seemed to get along in a way they hadn't in all the years they'd been married.

Since Marisa was pregnant, Colter worried about her doing too much, but he had only to look at her to know she was fine. The pregnancy had gone smoothly, with no problems. She had more energy than ever. In the mornings, before taking Ellie to school, she and Ellie fed Beauty, whom they'd set free, but the deer never wandered too far from the barn.

In the evenings Marisa played the piano, and he could see how much she enjoyed it. She'd joined the Dallas Symphony Orchestra as a guest soloist; a week before, she'd performed in the Christmas concert and invited family and friends—her parents, Reed, Cari, Hazel and Hélèna were among them.

When she was introduced and came on stage, she faced the audience and said, "I dedicate this performance to my mother, Vanessa Preston, whose dreams I never understood as a child. As a mother I see them clearly. So tonight I play for my mother and her dreams."

Marisa played brilliantly, and although he knew little about Tchaikovsky or Bach, he knew that he was hearing a very gifted young woman. He experienced a moment of guilt—that he had come between her and the career she so richly deserved. But he realized that career wasn't what she wanted. And these days Marisa knew *exactly* what she wanted.

When Marisa had made the announcement that night, Vanessa had begun to cry. Ellie had helped her find a handkerchief in her purse, saying, "Don't cry, Grandmother. Just listen."

Vanessa grabbed Ellie's hand and listened to the whole performance that way—holding on to Ellie. And that was wonderful to see. Ellie felt no resentment toward her grandparents, none at all.

When she'd met Richard and Vanessa for the first time, she'd asked in her usual, direct way, "Why didn't you want me?"

Vanessa had started to cry, and Ellie had done the same thing as she did later at the concert. She'd said, "Don't cry, Grandmother. Please don't cry."

Richard had sat down with Ellie and he'd told her how much they loved Marisa. He'd explained that out of their love, they'd made bad choices and decisions they regretted.

From that day forward, he and Vanessa had forged a relationship with their granddaughter. They took things slowly because that was the way Colter and Marisa wanted it. But as the weeks passed, he could see another miracle happening—the Prestons loved Ellie and the feeling was returned. Ellie now had grandparents.

He listened to Marisa's breathing and it wasn't steady anymore; it had become more labored. "You're not asleep, are you."

"No." She turned toward him, which was an effort because she'd gained a lot of weight. The doctor said the baby was going to be eight pounds or more. And they knew it was a boy. Not once had he heard her complain, though—both of them had thoroughly enjoyed the pregnancy. They were experiencing it together, and that made all the difference.

"Do you think Ellie's asleep?" she asked. "We have to put her gifts under the tree."

Colter crawled out of bed and reached for his robe. "You rest. I'll do it."

"No way, Colter Kincaid." She struggled to sit up. "I'm not missing any part of Ellie's Christmas."

He helped her up and held her for a moment. He didn't argue with her, since this was too important to Marisa.

Kissing the side of her face, he took her hand and they walked to the door.

"Wait," she said. "I have to go to the bathroom... again."

"I'll check and make sure Ellie's asleep."

Marisa came out of the bathroom and stopped abruptly as a sharp pain gripped her. She'd been having light pains lying in bed, but didn't want to alarm Colter or say anything until it was necessary. She grabbed the vanity as she realized water was running down her legs and pooling at her feet. *Don't panic. Don't panic. Be calm. Be calm.*

"Colter," she screamed, unable to still the anxiety in her. *Be calm. Be calm.* She squatted as another pain shook her.

Colter was inside the bathroom in a split second. "What is it? What's wrong?" he asked, kneeling beside her, his heart racing.

"My water's broken."

"What! OhmyGod!"

"The baby's coming," she breathed between pains.

He scooped her into his arms. "I'll get your bag and we'll go to the hospital."

Marisa shook her head. "No. We don't have time. The baby's coming *now!*"

Colter's eyes grew enormous. "No. It's too quick. We have to go to the hospital."

A pain ripped through her and it was a moment before she could speak. "Colter, listen to me," she said, each word slowly and carefully enunciated. "Put me on the bed and call 911, then call our doctor. The baby's coming. We don't have much time." The swift cyclic pains were the type she'd had right before Ellie was born. She wasn't having this baby in a vehicle.

"Okay. Okay."

His arms trembled as he laid her down, and she knew he was trying to be calm but failing miserably. Colter quickly dialed 911. She took several deep breaths, then a sharp contraction hit her. She bit her lip to keep from screaming again.

Tulley appeared in the doorway in his pajamas. "What's wrong? I heard screaming."

Colter slammed the phone down. "Marisa's having the baby."

"What!"

"Get dressed and drive to the entrance so the ambulance won't miss our turn," Colter said, the stress showing on his face.

"You got it." Tulley turned as Ellie came charging into the room.

"Why is everybody..." Ellie's voice trailed off as she saw Marisa in bed with her knees drawn up.

"Mommy, Mommy," she cried, running to her, but Colter caught her before she could crawl onto the bed.

"Mommy's having the baby," he told her. "So be gentle."

Sooner barked from the doorway.

"Shh," Ellie told him.

Colter released her, and Ellie leaned toward Marisa, who wrapped an arm around her daughter.

"Are you hurting, Mommy?" Ellie asked softly.

"It's a good kind of hurt, Ellie," Marisa said, trying not to cry out. "Soon your baby brother will be here."

"Oh boy, I gotta call Grandmother and Aunt Becky." She whirled around and Colter caught her again.

"First go with Tulley so the ambulance won't miss our turn."

Tulley came back, fully dressed, with a pan of hot water, fresh towels and sheets, and placed them on the dresser. "You might need those. Come on, shorty. We don't want to miss that ambulance."

As they left, Colter picked up the phone and called their doctor. Marisa let out a long scream. She had to. She couldn't hold it in as a strong contraction clenched her whole body.

"Remember the breathing," Colter said to Marisa, listening with one ear to the doctor and switching on the speakerphone. "Quick panting breaths."

Marisa just screamed.

"Marisa," Dr. Gates said. "Breathe, breathe, breathe. Don't push just yet."

"Okay," she answered, taking quick breaths and trying not to scream.

"Colter," the doctor continued, "take a look and tell me what you see."

He pulled up her gown, saw the blood and fluid and almost lost it. Then he noticed the crown of his son's head and he was revived with wonder and strength. "I… I see the head," he said, his voice cracking. "Ohm-yGod! The baby's coming!"

"Calm down," the doctor instructed. "And don't push, Marisa. Breathe, breathe, breathe. Looks like the baby's in a hurry to get here. Colter, get lots of clean sheets and towels and something to tie the umbilical cord. The paramedics will cut it when they get there."

"Like what?" Colter asked in a frantic tone.

"Some type of string, and get a bulb syringe. I'm sure you had one when Ellie was a baby."

"Yes." He dashed into Ellie's room. Where the hell was it? He ran to the utility room and found it in the medicine cabinet. He ran back. "I have the syringe and string from a kite. Is that okay?"

"Yes. That's fine. Cut a piece, then put several sheets beneath Marisa. Have towels ready and a wash-cloth to wipe the baby's face."

Colter worked quickly and efficiently. He cut the string and gently shoved sheets beneath Marisa, piling towels and everything else he needed on the bed.

"It's all there," he told the doctor.

"Now wash your hands and the syringe, and get ready to deliver your son."

A strong contraction almost overwhelmed Marisa, and she screamed and breathed at the same time. Sweat ran down her face and she clutched her knees with both hands. But as long as Colter was there, she'd be fine.

"Tell me what you see," the doctor said.

Colter crawled onto the bed and knelt between Marisa's legs. "The head's coming out," he shouted.

"Hold it with a clean towel. Do you see the face?"

"Yes, yes, yes. Oh my God, yes."

"Wipe his face, and clear his mouth and nose with the syringe."

Colter carefully held the baby's head and did as the doctor instructed, surprised his hands weren't shaking.

"Everything okay?"

"So far," Colter said raggedly.

"Okay, Marisa, time to push. Push hard. Push your son into the world."

"We're having a baby, sweet lady." Colter smiled at her. "How are you?"

"Gre—at. I love—you." Words locked in her throat as the pain became more severe. She would not pass out. She would not let go—that was a vow to herself. She had to be awake for her son's birth, and she had to see him, hold him.

"Honey, one more push," Colter said. "You have to push him out. Come on. One, two, three—push."

Marisa felt her strength waning. *Push. Push. Push.* She couldn't. She had to. Taking a deep breath, she pushed with everything in her. A scream left her throat and she fell back on the bed as their son slid into Colter's waiting hands.

Colter glanced at the clock and reached steadily for the string.

"Colter, is he okay?" Marisa asked in a faint voice. "Is he breathing? Colter, tell me!"

"Yeah, and it's definitely a boy."

"Tie off the umbilical cord," the doctor said. "The baby will be bloody and grayish, but don't worry about that."

Colter let out a long sigh of relief. He'd noticed the color, but everything was fine.

"It's done," Colter told him.

"Put him on Marisa's chest."

He placed their son on her chest and gazed at her face.

"Oh, he's so beautiful and so perfect," she whispered, her hands trembling against the small body.

"Take a towel and rub him vigorously all over." The doctor was still giving orders.

Colter began to rub him, and Marisa helped. Suddenly the baby started to cry loudly.

"That's what I wanted to hear," Dr. Gates said.

"Oh, oh, oh," Marisa cooed to him. "It's okay. Mommy's here." She kissed his face and touched his head, his stomach, counted his fingers and toes—and then she began to cry. She had her baby and no one would ever take him from her. In her weakened state that was all she could think about.

"Wrap the baby up. Keep him and Marisa warm."

Colter pulled a blanket around Marisa and the baby. He rested his face against hers. "How are you?"

"Wonderful and tired, but no one's taking this child. No one."

"Honey…"

Marisa grimaced.

"What is it?" Colter was immediately on the alert.

"I'm cramping."

"That's okay," the doctor said, still on the phone.

"The placenta's coming out. Colter, reach down and gently tug on the umbilical cord."

He did. "Everything's out."

"Good. Congratulations! You have a son and you both did great."

Colter kissed the side of Marisa's damp face. "*You* were great."

"Look at him, Colter, just look at him." Her voice held awe.

"I am. He looks a lot like Ellie."

"Does he?" Her voice wobbled, and he knew she was remembering Ellie's birth.

"I love you," he said, and she rested against him and smiled into his eyes.

"Hey, you two. I'm still here," Dr. Gates teased.

The baby began to squirm, moving his head as if he was searching for something.

"He seems hungry," Colter commented.

"He probably is. You can nurse him, Marisa." The doctor's voice was very clear.

Marisa opened her gown and the baby latched on, sucking hungrily.

"Colter, can you see him?" Marisa asked. "He knows exactly what to do."

"I see, honey. He's a Kincaid."

Marisa stared into her husband's eyes and knew that nothing in her life would ever match this moment— the moment of giving birth with her husband's help and then holding and seeing her child.

There was a clatter at the door just then. The paramedics came through and immediately took over. Colter gave her a kiss and moved from the bed, letting them take care of Marisa and the baby. Tulley hurried down the hall.

"Everything okay?" he asked sounding concerned.

Colter nodded. "He was born at 12:05 a.m. He's a Christmas baby." His body shook with all the emotions he was feeling, and Tulley put an arm around his shoulders.

"You all right, boy?"

He nodded again. "I've delivered foals before, but this is the first time I've helped deliver a baby—my own baby. It's a little overwhelming." He brushed away a tear. "Where's Ellie?"

"Talking to Mrs. Preston on your cell phone."

Colter looked down and saw Marisa's blood all over him. "I have to clean up for the trip to the hospital. I have clothes in the utility room, so I'm going to take a shower. I won't be long."

In less than ten minutes he was back. As he got clothes for the baby and handed them to the paramedics, Ellie ran up to him.

"Daddy, Grandmother wants me to call her as soon as the baby comes."

Before Colter could answer, the paramedics emerged from the room. "Your wife refuses to go to the hospital, so I've checked her and the baby, and everything seems to be fine. I spoke with the doctor and he's agreed to let her stay home for Christmas, but he wants her and the baby in his office first thing the day after Christmas." The paramedic looked down at the papers in her hand. "On your digital scale, the baby weighs seven pounds, fifteen ounces, and is twenty-one inches long. Did you by any chance get the time of birth?"

"12:05 a.m.," he said.

"Good. Your wife gave us his name. She's taken a shower, and we cleaned the baby per the doctor's instruction. We also changed the bed. We don't usually do that, but it's Christmas."

"Thank you. And Merry Christmas."

The paramedics left, and Colter entered the room with his daughter. Marisa was sitting up holding the baby who'd been wrapped in a blue blanket with pictures of ropes and spurs on it. She smiled, and Colter kissed her and then his son, now sound asleep.

Ellie stood staring with big eyes. Marisa looked at her. "Come meet your new brother."

"Are you okay, Mommy?"

"I'm fine, baby."

"I'm not the baby anymore," Ellie said moving closer to the newborn.

Marisa smiled at her. "You will always be my baby."

Ellie nodded happily and sat by Marisa, staring at her new brother. "Now you have two babies, Mommy. Can I touch him?"

"Yes, but very gently."

Ellie caressed his cheek with one finger. "He's so tiny and cute."

"Yes, he is." Marisa kissed the top of his head. "Now I'd like everyone to meet this young man. His name is Jackson Aaron Colter Kincaid. We'll probably call him Jack."

There was no question about what his first name would be. Colter wanted to name him after Tulley, and Marisa was fine with that. Aaron was her father's middle name, and the fact that she was able to call her son after her father meant the old wounds had healed. The scar tissue was still there, but it couldn't hurt her anymore. She'd forgiven her parents completely—and she prayed that she and Colter would never make decisions that would hurt their children.

"Lordy, lordy," Tulley said, his eyes filled with tears.

They hadn't told him what they were naming the baby. Colter had wanted to wait until the baby was born.

"You're crying." Ellie pointed at him.

"Yep, I guess I am." He cleared his throat, hugged Colter and kissed Marisa's forehead. "Thank you." He deftly took the baby from her. "Hi there, little buckaroo. I'm gonna enjoy getting to know you."

"Time for everyone to get to bed," Colter intervened. "Or Santa's going to miss this house."

Ellie shook her head. "Santa's already been here. He brought us Jack."

"It's still time for bed," Colter said, smiling.

Ellie gave lots of kisses. Tulley handed the baby back to Marisa and gathered up the dirty laundry. "I'll put this in the washing machine."

"Oh, no. I forgot. I gotta call Grandmother," Ellie said, and ran to her room, Sooner on her heels.

And then it was the two of them with their son. Colter went into the baby's room and brought the Christmas cradle, which he placed beside the bed. "Time for Jack to get some sleep, too."

"No. I want to hold him for a little longer."

Colter gently brushed back her damp hair. "Honey, no one's taking this baby."

"I know—it's just—"

"You're afraid you'll wake up and he won't be here," he finished for her.

"It's crazy, I'm aware of that, but I can't shake the feeling."

"With what you've been through in the past, I think it's a normal reaction." He kissed her softly. "Trust me. This baby isn't going anywhere." He lifted Jack out of her arms and laid him gently in the cradle.

Marisa shifted onto her side, watching him. "So many times over the years, I've looked at this cradle in Dalton's and imagined our baby in it. It's kind of surreal to actually have it happening."

Love brightened his eyes. "Have I told you how wonderful you are?"

She nodded, her eyes closing as exhaustion overtook her.

He looked at his son for a moment, knowing he'd witnessed another miracle, then slowly went to put out Ellie's gifts. First, he checked to make sure she was asleep—and she was. He got the gifts from the attic in the garage and arranged them under the tree. As he was about to turn out the light, he noticed a piece of paper lying on the table next to Santa's cookies and milk. He picked it up and read:

Dear Santa,
My friend Lori says there is no Santa Claus, but I believe. Even when I get as old as Daddy, I'll still believe 'cause you brought my mommy home

and you gave us a brand-new baby. Everybody's
happy. Thank you, Santa Claus. I believe.
Love,
Ellie Kincaid

A smile tugged at his mouth. Yes. They were
happy—finally. He drank the milk and took the cookies, along with the letter, to show Marisa. He stopped
when he entered the bedroom. Marisa was asleep on
her side, one hand on the cradle.

When he lay down by his wife, she let go of the
cradle and curled into him.

I believe, too.

* * * * *

SPECIAL EXCERPT FROM

H HARLEQUIN®

SPECIAL EDITION

USA TODAY *bestselling author Judy Duarte's*
The Lawman's Convenient Family
*is the story of Julie Chapman, a music therapist who
needs a convenient husband in order to save two
orphans from foster care. Lawman Adam Santiago fits
the bill, but suddenly they both find themselves longing
to become a family—forever!*

*Read on for a sneak preview of the next great book
in the Rocking Chair Rodeo miniseries.*

"Lisa," the man dressed as Zorro said, "I'd heard you were
going to be here."

He clearly thought Julie was someone else. She probably
ought to say something, but up close, the gorgeous bandito
seemed to have stolen both her thoughts and her words.

"It's nice to finally meet you." His deep voice set her senses
reeling. "I've never really liked blind dates."

Talk about masquerades and mistaken identities. Before
Julie could set him straight, he took her hand in a polished,
gentlemanly manner and kissed it. His warm breath lingered on
her skin, setting off a bevy of butterflies in her tummy.

"Dance with me," he said.

Her lips parted, but for the life of her, she still couldn't
speak, couldn't explain. And she darn sure couldn't object.

Zorro led her away from the buffet tables and to the dance
floor. When he opened his arms, she again had the opportunity
to tell him who she really was. But instead, she stepped into his
embrace, allowing him to take the lead.

His alluring aftershave, something manly, taunted her. As
she savored his scent, as well as the warmth of his muscular
arms, her pulse soared. She leaned her head on his shoulder

as they swayed to a sensual beat, their movements in perfect accord, as though they'd danced together a hundred times before.

Now would be a good time to tell him she wasn't Lisa, but she seemed to have fallen under a spell that grew stronger with every beat of the music. The moment turned surreal, like she'd stepped into a fairy tale with a handsome rogue.

Once again, she pondered revealing his mistake and telling him her name, but there'd be time enough to do that after the song ended. Then she'd return to the kitchen, slipping off like Cinderella. But instead of a glass slipper, she'd leave behind her momentary enchantment.

But several beats later, a cowboy tapped Zorro on the shoulder. "I need you to come outside."

Zorro looked at him and frowned. "Can't you see I'm busy?"

The cowboy, whose outfit was so authentic he seemed to be the real deal, rolled his eyes.

Julie wished she could have worn her street clothes. Would now be a good time to admit that she wasn't an actual attendee but here to work at the gala?

"What's up?" Zorro asked.

The cowboy folded his arms across his chest and shifted his weight to one hip. "Someone just broke into my pickup."

Zorro's gaze returned to Julie. "I'm sorry, Lisa. I'm going to have to morph into cop mode."

Now it was Julie's turn to tense. He was actually a police officer in real life? A slight uneasiness settled over her, an old habit she apparently hadn't outgrown. Not that she had any real reason to fear anyone in law enforcement nowadays.

Don't miss
The Lawman's Convenient Family *by Judy Duarte,*
available January 2019 wherever
Harlequin® Special Edition books and ebooks are sold.

www.Harlequin.com

Copyright © 2018 by Judy Duarte

HSEEXP1218

Looking for more satisfying love stories
with community and family at their core?

Check out **Harlequin® Special Edition**
and **Love Inspired®** books!

 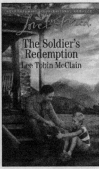

New books available every month!

CONNECT WITH US AT:

Facebook.com/groups/HarlequinConnection

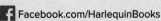 Facebook.com/HarlequinBooks

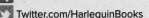 Twitter.com/HarlequinBooks

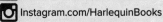 Instagram.com/HarlequinBooks

Pinterest.com/HarlequinBooks

ReaderService.com

**ROMANCE WHEN
YOU NEED IT**

HFGENRE2018

Need an adrenaline rush from nail-biting tales
(and irresistible males)?

Check out **Harlequin Intrigue®**
and **Harlequin® Romantic Suspense** books!

New books available every month!

CONNECT WITH US AT:

Facebook.com/groups/HarlequinConnection

Facebook.com/HarlequinBooks

Twitter.com/HarlequinBooks

Instagram.com/HarlequinBooks

Pinterest.com/HarlequinBooks

ReaderService.com

**ROMANCE WHEN
YOU NEED IT**

SGENRE2018

Looking for inspiration in tales
of hope, faith and heartfelt romance?

Check out **Love Inspired**® and
Love Inspired® **Suspense** books!

New books available every month!

CONNECT WITH US AT:

Facebook.com/groups/HarlequinConnection

Facebook.com/HarlequinBooks

Twitter.com/HarlequinBooks

Instagram.com/HarlequinBooks

Pinterest.com/HarlequinBooks

ReaderService.com

Love Inspired®

LIGENRE2018R2

Love Harlequin romance?

DISCOVER.

Be the first to find out about promotions,
news and exclusive content!

Facebook.com/HarlequinBooks

Twitter.com/HarlequinBooks

Instagram.com/HarlequinBooks

Pinterest.com/HarlequinBooks

ReaderService.com

EXPLORE.

Sign up for the Harlequin e-newsletter and
download a free book from any series at
TryHarlequin.com.

CONNECT.

Join our Harlequin community to share
your thoughts and connect with other
romance readers!
Facebook.com/groups/HarlequinConnection

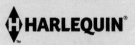

HARLEQUIN®

**ROMANCE WHEN
YOU NEED IT**

HSOCIAL2018